The Durbar's Apprentice

Remington Blackstaff

Published in North America and Europe by RIZE. Visit Running Wild Press
at www.runningwildpress.com/rize Educators, librarians, book clubs (as well
as the eternally curious), go to www.runningwildpress.com/rize.

ISBN (pbk) 978-1-947041-86-8
ISBN (ebook) 978-1-947041-87-5

To my parents for their heritage,
guidance and immeasurable generosity.

To my wife for her encouragement and unwavering support.

To my son for his limitless inspiration.

Chapter One

She was beautiful. The sunlight glistened off her flawless black skin as his fingertips traced a path from Sisoko's muscular thighs, mapping every contour along the way, to the nape of her neck. The gentle caresses from the palms of his hands were passively absorbed in alternating mesmerising strokes, each one coursing its own route along the velvet landscape. The slow corporeal connection between them hovered above Sisoko's racing heartbeat as the canvas was interrupted by his reflection in her dark eyes. For a moment they stood face to face, each silently transfixed by the affectionate gaze of the other. Appreciating the horse's beauty wasn't solely confined to admiring her at a standstill. In flight Sisoko glided gracefully, whether moving at a canter or at top speed. Maintaining such a fine creature was one of his greatest pleasures in life. One Isa relished every day. The hairs of her mane were delicately separated by the teeth of the wooden comb as if they were his own.

After tending to Master's steed, Isa's next task was considerably less gratifying. Cleaning the stable. As Sisoko wasn't entitled to an earthen hole in the ground, like Isa and his master, she habitually opened her bowels all over the stable. Armed with a shovel and intermittent breath-holding, Isa set about transferring the horse's nauseating bodily waste to a resting place beneath the topsoil. Master often said that Sisoko's excrement would help the soil grow. Questioning Master vocally was unthinkable, but Isa wondered how anything that smelled so bad didn't kill anything that it touched. After Isa swept the stable Master's lighter tools had to be arranged. Isa had clear instructions, in no uncertain terms, never to touch any of Master's weapons; including his swords, spears, daggers or his hammer. Master sharpened the blades of these weapons himself. Isa remembered when the temptation to feel the ornate pattern of a sword's hilt in his hand had overcome him. The sight of his opaque reflection in the steel had narrowly been surpassed by the exhilarating sound of the vibrating air as the blade cut through it. His playful air strokes had masked the sound of approaching footsteps. Having been startled by the sensation of cold sharp steel against his neck, the frozen boy dropped the weapon in a panic. Master caught the falling blade and Isa closed his eyes and clenched his teeth in fearful anticipation of the first blow.

No painful reprimand came. Not like before. Instead, Master sheathed the heavy sword and muttered something about not wanting to retrieve the weapon from Isa's belly after he'd accidentally impaled himself. Isa didn't know what it meant to impale one's self, but it sounded painful. The hanging bullwhip wasn't strictly off limits though. Isa had never seen Master use it on Sisoko or any other animal for that matter. Master said animals were better behaved, more trustworthy and generally needed less discipline than humans. It was humans that were prone to being idle, deceitful and benefitted from the odd lash to the nyash. As for Master's other equipment, only recently had Master shown Isa how to use the glass and metal eye that made far objects seem close. The needle that always pointed in a certain direction was another of Master's curiosities. Isa didn't really understand how it worked. Master had said to Isa that it would give him direction in life. This puzzled Isa. How could a round tool that fit into the palm of his hand tell him what an oracle couldn't?

Master routinely carried out the more laborious chores that Isa wasn't yet strong enough for. These included chopping firewood, grabbing two buckets of water from the well and catching and cooking their meals. Although Master washed his own robes after meticulously trimming his beard with the sharpest of blades, he had guaranteed Isa that when he was up to standard he could wash clothes for both of them. If his chores were finished early, Isa observed Master training on his own in the open air. His physique was like granite; solid with lean muscle throughout and smooth surfaces interrupted by fleshy cracks in his skin and scars, the physical remnants of conflicts past. Master's movements were supple, like a dancer, in all directions. He threw punches and kicks in the air and made short sharp breath sounds as he did so. It was as if he was fighting an invisible adversary. Sometimes he trained with weapons, like his sword or spear. Other times he trained with buckets full of water. Sometimes he even carried Isa on his back or his shoulders to make the exercises harder. Regardless of the exercise, Isa was certain his master was fast and strong, indestructible even. He dreamed of moving like Master, who had promised to teach him how to fight one day. First he would learn how to cultivate a good life, before learning how to end a bad one.

Master first came into Isa's life five years earlier. Their paths had crossed in Kirikiri marketplace in south eastern Katsina. Isa, the diminutive orphan, small in stature with eyes that spoke of sorrow, had been put up for sale. It wasn't the first time money had changed hands in exchange for his life. Isa had been through a couple of owners and had come to expect little from life up until that point. His penultimate master had been a pot-bellied farmer whose sole purpose in life had seemed to be to drink himself to an early death. Prior to this wish being granted, his daily routine had consisted of tending lazily to malnourished cattle while hurling abuse at Isa. Upon the final goatskin of palm wine passing his lips, Isa was sold to pay some part of the debt the lousy farmer had left for his family. Before he died, the man hadn't taught Isa much, apart from dodging the inebriated strokes of a wayward cane and steering hungry cattle towards grass.

Isa's last owner was both elderly and blind. His fragility and lack of vision was compensated for by his quiet voice and gentle manner. Unable to cook, Isa was relegated to being an additional crutch to lean on for the frail widower. On the surface, this hadn't seemed so onerous. It quickly became apparent that the old baba had neither the suppleness in his back and hips to squat over a hole in the ground, nor the stability to wipe his backside while in the stooping position. One of Isa's core responsibilities was to place a high bucket under the old man's buttocks when nature called. He was then a shoulder to lean on until he passed his master a rag to wipe himself with. Needless to say, it was Isa's job to wash the rag in a nearby stream afterwards. One of his master's daughters took care of the bucket. Toileting aside, Isa hadn't minded serving the old man. The man didn't say much but smiled occasionally, with his opaque irises fixed on the horizon and routinely thanked Isa for his support. Meals were provided begrudgingly by the man's other daughters. Much to the consternation of his children, the old man insisted that Isa ate with him to ensure that he was being fed at all.

When the old man passed away, it wasn't Isa's first encounter with death. The original heartbreaking milestone of bereavement was etched in his memory as a recurring nightmare. Isa's mother forced him into a cooking pot. He screamed, her hands trembled. His older brother Ibrahim and his father shared the same expression. Terrified yet vacant. Almost in acceptance of their inevitable fate. His mother was the catalyst to salvation. Others screamed nearby. Then darkness. Isa emerged a day, maybe two, later. His parents lay on the earth. Their wounds were open but their bloodied bodies were still and their spirits had left. There was no sign of Ibrahim. The village was no more.

Before Isa's elderly owner's death they sat by the fire at night in the open air. The old man had been more talkative than usual. He'd begun sharing vivid memories of his childhood with Isa. It turned out that the old man had never known his parents and had been raised by an uncle. The old man smiled and nodded his head slowly as he wistfully recalled a happy adolescence. His smile grew, his long white beard shook and his eyes widened as he fondly spoke of his late wife. Then silence. After a polite pause, Isa asked his master to continue. There was no response. It was only when Isa had leaned across the dying embers of the fire that he noticed that his elderly master's eyes, like his smile, were fixed open in the firelight. The old man's soul had departed peacefully and Isa had seen his first death.

Within days, Isa was passed on to a trader by the man's surviving family and put up for sale. His transactional departure came as no surprise, as the man's family hadn't hidden their disdain for Isa's existence. Isa had grown to take nothing personally and accepted his fate. If he had a wish it would be that his master fed him sufficiently, or at least be physically capable of squatting. The tall stranger in his elegant but simple garments, that then came gliding through the marketplace on a beautiful horse, had been far beyond Isa's wildest expectations. The man whom Isa would later call Master, with his perfect posture, appeared monolithically tall on horseback. Together with his horse, the two of them almost floated through the crowded market. As the mysterious horseman drew closer to Isa's post, traders jostled one another for his attention. One pair began a scuffle that left a cloud of dust in the air as they wrestled each other to the ground. The stranger and his horse continued their approach undeterred by the unwanted attention. As they came closer, the more composed market observers separated to clear a path for the horseman. It was then that Isa could clearly appraise the appearance of the would-be foreigner.

As they approached his post, the stranger's horse caught Isa's eye. Its hide was black and beautiful, with no blemishes and complemented by a dark leather bridle. It seemed undisturbed by the saddle and the large man on top of it who had no need to tug at the reins of his obedient mount. The rider was almost as dark as his horse, with prominent cheekbones and a finely trimmed beard that joined his moustache. Isa had never seen anyone dressed like him before. He looked nothing like the market rabble in their soiled tunics and wrappers. His clean clothes were a dignified dark grey. He tied a strange cloth around his head and neck and could easily have been mistaken for a court official that his dead master told him about. The leather-bound hilt of his sword projected from a scabbard that hung casually at his waist. Isa retreated as far back into his pen as his chains would allow.

"He's a durbar," said a thinner, older-looking boy next to him.

"A what?" asked Isa.

"A durbar," the boy repeated. He looked at Isa's puzzled expression and smiled. "For the Emir." Isa nodded but his blank expression betrayed confusion. He turned back to observe the approaching stranger.

"He has a sword. Is he a soldier?" Isa asked.

"No. They're peacekeepers," the boy replied.

"What's a peacekeeper?" Isa asked.

"*Quiet!*" the slave trader hissed as he wrapped the bars of their pen with a cane. Both boys went silent and waited until their temporary keeper's attention was back on the approaching stranger.

The older boy leaned in towards Isa and lowered his voice to a whisper. "Peacekeepers are like messengers for the Emir."

"If they keep peace, why is that man carrying a sword?" asked Isa.

The older boy paused, opened his mouth to answer and realised he had none. After a couple of moments of reflection, he gave his best attempt. "Maybe peacekeeping is dangerous. Especially around here. I've seen one of them before in Kano."

"Why do you think he's here?" Isa whispered. "Do you think he has a message?"

The other boy shrugged his shoulders. By then, the stranger was a few feet away from them. The rider briefly glanced at both boys before banking right. All eight boys in the cramped space followed the stranger with their eyes as he circled the pen, casting a shadow over them as he did so. Isa and his neighbour avoided eye contact as the stranger passed around their side. After making a second pass, the rider dismounted from his horse and slowly walked around the pen, holding his horse by the reins. He ignored the toothless smile of the slave trader following him at a safe distance.

"Do you see anything you like?" asked the slave trader. "I have boys of all shapes and sizes." The rider continued his inspection of the pen and ignored the advice. The slave trader waited a few seconds before continuing. "I have older boys, younger boys, fat boys, skinny boys, tall boys and short boys." The rider didn't respond. "I have boys for all purposes," the slave trader paused, "and pleasures." The slave trader's smile broadened and the rider stopped. He turned to face the slave trader with a scornful expression. The slave trader's smile faded, he swallowed hard, took a step back and for a few moments the observing crowd went silent. Isa and the older boy looked at each other. To the disappointment of the market crowd, the stranger's sword remained sheathed. He turned his back on the slave trader without uttering a word and resumed his inspection of the pen. The noise picked up in the market and the enslaved boys anxiously waited to see which one of their fortunes might change that day. Isa looked at the ground as the rider stopped at his post. He felt a warm breath on his face and looked up.

"It seems Sisoko likes you," said the stranger. Isa stared at the large dark eyes of the horse carrying out its own appraisal of him. "She's a good judge of character."

Through squinted eyes Isa stared at the silhouette of the tall dark stranger towering over him. The cloth wrapped around his head and neck made the man all the more intimidating.

"Do you want this one?" asked the slave trader, hovering around the stranger and eagerly anticipating a sale.

"Are you a peacekeeper?" asked Isa.

"*Silence! What did I tell you?*" shouted the slave trader. His face morphed into a mask of anger and frustration as he raised his cane. Before it could connect with the bars of Isa's cage, or even Isa himself, the cane arm was suddenly paralysed by immovable resistance. The iron grip that clasped around the slave trader's arm was so strong that he reflexively dropped the cane. The slave trader looked at the powerful stranger, then Isa, initially in shock. Panic then set in, as he feared the stranger might finally unsheathe his sword and relieve him of his arm.

"I keep the peace only when there is none," replied the stranger with a slight smile. His eyes remained fixed on Isa as he simultaneously released his grip on the slave trader's arm. "What's your name?"

"Isa sir."

"Isa? That's a fine name," commented the stranger. "How old are you?"

"I don't know sir," replied Isa.

"You don't know how old you are?" asked the stranger.

Isa shook his head. "Not exactly sir."

"Where is your family Isa?" asked the stranger.

"My parents are dead. Maybe my brother too," replied Isa.

The stranger nodded solemnly. "So you're alone?"

Isa looked around the pen at the other boys watching his interaction. "Yes."

The stranger studied Isa's face for a couple of moments. "Isa, can you read?"

"No sir."

"Can you write?"

"No sir."

"Can you ride a horse?" Isa shook his head.

"You'll learn." The stranger then reached into a pocket on Sisoko's saddle. He removed a small pouch and threw it at the slave trader. "I'll take this one." Preoccupied with nursing his bruised forearm, the slave trader barely caught the pouch. He immediately fumbled with a set of keys from his dirty tunic and unlocked Isa's shackles. Before he knew it, Isa had been hoisted up by the stranger onto the back of his horse. The stranger immediately mounted his horse and pulled at Sisoko's reins. As they gathered speed, a path cleared for their exit from the market. Isa knew he'd never see the slave trader or the boys in the pen again.

A short distance away from the market, Sisoko stopped. The stranger reached down into a saddle bag and removed some rope. Isa's heart began to race and his body stiffened. It had been far too good to be true. Such rescue and freedom only happened in dreams. The orphan slave braced himself for whatever maleficence had just been paid for. The stranger sensed the boy's unease and smiled at him reassuringly.

"Sisoko is faster than any horse you've ever seen," said the stranger. "You're no use to me if you fall and break on the way." The stranger passed the rope around Isa's torso, then tied the rope around his own waist. "Can you breathe?"

"Yes Master," replied Isa.

"Very good. Hold onto my waist and don't let go until I say so."

"Yes Master." Sisoko began to pick up speed but was stopped abruptly by a sharp tug of her reins.

"Isa?" The stranger turned his head towards his new travelling companion.

"Yes Master?"

"Consider today your birthday." Isa's new master barked an order at his horse and Sisoko broke into a gallop.

#

As the durbar's ward, Isa neither wore shackles again, nor was he ever on the receiving end of an abusive cane. The next few years were devoid of any mistreatment, although discipline still prevailed in Isa's life. Of all the great many things the durbar taught him, the most important thing was respect for himself and others. He was taught to value not being exchanged as a human commodity and seldom reflected on the harsh blows life had dealt him prior to that day in the marketplace. Despite his positive impact on Isa's life, the durbar wasn't quite the surrogate father. Their relationship lacked the tactile intimacy of a father and son and there were many things Isa didn't know about Master. The durbar could be aloof one minute and sharing pearls of wisdom the next.

The sound of hooves approaching in the distance snapped Isa out of his reflective daydream. He ran to the bottom of the lookout post of the compound and climbed up the ladder. Once at the top, he crouched down and extended Master's glass and metal eye. Looking through the eyepiece, he recognised the approaching figure on horseback.

Isa opened the compound gate and the visitor immediately entered the compound. The visitor's attire was similar to Master, as he also tied a turban round his head and neck. The man also carried a sword with an identical hilt to Master but a shorter blade. Where Master wore grey, white or other coloured robes depending on the occasion, the visitor always wore green. This was the colour of palace officials. The man was a royal emissary. He looked older and slimmer than Master but clean-shaven. The man dismounted from his white stallion and immediately gave the reins to Isa.

"Get your master," commanded the man. Isa guided the horse to a drinking trough and disappeared inside his master's quarters. Moments later he reappeared with his master. The two men nodded at each other. "The durbar council requests your presence."

"On whose authority?" asked Master.

"His royal highness the Emir," said the emissary.

"When?"

"Noon tomorrow."

Master nodded. "We have food and water. My ward will show you to my quarters if you need rest."

"I'm most grateful but I have further messages to deliver." The emissary bowed his head to acknowledge the gesture and turned to retrieve his stallion from the trough. Within a few minutes he was gone.

"Isa, get packing," said Master after Isa had closed the compound gate. "We're going to Kano."

Chapter Two

Kano city's impressive stone walls dominated the landscape from several miles out. With a height and depth of fifty by forty feet, Isa looked on in awe as they approached the imposing defensive enclosure. Also known as the heart of the emirate, Kano was the commercial and cultural capital of not only the northern regions but also the Hausa Kingdom. Although it wasn't Isa's first trip to the ancient city, he was still enthralled by the seething mass of people within the city walls once he and Master had passed through one of several gates. Merchants, traders, and ordinary citizens formed the congested human traffic that slowed Sisoko down to a trot. The odd curtained carriage shielded someone of presumed high importance from the late morning dust, bright sun and inquisitive looks. Master and his ward drew the odd cursory glance, but people were too busy going about their business to care too much about the durbar or his companion.

Just over an hour later, they came to the walls of the Emir's palace, the Gidan Rumfa. Completed two hundred years earlier in the late fifteenth century, by the Sultan Muhammad Rumfa, the palace was a walled city within the walled city, spanning thirty-three acres. From the outside, turbaned palace guards in red and green robes kept watch over the palace perimeter and beyond from high towers. Within the palace walls the Emir, his wives, concubines, children and their extended families, in addition to up to a thousand others, occupied the living quarters. A mosque, several courts, stables and a few nondescript low-rise buildings were visible from within the palace walls. Elsewhere a wide array of flora and fauna populated the palace gardens that took up approximately half of the palace ecosystem. One palace inhabitant in particular was conspicuous, not for its aesthetic appeal but for its contribution to palace security. Over time, hundreds of royal bats had occupied sections of the palace estate. Any unfamiliar or sudden disturbance within the confines of the palace grounds triggered the royal bats to take flight en masse, tipping off the palace guards to the possibility of an uninvited guest.

Two palace guards on horseback, posted side by side, blocked access to a palace gate. They were identical in appearance to the guards on the sentry towers but brandished a spear each, in addition to the long swords that hung at their waists. As Isa and Master approached the gate, the guards automatically separated to clear a path for them to pass. The heavy oak gate rumbled as it was opened from the inside. Isa, Master and Sisoko entered.

#

The grounds of the Emir's palace were calm, almost eerily quiet, the polar opposite of Kano city streets. The roads were mostly empty and free of the sounds of haggling and moving cargo polluting the air. One could hear the dirt crunching under their feet as they walked and if they held a breath, they may have heard the faint sound of a hoof hitting the earth or a child playing in the distance. Court officials conducted themselves quietly and efficiently, sparing any glances in Isa and Master's direction. When Sisoko and her passengers arrived at a stable, a young man in a brown kaftan and turban helped Isa from his horse onto a wooden box. Isa's natural inclination was to vault from Sisoko's saddle onto the ground. Instead, he stopped himself and accepted the assistance lest he should embarrass the stable boy who didn't look much older than him. Master gracefully dismounted his horse and passed Sisoko's reins to the stable boy who tied them to a post. The durbar and his apprentice continued their journey to the main court on foot.

"We're early," said Master, as they walked through a courtyard.

"How do you know Master?" asked Isa. Right on cue his master pointed to a sundial in the middle of the courtyard. Isa felt his cheeks flush and didn't wait for an answer that wasn't coming.

"We have some time to spare. Come, let me show you something," said Master.

Isa obediently followed Master through two atria and several more courtyards until they came to an open space next to the palace gardens. About twenty people had congregated on a patch of soil with little grass. A little bit away from the crowd were two men on stools, each of them facing a long drum. On each drum, several leather tension cords were stretched over the wooden body and connected the two opposite hide drum heads, allowing the pitch to be manipulated. In the middle of the huddle were two men. Both looked a few years older than Isa and were naked except for faded loin cloths. One was stocky while the other was lean. On closer inspection they each had an arm and a leg wrapped in rope. With the exception of a thick set man with muscular arms in a sleeveless blue tunic and matching turban, the small crowd dispersed to form a small circle. The sleeveless man stood between the two younger semi-naked men in the circle. Master and Isa joined the crowd of spectators.

"Have you seen this before," Master asked.

"No Master," Isa said while he shook his head and waited for something to happen.

"You're about to watch your first *dambe* bout," Master said. The sleeveless man checked the bound arms and legs of the two opponents. "Dambe is traditional martial combat." Master looked at Isa's blank expression. "*Fighting*," Master elaborated. Isa nodded and mouthed the syllables *dam-bey* to himself. "These men are training to be the Emir's royal bodyguard. They must excel in armed as well as hand to hand combat. The referee is checking the rope on their arms and legs, called the *kara*. The kara covers the attacking limb, known as the *spear*. Traditionally men would pack glass into the kara to inflict maximum damage." Isa grimaced at the thought. "These men would be useless bodyguards if they were already sliced to pieces."

The sleeveless referee retreated from the centre of the circle and the two men faced one another. The seated drummers began their rhythmic beat from the sidelines. The onlookers went silent. Both fighters immediately adopted an almost crouching posture, mirroring each other with their unbound hands raised and forward in a guard position and the spear limbs held back.

"Those men are beating the long drum, known as the talking drum, the *kalungu*," Master noted. "When the drum sounds the fight is in motion." The referee barked an order from the sidelines and the men slowly began to pace around each other in a calculated manner that resembled lions circling their prey. Without warning, the leaner of the two men suddenly kicked his opponent in his front thigh. The heavier-set recipient of the blow flinched and retreated back a couple of paces and switched his legs in his defensive stance as he did so. The leaner man continued his advance forward.

"The bout lasts three rounds, with no time limit and can be won in one of three ways," Master began. The leaner fighter fired another rapid arcing kick to the front thigh of his opponent who stepped back and maintained his defensive stance, absorbing the blow. "The first is knocking your opponent to the ground. All that's required is that the hand, knee, or body touches the ground." Isa nodded attentively. "This is affectionately known as *killing* your opponent as his contest is over." Isa squirmed uncomfortably at the brutality of the terminology. The fighters moved closer to the crowd. "The second way is by inactivity.

You'll lose if you do nothing." Isa studied the lean fighter moving on the balls of his feet. His opponent looked flat-footed with his weight predominantly on the back foot. "The final way is by decision of the referee. It's in your best interests to impress him instead of boring him." The stocky fighter threw a couple of wild swings at his adversary with his bound hand. None landed and the lean man weaved left then right with his hands down. Isa could've sworn the lean man smiled at the heavier man as he avoided the telegraphed attacks and the pair began to move away from the edges of the circle. The referee looked irritated and barked an order at both men to stop. The kalangu ceased its rhythmic drum beat, the volume of the audience rose and both fighters stood upright while the referee returned to the centre of the circle.

"The first round is over," Master said. He turned to Isa while the referee checked each man's kara. "Other variations of dambe include wrestling, known as *kokawa*, but as you can see avoiding the ground for today's fighters is a priority. If they hit the ground they lose. Fighters can grapple with the guard hand but they can only strike with the spear hand or spear leg."

The referee resumed his position on the side-line and barked an order for combat to resume. The kalangu began its beat once more. The only other competing sound was the opposing feet resuming their combative dance. The stocky fighter threw a punch in the air. The lean man swerved to one side. The stocky man feinted with his guard hand and stepped on the foot of his opponent to halt his retreat. With the foot trapped he lunged forward and launched a blow with his spear hand to the lean man's stomach. The lean man's guard arm was too slow to parry or stop the incoming blow. As the lean man's own spear arm desperately glanced at the shoulder of his assailant, a sharp exhalation of air was heard when he absorbed the first accurate strike of his opponent. The audience gasped. Isa winced at the thought of the pain being inflicted. The attack wasn't over. Sensing his opponent was heavily winded, the stocky man kicked the lean man on the outside of his back knee with his shin. His opponent's leg buckled long enough for his guard arm to drop and create an opening for the inevitable coup de grâce, the finishing blow, in the form of a fist bound by rope to the side of his jaw. Both legs buckled this time and the lean man stumbled until he was on all fours, dejectedly contemplating what had just happened. The muted nods of approval from the sideline confirmed his defeat. Having shut his eyes on the killing blow, Isa opened them. The referee barked an order, the drumbeat stopped and the referee stepped in between the two men. The lean man was helped to his feet by his assailant and after a few more nods from onlookers, the crowd dispersed.

"Brief but insightful," Master commented. "Do you know why he won?"

"The fat man hit the skinny man harder," Isa replied.

"True but that's *how*, not *why*," Master corrected. "He outthought his opponent." Being well-versed in interpreting Isa's confused expressions, Master continued. "The lighter man was faster, probably more skilful too. But speed alone will not win any battle. Nor will strength. Add in strategy and when you have the combination of all three, you will win the battle before it has even begun. The heavy man saw his opponent was overconfident and found his guard to be weak. Then he overloaded him to the point where he was unable to defend himself and the bout was over. Learning is using all your senses, what you see, hear, touch, taste, to increase your understanding of the world. Adapting is making a change based on what you've learned. If you cannot learn, you cannot adapt. If you cannot adapt, you'll be beaten by change. One way or another. Come, the council awaits us."

#

The feather's quill hovered over the ink pot until the excess droplets returned to their source. The scratching of their names being solemnly inscribed in the registration book was muted by the pigmented liquid solution. On the candlelit page their names glistened in the wet ink as Isa attentively watched the main court official record their arrival in the antechamber. Although Master and his ward were expected, it was mandatory that all arrivals and departures were accounted for. The dimly lit antechamber received light from high windows and lanterns along the corridors. Long shadows disappeared around a corner. Satisfied by the legitimacy of their reception, another official escorted them to a brighter side room.

An old man in a beige kaftan and green turban offered them tea. Pressed for time, Master declined the hospitable gesture and disappeared with another official in a gold kaftan and turban combination. Alone and invisible, Isa remained seated. Having drunk his tea as instructed, he studied the intricate designs of the pewter tea set long enough for boredom to set in. He scanned the spartan décor of the waiting room. Carvings, metal ornaments and more carvings. Mischief got the better of his imagination. He looked at the face of the old tea server. No eye contact. The old man's eyes appeared fixed precisely on a point in the middle of nowhere. After staring for long enough to provoke a response, Isa held up the pewter teacup level with the old man's weatherbeaten and expressionless face before squinting with one eye. Same complexion. Same entertainment value. After more time elapsed, the old man's eyes left their point of interest and met with Isa's open eye. The boy's cheeks flushed hot and prompted him to open his other eye and put the cup down immediately. When he looked up again, the old baba's gaze was once again elsewhere. Isa ran his palms along the armrests of the massive mahogany high-backed chair. The carved patterns bore a striking resemblance to the hilts of Master's swords. The tedium quickly returned. With his statuesque chaperone for company, as usual Isa would have to entertain himself until Master's return.

#

Light poured into the dark passageway as more stony-faced guards ushered the court official and the durbar through the gigantic double doors of the main courtroom. Like their numerous counterparts placed specifically around the ornate court interior, these guards were also armed with spears and swords. An unfamiliar visitor may have concluded that the guards were there to protect the dozen men spaced evenly in high-backed red velvet chairs on both sides of the aisle in the centre of the room. A keener observer would have seen that these men, in different coloured robes but all wearing turbans also wrapped around their necks, were also armed, albeit discreetly. Some had daggers concealed by sashes around their waists. Others concealed them on their arms or legs. All of them openly carried sheathed swords with identical scabbards. The convention of trained killers needed no protection. The guards were there for someone else. Someone occupying the vacant throne on the stage at the end of the aisle. Atypical in its appearance, the throne was elevated a couple of feet above the stage and wide enough to seat three average-sized people. It was entirely covered in red, gold and black patterned tapestries with large cushions completely obscuring the seat while it lay vacant. These tapestries complemented the lavish rug that lined the court aisle from the entrance up to the stage.

When the last of the twelve men on the aisle was seated, the court official remained standing in the centre. All waited patiently. Within minutes two men emerged from doorways from both sides of the stage and lined up on both sides of the throne. The pair were armed with a brass horn each, the *kakaki*, that was almost as long as they were tall. The long loud blast of these ceremonial horns cut through the atmosphere of bravado, chit-chat and social posturing. The horn-blowers immediately dispersed.

"His royal highness, his excellency Emir Ado Sanusi of Kano!" bellowed the court official from the centre of the aisle. The dozen aisle guests stood up immediately. A mixed procession, young and old, male and

female, clad in white and gold, emerged from the horn-blowers' doorways. The train took up positions on both sides of the throne. Amongst their number was a middle-aged man, small in stature. The white and gold embroidered cloth covering his turban set him apart from all the others, before he took his place on the throne. Once seated, the man removed the cloth to reveal two protrusions from the top of the turban fabric that resembled linen ears. His boyish face was swaddled by the turban fabric wrapped beneath his chin. The grey hairs sprouting from the pencil moustache on his slim face were the main clue to his approximate age.

"Wa as salaam alaikum," said the Emir, in a voice that seemed too soft to be regal.

"Alaikum as salaam," responded all but one of the twelve men seated by the aisle.

"Please be seated," said the Emir. His entourage and the dozen armed men took their seats. Once everyone was seated, the court official did an about face turn and left the courtroom. "Thank you for convening the durbar council at such short notice," continued the Emir. "It was imperative that I spoke to all of you at the earliest opportunity." The Emir paused and scanned each of the gathered faces in order to impress the gravity of the situation. "Something alarming has been brought to my attention. Something that is alarming to me and will be alarming to you and all those that reside in this kingdom if word of it spreads." A female entourage member with silver hair nodded as he spoke. The dozen armed men listened intently. "As you know, we have agents scattered throughout the kingdom to gather intelligence, should there be any indication that we are under threat." Silent glances were exchanged across the aisle.

One of the twelve closest to the stage stood. Older than the rest, with skin obsidian black and a neatly trimmed white beard. His attire was understated in dark orange robes and a brown turban. He waited for his summons to speak. "Speak Jibril Asari," ordered the Emir.

"Your excellency, who would threaten the kingdom?" asked Jibril Asari.

"Minister?" The Emir turned to the right of the aisle and another man stood up.

"Thank you, your excellency," began the minister. The scrawny light-skinned man turned to face the older durbar. "So far the details are scant. A messenger arrived two days ago from Sokoto. He warned of a threat to destabilise the kingdom. He wasn't making much sense before he lost consciousness, then died shortly after."

"*Died?*" asked Jibril Asari. "From what?"

"From his wounds," responded the minister bluntly. There was muttering among the durbar council before the minister continued. "He was feverish and the wounds to his body were infected, according to our physician. It seems that he'd been involved in an altercation of sorts prior to delivering his message and later succumbed to his injuries."

"So he died delivering a message," asked Jibril Asari.

"It would appear so," responded the minister matter of factly.

"Who was this messenger?" Jibril Asari asked.

"Nobody of any unique importance," scoffed the minister dismissively. Jibril Asari searched his face for some empathetic marker. He found none. "But a man loyal to the kingdom, nonetheless." The minister faced the throne as he clarified his statement.

"The murder of any royal official is punishable by death. Who would take such a risk? Who would threaten the kingdom? We've had peace with our neighbours in the south for over ten years. We regularly receive ambassadors from abroad with no ill will," mused Jibril Asari.

"All our foreign and domestic treaties remain intact," continued the minister. "Other than this messenger, there has been no warning of a threat to break the peace."

"Thank you minister," said the Emir. "This incident is extraordinary and needs further but cautious investigation," he continued. "We must not start retaliation without merit. Equally, we must not be caught unaware." All the members of the durbar council nodded solemnly as their ruler spoke. "The mandate of the durbar council is to identify the source of this information. Once the source has been identified the information must be clarified and the threat quantified. Each of you will investigate within your designated jurisdiction. You will have the full support of the palace. Time is of the essence. Do you have any more questions?"

Jibril Asari looked at the remaining council members. Each one of them shook their heads. The chairman turned back to the Emir. "No your excellency. We are ready."

Chapter Three

Consequences. Provide for your family. Start small, think big. A rich man is never hungry. Why doubt a rich man, an official no less? The proverb says that if not for someone else's influence, a man would die poor. After all, being born into wealth is the natural order of things. Opportunities like this don't fall from the sky. Take the money. These were the encouraging words of wisdom from those who wished Bawa no ill will. Those who wished him to succeed. Those who weren't faced with the consequences of his actions. Where were those people now?

Gambo was a braggart. A braggart with connections but a braggart nonetheless. When Gambo had approached him with a job, Bawa had naturally been skeptical. Especially when he told him it was for an official from the Gidan Korau. What would a big man from the emirate want with them? The job was reasonably straightforward, he was told. Detain a person of interest. Ask him some questions. Await further instructions. They would be considered unofficial agents of the emirate, Gambo had boasted. A little rough stuff might be necessary but they'd have one more pair of hands to assist them and the fee, pre and post completion of the job, would be worth it. Once Bawa had heard the mouth-watering fee for the job, the other risks Gambo then explained quickly became inaudible.

What little information they were given came via a go-between. This made sense. A big man was surely too busy to instruct them directly.

Details of the detainee were scant. Someone of high value. Someone from Kano. The last detail was a bonus. Getting paid to give a pompous goat from Kano a hiding? Definitely a bonus. Everything was relatively straightforward. Until it all went wrong.

Trepidation hung in the air like nooses around their necks, more suffocating the longer they sat there unsupported in the poorly lit antechamber. It was ironic that Bawa had dreamed of being in a palace, the Gidan Korau and now that he'd made it there, it was under precisely the wrong circumstances. He desperately tried to ignore his pounding heartbeat but his chest felt like it would explode and the sweat on his body was soaking through his tunic. He considered shutting his eyes but didn't want to give any element of surprise to the gigantic palace guards surrounding them in the tiny space. Making eye contact might also trigger a beating. The cracks in the stone floor seemed the safest space for his eyes for now. Bawa cast his mind back to the downturn in their fortunes. Once things had started to unravel, the summons to answer the big man had been expected. The sudden arrival of an armed escort had been persuasion enough to honour it. How were they to know the Kano man was from the emirate? He'd put up a good struggle but between the three of them, they'd managed to subdue him. The arrogant toad had taken his licks well. This had only spurred Gambo on to upping the ante and improvising with the rough stuff. In hindsight, perhaps the palm wine had blurred their focus, dulled their senses a little. Maybe that was when their captive had seen the window of opportunity to act and seized it. Perhaps if Gambo's accomplice hadn't passed out at his post, they wouldn't be in their current predicament. Perhaps all was not lost. It was possible that the big man might lend them a sympathetic ear, no blame would be apportioned and they might even be offered a chance to remedy the situation. If they were really lucky, they may be offered more work. The fact that they hadn't been shackled in chains and were still alive had to be positive news. The three dishevelled men sat in silence, all hoping that their recital of the chain of events that had unfolded would be consistent.

The chamber door creaked open, a guard stepped out and motioned with a jerk of his head for the outsiders to get moving. The three scrawny men entered the large well lit room as instructed. Had their lives not been at stake they would've marvelled at the otherworldly environment they stepped into. Exquisitely crafted furniture and precious stones aside, none of them had ever seen paintings before. The fascination was momentary. Guards, each a clear head height taller than Gambo, the tallest of their trio, lined up against the walls. A long polished wooden table at one end of the room was bare except for a pewter goblet. A heavy-set man in formal regalia sat at the table. Judging by the gold rings on his fingers, his full cheeks and bulging waist stretching the purple fabric to its limit, it was safe to assume that this was him, the oga at the top, the big man, *the* official.

The strangers shuffled forward uneasily, cautiously looking left and right for any threats or sudden attacks. The feeling of distrust was mutual. Fists gripped hilts as the guards eyed the malodorous alien trio suspiciously. The official held up the palm of his right hand to signal that they'd come far enough. He slid his chair back and stood up, eyeballing the visitors as he did so. The big man took slow measured paces around them, looking them up and down, wrinkling his nose as their foul stench invaded his nostrils and their tattered clothing offended his gaze. The guards watched in silence. After an eternity of inspection, the official stopped pacing and stood behind the three men.

"Kneel," the official commanded.

The three detainees looked around the room, at the narrow windows, the guards and then at each other. Making themselves even more vulnerable didn't feel right at all. The official sighed audibly behind them, clearly not in the mood to be disobeyed.

"Look around you. You're outnumbered and you'll easily be

outmanoeuvred no matter what you do. Your choices are limited," said the official. "If I wanted to harm you, you cannot stop me. I'm telling you for the last time. *Kneel.*"

Bawa, Gambo and their accomplice looked at each other, accepted that the odds were heavily stacked against them no matter what and slowly knelt on the cool hard stone floor in front of the table. The official remained standing behind them.

"Good. That's a start," began the official. He sounded a little less frustrated and more keen to get the post-mortem underway. "So, you three are the local talent that was employed to carry out a simple task." The official looked down at the men and scratched the stubble on his chin. "Who's in charge here?"

The strangers looked at each other hesitantly, before Gambo knelt taller than his companions, puffed out his chest and piped up.

"*Me,*" said Gambo confidently. Bawa felt even more uneasy. He'd recruited the others but Gambo was no leader. What was he up to? Was he trying to cut a deal for himself? Now was not the time for peacocking. The big rich oga didn't seem like a man that was easily impressed. The official walked around the men on their knees to face them and eyeballed their self-proclaimed leader. Gambo returned the stare, while his colleagues looked at the floor.

"Yes, you seem like the leader," said the official, nodding and smiling as he did so. He resumed his previous position behind the men and reached into the pocket of his robe. Gambo seemed buoyed by the acknowledgement of his elevated status but remained looking forward, despite the smirk on his face. The cloud of fear no longer hovered over him. Perhaps some kind of settlement or chance to make amends for their mishap was on the horizon.

"Were you paid in full?" asked the official.

"Yes s—" Gambo's speech abruptly morphed into a blood-curdling gurgle as a string-wire was forcibly wrapped around his windpipe from behind. His companions flinched but the sound of swords being drawn around the room froze them on the spot. Gambo's face was a mask of terror. His eyes bulged and rapidly turned red as the engorged capillaries of his eyeballs burst with the strain. Gambo grabbed at the garrotte but his frantic attempts to release the stranglehold were in vain, as a swift knee to his back forced him face down onto the ground. The significant weight advantage of his attacker pinned him to the floor. Instead of coming to his aid, his companions watched in horror as Gambo's arms and legs flailed helplessly and his bodily functions failed him.

Within a minute the struggle was over. Gambo lay still. The rotund official stood up and wiped sweat from his brow with his sleeve and threw the string-wire on the table. The braggart's blood dripped from the wire, staining the wooden surface. Bawa felt his bowels spasm, acid rise at the back of his throat and covered his mouth to stop vomiting. The official leaned over, swiped the goblet from the table and took a few gulps. He paused to catch his breath and wrinkled his nose at the smell of urine and faeces emanating from the now deceased Gambo on the floor underneath him. Despite the stench, he looked visibly more relaxed, the exorcism of his anger almost complete. As the official put the goblet to his lips again, one of the dead man's surviving companions visibly trembled with his hand over his mouth, while the other stared vacantly into space, as if stuck in a trance.

"I'll ask again. Who's in charge here?" asked the official.

The surviving two strangers made no eye contact this time. Bawa continued to tremble uncontrollably, while his accomplice appeared catatonic. Bawa looked at Gambo's soiled body and began to panic. Was he next? The official sighed his bored sigh once again.

"Y-y-you are sir," mumbled the tremulous Bawa. He didn't dare look the big man in the eye. The official walked around the table, sat down, put his goblet down and smiled.

"Very good. Now we're getting somewhere," said the official. "Your friend thought he was in charge," the official pointed at Gambo's corpse, "but he was just a consequence of your collective failure to complete the task that you were paid very handsomely for." The official clicked his fingers and signalled to a guard to remove the body. A sword was sheathed, Gambo's feet were picked up and his surviving companions watched his limp body being dragged out of the room. A short trail of blood and excrement was left in his wake. The captives immediately turned back to face the floor in front of them. Bawa took a deep breath and tried to steady himself. It didn't work.

"You were supposed to extract information from the man from Kano, then await further instructions," continued the official. "Instead, you let him escape." The official frowned and let his words hang in the air for a few moments. "If he's still alive, he may come back and if he does, after what you did to him and what you failed to do, he won't be alone." The official sighed. "Even if he doesn't return, someone will come in his place. I can assure you of that. As you can see," the official pointed to the late Gambo's body fluid signature, "mistakes cost lives."

Bawa looked at the bloody garrotte on the table. His surviving partner looked at the patch of human detritus where their companion had been executed.

"*Look at me*," demanded the official. Both men slowly looked up at their captor. "A heavy price will be paid for your failure. Do you know what that price will be?"

Both men shook their heads apprehensively. Bawa managed to keep still.

"Luckily for you I'm yet to decide your fate, as I have some pressing business to attend to." The official smiled his insincere smile. "Stand up."

The two men obeyed the command and clumsily got to their feet as the circulation returned to their legs. "You're going to tell my men everything the man from Kano told you. The longer you take, the more...uncomfortable this whole process will be. Lives depend on it, including your own. Do you understand?"

The two men nodded emphatically.

"*Now get out.*"

Four guards escorted the terrified twosome out of the room. Bawa's legs felt alien and sluggish, as if they belonged to someone else. He almost stumbled after a few steps. Fearing they'd be hacked down before reaching their exit, his partner in crime caught him by the arm and held him up. Gambo was dead but they were still alive. That had to count for something. The chamber door creaked shut behind them.

The official leaned back in his chair, yawned, beckoned a guard to the table and placed the bloody garrotte in the palm of his hand. It had been a while since he'd gotten his own hands dirty, actually killed someone with his own bare hands. Especially such low-rent scum. But the occasion warranted it. The last time he'd relied on others he'd been rewarded with the current mess. Not that he'd had much choice, given the nature of the operation. Loose ends had to be tied up. Besides which, he needed the release. The Boii priestess wasn't due until the next day and there were several hours to go until the evening's other entertainment.

"Get someone to clean this mess," demanded the official, waving his hand dismissively at the stained stone floor. "Then, take your time with those two. They'll say anything to get you to stop. Once you're satisfied that they've told you everything they know, work them over some more. Then scatter their remains where nobody will find them." The official placed his elbows on the table, interlocked his fingers and placed them under his chin. "Then, we must prepare for what comes next."

Chapter Four

Kano was the fortressed heart of the north, in healthy pumping order, with copious rich flow to, from and through it. Katsina was bloated, barely functioning and starved of the healthy circulation and balance that its neighbour thrived upon. Once a prosperous walled city that flourished on agriculture, Katsina was nourished by violent crime, poverty and general desperation. Under the harshest rule of the Katsina emirate, inequality was as prevalent as ever. Those of any means had been driven to the outskirts of the city, while the poorest festered in the city centre. The comparatively less dangerous southern part of the city was a hive of trade in commodities and people, including the infamous Kirikiri market. Travellers unable to circumnavigate the city and take the much longer route to Sokoto, used Katsina as a brief stopping point only. To stay any longer, without the necessary nous to avoid exploitation or other calculated maleficence, was at one's peril. Katsina was a rogues' paradise and a breeding ground for opportunists.

As nightfall crept in, Master opted for himself and Isa to stop over at the city's nucleus. Then the investigation would begin in earnest. Curious eyes followed the well-dressed stranger and his young companion on horseback. Some of the watching faces were familiar to Isa as they wandered the streets looking for suitable accommodation. He recognised the familiar faces of hunger, hopelessness and destitution. Sensing the unwanted attention, Master casually pulled back his robe to reveal the scabbard of the sword hanging at his waist. Some of the prying eyes took heed of the warning and looked elsewhere for their opportunity. Eventually, less than modest lodgings on a noisy street corner were decided on.

"Wait here with Sisoko," said Master, as he dismounted the horse.

"*Here,* Master?" asked Isa indignantly. Ignoring him, Master removed a pouch from Sisoko's saddle and concealed it inside his robe. He then took a dagger hidden around his waist and placed it in the palm of Isa's hand. The dagger was a mini-replica of Master's sword. Isa stared at the dagger dumbfounded.

"Is there dust in your ears Isa?" asked Master impatiently. "Wait right here. I'll be back shortly." Master set off then stopped after a couple of paces before turning around. "Oh and Isa?"

"Yes Master?"

"If you stop staring at the blade, perhaps people might actually think you know how to use it."

"Yes Master." Isa ostentatiously held the dagger upright and at arm's length, while self-consciously looking at his surroundings, as his master disappeared into the noisy building next to them. The odd less than friendly onlooker milling outside the establishment eyed Isa suspiciously. Was he meant to point the dagger at an attacker, stick it in them or throw it at them? He'd only ever seen Master throwing knives, jabbing the blade into thin air or stabbing a tree on the compound. As he looked around, common sense told him that if he got attacked in this wretched place, it wouldn't be by a tree.

An excruciatingly long ten minutes later, Master returned and nonchalantly retrieved the dagger from Isa in a pincer grip. Having hidden the weapon in his robe, Master then set about untying their belongings from Sisoko's saddle, ignoring Isa's visible relief as he did so. Before Isa knew it, Master was carrying all their belongings and staring at him impatiently.

"Do you intend to sleep out here tonight?" asked Master, with both arms full. With a staff strapped to his back, his silhouette cast an interesting shape in the setting sun.

"No Master." Isa sheepishly dismounted Sisoko and took her by the reins.

"Good. We have somewhere for the night. Follow me."

#

The rowdy tavern resembled an indoor market. Unlike a market, there was shelter for drunkards staggering all over the place. Items on sale varied from plentiful palm wine to goat meat with stew, to plantain and chin chin. The crunching of the latter in peckish mouths and the slurps of wine punctuated the cacophony of slurred speech and discordant singing. The overpowering stench of different blends of saturated body odour and other putrid smells was suffocating. The establishment was also conspicuous for a visible lack of women in the vicinity. Given the surplus of testosterone at close quarters, Isa thought it was probably safer that way. For the first time since they left Kano, his sense of excitement was deflated. If they were going to keep visiting places like this, Master's big investigation felt less like an adventure and more like a chore. Being a durbar suddenly didn't seem so glamorous. The establishment's proprietor and his staff, most likely working in servitude, seemed to be in the minority of sober people. Master chose a table on the periphery of the fog of human aroma.

"Don't judge them too harshly," said Master, breaking Isa's train of thought.

"Master?"

"I can see it on your face, the way you look at them."

"But Master, they're drunk and acting like animals. Aren't they idle, useless even?" asked Isa.

"Right now, yes but do you know any of these people?" countered Master, as he observed the contained chaos.

"No Master." Isa wrinkled his nose. Normally Master was far more critical of far less. Why did he find this behaviour acceptable? "I don't understand."

"Isa, do you consider yourself a slave?" asked Master.

"Hmm…well, I *was* a slave…but that was before," replied Isa, not seeing the relevance of his master's point. He guessed that a drunk slave was a rare phenomenon.

"Very good. My point exactly," replied Master. "You see that man sitting on the ground?" Master pointed to a man with half-open eyes wiping drool from the corner of his mouth and barely supporting his head above a table. "He could be a farmer, a trader, a father or anything else. We don't know anything else about him and we may never know. All we see now is a drunk." There was a small pool of vomit beneath the man's table. Isa's confused expression resurfaced. "What I can tell you is that things in Katsina are tough. Worse than they've been since I can remember. It's ever so easy to pass judgement without looking at the bigger picture. That man may be drowning his sorrows, he may be celebrating good fortune for himself or others. We don't know. Don't be so quick to pass judgement on others."

"Yes Master." Isa wondered whether it was worth celebrating to the point where you threw up all over yourself, but kept that thought to himself.

"On a more practical note, tongues will be loose in this establishment."

"Master?"

"Lies can pass through the lips of anyone but for the intoxicated, the wine makes the truth much easier to swallow."

Isa nodded slowly. For once he understood one of his master's many pearls of wisdom.

"Furthermore, our appearance might attract just the right kind of attention to help with our investigation," continued Master. "As you've correctly acknowledged, we're not the typical clientele of this establishment and neither of us have a drink in our hands."

"So what do we do now Master?" asked Isa.

"We watch and wait for an opportunity to present itself," replied Master.

Isa wasn't sure whether this was Master's coded language for not having any specific plan but he knew that it was in his best interests to keep his own pearl of wisdom to himself. He chose to nod sagely to himself instead.

An hour later the patron of the establishment approached their table. Master accepted the bowl of plantain and yam with stew but politely declined the palm wine. The patron gave Master and Isa a brief but quizzical look.

"No wine for you?" asked the patron. Master shook his head and smiled. "What about the boy?" The grizzly looking patron then broke out into wheezy laughter, exposing rotten teeth. His stale breath made Isa hold his. "We normally don't see your lot in these parts very often. You must have a lot of business this way."

"Our lot?" asked Master.

"You official people," replied the patron.

"We're very busy indeed. I'm sure a man with your seasoned eye can easily spot an out of towner," noted Master.

"Yes, I guess so," said the patron.

"When was the last time you saw one of us?" asked Master directly.

"One of you?" asked the patron. Isa observed Master maintaining a smile but looking the man dead in his eyes.

"There was someone, dressed just like me," said Master, "but in green and probably alone. He must've passed through Katsina not that long ago. Maybe in the last week or two."

"Last week or two?" muttered the patron. "Oh, my memory fails me, must be my age." In an instant his demeanour switched from personable to awkward.

"But you were able to recognise me as someone official," pressed Master. "I'm guessing your memory can't be as bad as you say. I'm guessing you would've seen some other official people passing through here recently."

The patron looked flustered, avoided all eye contact and began to fiddle with items on their table, as if suddenly under some new time pressure to clear it. "Maybe. Maybe I saw someone like you some time ago. As I said, old age."

"Well here's to old age then." Master raised his cup to the man and smiled.

"Yes indeed. Old age." The patron nodded. "Please excuse me, I have some urgent business to attend to." Without waiting for a response, the man shuffled off to another section of the tavern. Master followed him with his eyes and then shifted his gaze to Isa, who watched the uncomfortable exchange with renewed enthusiasm.

"Your thoughts Isa?" asked Master.

"He's lying."

#

After another hour of people-watching and gentle probing of anyone who came into their orbit, Master called time on the day's investigation. He shouldered the heavier items, while Isa carried the rest. As they approached the doorway, a man in soiled clothing with a toothless smile blocked their exit. The malodorous man barely came up to Master's chest height.

"Excuse me sir, is this your son?" asked the man.

"That isn't your concern. Excuse us," replied Master politely. He moved to step around the obstacle but the peculiar man took another step to block his path. The din in the tavern quietened as the exchange was observed by the minority of the less inebriated clientele.

"He doesn't look like your son," said the man suspiciously, eyeing up Isa with a look that made his skin crawl. "How much for this fine boy?"

"He's not for sale." Unfazed by the sleazy proposal, Master stared at the man and waited patiently.

"I'm reasonable. How about just for the night?" persisted the man.

A shiver went down Isa's spine. He stood behind his master as his breathing became shallow. Master didn't flinch.

"He's not for sale. I won't tell you again. Let us pass or you will be moved." Master spoke in a firm tone without raising his voice. "I must warn you, if I have to move you, I cannot guarantee a soft landing."

The darkness lifted off Isa and the perpetrator focussed on Master. It took only a couple of seconds for him to weigh up the different permutations of a soft landing, courtesy of the much bigger man in front of him. He moved to the side and muttered to himself angrily as they passed by. "You durbars think you're better than everyone else. Well you're not!"

Without looking back, Master and Isa carried on to their quarters. The racket in the tavern picked up again.

#

Outside, light spilled over from the noisy tavern into the dark street. The immediate vicinity was shrouded in darkness, with the odd lamp or house fire glowing in the distance. Master and Isa's designated quarters were accessible via a separate entrance around the corner and across a small pathway.

"What do you think that man wanted with me Master?" asked Isa as they lugged their belongings to their temporary home.

"It's better that you don't fully understand the mind of a deviant Isa."

"What's a deviant Master?"

"A very bad person," responded Master.

"But why not just call him a very bad per—"

"*Quiet!*" whispered Master. He froze in his tracks. Isa stopped immediately. Master's head moved slowly right then sharply left, scanning the darkness. He carefully squatted down and quietly placed their belongings on the ground. He immediately raised his right hand to signal to Isa. Obeying his master, Isa remained right behind him and didn't move a muscle. With his left hand, Master reached back and slowly pulled his staff from its harness. He held the weapon in two hands, one end of the staff pointing forwards and took a step and a half backwards into a low stance. They both heard footsteps on the earthen path. Then, in the moonlight, Isa and Master saw an all too familiar face.

"You should've given me the boy when I asked," said the toothless stranger. This time he'd come prepared. He was brandishing a long knife and he'd brought back up. Considerably larger backup. In the moonlight, Master made out the silhouette of a man of identical build to himself and another, shorter and wider. They too had long bladed weapons at hand. A friendly warning wouldn't pass muster this time. The backup slowly separated from the ringleader to surround the durbar and his apprentice. The three men slowly began to circle their prey. The deviant sneered at Master knowing that this time there would be no offer of a soft landing.

Maintain distance. Keep the boy safe. Disrupt. Master's reptilian brain was already at play without hesitation. He turned slowly in time with their assailants, keeping them in his field of vision at all times.

"Isa do exactly as I say," ordered Master. "Stay close to me and keep them in front of you at all times. Understand?"

"Yes Master." Fear was sucking the air out of Isa's lungs. He felt lightheaded and his voice quivered as the predators slowly began to narrow the circle. He and Master stood back to back. Luck was not on their side. Master had lowered the tip of his staff and slid it along the ground as they faced their encircling threat. Was he marking their territory? If ever Master possessed any magic powers, Isa prayed he would use them to keep them safe inside this circle.

Eliminate the weakest link. Master watched all three opponents, turning his head left and right as the advancing circle grew smaller. Then at just the right moment, with the tip of his staff, Master flicked some loose soil at his largest opponent. As the man stumbled back and rubbed his eyes, Master immediately stepped in the direction of the next big man and feinted a jab of the staff in his direction. The man automatically retreated a couple of steps, creating further breathing space. The next step went reassuringly as predicted. Strategy, cowardice or a combination of both had kept the deviant ringleader at bay thus far. Unfortunately for him, his overeager desire to settle the score was to Master's advantage. Sensing the oncoming attack, Master cut the distance between them with a couple of rapid paces, spun around and thrust the end of the staff into the throat of the deviant with a reverse strike. Paralysed by uncontrollable pain and panic at the sudden inability to breathe or make a sound, the man dropped his knife, reached for his bruised larynx and doubled over. Before the blade hit the dirt, Master had stepped back inside and parried an arcing slash from the other short man's blade. Pushing the man off balance, Master followed up with a stamp to the man's front knee. Isa winced as the man's knee ligaments ruptured with an audible *crunch* and the man howled in agony. While the felled opponent rolled around on the ground, Master faced forward, spun his staff overhead and dumped the momentum in a blow to the temple of the deviant ringleader behind him. The deviant dropped like a sack of old yam. Master held the staff in his right hand in an open stance, ready to deal with the last opponent.

The altercation flashed before Isa's eyes in seconds. Without realising, he'd taken refuge off the pathway by a bush. Despite disobeying Master's instruction to stay close, the carnage on the pathway proved that his prayers had been answered. Master had kept them alive, albeit with collateral damage in the process. One man was unconscious, possibly dead. The other was crippled like a lame dog. Isa almost felt sorry for Master's final foe. As the stranger angrily charged towards Master, it was clear to Isa that Master exuded something that the man didn't. Pure controlled aggression. In Isa's mind the outcome of the fight had already been decided.

Overcome. The third opponent would be both disheartened by the rapid dispatch of his comrades and emboldened by his own humiliating start to the altercation. The man charged towards Master like a feral beast. He immediately sidestepped Master's first thrust of the staff. Then he weaved under the next one. At the third attempt the man stepped inside, grabbed the staff and pulled it towards him with his free hand, closing down Master's reach. He simultaneously lunged forward and thrusted his blade towards Master's torso. Master had little choice but to release his grip on the staff. *Adapt.* Reducing his opponent's reach with the blade would give him a hands-free advantage. Master immediately stepped perpendicular to the attack, leading with his right shoulder. He struck his attacker's blade-carrying forearm with his own right forearm, knocking the weapon off target. The durbar then launched his entire body weight, shoulder first, into the man's sternum. Master's opponent released the staff and landed a powerful blow to Master's kidney with his freed-up hand but the execution of his counterattack was too poorly timed. The air left his lungs as Master's shoulder smashed into his chest and the man stumbled backwards. *Finish.* Master followed his momentum then accelerated his right elbow upwards through the man's chin. The blade and the staff fell to the earth. The man's eyes rolled back in his head, his legs went limp and with an almighty *thud*, he fell backwards onto the ground.

Master picked up the man's blade and tossed it as far away as he could. He then picked up his staff and walked over to where the crippled man was still writhing around on the ground, trying and failing to stand on his damaged knee. To his credit, the man hadn't yet let go of his weapon. The man looked angrily at Master before he too was engulfed by darkness, courtesy of the end of Master's staff.

#

Maintain vigilance. Master sat cross-legged facing the door of their lodgings from the inside, with his back to the wall, in anticipation of the next wave. He held his unsheathed sword in one hand and a naked dagger in the other. The remaining daggers were laid out on the floor next to him and the staff was behind him within easy reach. If they came, he was ready.

"Get some sleep Isa." Master looked at the boy. "If we make it through the night, tomorrow will be a long day." It was unusual to hear Master sound so weary.

"Do you think they'll come back, Master?" asked Isa.

"Not them necessarily. At least not tonight and not all of them." Master paused and then looked again at Isa. "What happened tonight was no coincidence Isa."

"Master?" Isa stifled a yawn as his adrenaline levels returned to normal.

"How would a low-life like that find two accomplices like them so quickly?" Master shook his head slowly. "As valuable as you are to me Isa, are you really worth the price of two trained fighters?"

"Trained fighters Master?" asked Isa.

"Don't be fooled by the outcome. Those two knew how to fight. I'm guessing they're soldiers."

"What does that mean Master?"

"It means somebody doesn't want this investigation to begin."

Chapter Five

Contemptuous looks replaced the curious ones Isa and Master had thus far been subjected to. The foreigners looked hungry and bitter. From the moment they entered the grounds of the Gidan Korau, the royal palace of the Katsina emirate, Isa felt more secure but no more welcome than the day before. The safety of daylight and dearth of intoxicated people in the vicinity offered meagre comfort amongst the disdainful looks of the palace populace. Even the lowest common denominator, the stable boy, had a mild contemptuous air. After the previous night's ordeal, the day had reassuringly lacked any excitement. Sisoko buried her head in a trough and quenched her thirst while Isa mastered the art of avoiding eye contact with anyone that passed them by.

Considering he hadn't slept at all the night before, Master hadn't lost any focus when they left for the palace. He hadn't spoken of the attempt on their lives. If anything, with isolating calm, he seemed more determined than ever to pursue the investigation. As detached as he could be his clarity for the task ahead was both unsettling and irregular, even for him. His first official engagement in the Katsina emirate Council building, an island in the palace grounds, beckoned.

"What happened to your messenger is most distressing." The bulging belly beneath the purple fabric rumbled like an earthquake as he coughed into his hand before continuing. The gold rings on his fingers were an ostentatious sign of his wealth. "But of course, no less distressing than what happened to you and your son."

"Thank you minister," replied the durbar. "The boy is my ward, but your sympathy is still greatly appreciated."

"There is seriously something wrong with anyone who would even consider harming a child," continued the official. "These are desperate times. I suspect you were attacked by local vagabonds. Desperate times indeed."

The situation wasn't yet desperate but the durbar's arrival was official confirmation that the botched job had complicated matters unnecessarily. The counter-measures to buy extra time had apparently also failed. Minister of Information Atiku Danladi was becoming acquainted with failure with increasing frequency. And he didn't like it.

"The local vagabonds seem very robust in this city," commented Master casually.

"Robust?" The minister raised an eyebrow as if Master's comment was somehow peculiar.

"It was a very minor detail that I noticed during the thankfully brief altercation," volunteered Master.

"Please elaborate, master durbar. One man's minor detail may be another man's major discovery," said the minister. The rotund man leaned forward in his chair, his interest piqued by Master's casual reference to this minor detail. The large wooden chair creaked as his considerable weight shifted.

"As you wish, minister. The ringleader of our attackers was undoubtedly wretched and useless. A deviant with a penchant for small boys nonetheless."

"Terrible." Minister Danladi shook his head. "Continue."

"But his two accomplices were a different matter."

"How so?"

42

"One could say that both were in formidable physical condition, with the prowess to match. One was more tactically astute and required more skill to subdue than the other, but both were most certainly robust."

"Where do you think they came from? Was there anything on them that may have hinted as to their origin?" asked Danladi.

"I searched both men thoroughly." Master studied the official's face for a response. "Including their weapons and found nothing." The official didn't flinch when he raised the matter. "I found nothing to suggest anything other than, as you say, local vagabonds operating in desperate times."

The official nodded slowly and read Master's face for any giveaways. Nothing. The durbar had an icy calm about him that was as unnerving as it was reassuring. Danladi imagined the durbar giving those men a hiding they wouldn't forget. He probably hadn't broken a sweat. Confident, skilled fighter and unflappable. The durbar was extremely dangerous indeed.

"But of greater concern to Kano is the mysterious death of our royal emissary," said Master.

"Indeed," acknowledged Danladi. "You say he died on his return from Sokoto?"

"Yes."

"But you feel he passed through Katsina before he reached you?"

"We can only assume," Master answered.

"But you have no proof," countered the official.

"Given the grave nature of his injuries, the most likely route of someone in such a state would've been the shortest one. A man of his responsibility would've sought help at the earliest opportunity. If he knew the futility of his situation, he would understand his obligation to deliver his final message." Master raised his eyebrows deferentially. "As you correctly say Minister, there is no proof. One can only assume he passed through this city."

"Hmmm," the official scratched the stubble on his chin, "did he give you any information at all before his passing?"

"Yes minister," responded Master. "The royal messenger did give us one last important message."

"Go on, what was it?" asked Danladi eagerly.

"He warned of a threat to destabilise our kingdom."

The official paused, scrutinised the durbar for a few seconds, frowned and then continued. "This is most perplexing. This threat, did he say anything more specific? The nature? From whom?"

Master shook his head. "Nothing."

The official sighed. "That is most unfortunate."

"Most unfortunate for everyone," said Master. He glanced at the guards in dark purple and blue, the colours of Katsina, surrounding the official. Unlike some other palace staff wearing turbans, these men all wore helmets. They were all tall, muscular and athletic, with no distinguishing features. Much like any royal protection would be. Very robust indeed.

"And what action has Kano taken, in anticipation of this threat, should the messenger's warning be of sufficient concern?" asked the minister.

"His excellency has instructed the durbar council to investigate the demise of the emissary with the full cooperation of our allies. I can assure you his demise is of sufficient concern to the kingdom, hence my presence here."

"I would not presume to speak on behalf of my excellency but I can assure you that Kano will have the full assistance of everyone at my disposal," said the official. "Unfortunately, your presence is the first I'm hearing of this alarming news. Is there anything else to feed back to my excellency?"

"I have no further instructions."

"I'm sure your investigation will be very thorough. I will update my excellency at once. In the meantime, please enjoy the hospitality of our kingdom master durbar," said the minister, with his diplomatic smile.

"Kano is most grateful." Master nodded. "However, I must resume the investigation as a matter of urgency and leave for Sokoto immediately."

"As you wish, master durbar. As you wish."

#

Master returned in all his aloof glory. Aside from the instruction to mount Sisoko for their departure, he relayed nothing of the meeting and didn't utter a word until they were well beyond the sensitised ears of the palace walls. Isa was happy to leave the miserable city behind in the late morning dust.

"From now on we must keep our wits about us Isa." Master finally broke the silence. "I believe that malevolent forces are at play."

"Who are malevanant's forces, Master?" Isa asked, glad that the gift of speech had returned, even if he didn't understand it.

"*Ma-le-vo-lent*...hostile forces...people that may want to cause harm. Bad people."

"Did the palace people tell you something Master?"

"No and that's precisely why I'm concerned. Something seemed off. Another attempt on a servant of Kano within such a short timeframe should concern a Katsina official."

"Was the man not concerned about us?" asked Isa innocently.

"Not exactly. Three things seemed to concern this Katsina official." Master didn't wait for an invitation to spell out his theory. "The first was the identity of our attackers. He seemed more concerned about *who* attacked us, rather than *why*." He paused to allow his pupil to absorb the information. "The second was the message of our dead emissary. This wasn't an unusual concern, but he seemed disinterested in how the emissary met his end. Not one question about how he died. The final thing was Kano's response to this mysterious threat to the kingdom. Again, not an atypical concern. What might we conclude from this exchange so far Isa?"

Isa searched for an appropriate response to Master's revelations. "That one response was abnormal and the other two were normal?" he asked.

Master ignored his attempt. "We might conclude that the Katsina official was concerned about any affiliation, suspected or proven, our attackers may have had with the Katsina emirate. A failed but confirmed attempt on servants of Kano would have far reaching and serious consequences. But this is the least important point, Isa. Although we have little to no proof, there was something of much greater concern to this Katsina official."

Isa's attention was captured by vultures feasting on an equine carcass on a rocky outcrop in the distance. He stroked Sisoko's hide and wondered whether they would've nourished a separate vulture family, had things turned out differently the night before. Master's lesson continued, unabated by his temporary lapse in concentration.

"We might also conclude that the official is concerned about a warning to Kano and time to prepare," continued Master.

"Time to prepare for what Master?" asked Isa.

"War."

Chapter Six

The tunic was too damn tight. Danladi's armpits gushed like burst dams every time he moved his elbows and with every step he took, the sweat uncomfortably trickled between his buttocks. But the incongruence of his body habitus and an incompetent tailor wasn't solely to blame for his excessive perspiration. The information minister's nerves were jangled for another reason. As he sat waiting for his courtroom summons, he dreaded the humiliation that lay in waiting on the other side of the double doors. No amount of fidgeting or fanning his uncomfortable clothing would alleviate that. He wiped his moist palms on his lap and silently cursed himself for soiling his best tunic when he'd taken matters into his own hands. Who would've thought the blood of lowlifes could leave such a stain? Minister Danladi's musings on a definitive solution for this new durbar problem were interrupted by the opening of the double doors. A sullen official emerged from the courtroom.

"*Minister Danladi,*" bellowed the court official.

The Minister of Information stood up from his pew. The other courtroom attendees, at least those who were awake, focussed their attention away from Danladi onto the stage.

"State your business," commanded the court official before stepping aside to give Danladi a direct line of sight to his audience on the stage. Danladi cleared his throat.

"Your excellency, I received a message from Kano earlier today. Something I believe to be of particular concern," said Danladi.

"Speak Minister Danladi." The Emir of Katsina's voice wheezed as if his lungs could barely service his gargantuan frame. Despite the opulence dripping from every corner of the courtroom, the sheer size of the Emir was its dominant feature. The information minister's girth was no comparison. The Emir was kept cool by a lean servant waving a large fan with a long handle to the side of him.

"As you wish, your excellency," Danladi replied. "A durbar came to our council today, with news of his mandate to investigate a death."

"Whose death?" asked the Emir.

"A royal emissary."

"One of ours?"

"No your excellency. A royal emissary from Kano."

Danladi could see the Emir's small eyes in his large head already glazing over.

"How does this concern Katsina?" grumbled the Emir. "How does this concern me?"

"If you would be so gracious as to indulge me, your excellency." The Emir waved impatiently for Danladi to continue. "Before he died, this messenger passed on a message that this durbar believes to be of great importance. Something very vague about some kind of threat to Kano. It was all very vague. The durbar had no other details."

"How did this messenger die?" asked the Emir.

Danladi felt his cheeks warm up slightly and silently cursed himself. He'd been so focussed on sounding out the durbar that he'd forgotten to ask one very simple but important question. "The durbar didn't share any specific details regarding the death of the emissary," said Danladi. "Only that he believed he had passed through our kingdom on his return from Sokoto before his untimely demise."

The Emir raised his right hand to pause proceedings. A servant carrying a tray shuffled from his post in the corner and held a goblet to the Emir's lips. The monarch audibly drank from the goblet like an animal with its head in a trough. He lifted his head when he was done and the servant dutifully dabbed his mouth with a napkin. Danladi wondered when the Emir had last wiped his own nyash and if he could even reach it.

"Continue Danladi," said the Emir before belching.

"As you wish excellency. The durbar's conclusion that the messenger passed through Katsina is only an assumption."

"How so?" asked the Emir.

"He had no evidence, no eyewitness accounts, nothing to support his theory. There is no objective evidence to indicate that this messenger passed through our city."

"Hmmm. Do *you* have evidence that supports your conclusion? Anything from Sokoto?" countered the Emir.

"Nothing, your excellency. The durbar's arrival was the first I'm hearing of this situation," conceded Danladi.

"So you don't know whether this man did or didn't come through our kingdom before he died in his own kingdom. Furthermore, you haven't heard anything from Sokoto or elsewhere about the supposed murder of a Kano official." There was a long uncomfortable silence. The members of the Emir's entourage looked everywhere but Danladi's direction. "For a man who's supposedly my Minister of Information, you seem to have an alarming lack of any. Maybe I should demote *you* to a royal emissary," scoffed the Emir.

"Excel-"

The Emir raised his right index finger from his armrest to silence him. "At least you know one thing Danladi," said the Emir. "You know that we have a problem. Kano came to Katsina looking for answers to their problem and until we provide them with answers, it is also our problem. Did the durbar tell you anything else of note?"

Danladi recalled the attempt on the durbar's life. "Nothing, other than that Kano is sufficiently concerned by this matter. Those were the durbar's exact words."

"Where is he now?"

"He's already on his way to Sokoto." Danladi cleared his throat. "But prior to his departure I assured him that Katsina will offer Kano its full cooperation in this investigation and I offered him the full hospitality of the kingdom, should he wish to delay his departure."

There was another uncomfortable silence. The Emir frowned and stared at Danladi. Danladi looked at the floor. The wafting of the fan was the only sound in the room.

"Maybe I should demote you to my houseboy because of your hospitality." The Emir gave Minister Danladi a wry smile. "The durbar is irrelevant. My question for you Minister Danladi, is what do you intend to do about this situation?"

"I propose a two-pronged approach. First, we send word to Kano that we shall assist them fully in their investigation. The peace between our kingdoms must be maintained at all costs. If I may continue?"

"Go on," said the Emir.

"I also recommend that we send word to Sokoto, in case for any reason the durbar's message is delayed or fails to materialise. An alliance with Sokoto, I must stress, may be a good option. Purely to share information, spare any embarrassment or more serious consequences in the future."

"Very well, Minister Danladi." The Emir nodded his approval. "Get it done. See to it personally."

"As you wish, your excellency."

The court official escorted information minister Atiku Danladi out of the courtroom. He immediately sat down on a nearby bench, let out a sigh of relief and wiped the dripping sweat from his forehead with his sleeve.

#

A knock roused Danladi from his sleep. Upon instruction, the sergeant at arms ducked under the door frame and entered Danladi's private chamber. The man mountain partially blocked the natural light coming in from a small window.

"My lord," said the sergeant at arms.

"I trust you took the usual precautions in coming here?" asked Minister Danladi.

"Yes, my lord."

"Very good," said Danladi. "As predicted, external forces have brought our plans forward. This new obstacle must be eliminated. Prepare two teams. I want your best men."

"Yes, my lord."

"Each team will take a separate route to Sokoto."

"And word to Kano, my lord?" asked the sergeant.

"Forget Kano. That will be all."

The burly soldier left Danladi alone in his chamber to ponder the future. The durbar problem would be remedied imminently. Soon all the ritual humiliation he'd endured for far too long would be over and he'd enjoy the fruits of his labour. By the time Danladi had his way with the Emir, the uncouth beast would have to eat his own entourage just to stay alive. Or better still, his own flesh. There was plenty of it. Minister Danladi smiled to himself. Perhaps he would make *him* his houseboy.

Chapter Seven

The opportunity for change outweighed the call of duty. Two teams. The sergeant at arms of the royal palace of Katsina, Yusuf Dankote, had always justified his loyal service to morally bankrupt men as duty. The stakes couldn't be higher, the penalty being death, but in his heart he knew he was one step closer to a better life. A better life for his family. A better life in which he'd no longer justify tolerating such vile men. This overwhelming desire was at the forefront of Dankote's mind as he assembled the cadre of highly skilled professional soldiers in the underground passageway leading to the outskirts of the city.

The meeting point maintained operational secrecy while providing the cover of darkness. Only a handful of people outside the military chain of command knew of the existence of this particular passageway. According to military folklore, tunnels had been built three hundred years earlier during an era of peace in anticipation of when that time would inevitably come to an end. A basic principle of any war was that combat was one of many tools to defeat an enemy; blocking trade and destroying an economy were others. History had proved that cutting off essential supplies to the seat of power and starving those most well fed was the most cost-effective way to enforce a surrender. The historic rulers of Katsina were well aware that the walled city's greatest strength, its limited points of access, was also its greatest weakness. Consequently, the passageway was constructed as both an escape and a supply route to and from the palace.

Dankote's change-makers gathered in the tunnel. He knew each of the men, in nondescript unidentifiable clothing, personally. A couple had been handpicked from the royal bodyguard, others from posts in palace security. He'd earned their trust and some had even shed blood with him quelling uprisings over the years. They all understood what was at stake and had accepted the risks involved. Dankote wouldn't be joining them. His absence from palace duties would raise suspicion and jeopardise the mission. He knew that only when the time was right, when all moving parts were in play, could he reveal his true hand in things to come. For now, he was the coordinator of change, with full deniability should things go wrong. Even the team's weapons had been sourced externally from outside the palace armoury. Nothing short of a confession could identify each man.

Two teams of four would deploy along separate routes to Sokoto. The targets would be acquired on either of the two functioning routes, one much longer than the other, to the neighbouring kingdom. The targets were a man and a boy. The boy was described as small. Nothing more, nothing less. Not particularly dark, not particularly fair. Completely unremarkable. The man was described as tall, athletic, bearded and most important of all, extremely dangerous. He would be recognised by the turban wrapped around his neck and his long beige robes. A durbar. The verbal description sufficed. The mission brief was simple. Eliminate the durbar and the boy then leave no trace of them. If a case of mistaken identity should befall an unfortunate man and boy fitting the same description along the way, then they'd be another casualty of war.

Dankote and his men parted company in opposite directions. He returned to the palace, while they advanced on foot to the outside world. In two days everyone would rendezvous at the assembly point. When the eight emerged at ground level, both teams went their separate ways, initially by foot and then on horseback. Stoppages notwithstanding, the durbar and the boy had a substantial head start of several hours. Interception of the pair within Sokoto was undesirable, not least because the covert nature of the operation would be compromised but also because the risk of outside forces being caught up in the melee would be increased, potentially complicating the matter even further. One thing had been made abundantly clear. If any of the eight were wounded or captured, no help would come. It was in everybody's interests for the mission to succeed.

In the distance, a figure in black observed one departing team through a magnifying lens. Satisfied from the elevated vantage point, the figure closed the pocket-sized telescope, placed it in a pouch and tugged at the reins of the horse. The figure in black descended the hilltop and pursued the men on a mission, at a safe distance, as the late afternoon sun set.

#

Two hours later, the sweeper team stopped in a field to rest and rehydrate. Their horses were secured to a tree and a campfire was lit in the darkness. The group congregated around the fire and ate nuts to pass the time. As they were all of similar ability, they drew branches on which three would take the durbar and who would take the boy. The unlucky recipient of the short branch accepted his role without complaint. The boy was technically an enemy combatant and besides which, he was apparently old enough to wield his own weapon. As a trade-off the recipient of the short branch was granted first nap, while someone else kept watch and the other two exchanged war stories over the fire.

The crackling of the campfire, the low rumbling of deep voices and the sound of crickets conversing in the moonlight had soothed the short branch man into a deep sleep. The horses would soon be sufficiently rested and the team would resume the outward leg of the mission. A full bladder roused the short branch man from his brief slumber. He got up and unfastened his clothes. As the gentle discomfort in his bladder eased, it was substituted by another unsettling sensation. While his two comrades jisted over the campfire, he noticed a missing third silhouette. Short branch man fastened his clothes and scanned the horizon. There was no sign of the watchman. In the dark he eventually made out the shape of a motionless body on the ground. Something was sticking out of the watchman's head. Short branch man spun around, on the verge of alerting the others when he felt a sudden sharp severe burning sensation in his chest.

"*Aargh!!!*" he screamed as he dropped to his knees. His chest felt like it was on fire and he began to hyperventilate with the severe pain. The man clutched his chest in agony and fell onto his side. From the ground he looked up at the campfire. Both men had heard him scream and looked in his direction. A moment later, he witnessed the silhouette of an object suddenly lodge in the neck of the nearest man by the campfire. The force of the contact snapped the man's head back and he fell backwards onto the campfire. The man didn't move thereafter. His campfire companion instinctively jumped back and to the side. A fast-moving object whizzed past the man cooking on the fire, missed its newly acquired target and hit the earth. The surviving campfire man grabbed his weapon and dashed away from the pyre.

"*Wait!*" screamed the wounded short branch man.

His colleague ignored his plea for help and scrambled for a horse. Before he got close, another fast-moving object hit the horse he was running towards, squarely in the head. The horse's legs buckled immediately and the beast crashed to the ground in a heap, with its head held above ground, still tied to the tree. In the moonlight the object protruding from the dead horse's head resembled the shaft of an arrow. The fleeing campfire man darted to another horse. This time the arrow whizzed past him and hit the next steed in the right buttock. The horse thrashed around in agony and the man reflexively swerved to avoid being kicked by the distressed animal. This manoeuvre turned out to be lifesaving, as he felt another rush of rapid air thrust past his ear. This last arrow landed in the neck of the agitated horse. The steed was suddenly incongruently calm. It stumbled to one side, then another before its front legs collapsed awkwardly and the horse slowly succumbed to its fate. Meanwhile, the fleeing soldier had dropped to the ground and rolled away from the horse, making himself a smaller target in the darkness. There were two horses left and he had little time to decide which one to cut free. The longer he left it, the less choice he'd have. Both surviving horses were already suitably agitated by the commotion so far. The soldier unsheathed his weapon in the prone position and breathed in before he sprang to his feet. He hacked away at the rope tying the remaining two horses to the tree. The nearest horse bolted immediately but shielded the soldier long enough for him to mount the remaining horse. As the horse galloped away, his relief was cut short by a searing pain in his right thigh.

The short branch soldier crawled along the ground towards the dying embers of the fire. His legs felt unusually weak. Getting to his feet didn't make sense for now anyway. If he did, he'd be easy pickings for whoever had taken out his teammates. He was a much harder target to hit lying flat and he needed time to appraise the situation. Who was firing at them? He had no immediate means of escape but if he could at least defend himself, he might last until the assassin left, help came, or the sun came up. On reflection he'd have a long wait for the latter. Furthermore, there was no help coming. Finally, if this was a true assassin, he'd come sooner rather than later and make sure he was dead. Short branch man dragged himself by the arms next to where his comrade was still roasting on the campfire. Under other circumstances he may've laughed to himself at the absurdity of the situation. His dead teammate had an arrow protruding from his throat, while he still had an arrow in his chest. Removing it now would further complicate his already dismal chances of survival. He felt along the ground in the dark and found his scabbard. He unsheathed his sword and waited.

#

The sound of approaching hooves roused short branch man back to consciousness. His breathing was laboured and fast, as the blood filled his right lung and closed the space in his chest cavity for his left lung to expand. He felt lightheaded, his arms were heavy and he could barely hold up his sword to defend himself. At first he thought he'd heard the sound of a rescue, then remembered that it was actually the sound of the timekeeper. And his time was up. The approaching horse stopped and its rider dismounted.

Despite the acceptance of his fate, the first thing that struck him during this final encounter was the appearance of the assassin. In the darkness and in his semi-conscious haze, the assassin appeared to be wearing dark clothes that blended in with the shadows. Unlike the assassin's clothing, the moonlight reflected off the assassin's face, highlighting a fairer skin colour. But it wasn't the hue of the assassin's skin that was most peculiar. The assassin was small in stature, with a narrow waist and wide hips. *Impossible.* Was this some delirious death fantasy to ease his passage into the next life? That question was answered immediately, as the assassin came closer and immediately stood on his arm. The arm was already almost numb due to his rapidly dropping blood pressure. Under the weight of the assassin's heel, his fingers easily released their grip on his sword and his limp arm dropped the heavy weapon with little resistance. The assassin picked up his sword and tossed it into a nearby bush. Then the assassin stood over him and silently appraised his critical state. Short branch man thought of all the armed conflicts he'd taken part in throughout his life and *this* was who'd send him to his maker? The narrow-faced assassin stared at him. Short branch man's first attempt to speak was muted by the sound of blood being coughed out of his mouth to clear his airway. He took another laboured breath and tried again.

"I don't believe it...you're a-"

His final words were cut off by the shock of a long blade entering his abdomen. As his remaining blood rapidly drained from his aorta and soaked the soil beneath him, his final thought wasn't that he'd been bested by a woman. It was the familiar insignia that he felt on the leather-bound hilt of the sword sticking out of his belly.

#

Sergeant at arms Yusuf Dankote heard a knock at his door. It was late at night. He groaned and looked at his heavy belt and weapons on the floor. Surely any palace disputes could wait until morning and if there were any serious security concerns then the alarm bell would've been rung. Any disorderly ministers would either be drunk, asleep, up to mischief with a companion or all of the above. He chose to ignore the disturbance, put his hands behind his head and closed his eyes. *Knock, knock.* The custodian of palace order grumbled to himself and reluctantly got off his bed. He was about to launch a verbal assault on whomever was behind the door, when he got an unexpected surprise.

The man on the other side of the door almost fell through the open doorway. Dankote stuck his head outside the door and looked left then right to make sure nobody had seen his uninvited guest enter his quarters. He hastily closed then locked the door.

"*What are you doing here?*" hissed Dankote angrily. "This wasn't the plan. You were supposed to meet with the others in two days."

The guest held onto the wall to steady himself. He was dripping with sweat and had a bloody rag wrapped around his right thigh. This guest, the last surviving member of the sweeper team, had left the palace in secret several hours earlier. The soldier, Lateef, was in a very bad way.

"I'm sorry, sir...things went...things went wrong...very wrong," said Lateef. He was perspiring uncontrollably.

"You've jeopardised the entire mission coming here," said Dankote unsympathetically. "Why did you break protocol?"

"I'm sorry sir. No-one saw me coming here. I…I even changed back into my uniform," panted Lateef. Dankote looked at his uniform and shook his head.

"Your uniform? Your leg is soaked with blood. By the state of you, that looks like *your* blood," remonstrated Dankote.

"I had to let you know tha-"

"*Stop*," interrupted Dankote. He lowered his voice to a whisper. "We don't discuss anything here. Go to the meeting point. I'll be there shortly."

Lateef nodded, wiped his forehead and gingerly stood up. Dankote opened the door, checked that the coast was clear and ushered him out of his quarters. This was exactly what he didn't need. At least Lateef had returned to the kingdom and his body hadn't been shipped back from Sokoto in a box. Perhaps things hadn't been completely compromised. The situation could now be contained.

#

Sergeant at arms Yusuf Dankote quietly walked down the old stone stairs into the passageway beneath the foundations of the Emir of Katsina's palace. He carried with him a shovel, a lamp and a sack. Directly in front of the bottom of the stairway lay Lateef. He was propped up against the wall of the passageway with his legs splayed out in front of him. Dankote moved closer to him with the lamp.

"Don't worry, I'm still alive," said Lateef. He'd removed his weapon belt and his sheathed sword lay by his side. He saw the shovel in Dankote's hand and immediately unsheathed his weapon.

"Relax Lateef," said Dankote. "I'm not here to hurt you."

"Why did you change your clothes? What's in the bag?" asked Lateef suspiciously.

"I can't be recognised coming down here. You know the mission protocol Lateef. I brought you a change of clothes."

"And the shovel?" enquired Lateef.

"The shovel is to bury your uniform. It's covered in blood. That'll easily draw attention." Dankote lowered the lamp to Lateef's thigh. "That leg looks bad. Tell me what happened." Dankote's tone was more sympathetic than earlier.

"An arrow. I got shot in the leg with an arrow. I think it's poisoned. I don't feel well at all. I think I have a fever." Lateef looked pale, even in the lamplight. His purple tunic was drenched, the rag tied around his thigh was now completely soaked through with blood and he was sweating profusely. Perhaps he was already dying.

"Tell me who did this."

"I think I need medical attention."

"Lateef, it's very important that you focus. Tell me exactly what happened and who did this to you."

"Yes sir…two hours out," gasped Lateef, "we took a break…someone killed the others…with arrows…an archer." He paused for a breath. "I didn't see them…it was dark…very fast…killed the horses too. It was better to come back…to report back…mission compromised."

"Everyone?"

"Everyone in my team…don't know about the others. I came straight back."

"Any idea if you were followed?"

Lateef shook his head. "I didn't see anyone on the way back. None of us saw anyone on the way there either…they had to know we'd be there…sir…why did you bring your weapon?"

"What?" Dankote looked down at the sword hanging off his belt. "Force of habit."

"How will you explain if someone recognises you in civilian clothes?" asked Lateef.

"I'll simply tell them that I left the palace grounds for some female company." Dankote smiled. He was impressed. Not only had he survived his entire team getting wiped out, the young man was still sharp, even on his last legs. Lateef still gripped his sword tightly.

"Sir…who else knew about the mission? How else could we be compromised?"

"Those are very important questions Lateef. Questions I intend to get to the bottom of. All in good time. You can relax now. I'll get you some help. Look, I'm going to put my sword down, just so you trust me."

Dankote ostentatiously placed the lamp and shovel on the ground, then removed his belt with his sword and scabbard and also placed them on the ground. Lateef let go of his sword.

"Very good, Lateef. Have a look in the bag for some clothes, I'll have a look at that wound." Dankote dropped the bag on the ground in front of Lateef and stood by the downed soldier. Lateef pushed himself away from the supporting wall, grabbed the bag and opened it. At the precise moment he realised the bag was full of hay, he felt a forearm envelope his neck in a rear chokehold. Lateef tried to grab at the vice-like hold but his arms were too weak. He reached for his sword but it was too far away.

Dankote reached into his robes, withdrew a dagger and plunged it into Lateef's chest. The blade met little resistance. As he held it in place, he released his chokehold and covered Lateef's mouth. The soldier's flimsy struggle continued for a few more seconds before he went limp. Dankote removed the blade and wiped it on the dead man's clothes. He then lowered Lateef's body to the ground and undressed him. Dankote then picked up the shovel, the lamp and carried the naked corpse along the passageway to the outskirts of the city.

#

Did knowing the face of one's victim make them a murderer? Or were his actions merciful? Did Lateef deserve better than an anonymous grave? Yusuf Dankote could neither answer nor ignore these questions. The first fact was that a loose end had been tied up. Justify the greater good. The second fact was that a meticulously planned operation had already been compromised in its infancy. Time would tell of the other team's success. If they succeeded at all. It would be a very long wait. In the meantime, there was one minister he'd have to wake up.

Chapter Eight

Metamorphosizing shapes and colours. Oscillating sounds. Effervescent tastes. Tantalising touches. The senses coalesced into an overwhelming experience of euphoria and enlightenment. The musical chanting of the Bori priestess accompanied the fumes of the burning boka infiltrating Minister of Information Atiku Danladi's nostrils. Shut off from the outside world, a cloth covered his head, buried in the bowl of burning medicinal herbs. The priestess was wretched, with matted grey braided hair and a wiry frame clothed in a faded brown wrapper. The multiple scars on her raised arms and symmetrical markings on her face were indistinguishable between self-inflicted and ritual wounds. The acoustics of the small chamber accentuated her commanding voice as the room filled with the hallucinogenic vapour emanating from her concoction.

Light overpowered his visual fields as the priestess removed the cloth from Danladi's head. Disoriented, she flung his head back, causing him to fall into a pile of pre-arranged cushions. Danladi was jolted by the deafening thunderclap of her palms slapped together. She raised the volume of her chant and slowly began to stamp on the chamber floor.

"*Iskoki!!!*" hissed the priestess, calling on spirits as she swayed side to side in front of Danladi.

The information minister's body stiffened then relaxed three times before he was still again. Danladi stared vacantly into space as the adorcism continued. The priestess resumed her chanting but this time with a different timbre. The sound of her voice was more melodic, the volume lower and her movements softened into a flowing dance. She raised her arms then touched the floor, as if commanding heaven and earth. Her supple torso wound sideways as if battling the wind and the ocean. The priestess flicked her fingers at Danladi, as if casting fire from the tips.

Rigid to the outside world, visceral imagery formed in his mind. The colours evaporated and everything went dark. Suddenly Danladi was bathed in blinding bright light. At first he shielded his eyes. When he uncovered them, his eyes filled with tears of joy at the sight in front of him. He was in a fertile field, lush green with crops. He ran his fingers through them and breathed in the familiar smell of the farm in Daura where he'd spent his childhood. In the middle of the plot were Danladi's parents, accompanied by his siblings Seku, Fatima, and Atikah. His mother and father were the same age as when he'd last seen them in boyhood. He barely recognised the siblings he'd never encountered as adults. Seku had survived the fatal famine and was tall and muscular. Fatima and Atikah hadn't been sold into slavery and were beautiful women. As he tearfully embraced them all he inhaled the smell of his mother's cooking on her clothing and felt his nostrils tickled by the hairs of his father's beard.

The perfect family portrait dissolved into its constituent colours. The gold, blue, and red colours coalesced to form a golden throne on a red carpet in the sky. Green and white colours morphed into emerald and ivory statues on both sides of the throne. The outstanding colours merged to form a modified image of Danladi. The Atiku Danladi that sat on the golden aerial throne wore a radiant white babanriga. In his flowing white robes, he resembled a Hausa king.

The vision took an unusual dark turn. Adjacent to the floating throne was a cage. Inside it was a familiar man, eating from the ground like an animal inside the cramped prison. Where the image of Danladi, resplendent in his regal attire, was imperious, this man was naked except for a loin cloth and resembled a lowly beggar. The man's obese frame created the illusion of the cage being too small to accommodate him. His arms and legs hung outside the cage bars like an ape. Danladi leaned forward from his throne and a white slipper fell from his foot. Without hesitation the caged man retrieved the slipper from inside the cage and began to eat it. The onlooking sovereign Danladi extended a hand and petted the caged man like an animal before cruelly beating him with the back of the same hand, until it was bloody. It was then that Danladi recognised the pitiful creature he was mistreating as the Emir of Katsina.

Suddenly there was no aerial throne. Danladi wielded a spear in one hand and a sword in the other. To his right were the sergeant at arms, ministers, and loyal servants. To his left were multiple wives and concubines. Behind him stood an army several hundred thousand deep and wearing the purple and blue colours of Katsina. Danladi looked up. Another man was suspended above him, impaled on Danladi's weapons. Danladi held the impaled man above his head like a trophy while his allegiant troops cheered him on. The man's blood gushed from his puncture wounds onto Danladi's face and mouth, until he was waist deep in it. The impaled man was instantly recognisable as the durbar from Kano.

Danladi woke up. The priestess was mumbling almost inaudibly and held her hands over him as if warming them over a fire. His vision was blurred with a faint ringing in his ears. The priestess stopped mumbling and clapped her hands one last time. By the time Danladi had fully regained his senses, the Bori priestess was already packing up her bowl and other paraphernalia into a sack. Danladi wiped the saliva from his mouth and chin. It was normal to feel light-headed for a few minutes after these sessions. He nodded at a pouch on the table in the chamber. The priestess nodded her gratitude, retrieved the pouch and left Danladi in his room.

Outside the information minister's chamber, sergeant at arms Yusuf Dankote patiently waited for the unholy ritual to finish. The last person to interrupt the minister's occult practices had been chased into the courtyard with a brass cane. Dankote was already unsettled by the recent turn of events. Being around such heresy, even though he took no part in it, put him even more on edge. As the witch left Danladi's chamber and walked past him, Dankote's face registered disgust at the abominable acts she'd most likely performed on the other side of the door. The juju woman ignored him completely and carried on her way. Dankote knocked on the minister's chamber door and waited.

Information minister Danladi was dazed. He looked at his sergeant at arms without moving his head, uncharacteristically smiled and waved for him to take a seat. Dankote obeyed. The minister's eyes were glazed over and he was sprawled over some cushions. Dankote dared not comment but was certain his information minister was still intoxicated. The room stank of whatever foul potion the witch had been cooking.

"Sit sergeant," said Danladi. "I see you're not bearing gifts, so what else have you brought for me?"

Had the minister already forgotten their brief conversation before the juju witch's arrival?

"Would you like me to come back later my lord?" asked Dankote uneasily.

"Why?" asked Danladi. He raised an eyebrow but didn't look offended.

"I...I thought-"

"You thought what?" interrupted Danladi. "That I might need more time?"

"No, my lord, it's just that y-"

"I what? Look out of it?" Danladi's head rested back while he looked at the ceiling. "High? *Intoxicated*?" he teased. "Come on man, speak up. I won't beat you. At least not today." Danladi smiled at his sergeant at arms, goading him, fully aware of just how ridiculous the mock threat sounded. In reality Dankote could easily snap his neck like a twig.

Dankote considered his response very carefully, while wondering if the minister was even capable of standing. "No, my lord. I'm just concerned that I may have come at an inconvenient time."

"*Rubbish*," scoffed Danladi. "When is it ever convenient to discuss what we have to discuss?"

Dankote said nothing and looked at the floor. Maybe he wasn't intoxicated after all.

"Actually, you couldn't have picked a better time," continued Danladi. "I've just experienced the most powerful signs of things to come, from my spirits. You really should try it some time. Most reassuring."

Dankote couldn't resist frowning but said nothing and avoided eye contact. Minister Danladi looked at his sergeant at arms, caught his expression and cocked his head to one side. "You disapprove, don't you? You disapprove of all of this. What do you call it? *Juju*? *Black magic*? Come on, speak freely. I grant it on this one occasion."

Dankote took a breath and chose his words wisely before responding to the smug official. "That woman's practices are against my religion, my lord."

"*Your* religion? You mean that eastern religion that our people borrowed. That same eastern religion with its offshoots and mutations. That same eastern religion that is apparently a mutation of the religion that I hear the white man now claims as his own. I'm sure you know *my* religion predates your borrowed eastern religion."

"I thought such things had been outlawed by the kingdom."

"Really?" Danladi chuckled to himself. "You should know better than anyone that if whores, alcohol and other such addictions can be smuggled into the palace, what makes religion so different?"

"The witch's practices are ungodly," Dankote argued defiantly.

"And killing your brother in arms in cold blood isn't?"

Dankote said nothing. The words wounded him. The cold harsh truth of his actions hit him with piercing clarity when vocalised by another. The minister smiled at him.

"Relax. I'm not judging you," continued Danladi. "What you did was absolutely necessary and unlike the sheep one often encounters in all these so-called religions, you took action and changed course when you needed to. That's what I like about you sergeant. You're not afraid to mix things up. That is why you're instrumental to the change that's coming. That is why you and I are inextricably linked from now on. And as I've seen in my vision, this temporary setback, whatever it is, won't have any bearing on our success."

The juju he was under must have been powerful. Nevertheless, Dankote wasn't going to argue. "What do you recommend next, my lord?"

"Rendezvous as planned tomorrow."

"And if the other team has also been wiped out?"

"Then things really will become interesting." Danladi sighed. The euphoric feeling was well and truly over. "Really interesting indeed. There are contingencies in place and things are already in motion. Eliminating the durbar and this boy is just to buy us time. I am curious about this assassin though. Your man saw nothing?"

"Nothing, my lord."

"Perhaps the durbar has help. Then again, poisoned arrows? Not really a durbar's style with all their sanctimonious honour. Perhaps Kano has sent reinforcements and the time for our advantage is over."

"Is it worth retrieving the bodies of the men from the sweeper team?" asked Dankote.

"No. Someone else may get there first and we can't have those men identified as coming from here. Those men knew the risks and their sacrifice won't be forgotten. I can assure you."

Dankote wondered whether the minister spoke the truth only when it served his agenda, like all politicians or whether his witch-medicine had rendered him incapable of lying. Either way he was right. Those men would have to be buried in the next life.

"Let's be patient sergeant. Even if your men fail, the durbar loose end will be tied up one way or another. There are other ways and means."

"Yes my lord."

"Now sergeant, I've had quite the soul-searching session with my priestess tonight and I'm rather fatigued. Good night sergeant."

"Good night my lord."

Dankote left the information minister to sleep off the effects of his soul-searching and returned to his own chamber.

#

As he lay his head down to sleep, Dankote was troubled by more thoughts. *Other ways and means.* Was it the juju talking or was he serious? Dankote was supposedly integral to the machinery of the looming new order, not least because he headed palace security, yet he wasn't privy to the contingency plans Minister Danladi had alluded to. If he really did have other ways and means of eliminating the durbar and the boy at his disposal, what were they? Dankote knew that the information flow was limited for a good reason. The more each person knew, the more of a liability they became. *Loose end.* Who else knew the entire plan from start to finish and what were they sacrificing for this great change? *He* had sacrificed everything. His life. The lives of his family, relocated far from the city in the interim. Inshallah he'd see them again soon. What was the information minister sacrificing? Had the minister known about this assassin all along? That could explain why the team was completely dismantled so quickly. No, that was fatigue, a dangerous bedfellow of paranoia, whispering nonsense in his ear. He put the thought out of his mind as quickly as it had entered it and closed his eyes.

#

Arrogance and complacency had hastened their downfall. Not one of them had weapons to hand, apart from the man on watch, who was probably the most arrogant and complacent of them all. His fallen comrades would never know that part of the reason they were so easily picked off was because the fool had fallen asleep at his post. The perfect stationary target. Silent and blind. The campfire was another fatal mistake. A beacon in the darkness. What more could an archer ask for? By the looks of the weapons they'd brought with them, they hadn't anticipated anything but close quarters combat. Another short-sighted and ultimately fatal mistake. Of the downed targets, one was foolish, two were too slow to react and one was a coward. The coward would bleed out or the poison would get him slowly. Some would consider it just desserts for his lack of courage. Others might say he had the brains to realise he was outclassed and took his only option. Too generous. The horses had made his escape easier. Of all of them, the one man the assassin had any respect for was her final kill. Although beaten and pathetic, he'd held his weapon until the end and stared death in the eye. Even if death came in the surprising shape of a woman. So much for the fabled might of the Katsina royal guard.

After completing her assignment, the assassin surveyed the kill zone. The flies were already congregating on one horse and the air reeked of roasted flesh on the campfire. She felt some sympathy for the horses. They'd made the ultimate sacrifice for their hapless riders. The two that she'd shot were still tied to the tree with their heads unceremoniously suspended by their reins above the ground. The horse hit twice, whimpered it's last few breaths and twitched as it clung onto life desperately. The assassin looked at the arrows in its buttock and neck. The double dose of poison would course through its veins while the horse bled internally. The assassin unsheathed a sword hanging from its saddle and cut the horses loose from the tree. Both dropped to the ground with a heavy thud. In a moment of mercy, the assassin stood over the dying horse and drove the sword of its recently deceased rider through its neck. She held it in place until the horse was still and clung onto life no more. Satisfied that the horse was out of its misery, the assassin withdrew the sword and tossed it away.

The assassin then searched each man meticulously. With her boot she rolled the roasted corpse off the burnt-out campfire. The arrow protruding from his throat caught in the soil and halted his momentum. She patted him down. Nothing. She then moved on to the watchman. His eyes were still closed. The only possession he carried was the arrow sticking out of the side of his head. She moved onto kill number three. His face was a mask of shock and confusion. His mouth was still agape and his eyes were fixed open, looking up at the stars. As his clothes were soaked from the torso down with his blood, the assassin carefully felt along his limbs and his body with the ball of her booted foot. Nothing. As predicted, there was nothing identifiable on the men, except for the sword she'd purposefully left in the belly of the last man. Even if they weren't well drilled, some planning had gone into their failed operation.

The assassin returned to the downed horses and rummaged through their saddlebags. She pocketed whatever sustenance and money was available. She then surveyed the scene one last time. Eight arrows down. Not bad, but four had missed their mark. There were plenty left over but there was still room for improvement. She then unhooked her bow from the saddle of her own horse, put it over shoulders and mounted her ride. The assassin galloped away in the moonlight onto her next assignment.

Chapter Nine

The journey to Sokoto was uneventful. Arriving in the late afternoon, Master had secured shelter for the night, not far from the Sultan of Sokoto's palace. Although he slept with one eye open and one hand on his sword, his loud snoring indicated that he had at last gotten some much needed rest. Isa was stirred from a deep and refreshing sleep by the muezzin's call to prayer and the warmth of the rising sun's rays on his face. As usual, Master was already up. Isa rubbed his eyes to check his orientation in the room. His vision was correct. The world hadn't turned upside down. Master was doing his push-ups against a wall in the handstand position. With his heels sliding up and down the wall, Master's feline prowess was only marginally surpassed by his breath sounds through pursed lips. He sounded like a submerged hippo with its nostrils half in and half out of the water. Upon finishing this particular exercise, Master kicked his legs away from the wall, landed on both feet and sprang up to face his groggy ward.

"Good morning Isa."

"Good morning Master."

"After breakfast get Sisoko ready. We need an audience at the Sultan of Sokoto's palace. Hurry up. The day's already growing old."

"Yes Master."

Without further ado, Isa skipped his plans to emulate Master's early morning athletic feat and did as he was told.

#

A remnant of the Songhai empire, Sokoto was located at the junction of the Gublin Kebbi and Rima rivers. Following the fall of the empire a hundred years earlier, power had shifted hands back and forth through several bloody conflicts between Sokoto and Kano. Since then the peace had been kept through treaties between the sultanate and the emirate. Old heads maintained that prosperity had swung the same way as the balance of power, with Kano currently in the ascendency. Beneath the surface, resentment festered alongside the rivalry between the two regions. The recent relative tranquillity was perceived by some, on both sides, as the calm before the storm. But both sides agreed on one thing. Sokoto was the cradle of Islam in the northern regions. Beyond trade, this had been the lasting legacy of the extinct empire. No other kingdom adhered to religious practices as diligently as Sokoto.

Although larger in size, Sokoto was even quieter than Katsina. The Sokoto locals were slightly better off than their neighbours but more reserved and modest folk. Limbless beggars lying in the road were few and far between. There was no congregating mischief on any street corners and if they existed at all, rowdy taverns were considered safe spaces in tiny pockets in the distant outskirts of the city. Unusually for the times, the sight of slaves in transit through the city was a rare occurrence. For those slaves that stayed, it wasn't uncommon for them to spend a lifetime with one master. Many had even earned their freedom and risen to positions of good standing. Noise pollution was also kept to a minimum. In comparison to other cities, the relative silence of the market traders was deafening. Sokoto could be summed up in one word. Order.

The durbar and his apprentice reached the Sultan of Sokoto's palace in the northern part of the city. Despite the homogenous local architecture, the palace was an impressive structure. It was fortified with high white stone walls and an imposing central tower, hosting the main gate. Sentry towers flanked the central tower at intervals along the wall. The palace guards in blood red uniforms and matching red turbans kept a watchful eye over the surrounding city. Isa and Master dismounted Sisoko no more than twenty feet from the main gate.

"Wait here," instructed Master.

"Yes Master," replied Isa.

Isa watched Master approach the four palace guards in front of the main gate. Even though Isa looked up to him, Master was dwarfed by the guards on horseback who looked ten feet tall next to him. The standing pair on either side of them didn't look particularly inviting either. Master went straight for the horseback duo. They looked down at him from high up but appeared to engage. Isa rubbed Sisoko's mane gently, more for his own reassurance than hers. A couple of minutes later, the same horseback guard turned towards his ground level colleague and said something. The guard on terra firma responded and turned around. He knocked on the main gate with the blunt end of his spear and waited. The noise was audible from Isa and Sisoko's position. A few moments later the heavy main gate slowly opened from the inside. The two horsemen cleared a path. Master turned to Isa and beckoned for them to follow.

#

Distrust. From the moment they set foot in the Sultan of Sokoto's palace, all eyes were on the visitors. Their every move was watched with the utmost scrutiny, albeit without open hostility. Even the stable boy kept a mindful distance from Isa. Master kept his usual cordial demeanour without overfamiliarity. None of this surprised Isa, given their previous experience the day before and Master's brief history lesson. Everyone, including Master, had their guard up.

#

The meeting with the council of elders was chaired by a thin, stern-faced middle-aged man in a white turban and red robes. His high cheekbones and angular jaw dovetailed into his pointed beard, whose flecks of grey hair matched the stonework surrounding them. The twelve men in blood red robes and matching turbans, evenly spread in high-backed chairs arranged in a semi-circle on both sides of him, also wore equally serious expressions. Some looked older than the chairman, with longer and whiter beards. A minority were younger. All of them focussed their attention solely on the man stood before them.

"You are welcome, master durbar," said the chairman.

"Thank you Grand Vizier. Kano is most grateful," said Master, with a deferential head nod.

Gidado Buhari, the Grand Vizier to the Sultan of Sokoto and chairman of the Sultanate Council, was officially the Sultan's right-hand man, the de facto ruler in his absence. Nothing got to the Sultan without first getting past the Grand Vizier. A man who rarely smiled, he wasn't just a barrier to the seat of power in Sokoto, he was a wall.

"I'm told an urgent matter has brought you here," began Vizier Buhari. "I'm told that you have something of vital importance to discuss. What pray tell is this urgent matter of vital importance that has brought you to our kingdom without invitation?"

The man's passive aggressive tone registered clearly with the durbar, who did what all great negotiators did. He ignored it. "A short time ago a messenger left our kingdom for Sokoto," began Master. "When he returned some days later, he was critically wounded. As his health deteriorated rapidly, he warned of a threat to destabilise our kingdom. The messenger succumbed to his wounds not long after."

"A threat to destabilise your kingdom," mused the Grand Vizier, after a lengthy pause. "Did he give you any more specific information?"

"No, my lord. According to our physician the rest of his speech was incoherent," said Master.

"Incoherent?" The Grand Vizier raised an eyebrow.

"Yes, my lord," responded Master. The long silence after Master's response was punctuated by a cough from an elderly member of the council.

"So it's possible that you may have been privy to the nonsensical ramblings of a delirious man before he expired?" asked the Grand Vizier. *Discredit the delegate with mockery.*

"Possible my lord, but unlikely," responded Master. *Defuse the mockery by giving it vague legitimacy.* His response drew rumblings from the council members. Master waited for the noise to die down. "If I may continue?" he asked. *Cement your legitimacy with grace.*

The Grand Vizier blinked slowly and nodded his head in agreement. *Reset.*

"Our palace physician confirmed that the messenger had been subjected to significant physical trauma. His wounds were consistent with severe beating, cutting and burning. Essentially, he'd been tortured."

Some of the council members shook their heads in disgust. Others shook theirs in sympathy.

Vizier Buhari upturned his lips in acknowledgement of the heinous act and waited for the muttering from either side of him to stop. "Our sympathies and those of the kingdom lie with this man and his family. Inshallah, he is at peace now." The other council members muttered their staggered agreement. "Who do you suspect would commit such a vile act?"

Master paused before answering. "We do not know my lord. That is why the durbar council has been ordered by the Emir of Kano to carry out an investigation."

"An investigation into what?"

"The death of the royal emissary," began Master, "and an investigation into the allegation of a threat to destabilise our kingdom."

"And you are here for which one, master durbar?" *State the true agenda.*

"Both." *Counter suspicion with clarity.*

The muttering from the other council members resumed. They all exchanged glances with one another. All except the Grand Vizier. His expression didn't change. Instead, he kept his eyes fixed on the durbar warrior. Master did the same to him. *Stand your ground.*

"*Silence*," demanded Vizier Buhari, marginally raising the volume of his voice. The council went quiet again. "Master durbar, you must be absolutely clear. Potentially serious allegations could be made with dire consequences." *Threaten us at your peril.* "Are you saying that you believe Sokoto had something to do with the death of your messenger *and* has threatened to destabilise Kano?"

The council waited in silence for Master's response.

"My lord, I am in Sokoto to conduct my investigation. An investigation which has not been concluded." *We mean you no harm until you mean us to.*

Vizier Buhari's brow furrowed at Master's evasive answer. "Master durbar, are you able to tell this council if you believe Sokoto is implicated in any way with this murder or this alleged threat to Kano?" pushed Vizier Buhari. *Last chance to back down.*

The air turned silent again while Master planned his next manoeuvre.

"Grand Vizier, so far I have no evidence to implicate Sokoto, the Sultanate or its servants, in any heinous actions or threats against Kano or its servants," said Master. *Stand down.* "However, I would be negligent in the execution of my duties as a servant of Kano, if I did not inform you that thus far no hypotheses have been exhausted and there are still many avenues to explore." *For now.*

The frown on Vizier Buhari's face relaxed and the corners of his mouth almost creased into a barely detectable smile. He was impressed. The young upstart was smart. Certainly smarter than most of the fools he'd encountered from Kano. The young man was a proven politician in the making or at least in everything but name. The durbar had cleverly avoided a declaration of war, while maintaining the cloud of suspicion. "So master durbar, what are these hypotheses?"

"Given the timelines involved, we're confident the messenger reached Sokoto and came back via Katsina. Had he taken any other route he would surely have perished before his return. The first hypothesis is that he met his downfall either in Katsina…or here."

"And what of Katsina?"

"Katsina had no knowledge of the emissary's death or any threat to our kingdom."

Of course they didn't. How convenient. "Have you any reason to suspect Katsina of any intent to destabilise Kano?" he asked.

"Poverty is rife in Katsina and it has its problems, but these are not cause enough to suspect treachery," responded Master. "However, our physician was confident that the emissary could not have survived a straight journey back from Sokoto in his condition."

"So it *is* possible that he was attacked in Katsina," commented Vizier Buhari.

"It is possible," conceded Master. "I must tell you my lord that there is another detail, not disclosed by the emissary himself, that supports the theory that he was murdered."

"Oh, what is this detail?" asked Vizier Buhari.

"When the emissary returned to Kano, he came back on a different horse to his usual stallion. Several stable hands have independently verified that the emissary left the Emir's palace on his usual horse. One that he used every day for the past few years."

"Go on, master durbar."

"This would lead one to the sub-hypothesis that the emissary was separated from his own horse when he was set upon, possibly captured. One could surmise that when the emissary was unbound from his predicament he took an alternative horse, possibly even seized one. It's possible he seized it as part of his escape. The emissary's horse has not been recovered."

"A missing horse and a dead man." Vizier Buhari sounded bemused. "This could all be the fate of a gambler, a man in debt or just a bad man with bad luck."

A few council members smirked at the last remark. One or two sighed as if they were bored.

"These are all possibilities Grand Vizier. I must admit that even I have had the worst luck since this investigation began."

The Grand Vizier's facial expression was static. Perhaps he really knew nothing about the attempt on Master and Isa's lives in Katsina. After all, Katsina was a long way to send assassins. Or perhaps his face was a mask of impenetrable inscrutability.

"Ah, before I forget, there is one important piece of information that I must share. I'm ashamed to admit that this slipped my mind in Katsina and I failed to share it with their Minister of Information. If I may continue, my lord?"

The mumbling among the other council members had resumed. The council members had already mentally moved onto other business, even before their chairman had responded to the durbar's testimony.

"*Quiet.*" demanded Vizier Buhari. "Please continue master durbar. Then hopefully we can assist you in wrapping up your investigation. I'm sure Kano has more pressing matters," scoffed Vizier Buhari dismissively.

"I'm most grateful, my lord," responded Master. "When the emissary left Kano, he was in possession of something private. I'm told it was a letter or a document. Truth be told, I have no knowledge of the contents of this document. There are some matters that are so private within the Kano emirate that even the durbar council is not privy to. Especially direct communiqués between the Emir and the Sultan."

Master almost missed it. Almost but not quite. There was an extremely subtle shift in the general demeanour of the Grand Vizier. It only lasted a couple of seconds but the self-assuredness wavered very briefly. For the first time during their exchange, he'd caught the Grand Vizier completely off-guard. The man knew something the other council members didn't.

"When the emissary returned on this strange horse, prior to his death, there was no sign of this document," continued Master. "There was no sign of this very sensitive document that, I'm told by my superiors, could have drastic consequences if it were ever misplaced or ended up in the wrong hands." *We mean you no harm until you mean us to.* "This disappearance of the document and the dying words of the royal messenger are the basis of the second hypothesis of the threat to destabilise Kano."

The Grand Vizier and the rest of the Sokoto Sultanate Council were silent. The council members turned to Vizier Buhari but said nothing. Vizier Buhari's eyes narrowed and he scratched his beard. Master waited patiently for a response, fully aware that he'd ruffled some very important feathers and had the undivided attention of everyone in the room.

"We received the document," admitted Vizier Buhari with resignation. The rumbling chatter amongst the council members resumed and there was genuine consternation on the faces of several council members.

"*We must have order in the council!*" demanded Vizier Buhari, raising his voice a touch for the second time during the meeting. The council members obeyed and went silent again. "Master durbar, as you have correctly stated, the contents of this document are of such a sensitive nature that the content cannot be disclosed in this forum."

"Grand Vizier, I can assure you that I will inform Kano that this document has been received by the Sultanate," said Master.

"Sokoto is most grateful, master durbar," replied Vizier Buhari. "I believe the council has heard sufficient testimony from you. Is that correct?" *Retreat.*

"Yes, my lord," responded Master. *Regroup.*

"In that case, I believe your hypotheses should be granted a response," continued Vizier Buhari. He looked right then left at the other council members. All of them nodded in agreement. "The council will discuss the matter with the Sultan as a matter of urgency. To give you a preliminary response would not only presume we know the mind of our supreme leader but would also betray the due consideration that this matter deserves. You will be summoned for an update today."

"Kano is most grateful," responded Master with a slight head nod. The Grand Vizier made hand gestures towards the palace guards in the room and Master was escorted elsewhere in the palace grounds.

Grand Vizier Gidado Buhari frowned in his chair. The other council members stood up to stretch their legs, leave the room, and exchange opinions face to face. Vizier Buhari remained seated. The unannounced arrival of a durbar was always ominous. The durbars, these agents of Kano and extensions of the Emir's power, brought problems with them. This one was no different. He had to be dealt with immediately.

Chapter Ten

"What is his condition?"

"In terms of his body, he is stable, my lord," replied the physician.

"And his mind?"

"There are periods of lucidity today. Yesterday he called me by his fourth son's name, Mustafa. The day before that he called me Hauwa, the name of his third wife. Today he calls me *witch doctor*." The royal physician smiled. "His majesty hasn't lost his sense of humour."

The Grand Vizier stood over the ailing monarch, as the royal physician illuminated the Sultan of Sokoto's face from the other side of the bed with a lamp. The only other occupants of the Sultan's vast chamber were two guards. Vizier Buhari was filled with great sadness whenever his shadow was cast over their frail leader, who was now supreme in name only. The Sultan's sixth wife had succumbed to a similar illness. Her body had gradually failed her, while her mind demented until her death. As the Sultan's other wives shared the same quarters, ate the same food and drank the same water but were well, the royal physician concluded that their leader may be afflicted with a venereal disease of some sort. The fact that the Sultan and his late wife had not been blood relatives added weight to this theory. There was no known cure for the suspected illness. Sokoto's once formidable leader's limbs had been reduced to flaccid appendages that no longer functioned. He hadn't walked for months and he was now too weak to be wheeled out in front of any court or for any public appearances. The flow of information regarding his illness had been limited to the Sultan's immediate family and a handful of others. To further protect the secret, the same guards had been rotated and sworn to secrecy under pain of death. Even the Sultanate Council didn't know the full extent and prognosis of their leader's mysterious illness. Vizier Buhari was aware of the rumours of the Sultan's death floating in the ether. The spread of such malicious gossip had been swiftly quashed in the harshest manner wherever possible. However, Vizier Buhari knew that the longer the Sultan remained out of the public eye, the more such hearsay would feed the appetite of the Sultan's enemies to strike. And the Sultan's enemies were the Grand Vizier's enemies.

"How long has he been asleep?" asked Vizier Buhari, anxious for his leader's welfare.

"Since morning, my lord," replied the physician.

Vizier Buhari looked perplexed. "Was he up all night?"

The physician shook his head. "No, my lord, but he was extremely restless this morning. He thought there were snakes under his bed and the walls were on fire, so I gave him a tonic to calm him down."

"And you're sure you didn't give him too much?" Vizier Buhari shot the royal physician a suspicious look.

"Yes, my lord. I gave him the correct dose."

"How do you know it's not too much?" asked the Grand Vizier.

"The tonic is measured by weight, my lord," responded the physician bluntly.

"And his weight is decreasing," noted Vizier Buhari skeptically.

"Exactly, my lord," said the physician. The de facto ruler flashed him an irritated glance. The royal physician took the Grand Vizier's tone and facial expression as a subtle reminder that he wasn't the only physician in Sokoto. "What I mean, my lord, is that I reduced the strength of the tonic to account for his majesty's weight loss."

"Very well," said Vizier Buhari. He ceded his suspicious tone momentarily. The physician could be replaced with the click of a finger, but his departure would ignite fresh rumours within the palace and beyond. There were far more pressing matters at hand. Not least of all the durbar problem. "Can you wake him?"

"My lord?" The physician looked up from his lamp.

"Can you wake him?"

"My lord, I must strongly advise you that his majesty must rest," began the physician. "Rousing him from his sleep could have consequences on his physical and mental state."

"These consequences, can you quantify them?" asked Vizier Buhari.

"I…it's difficult to say specifically my lord but—"

"Can you quantify them?" Even in the shadows, the Grand Vizier's look of consternation was as severe as in any court room.

"No, my lord," conceded the physician.

"Then if they're not quantifiable, perhaps these risks are not as catastrophic as you fear they are. I have urgent business I must discuss with his majesty at once. I need him awake. Right now."

"My lord, if you were to advise me that lives were at stake, including that of his majesty," continued the physician, "then I would be reassured that the benefits of interrupting his majesty's restful state outweighed the risks."

Vizier Buhari leaned over the Sultan's bed, closer to the physician. His illuminated face looked larger than life, the shadows of his cheekbones accentuated in the bright light. "I can assure you that this is a matter of life and death for the Sultanate. Starting with the life of the Sultan himself. *Wake him up.*"

"As you wish my lord," replied the physician, satisfied that he'd been absolved of responsibility for any deterioration in the monarch's health. Vizier Buhari watched him set down his lamp on a bedside table and open a compartment in a wooden cabinet next to the bed. Since the

Sultan's decline, the royal physician had set up shop by his bedside for quick access to his patient. After rifling around in the dark, the physician withdrew a pinch of white crystals from a compartment in the cupboard and laid them on a cloth on top of it. He then produced a small bottle of transparent liquid. He uncorked the bottle and carefully dabbed a few drops of the odourless liquid onto the crystals. The crystals immediately began to effervesce. The royal physician carefully placed the cloth on the Sultan's emaciated chest, just beneath his collar bones and waited. The Grand Vizier withdrew from his leader's bedside, such was the potency of the effervescing crystal vapour.

"What happens now?" asked Vizier Buhari.

"Now we wait."

#

His chest rose and sank a little faster than before. Then the muscles at the angle of his jaw tensed as he clenched it. Their fibres were clearly defined on his gaunt face. The jaw-clenching was immediately followed by the unpleasant sound of grinding teeth. Next came twitching fingers, shortly followed by twitching nostrils. The guttural groan, rattling chesty cough and fluttering eyelids, were the final signs that the Sultan of Sokoto was regaining consciousness. There were sighs of relief from both sides of his bed.

The Sultan opened his eyes, looked up above his head and then slowly rolled his eyes clockwise from the Grand Vizier, past his own nose, to his physician. Both men stared back at him. Their faces were long, weighed down by concern and anticipation. The monarch's gaze returned to its centre and he closed his eyes. Vizier Buhari flashed the royal physician a perturbed glance. The royal physician gave his moribund patient a perplexed look. The Sultan's chest rose then sank slowly.

"If this is the first thing I see in the afterlife, I beg you Allah, return my soul to its rotting body, where my bed was my toilet and my toilet was my bed," said the shell of a man.

The royal physician exhaled audibly. The Grand Vizier smiled a relieved smile. The Sultan opened his eyes and frowned. "Witch doctor, is that pungent odour my flesh actually rotting or one of your ghastly concoctions?" The physician opened his mouth to respond but was too slow. "Whatever it is, either cut it out, cut it off or remove it."

"Yes your majesty," replied the royal physician. He hastily folded over the cloth of crystals and put it into a cloth bag.

"Water. I need water," rasped the frail Sultan.

"At once, your majesty." The royal physician placed a golden goblet at his leader's lips with one hand and supported his head with the other. The Sultan slowly slurped the water and turned his head marginally to the side when he'd had enough.

"Your majesty, praise Allah that you are well," said Vizier Buhari.

"Grand Vizier Gidado Buhari." The Sultan's eyes shifted towards his stand-in. "My eyes and my ears, my fist and my tongue, my shadow. Allah will tell you that I am not well. Allah will tell you that I'm dying a slow death. And it will be an even slower death if my witch doctor friend has any more to do with it."

The royal physician stifled a proud smile and instead looked down at the floor.

"Majesty, even though Allah tests your patience in this difficult time, we are grateful he hasn't taken you from us just yet," said Vizier Buhari.

"Speak for yourself," replied the Sultan.

"Majesty, I am especially grateful," responded the Grand Vizier. The royal physician watched the curious exchange between the two most powerful men in Sokoto. Although weak and pathetic, one man still had the ability to soften the other one. A softening that probably no-one outside the Sultan's chamber would ever witness. A softening of perhaps the most callous man in Sokoto.

"Grand Vizier, as flattered as I am by your gratitude and despite my incarceration by fleeting madness, I know you are not one to be paralysed by praise. Something is bothering you. Tell me what it is or return me to my mental prison."

"Majesty, I have an urgent matter I must discuss with you." Vizier Buhari looked at the royal physician. "Leave us."

The royal physician looked higher up the food chain at the Sultan for confirmation of the order "Your majesty?"

"Go," said the Sultan.

"As you wish your majesty." The royal physician bowed his head to the Sultan. He turned to the Grand Vizier and gave no physical acknowledgement of the order. "Grand Vizier."

"Royal physician." Vizier Buhari gave an equally dispassionate response.

With that, the royal physician moved from the Sultan's bedside and left the chamber. Vizier Buhari waited until the chamber door was firmly shut and the guards had resumed their positions by the door.

"Majesty, the palace received a visitor today," began Vizier Buhari. "An unexpected visitor."

"An unexpected visitor? Go on Vizier."

"The visitor was a durbar. From Kano."

The frail monarch turned his head slightly towards his subordinate. He had a curious frown. "A durbar from Kano. The Emir's enforcer. What did he want?"

"He claimed he was here on official business, at the Emir's behest. He claimed he was here to investigate the death of a royal messenger that had come to our kingdom. Apparently, this messenger died shortly after returning to Kano. The durbar and his people believe this man was tortured before his death."

"Tortured?" asked the Sultan.

"Yes majesty, tortured," replied Vizier Buhari. "According to their physician, the messenger was beaten, burned and cut before he died."

"This is most unfortunate, but a messenger from Kano is nothing extraordinary. A potential nuisance yes but out of the ordinary? No. What does this have to do with our kingdom?"

"Majesty, according to the durbar, before his passing the messenger warned Kano of a threat to destabilise their kingdom," continued Vizier Buhari.

"A threat to destabilise Kano?" asked the Sultan. His wide eyes were the most vivid sign of life since the royal physician had roused him from his deep sleep.

"Yes majesty," confirmed Vizier Buhari.

The Sultan immediately erupted into wheezy laughter. The laughter lasted a few seconds before it became spluttering, then coughing. Vizier Buhari was on the verge of calling the royal physician back into the room when the Sultan managed to regain control of himself. He walked round the bed and gave the Sultan some water.

"Kano is the most stable region in the north," protested the Sultan. "Kano continues to castrate us from afar and yet they have the nerve to accuse *us* of destabilising *their* kingdom. Whoever believes this is proof that I'm not the only one losing their mind."

Out of fear of his supreme leader choking on what little spittle he had left, Vizier Buhari waited some moments before continuing. "Majesty, I did question whether these were the ramblings of a delirious dying man but from what the durbar relayed to the council, the Emir has taken both this murder and this threat seriously."

"Murder?"

"Yes, majesty. That is how they perceive it."

"And what proof do they have of this so-called murder?" scoffed the Sultan.

Vizier Buhari chose his words carefully, so as not to rouse more laughter. "The first piece of evidence is flimsy at best. When this dying messenger supposedly returned, he returned on a different horse to the one he left the kingdom with. Apparently, this vanishing horse was the messenger's only horse for several years. Kano believes that the messenger most likely fled his captors and sequestered this new horse along the way."

"A dead man and a missing horse," mused the Sultan. The corners of his mouth creased into a smile and the Grand Vizier reached for the goblet of water. The Sultan maintained his composure. "This is hardly compelling evidence of a great conspiracy to overthrow the great oppressors of the north."

"Indeed majesty," concurred Vizier Buhari. "Even the durbar surmised that the messenger most likely sustained his fatal injuries in Katsina, such were their severity."

"Well there you have it," concluded the Sultan. "This man was probably abducted and tortured in Katsina. Not only is it a godless place, it is a lawless place. A deviant's paradise. It doesn't surprise me."

"Well majesty, the durbar began his investigation there."

"And?"

"He found nothing to suggest Katsina is implicated in this alleged conspiracy."

"*Alleged conspiracy?* A very specific choice of words. Speak your mind Grand Vizier. Do you think the Emir is shaking his spear? Seeing if he can irritate the lion just enough for it to bite?"

"Then he can justify killing the lion, majesty? I don't know. As silky-tongued as he was, the durbar couldn't hide the fact that he was carrying suspicion in his pocket and suspicion left with him after the council meeting."

"If the Emir wants to fight…if only I had a suitable heir that could lead an army to reclaim our power. Instead I'm surrounded by women who breed women and of my few sons, the one who has by far the most military competence, has shown no fondness for the pleasure of a woman. He is incapable of reproducing. What legacy will he leave? A true disappointment. Where is this durbar now?"

"In a secure waiting area within the palace."

"Does he have any proof that this messenger was ever here to begin with?"

There was a long pause before the Grand Vizier of Sokoto answered the Sultan of Sokoto. "Majesty, the messenger was here."

The flatness in Vizier Buhari's tone surprised the Sultan. With whatever strength he had left, he craned his neck towards his most senior official. "How do you know?"

Vizier Buhari cleared his throat. "The messenger from Kano had in his possession a document. A document with a special seal. Such a document could only be sealed by a sovereign and broken by another sovereign upon receipt. Specifically, in this case, a direct communiqué from the Emir of Kano to the Sultan of Sokoto."

The Sultan's face looked blank, almost sheepish as he struggled to comprehend what Vizier Buhari was telling him. "I do not recall being in receipt of such a document," conceded the Sultan. "I know madness has consumed me in recent times, so my memory is unreliable. I must confide in you Gidado that I'm ashamed that I'm a shadow of my former self."

Looking at the flummoxed Sultan, Vizier Buhari felt something uncomfortable, almost alien, that he hadn't felt in a very long time. Something in the pit of his stomach. Something that prevented him from looking the Sultan directly in the eye, if only for a second. Guilt.

"Majesty, you never received this document."

"I didn't?"

"No." Vizier Buhari shook his head. "I did." The admission hung uncomfortably in the air.

"But why is this the first I'm hearing of it? Something this important?" asked the Sultan, astonished by the revelation.

"Majesty…you…you were not in a capacitous state for me to share this document with you."

"And the council, what do they make of this?"

Vizier Buhari took a deep breath. "Majesty, the durbar's arrival is the first they've heard of this."

"You mean you didn't even tell *them*?" The Sultan looked bewildered. "Gidado, what's going on?"

"Majesty, I couldn't trust or rely on anyone else knowing the details of this communiqué while being certain of your absence from the public," confessed Vizier Buhari.

"Lest we should look weak?" asked the Sultan.

Vizier Buhari couldn't bring himself to repeat the word. "Lest we should look vulnerable."

There was a long uncomfortable silence. The Sultan stared into space. Eventually he spoke. "What message from Kano could have such dire consequences?"

"Let me show you majesty."

Vizier Buhari unfastened his robe and removed a scroll that had been concealed around his waist. He put the scroll down on the Sultan's bed, reached for the lamp and placed it next to him. The Grand Vizier unravelled the scroll and began to read.

#

The Sultanate Council, with its chairman and Grand Vizier at the helm, debated for a good while. With strength in numbers, the members collectively questioned Vizier Buhari's decision not to disclose the contents of the royal communiqué earlier. The remaining council members were careful not to address why the document had been actively withheld, thus openly accusing their chairman of maleficence and instead focussed on the lack of disclosure. They all knew that only a fool would gamble with even the slightest hint of sedition, knowing full well that the consequences could be fatal. *Ruthless* was one of the more common descriptors of the Sultanate Council chairman, whispered only in intimate circles. Regardless of the Grand Vizier's motives, the Sultanate Council ultimately agreed by unanimous decision on a definitive solution for the durbar problem.

Following the consensus, Vizier Buhari summoned a guard to their crescent-shaped table.

"Bring back the durbar."

Chapter Eleven

Failure. Suffocating humidity. No windows. No light. Night equalled day and day equalled night. If this was how things were to end, he'd failed. The Grand Vizier was riled yet he, the durbar, was incarcerated. Word wouldn't get back to Kano in time to prevent whatever was brewing and his mission would end in failure. The most galling aspect of his failure was abandoning Isa. The boy was innocent. The life he'd given him, the life he could have, the promise of a better life, would end as a casualty of war. The boy deserved better. An abject infuriating failure. He opened his eyes. No solutions.

As the key turned in the lock, Master braced himself for every possible outcome. He was either walking out of his temporary prison to rejoin the outside world, or his release would be a very short affair, perhaps a short walk to a hole in the ground. A hole in the ground that he'd be forced to kneel over, prior to the hole becoming the permanent resting place for his body and his separated head. An undignified end.

The door swung open and light poured into the room. Master squinted as his vision adjusted. *Assess the situation.* One guard flanked by four others entered the room. Strength in numbers. Not a good sign. Each one with a considerable height and weight advantage over him. Speed and agility might even the odds. On one hand their swords were all sheathed. *Buy time.* But on the negative side, there was little room to manoeuvre in the confined space and the corridor beyond. At best he could shoulder charge one guard and have limbs free for one or two more. While the remaining guards scrambled for their weapons he might get a chance at one more while using another as a shield. Realistically, the odds were not in his favour. Even if he overcame five armed men, how would he find Isa?

"The council wants you now," demanded the lead guard. Wary of an ambush, Master nodded. "Come with us."

Be aware of your surroundings. Slowly and suspiciously the guards separated to form a tunnel, with the lead guard at one end. Master cautiously followed the leader. The remaining guards closed the tunnel to follow him out of the room in single file. The corridor was silent. Master had almost finished mentally mapping out his initial attack by driving his body weight and rear elbow into the face of the guard behind him when something occurred to him. The route he was being taken along was familiar. After a few turns, the corridor opened up into a passageway with windows. Through the windows he recognised the last building he'd entered before his confinement. Contrary to his suspicion, they were in fact heading back to the Sultanate Council building. It seemed highly irregular that an execution would take place in such a lavish setting. Men of power usually had no problem with the blood of others being spilled. They just had a tendency to be as far away as possible from it when it happened. Master gambled on postponing his fight for their freedom and continued walking.

#

"Master durbar," began the Grand Vizier, "Sokoto appreciates your patience in this matter."

There it was. The subtle but effective facial gesture. A smirk, in case Master had forgotten he'd been held captive for the best part of a day without light, food or water. A reminder of who was in charge.

"Kano is most grateful Grand Vizier," replied Master. Outwardly, he had the relaxed graciousness of someone who'd enjoyed a restful afternoon nap. Inwardly, given the opportunity, he would beat the Grand Vizier like sugar cane.

"The Sultanate Council has reviewed all the so-called evidence you have presented. We have discussed the communiqué from the Emir. Our conclusion is that there is no evidence of any conspiracy to destabilise Kano involving the Sultanate of Sokoto. Furthermore, there is no evidence of the Sultanate's involvement in any plot to kill any servants of the Kano emirate. This includes a royal emissary. It is the recommendation of this council that you return to Kano and convey our findings to the Emir. What is your response master durbar?"

"Are these the conclusions and wishes of his majesty, the Sultan?" asked Master.

The smug expression on the Grand Vizier's face withered for a second. "The thoughts and words of his majesty the Sultan have been channelled through the Sultanate Council."

"Then I shall convey his words and thoughts to my Emir, my lord," responded Master. "If it doesn't trouble the council greatly, I would be grateful to know the welfare of my ward."

"The boy is well, master durbar. You will join him shortly," responded Vizier Buhari.

"I am most grateful, my lord."

"Night is coming and you have a very long journey ahead of you. The roads can be perilous in the dark," warned Vizier Buhari. "You and the boy will stay the night in the palace and will leave first thing in the morning."

Master reluctantly obliged the order. "My ward and I are most grateful for your hospitality, Grand Vizier."

"There is one more thing master durbar," said Vizier Buhari.

"My lord?"

"Regarding the royal communiqué," continued Vizier Buhari, "tell the Emir the answer is *no*."

Master let the man's message sink in for a few seconds before responding.

"Grand Vizier, if I may be so bold as to ask what specifically the response is in relation to? Communicating this may avoid any later miscommunication that may hinder a matter of such importance."

The Sultanate Council members shifted in their seats and collectively turned to the Grand Vizier. His patience had worn thin with the durbar's diplomatic but irritating persistence. Vizier Buhari's eyes narrowed but remained fixed on the durbar.

"You would do well to know your place, master durbar," he said. "A little knowledge can be a very dangerous thing."

"As you wish, my lord. I meant no disrespect."

"As far as Sokoto is concerned this matter is concluded. The time to extend you courtesy is nearing its end." The Grand Vizier raised his hand but kept his eyes locked on Master. A guard left his post and came to his side. The guard bent down and awaited his command. "Take our guest to more appropriate accommodation."

#

Isa woke to the sound of the muezzin's call to prayer, at first believing it had all been a dream. The room was simple in its décor but large and airy. The soft animal skins padding his bed were so comfortable, getting up was a challenge. They'd been fed well the evening before, with an assortment of different meats and stew. Isa didn't know what the meats were, but the giveaways were the different textures and the varying degrees of difficulty chewing them. He ate so much his stomach felt like it would burst. The Sultan's palace accommodation was his first proper taste of luxury. The journey had definitely been worth it.

Master had eaten and drunk in silence. Considering he'd spent hours in the palace while Isa had been stuck in the stable, being watched like a criminal no less, Master had very little to report. The meeting had apparently been a productive dialogue between two kingdoms. Isa had no idea what a dialogue was but guessed that it was something important people must want. After that, Master sat facing the door until Isa went to sleep and was there again when he woke. Unlike the last vigilant watch in Katsina, he was weaponless and as far as Isa was concerned, they were being pampered.

The conversation was just as lacklustre in the morning. The durbar was clearly still on edge and had already packed their belongings by the time Isa was up. Master pointed to some food that a servant had left on a table. Isa inhaled everything in front of him except the berries that Master had told him not to, as he was unsure they were harmless. Isa wondered what harm they could do if he chewed them thoroughly and drank enough water but wasn't going to argue with his master. Especially not when he was in this kind of mood. The durbar and his apprentice left the palace without fanfare. They left the Sultan of Sokoto's palace with no pleasantries exchanged at all.

#

Finding the boy and the durbar had taken two full days. They'd scoured the city, checked every tavern, mosque and marketplace and left empty handed. As a first and last resort, knowing the only confirmed stop on their targets' itinerary, they'd waited by the Sultan's palace. As frustration surpassed fatigue, the targets emerged from the fortress back into the open.

The durbar fit his description perfectly. With the staff on his back and the scabbard at his waist, he was sufficiently armed. Sufficiently armed and sufficiently dangerous. The boy was too small to pose any risk. Taking them in public under the watchful eye of the palace wasn't an option. Instead, they followed the durbar and the boy at a safe distance and waited for an opportunity to present itself.

#

Master remained lost in his thoughts on the return journey to Kano. Occasionally Sisoko reminded them of her presence and broke the uncomfortable silence with a snort of her nostrils. Isa rubbed her hide reassuringly. A short while later, the three of them stopped for a rest on the outskirts of the city. Isa guided Sisoko to a drinking trough, then tied her reins to a post in the shade. Given the brevity of their stay, the staff and Master's sword were left with the rest of their belongings mounted on Sisoko. The adjacent tavern provided some respite from the unforgiving sun. There, unprompted, Master spoke candidly.

"They claim they know nothing about the emissary's murder and the threat to Kano," pondered Master. He looked perplexed.

"Do you believe them, Master?" asked Isa, unsure how to drag his master out of his funk.

"I can't say they mean us harm, but I can't say they would come to our aid in our moment of need."

"Why, Master?"

"The Grand Vizier, the Sultan's deputy and ruler in his absence, spoke with a bitter taste in his mouth. His contempt for me, us, was indubitable." A beat skipped. "Clear."

"But he doesn't know you or us, Master."

"It's not just me Isa. It's *anyone* from Kano. The history between our two kingdoms is long and very complicated. There have been sacrifices and losses on both sides. Some people feel they've lost more than others. Some people feel this was unjustly so."

"What does the Sultan think?"

Master opened his mouth to speak, then closed it. He shook his head then smiled, like a madman enjoying a conversation with himself. Isa stared at him, confused but wise enough not to comment.

"That is your best question yet Isa," said Master, with a glint in his eye.

Isa was even more confused that a man as smart as Master considered this his masterpiece.

"The fact is I don't know. But who truly knows what the Sultan thinks? For some time, there have been rumours that the Sultan is incapacitated."

"In-ca-pa—"

"Not functioning. Possibly even dead," interrupted Master. "I saw nothing to truly confirm or refute these rumours, *however,* one thing was very clear." Master leaned forward a little before continuing. "The Grand Vizier knows more than anyone else in the Sultanate Council. If he's really controlling the flow of information to and from the Sultan, this will at some point become problematic. Knowledge is power Isa and he who is the most knowledgeable will become the most powerful."

Isa was reflecting on Master's latest pearl of wisdom when his train of thought was suddenly interrupted.

"Wait here Isa. I need to empty my bladder."

Before he could respond, Master had already left their table and gone outside. The tavern was characteristically quiet for the time of day. Like them, the few people inside seemed to be taking refuge from the heat outside. While scanning the room to pass the time, Isa noticed a man staring at him. Isa politely looked away and then looked back. The man was expressionless, with numerous facial scars but he was definitely staring at him. Isa felt uncomfortable. Not in the same way as with the deviant in Katsina but in a way he couldn't quite put a finger on. After a minute of being stared at, Isa decided the risk of being disciplined for disobedience outweighed being left alone with this unsettling stranger and went to find Master.

#

The durbar had disappeared. His horse was secure and the boy was inside. How had he slipped away so easily? The man was about to double back on himself when something stopped him in his tracks. He felt the cool steel of a sharp blade across his throat. His natural instinct was to reach for his weapon but he knew his windpipe would be cut open well before his own blade was drawn.

"Why are you following us?" asked his hidden assailant.

"I mean you no harm," said the man, frozen on the spot. "I have no money. Take my sword. I have a horse too."

"Last chance. *Why are you following us?*"

The pressure on the blade increased ever so slightly but just enough to remind him that the pressure required to draw blood was minimal. Any more would cut flesh.

"I was asked to follow you," said the man.

"*By whom?*" The blade pressure didn't let up.

"On the order of my lord, the Grand Vizier of Sokoto," said the man.

The man closed his eyes, held his breath and said a silent prayer. A moment later, the blade contact with his throat was released. When he opened his eyes, the elusive durbar stood in front of him, with a sheathed dagger. The grip of the hilt was fine leather and the hilt's pommel was intricate in its design.

"You have a lot to learn my friend," said Master.

"Bashir, my name is Bashir," said the man.

"Well Bashir, I saw you twice in the city centre and once more before now. You're as subtle as a rattlesnake," said Master. "Luckily for you, you aren't one." Master pointed the tip of his dagger at the man's neck. "The Grand Vizier demanded we leave Sokoto, so why are you here?"

"Master durbar, I was tasked only to observe you."

"For how long?"

"Until you reached Kano."

"Well you can go home and tell your Grand Vizier that we have no intention of remaining in Sokoto."

"Master durbar, my orders are to follow you and the boy until your arrival in Kano," said Bashir defiantly. His puffed-out chest meant that he'd gotten over his near-death experience.

"Do what you need to do Bashir. I suggest you pay better attention to your surroundings. I must go and find the boy."

As he feared, the stranger stood up when he did. He wouldn't take his eyes off Isa. No smile, no frown, just a stare. Isa slowly moved towards the tavern doorway, while the man mirrored his movements like a shadow. When he got outside, he waited to see if the man followed. A few moments later the man emerged from the tavern. His focussed expression hadn't changed but there was something different about him, something different about his posture. Isa's heart began to race. As he stepped further out into the late morning sun, the light reflected off what was different about the man. He was carrying a blade in his right hand. Isa turned around and ran.

#

Master heard footsteps coming towards them and immediately stepped away from Bashir, unsheathing his dagger in the process. Stunned by the durbar's sudden aggression, Bashir unsheathed his own sword. The two men squared off against each other.

"*Master!*" screamed Isa, as he came around the corner of the building. He immediately slowed down, looked at Bashir and veered towards his master.

"Get behind me Isa," ordered Master. He was already in a low fighting stance, with the dagger blade facing downwards and his free hand raised to shoulder height with the fingers apart. Isa did as he was told.

"I told you I mean you and the boy no harm, master durbar," said Bashir defensively.

Both men eyed each other suspiciously. Neither backed down. Then there were more footsteps. Not just one pair but several. Seconds later there were four more men in the small courtyard. They all wore nondescript, almost shabby but identical clothing. They were heavily built with haggard faces and armed with blades. The most facially scarred of them eyed Isa. His blade was shorter but no less sharp than the others. Bashir kept his weapon raised but turned away from Master to face the four new would be assailants. He'd been startled by Isa's panicked arrival. Now he looked scared. It was a gamble but trusting Bashir might improve their odds of survival. Master gave Isa his dagger. Isa took it with a trembling hand.

"Stay close to me," said Master. *Protect the boy.* He reached into his sleeve, then his thigh with opposite hands and withdrew two more daggers. Master maintained his low fighting stance with the dagger blades in each hand pointing downwards. Then the attack came.

The four strangers charged at the three of them. As predicted, the man with the short blade went for Isa, while his companion hacked at Master with his sword. Amidst the flurry of oncoming attacks, weaves and counterattacks with his dagger blades and limbs, Master shielded Isa from the onslaught. Their attackers were skilled, direct and barely fazed by the blows Master landed with his elbows and the lacerations from his daggers. Only once did the short blade man falter, when Master landed his right heel in the man's chest. He stumbled backwards, temporarily winded by the force of Master's front kick. Unbalanced on his supporting leg, Master barely managed to pivot and parry the thrust from the second man's oncoming blade. As he simultaneously stabbed his attacker's sword arm with his other dagger, he felt a searing pain as the sword blade cut through his clothing and glanced off his left flank. As his opponent dropped his sword, Master felt a powerful blow to the left side of his face and fell onto one knee.

#

Focus. The combination of dizziness and loud ringing in his left ear was both deafening and disorientating. The pain beneath the left side of his rib cage was excruciating. The unarmed man launched a knee at Master's head. Despite blocking the attack with his forearm, the absorbed impact felt like a kick from a horse. From the crouched position Master simultaneously swiped his dagger across the back of the man's supporting leg ankle, severing his Achilles' tendon. This time the man screamed and fell awkwardly onto one knee. At the bottom of his descent, Master plunged one dagger up into the man's solar plexus and the other dagger down into his neck. The two men momentarily mirrored one another in a deadly embrace before one collapsed in a bloody heap.

Reassess the situation. As Master withdrew his blades from the dead man he saw that the short blade man was already back on his feet and slowly advancing. He also witnessed Bashir's demise in its entirety. Having circled their opponent, the other two men coordinated their attack on the observer from Sokoto. Bashir managed to parry one attack but blocked the next one, an overhead attack, with two hands on his blade. The mistake proved fatal. While Bashir was committed overhead his other assailant thrust his long blade deep into Bashir's abdomen. The young man staggered backwards in disbelief, with his left hand over his abdomen, gushing from the penetrating injury. The two attackers slowed down their attack and resumed circling their prey. Bashir's sword flailed hopelessly in their general direction. The final blows were definitive and brutal. The first man hacked at his right arm and cut it deep just above the elbow. Bashir screamed and dropped his sword immediately. The second attacker immediately stepped in and drove his sword through Bashir's torso with such force that the tip protruded from his back. Bashir slumped to the ground in a pool of blood. His second executioner pushed Bashir backwards with his foot and retrieved his sword from the dead man's torso.

Maintain focus. The situation felt hopeless. Master's abdominal wound reminded him of its presence with burning ferocity every time he moved. The ringing in his ear and the dizziness were clouding his coordination. The courtyard walls were too high for Isa to scale. The most that Master could do was buy him time. Even if he created an opening for Isa to run, there were two men to close it. They were cornered and outnumbered. Master picked up his dead assailant's sword with one hand and with his dagger blade in the other he gingerly got to his feet. All three men slowly advanced towards the durbar.

Persevere. Distance was key. Master had the advantage of leverage over the short blade man. Isolating him was the best option. But the man seemed all too aware of his tactical disadvantage and hung back from his companions. Their collective focus was on finishing off Master before moving onto the frozen boy's disposal. The nearest man jabbed his sword at the durbar's mid-section. Master easily pivoted and slashed the man's forearm with his dagger blade. The sacrifice proved fortuitous for the attacker as he landed a round kick with his shin, connecting with Master's left flank. The pain was agonising. Master stumbled to the side and immediately attempted to parry the follow-up inbound front kick to his abdomen. He was too slow. The kick launched him backwards, causing him to drop his weapons and land on his back next to Isa. *Fight until the last breath.* As Master groggily rolled onto his side and propped himself up on one hand and one knee he rubbed his palm against his left flank. It was wet with his blood. By the time he was steady on all fours, his assailant was almost on top of him, with his sword held high. Then, everything seemed to pause.

As he reached the apex of his killing blow, the man froze for a couple of moments. His eyes went wide in apparent shock, then disbelief. Taking the opening, Master side-kicked his knee, causing the joint to bend from front to back and beyond with an ear-splitting *crunch*. The man screamed, overloaded with pain from different parts of his body. He hobbled on his good leg with one arm out to the side as if he were reaching for something. The reason for his temporary paralysis became clear. There was an arrow sticking out of his back. *Adapt.* Master immediately scrambled along the ground for his dagger, sprang to his feet, blocked then trapped the man's sword arm in one fluid motion with one arm and with his other arm plunged his dagger into the man's abdomen and pulled the blade up to his sternum. Master pulled his blade out of the man and dropped him to the ground.

Wary of the unseen archer, the last two men frantically went for Master and Isa. An arrow immediately landed where the furthest man stood as soon as he moved. Master picked up a sword and closed the gap on the nearest man. Their swords clashed and locked. The man had Master's dagger arm by the wrist in an iron grip. Master was no match for his strength. Then his opponent immediately kneed Master in his left side, knocking Master off balance but still able to maintain the power struggle. *Maintain focus.* The pain in his side was unbearable. When the man kneed Master for a second then third time, Master kicked at the man's supporting ankle, causing the man to lose balance and fall on top of him. On the ground, the man repeatedly attempted to punch Master in his wound with his free hand while using his bodyweight to advance his blade into Master. With his dagger blade free, Master repeatedly stabbed the man in the back, frantically targeting his kidney and his lung. Within a few seconds, the man's punches became limp and he punched Master no more.

Overcome. Master rolled the dead man off him and anxiously looked around. There were at least two more arrows in the ground. Then horror set in. The last man standing, the man with the short blade, lay face down with two arrows in his back. Something lay between the man and the ground. Or someone. Isa was nowhere to be seen. Master scrambled to his feet and rushed over. He pulled the heavy man away from his deathbed and found Isa. He was covered in blood. Covered in blood but breathing. His eyes were closed and there was a blood-soaked dagger in his hand. Master quickly scanned Isa's body for wounds and looked at the dead short blade man. There was a gaping hole in his throat.

"Isa! Isa! Wake up!" shouted Master. Isa opened his eyes partially then opened them wide with terror. Master gently removed the blade from his grasp. "You're alive. Are you okay?"

Isa stared at him vacantly.

"It's not your blood Isa. We have to get out of here. Let's go."

Master winced as he got to his feet and put his ward over his shoulder. He staggered past the crowd that was gathering to witness the aftermath of the bloodbath. As he pushed through the onlookers en route to Sisoko, he briefly glimpsed a slender figure in the distance, perched on a rooftop. The figure in black carried a bow over her shoulders. The durbar carried on running as the figure disappeared from the rooftop.

#

The flame quivered in the oil lamp as his breath blew it out. Sergeant at arms Yusuf Dankote was alone in the darkness. It was the second day in a row that the remaining team had failed to materialise for the rendezvous in the underground passageway. Something had gone very wrong with the operation. Loose ends. As he walked up the stairs in the darkness, he feared things were about to get more complicated and his headache was about to get much worse.

End of Part One

Chapter Twelve

Salty blood choked him. His ears were occluded, amplifying the sound of his laboured breathing and his vision was blurred by the relentless sanguine fountain obscuring it. The immovable weight pinned him down. The struggle was futile. The panic was intensifying. He was going to die. He heard his mother's muffled voice and felt her submerged hand. As he grew tired, she told him not to fight, to let go. Her grip got stronger. The death throes began to consume him. Then the weight lifted. His breathing eased. His hearing quietened. His vision cleared. Her grip loosened. His mother was gone. He faced the source of his struggle, the source extinguishing his life force. The silent killer, the anonymous stranger, showed no emotion. The gaping hole in the stranger's neck filled with darkness. The dark hole became bigger and bigger, until everything went dark. Then the screaming began.

Isa opened his eyes and immediately sat up. He was covered head to toe, soaked with sweat. He held his throat and looked around the room in the darkness.

"You're safe Isa," said Master. Isa was more relieved than embarrassed that his master was by his bedside. Even if it had been every night for the past week.

"I'm sorry Master."

"Sorry for what? These things happen," Master said gently. "They remind us that we're human."

"How long will it take for them to stop?" asked Isa.

"They'll stop in good time. Go back to sleep. I'm here."

Isa lay back down and rolled onto his side with his back facing Master, too frightened to close his eyes.

#

The tranquility of the botanical gardens of the Emir of Kano's palace provided the perfect backdrop for their stroll. It was the first time the two durbars, Master and Jibril Asari had spoken alone in some time. Events in Sokoto had clearly affected the younger man. Normally so focussed, so single-minded, at times his mind seemed adrift. The older man, his mentor, could see this better than anyone else. The diverse flora and high walls of the enclosure provided ample shade from the bright sun.

"How is the boy doing?" asked Jibril Asari.

"Still having nightmares," replied Master, "but recuperating here has been a very welcome kindness from his excellency."

"The first kill is the hardest. I wasn't much older than him when I had mine. Under different circumstances of course but I remember it vividly to this day. Taking a life affects us in different ways, but it does affect us all. The bad dreams will pass. But I see something else is bothering you. What is it?"

"It's nothing Master Asari."

"Come on, you forget who you're talking to, my former apprentice. It's not your injuries. I recognise that look."

"What look?"

"The look of a man who won't rest until he's satisfied. It's not anger. What do they call it? *Determination*. The twin sibling of perseverance," said Jibril Asari. He searched the face of his former pupil and gave him a warm smile.

"Don't the Igbos still murder their twin children?" asked Master.

Jibril Asari ignored the weak attempt at levity.

"Sokoto, things didn't add up in Sokoto," continued Master. "The ambush is probably troubling me the least."

"Ambush?"

"What happened in Katsina may've been bad luck but Sokoto was different. Those men were good. Very good. Four of them? At the same time? It was no coincidence."

"But you didn't see them following you."

"Exactly. I didn't even see them coming," Master said.

"But why would they want to kill you?"

"I don't know. Killing a durbar might be a trophy for some people but the boy? It makes no sense. It makes no sense unless they had specific orders to kill both of us."

"What of the observer from Sokoto? What would be the purpose of killing you, the boy and a servant of Sokoto?" asked Jibril Asari. His former apprentice was indeed troubled.

"The observer from Sokoto was unlucky. Collateral damage. Wrong place, wrong time for him. Us? Maybe slow down the investigation, I don't know. I do know that if not for this mysterious archer, Isa and I would probably be dead."

"Yes, this mysterious woman in black." At first he'd entertained the account of the encounter but the younger man was becoming alarmingly preoccupied with this mysterious saviour. "Are you sure you saw a woman? On a rooftop? You were badly injured and fleeing for your lives."

"Although rare in these parts, female warriors can and do exist Master Asari," said the younger man defensively. "The archer was slight. A young boy or girl couldn't have attained the skill to be that accurate from that distance at that height. It was a woman."

"Assuming this archer was a woman, whose face you did not see, why would she help you?" continued Master Asari. "How would she even know you were there?"

"Unless she'd also been following us."

Master Jibril Asari sighed a deep sigh. A blue swift landed a few feet away from the garden path and casually observed the exchange between the two men for a moment before flying away. "The details of your investigation were limited to small numbers of people and at very specific time intervals. Why do you want to start chasing shadows?"

The former apprentice ignored his mentor's cautionary tone and continued to air his views. "This business with the royal communiqué. We're not being told the full story."

"Are we ever told the full story?" countered Jibril Asari.

Master was about to speak but instead bit his lip, took a breath and changed track before continuing. "You're going to tell me that I should know my place."

"I shan't insult your intelligence," said Jibril Asari, "but I will remind you that we're not politicians."

"But kingmakers when needed."

Master Jibril Asari stopped walking to face his former pupil. As much as he cared for the younger man and he cared for him deeply, his patience had limits. He was visibly irritated and took a deep breath before speaking. "You'll need a clear head before the council meeting. Perhaps some time alone is in order?"

Without another word, Durbar Master Jibril Asari left his former protégé alone with his thoughts in the royal botanical gardens.

#

The heavy sacks hit the long table, each with a resounding *thud*. Each one was cut open by the assistant, lengthways down the middle of the goat's hair material. Flies immediately escaped from the apertures and the overpowering stench of putrefying flesh rapidly followed. The onlookers tried their best not to vomit. Their success was variable. One dashed out of the windowless room, while another retched on the spot.

Apart from the assistant, one other person was immune to the nauseating smell. He was immune to the smell of death. He casually swatted away the flies buzzing between his face and the lamp, while his assistant cut away the bloodstained clothing of the five bloated bodies on his table.

Once the bodies were exposed the assistant held the lamp over each body while the royal physician made his notes. First he noted a general description of each specimen. Adult male. Approximate age twenty to thirty years old. Facial hair, specifically beard and moustache, with some facial scarring. Strong build with no obvious congenital deformities. No specific distinguishing features. Based on current rigidity and decay death was probably several days ago. Next came the more gruesome detail. Bruising and superficial lacerations to both upper limbs. Penetrating injury to the right shoulder. The epigastric wound signposted a perforated stomach, mostly likely caused by a similar blade that caused the deep penetrating wound to the left anterior triangle of the neck, judging by the size of the penetrating wound. The physician's assistant rolled the rigid body onto one side while the royal physician examined the posterior aspect of the corpse. Some insects crawled out of the buttocks of the corpse. Another onlooker left the room holding his mouth. The physician turned his attention back to the corpse. Interesting. Severed left Achilles tendon. The cut was almost clean with no jagged edges. The royal physician admired the handiwork of whoever had made the cut. *Most definitely skilled with a blade*, he thought. The physician moved on to the next specimen.

From a pathological point of view, the next specimen was far more interesting. Like all the other specimens, this was a deceased male of similar age. What made him more interesting was the escalating severity of his injuries. Deep laceration to the left forearm. Right knee hyperextended beyond the normal range of movement, apparently by blunt force. This was in marked contrast to the deep longitudinal incision, apparently by blade, from his umbilicus to his sternum. The large and small bowel were perforated and the aorta was severed. Catastrophic blood loss would have resulted almost instantaneously. The royal physician smiled to himself upon discovering the most curious thing about this particular corpse. The arrow shaft, protruding from just between the spine and the right scapula, indicated a punctured lung and possibly the primary injury before the death by exsanguination. The man had probably faced more than one assailant.

The other three corpses were dull in comparison. One had two arrow shafts protruding from his back and a penetrating injury to this throat. If he hadn't died by asphyxiation from the blood pooling in his throat, the blood and trapped air in his lungs would've killed him. The next corpse had multiple penetrating wounds to the back, most likely from stabbing. The last man had a deep wound above his right elbow, exposing the bone and two deep penetrating wounds to his abdomen. One was a full thickness injury with an exit wound. The physician was about to begin dissection of the corpses when one of the observing soldiers, who had thus far appeared on the verge of vomiting into his helmet, piped up.

"Stop. I need to see that last one on the end," said the soldier.

The physician's assistant looked at the physician. The physician raised his eyebrows. The soldier didn't wait for a response and approached the end of the table. He covered his mouth and nose as he did so. He stopped at the final corpse and studied it.

"How did he die?" asked the soldier.

"Deep abdominal wounds. Most likely from a bladed object," replied the royal physician, pointing to the wounds as he did so. "The brachial artery of this arm is also severed. As no tourniquet was applied, perhaps the eventual blood loss would have been catastrophic."

"A bladed object like a sword?" asked the soldier.

"It's possible."

"Did the same person do all of this, to all of them?" asked the soldier, baffled.

The royal physician scratched his grey beard and ostentatiously paused before continuing. "There are one of two possibilities." The man clearly liked an audience. The frowns on the faces of the other nauseous onlookers indicated that perhaps they didn't appreciate his drawn out postulating. "The first is that the perpetrator of these injuries fired these arrows from afar." The physician pointed at the broken arrow shafts and their rigid recipients. "Then, once the initial attack was complete, they switched to a close quarters blade. Most likely, as you correctly state, a sword. The second possibility is that there were two perpetrators and one fired the arrows while the other completed the job. The craftsmanship is definitely identical. Clean cuts, vital points struck. Whoever inflicted these penetrating wounds is truly skilled."

Awkward looks were exchanged between the military onlookers. The royal physician was clearly the only one revelling in the post-mortem. The inquisitive soldier brushed past him and left the room. His comrades hastily followed. The royal physician's assistant looked at his master and shrugged his shoulders. He then passed him a bone saw.

#

"My lord?" said the soldier standing at the Grand Vizier's open chamber door.

"Enter Captain Fujo," ordered Vizier Buhari. The servant of the sultanate entered and in the presence of his de facto leader, privately recounted the royal physician's autopsy findings. At an appropriate moment he acknowledged the discovery of his brother in arms Bashir, who it seemed had been killed in the line of duty. The Grand Vizier registered Bashir's passing but paid not even lip service to the news. He wasn't in the mood to indulge such sentimentality. Most important to him were the details of the four dead foreigners and the assassin. Bashir was of no consequence.

"Do we believe they met their end by the same hand?" asked the Grand Vizier.

"My lord?"

"Did the same person kill all five men?"

"The royal physician believes that either the same person killed them all or did so with an accomplice," replied the soldier.

"An accomplice?" Vizier Buhari looked surprised.

"He wasn't certain my lord but it was a possibility."

"The durbar leaves our city, five men die," mused Vizier Buhari to himself. "This is no coincidence. Who else is aware of the bodies?"

"The royal physician, his assistant and two of my men."

"I will speak to the physician, then I will speak to the Sultanate Council. You and your men are to speak of this to no one. To do so will be considered treason. Is that clear Captain Fujo?"

"Yes my lord."

"You're dismissed."

Captain Fujo turned to leave the Grand Vizier's chamber.

"Oh Captain Fujo?"

"Yes my lord?"

"Once the royal physician has completed his examination, ensure the bodies are cremated."

"*My lord?*" The soldier was stunned by the request. "But this is not the custom," protested Captain Fujo.

"*Burn the bodies,*" demanded the Grand Vizier, looking out of the window as he spoke.

"Yes my lord."

Captain Fujo left Vizier Buhari's chamber feeling dejected. The order weighed heavily on his conscience. He could handle the secrecy but burning the dead? This was strictly *haram*, forbidden by Islamic law and the Grand Vizier knew it. A loyal soldier and observant Muslim deserved nothing short of an appropriate send-off to the next life.

Especially from the man who'd sent him to his death. For Captain Fujo, it boiled down to a simple question. Was his own life worth disobeying the Grand Vizier of Sokoto?

\#

A short while later, there was another knock on Vizier Buhari's chamber door. He continued writing at his desk. "Enter," he responded.

A guard entered. "My lord, the royal physician is here."

"Send him in," ordered Vizier Buhari. The guard stood to one side and the royal physician entered. "That will be all." The soldier left them alone. Vizier Buhari replaced his quill pen in its ink pot and placed the document he was attending to, to one side. The royal physician stood in front of his desk. He was not offered a seat.

"My lord. You requested my presence?"

Vizier Buhari looked up from his desk, leaned back in his chair and placed his hands on his lap. "Yes, I did." He scrutinised the medical man in silence for a few seconds before continuing. "You've served the Sultanate for a long time and you've served it well. His majesty's perseverance, despite the inevitable decline in his condition, is undoubtedly in part due to your attention and care." The royal physician at first struggled to keep a straight face. When a serpent sang your praises, that was when your guard should be at its highest. Nevertheless, mocking the serpent, regardless of its intentions, rarely ended well.

"I'm most grateful for these kind words Grand Vizier."

"As painful as it is to acknowledge it, the reality is that the seat of power will have a new occupant shortly. It would be a shame to clean house completely, when the time comes." Vizier Buhari looked the royal physician in the eye and paused before continuing. "Familiar, reliable and loyal faces will ease that transition."

"The Sultanate has my undying loyalty my lord," said the royal physician, fully aware of the thinly-veiled threat.

"Good. You'll testify before the Sultanate Council that you believe the wounds inflicted on our murdered soldier may also have been inflicted on the four unidentified men, by the same perpetrator, with or without an accomplice."

"Yes, my lord. It is indeed a possibility. Whoever inflicted these wounds was highly skilled with a blade. I haven't seen anything like it for quite some time."

"You will then tell the council that the bodies were infected with some," he paused, "some...whatever you think is appropriate and you had no choice but to burn the bodies after your thorough examination, so as not to infect the soil or others with this highly contagious agent."

The self-satisfied smile on the royal physician's face faded with surprise and his fair complexion almost turned yellow. He swallowed hard before opening his mouth. "Yes, my lord."

"Very good," said the Grand Vizier. "Good that you're on board. The alternative would be most...unfortunate." Vizier Buhari nodded at the royal physician. "That will be all."

"Yes my lord."

The royal physician sighed heavily after closing the door to the Grand Vizier's chamber. Men had their tongues cut out for lying to the Sultanate Council. He'd just committed to a lie, and undoubtedly several more, in order to keep not only his position but his life. The royal physician prayed that the Sultan clung on to his life for as long as possible.

Chapter Thirteen

Svit. Svit. Svit. Tree bark splintered into the air. Each of the three consecutive blades angrily hit its mark with definitive impact. The thrower of said knives winced as he threw the fourth. The wayward projectile missed its intended target and scuffed the side of the tree. The knife-thrower was holding his breath, bracing unnecessarily, tensing the muscles around his wound and feeling the unpleasant end result. Isa said nothing but waited until Master nodded for him to safely retrieve the knives. Since the events in Sokoto, Master had avoided his arduous training regime and instead focussed on skill-based exercises. The bandage had been removed from his side and there were no outward signs of their recent brush with death. At least not to the casual observer. Isa's nightmares persisted to his great shame. Their frequency had diminished but the intensity was just as disturbing as at their onset. Try as he might to hide it, Master was frustrated, even angry at times. Whether it was the enforced break from active duty, the change in his daily routine or the many unanswered questions that only Isa seemed willing to entertain, only Master knew. The atmosphere in their compound was decidedly downbeat.

Mysterious archer. Mysterious archer in black. Mysterious woman in black. The identity of the mysterious figure, whom they were undoubtedly indebted to, remained elusive. While Isa had buried some details of the attack deep in his subconscious, only for them to resurface in his dreams, Master seemed haunted by their anonymous saviour in clear consciousness. This anonymous woman. This highly skilled stranger whose existence others secretly doubted behind closed doors. There *was* a place where female warriors flourished. It was far away and some believed it to be the stuff of legend. Not Master. This was no false memory. No cerebral justification of lady luck's part in their survival. He'd been there and knew it was real. But how would they know of his mission to Sokoto? How would they know he was in danger? Who were they working with? Pursuing this exasperating line of enquiry meant directly disobeying instructions. The durbar council had made their position crystal clear. Master Jibril Asari had recommended some *constructive reflection* during Master's period of convalescence. The chain of command would deal with the outcome of his investigation and formulate the next steps, if any. In summary, when he was needed, someone would let Master know.

Master held a knife blade in his fingertips. He was about to resume target practice, when he glanced at his apprentice. The boy now habitually avoided eye contact unless spoken to. Obedient but distant, his spirits were obviously low. Even Sisoko looked glum. Enough was enough. The mood in the compound wasn't going to change unless Master instigated it.

"Enough focus on death," said Master. He snatched the remaining knives out of Isa's hands.

"Master?" Master's abrupt manner snapped Isa out of his funk.

"We should be glad we're still alive, yet we're mourning death," said Master. "The sun is shining and the sky is clear, yet we're lamenting thunderstorms. *Enough*."

Isa watched Master hastily stride over to a work surface and toss his knives onto it. He was normally very meticulous with his weapons after using them. Isa wondered whether the untidy impostor who'd taken possession of Master's body might put the hanging bullwhip to good use and flog himself until his real Master returned.

"We're going to appreciate life. Right this minute," said Master. "Get Sisoko. She could do with some attitude adjustment too."

Isa looked at their equine companion. She looked as confused as he did but when did not understanding Master mean disobeying him? Within five minutes Sisoko was saddled and the three of them were out of the compound, galloping to an unknown destination.

#

Twenty minutes later they came to a secluded river, with only shrubbery for company on the flat riverbanks. Master tugged at Sisoko's reins and the two of them dismounted. The durbar led his ward to the edge of the riverbank and they sat while Sisoko helped herself to the river water, hazy with floating sediment. Master stared at the horizon. Isa's eyes flitted between Master, the river and the landscape. The durbar master and his apprentice sat in silence for several minutes.

"What's missing?" asked Master. His voice was as quiet as a whisper.

"Master?" replied Isa.

"What can't you see? What can't you hear?" Master's inquisitive smile reminded Isa that perhaps his real Master was still missing. The more patient imposter waited for his response.

"I don't understand, Master," replied Isa blankly.

"Exactly," said Master. His smile grew wider and he turned his face from Isa back to the horizon. The silence returned and was intermittently broken only by the sound of Sisoko snorting beside them. The smile remained plastered on Master's face as if he'd gone mad. A full minute later he spoke again. "Sometimes we have to escape from every stimulus drowning our senses to appreciate what it is we're missing."

Isa had no idea what Master was talking about but it was nice to see him smile, even if he looked mad. Since Sokoto, neither of them had smiled.

"Isa, the last few days have been difficult. For both of us. I know the nightmares still trouble you." Isa looked at the soil, embarrassed as Master spoke. "But let me tell you something. To run is the couch of the coward, to stand fast is that of the brave man. In Sokoto you chose not to run. You stood your ground and you became a brave man."

"Master," began Isa, "if I'm so brave, why am I afraid to sleep?"

"The journey of the brave man is not an easy one. To fight fear and be victorious takes tremendous courage but is an ongoing struggle. Your enemy will be doubt, from others as well as yourself."

"How do I beat doubt from myself?" asked Isa.

"Pride, perseverance and patience."

"Per-se-v—"

"Per-se-ver-ance," interrupted Master. The imposter had finally gone. "It means you don't give up trying. Be proud of who you are and have the patience to believe in who you can become."

"Yes Master. I'll try."

"Taking a life is a responsibility many cannot bear," continued Master. "After my first kill, I didn't sleep properly for weeks. I saw his face every night and questioned whether he was destined to haunt me for the rest of my days. Then one day it just stopped. Look over there." Master pointed to a pack of hyenas mauling one of their own. "Do you know what separates us from them?"

Isa shook his head. "No, Master."

"Very little." Master picked up some soil and blew it out of the palm of his hand towards the water. The defending hyena desperately struggled for its life with admirable vigour. "Holding dominion over others," Master shook his head, "expanding one's territory while destroying others'. Very little." Master sighed. "Sometimes we're so blinded by obsession and desire that we lose sight of what's truly important and lower ourselves to that." Master pointed at the hyena losing its fight for survival. "Those men who tried to kill us in Katsina and Sokoto are even lower than these animals. As you know, I'm not one for religion but what elevates us from those creatures is in here." Master pointed to his chest with his left thumb and pointed to his head with his right index finger. "And in here."

Isa nodded. The hyena had lost its fight. The triumphant pack ravaged its lifeless carcass. Master stood up and patted Isa on the shoulder as he did so. "You'll be alright Isa. Remember my advice and you'll never lose your way. Sisoko, come."

On the return journey their spirits were elevated. A burden had been lifted from Isa's shoulders. An unforeseen side to the durbar had emerged. Contented, Master didn't speak at all on their way home. The whole time he thought about nothing else but the mysterious woman in black.

#

Arms up. Tolerate the pat down. The bad breath. The body odour. Ignore the unnecessary closeness. The smelling, the squeeze here, the rub there. The grope hidden in the security protocol. Comply. The burly bodyguard retrieved two daggers from inside the hooded figure's cloak, another one from a holster above the ankle and passed the three blades to an equally hefty bodyguard standing beside him. One had to take precautions when passing through the city at night. Especially as a woman. The first bodyguard opened the tavern door and grunted for the hooded woman to proceed to the back room.

Another hooded figure. In the dimmer light, the shadow obscured the face. The fat-fingered ringed hands resting on the table revealed his masculinity. Upon entering, the visitor repeated the same demeaning invasion of her personal space with two more stout bodyguards by the door. Satisfied that the nocturnal guest posed no armed threat, the guards turned to the hooded figure at the table.

"Leave us," said the hooded man.

The guards nodded and left the room. The hooded woman stepped forward and dropped her hood to reveal a thin face. The grey and black interwoven hairs gave an air of elegance to her cornrows arranged in a tight bun. The candlelight and darkness hid the facial scars that reflected a lifetime's worth of hard fought independence.

"Good evening, my lord," said the woman.

"Adesua, what news do you have for me?" Information minister Atiku Danladi dropped his hood and appraised the appearance of his spy. She was in good physical shape but to be good at her job she was far too independent for his liking. Even though they were presumably the same age, he preferred his women much younger.

"My sources tell me five men were found dead in Sokoto," said Adesua.

"Five?" asked Danladi.

"Yes, my lord," confirmed Adesua. "Four strangers and a low level official from the Sultan's palace."

"Who killed them?" asked Danladi.

"Nobody can be certain my lord, as there were no witnesses but the killings took place not long after a durbar left the palace. The rumours going around the palace are that the durbar may be linked to the killings."

"A durbar?" Danladi's eyes widened. This was an unexpected surprise. His visions had predicted good fortune but he hadn't expected it so soon.

"Yes my lord."

"Is there any more information on how they died?"

"No, my lord. But there has been another interesting development."

"Go on."

"Not long after, the bodies of three men were found outside the city, near a farm."

"So? Men die all the time."

"These were three heavily armed unidentifiable men. Possibly mercenaries or some kind of militia, perhaps operating between the kingdoms of Katsina and Sokoto. It's unclear whether the men were travelling to Sokoto from Katsina or from Katsina to Sokoto." Adesua gave the minister a curious look. "Unsanctioned soldiers entering one region from another could be considered an act of war. The sultanate denies sending any men."

The blood temporarily drained from Minister of Information Atiku Danladi's face. Full deniability had been central to their planning but hearing out loud the possibility of being linked to the dead men made the hairs stand up on the back of his neck. It was a rare sight but Adesua's journey had been worth it, even if only to see the lecherous pig squirming in his seat. Getting paid for the pleasure was an added bonus.

"Know your place Adesua," snapped Danladi. "I know full well what constitutes an act of war. Katsina did not send any men."

"I meant no disrespect, my lord." It was hard not to smile at the riled information minister who was so used to abusing and extorting others. "The farmer was apparently going to bury the bodies and chop up the dead horses for meat but something stopped him."

"*What?*" asked Danladi.

"The farmer found a sword in one of the bodies. At first he was going to keep it. Then he considered selling it, as this was no ordinary sword. So he asked around to get a good price. It seems the farmer asked one too many people and before he knew it he was being hauled in front of the Sultanate Council to report on how he came into possession of such a sword."

"Such a sword?"

"Yes, my lord. This sword had a very unique design, specifically the design of the hilt. A design that identifies the sword as coming from one very specific source and belonging to one very specific group of people."

Danladi was on the edge of his seat. Under other circumstances Adesua would've relished keeping him in such impotent anticipation. From painful experience, she'd learnt that men in positions of power had little patience in reminding others of their propensity to wield it.

"It was a durbar sword, my lord."

The minister audibly exhaled and sat back in his chair, having reached the climax of his information gathering and realised predictions in one go. He smiled to himself. "A durbar sword."

"Yes, my lord, a durbar sword."

"Where is the sword now?"

"I'm told it's kept somewhere inaccessible within the Sultan's palace."

"What does Sokoto make of all this? Do they think the durbar is responsible for killing both groups?"

"That I do not know, my lord. The flow of information regarding these bodies and the sword has gone quiet. This is usually an indication that the information flow is deliberately being halted."

"Indeed. What of troop movements, exercises in and around Sokoto?"

"There has been an escalation in troop movements and conscription over the past month, even more so after the past week. Taxes have also increased."

"They're preparing." Danladi smiled to himself.

"My lord?"

"They're preparing for war."

"My lord, I cannot speculate on any imminent military strategy wi—"

Danladi put his hand up. "Nor should you. That isn't what I pay you for. You've done well Adesua." Danladi reached inside his cloak and retrieved a small pouch. He threw it onto the table in front of her. "Keep me informed via the usual channels if you hear anything more."

Adesua picked up the pouch. It was heavier than usual. "Thank you, my lord."

\#

Milling through the front of the tavern, Adesua caught the eyes of more than one lascivious patron. Even with her cloak hood up she still sensed their hungry stares. The information minister and his security detail were long gone by then but thankfully her horse was nearby. It was wise to avoid the risky road back to Sokoto and remain in secure accommodation for the night. Any uninvited interlopers would feel the sharp tip of a dagger blade for their troubles. As she approached the tavern exit, Adesua felt a hand on her shoulder.

"A fine thing such as yourself must be careful in these parts. Perhaps you need some company for the night to keep you safe." The man grinned to complement his indecent proposal. His breath reeked of crayfish and most of his ogbono soup seemed to have missed his mouth and decorated his filthy tunic. The man's oblong shaped head, chipped brown teeth, eyes that were too close together and long nose hairs, completed the unattractive picture. He let go of Adesua's shoulder, in some laughable gesture of offering consent for further molestation.

"Thank you but my husband is waiting for me at home," replied Adesua. She turned back to the exit and continued her departure.

\#

Accelerating footsteps. Even though she'd picked up the pace, Adesua's pursuer was much closer than her horse. A confrontation was inevitable. The alternative was being followed to her room for the night. Adesua stopped and turned around. The sleazy man from the tavern smiled at her from a few feet away. His companion didn't feign any romantic intention and stared at Adesua like a ruthless predator.

"What kind of husband lets you out at night?" said the sleazy man.

The three of them were alone on the moonlit empty street.

"I don't want any trouble," said Adesua.

"Then don't struggle."

"Okay. If that helps. Please just don't hurt me."

The sleazy man's companion stepped forward but his path was blocked by his counterpart's arm, laying claim to the first pick of their victim. There was no objection. The sleazy man advanced towards the submitting woman. He grabbed her by the wrist and pulled her towards him. Adesua didn't resist her attacker but instead clamped her free hand firmly on his strong grip, following him in the process. Without breaking his momentum, Adesua rolled her engaged side forearm over the sleazy man's wrist and immediately dropped her elbow. The perpetrator was suddenly trapped in an excruciatingly painful wrist lock mid-stride that jolted him to a halt. The intolerable pain in his wrist forced him down to one knee but it was too late. As the unbearable pain reached its peak, Adesua continued driving through with her forearm until she felt resistance then his wrist break with an audible *crack*. The sleazy man's brief howling scream was muted by a follow-up teeth-shattering knee to his face. Adesua let go of the unconscious man and his flimsy broken wrist.

She wasted no time disposing of the remaining perpetrator. The sleazy man's companion was so panicked by the swift dispatch of his partner in crime, that when he overcame his paralysing indecision over fight or flight, his fumbling fingers barely retrieved his tiny blade from his tunic. His weak thrust was easily parried and almost simultaneously punished by a jab to his windpipe. While the perpetrator gasped for air, Adesua landed a reverse knife-hand strike to the side of his neck. The subsequent shockwave surging through his body shut down his peripheral nervous system and he collapsed like a sack of yam.

The perpetrator's life lesson didn't end there. He was roused back to consciousness by the unique sensation of the bones in his hand breaking under the weight of Adesua's heel.

As the two perpetrators whimpered in the distance, Adesua mounted her horse and sighed. At least there would be two more people in the city that would think twice about waving their weapons at women without their consent. At least in the short term. She'd briefly considered killing them but saw no point in forcing retribution on other women in the vicinity. Especially those least equipped to deal with the advances of a rapist. Adesua looked forward to the time when she'd no longer have to come to this predator's playground. The woman in the hooded black cloak rode off into the night.

Chapter Fourteen

The synchronised chaos of the dancers moved to the rhythm of the kalangu. The drum beat marshalled the frenetic movements of their bodies and the bamboo canes they brandished. The dancers, in their vibrant multicoloured clothing and painted faces, captivated the live audience, including their esteemed guest. As their feet pounded the red earth, their infectious energy rose to a fever pitch that was palpable amongst the crowd at the open air ceremony. A shirtless adolescent boy danced his way from the crowd, unhindered, towards the performers. His arms were slung over a long tree branch resting behind his neck. As the onlookers cheered on, the dancers continued but cleared space for him until he was centre stage among them. The space around the young boy widened and he was joined by another boy, not much older but fully clothed and carrying his own bamboo cane. The younger boy stood his ground and the pace of the drum beat slowed down. The dancers stopped and looked on. The older boy dropped to a low stance, held his left hand ceremoniously above his head and with his other hand dragged his cane along the ground. He stared at his younger counterpart intensely as he circled him. Then the first blow came.

The young boy winced, paced side to side and muttered to himself as the bamboo lashed the skin across the top of his shoulders. The sound of the painful contact was drowned out by the surrounding noise. The crowd roared and the kalangu beat picked up. The ceremonial dancers sprang back into action and closed the circle. The boy's tormentor danced with his cane aloft, as if part of their regular ensemble. A few moments later the dancers separated once more, the kalangu slowed down and the older boy resumed his theatrical prowl around his target.

The second blow caught the young man around the small of his back. He wriggled his waist and muttered to himself to distract himself from the stinging pain. The crowd cheered once more as he stood his ground. The collective dancing resumed and the drum beat accelerated. As the cycle continued, the boy was struck just beneath his shoulder blades, just below each armpit and finally across his low back once again. With each successive strike of the bamboo cane, the boy shook his head more fervently, as if to outwardly deny any acknowledgment of the pain being inflicted. By the end of the ceremony his tormentor's cane was stained with the blood and skin off his back.

Having survived his public flogging as the main event of the Sharo festival, the young man was victorious. He hadn't disgraced his observing family and had successfully transitioned from boyhood to manhood. He was now fit to marry, according to traditional law. The tree branch beneath the young man's shoulders was removed by the older boy, given back to him and the celebrant triumphantly waved it above his head. The dancers reconvened, the kalangu accelerated and the newly minted young man joined their procession.

The special guest of honour looked on from his enclosure, impressed by the boy's resilience to successfully complete the painful rite of passage. The boy's parents had joined the throng and acrobats performed on the periphery of the dancers. The special guest was undisturbed by the festival crowd, partly due to the elevated height of his enclosure but also due to the small army of royal guards, in red and green uniform with red turbans, surrounding him. Emir Ado Sanusi of Kano, in his white and gold babanriga with green turban, was pleased with the festivities so far.

"Our assets tell us conscription has risen dramatically in Sokoto," said the Minister of Defence. He sat behind the Emir. Close enough to be heard but far away enough not to encroach on the image of the Emir's entourage, in bright white attire, from ground level. "Food supplies to the Sultan's palace have reportedly tripled."

"I didn't realise there was a famine in Sokoto," deadpanned the Emir while maintaining a keen eye on his subjects enjoying the festivities beneath him. The Minister of Defence looked uncomfortably at members of the Emir's entourage. His weary expression failed to register with the group, who seemed either distracted by the festival or distracted by boredom.

"A time of great strife is when a sense of humour is needed most," replied the Emir. "Besides, everyone knows that conscripts don't get fed."

Smiles came from some vaguely curious members of the Emir's entourage. The minister smiled awkwardly. He waited a couple of moments before continuing. "We have no word on any troop movements through or around Katsina but given the murder of our emissary and the events concerning the durbar—"

"The events in Katsina, Sokoto or both?" interjected the Emir.

"Both," replied the minister. Beneath the enclosure dozens of royal servants carried hog-tied flayed and roasted cows amongst the crowd. The procession of cooked meat quietened and broke up the seething mass of people.

"And what, other than the durbar and the theoretical passage of our dead emissary, links the two?" asked the Emir. Disinterested in the hungry people beneath them anticipating a feast, a couple more of the Emir's entourage had taken an interest in the conversation.

The Minister of Defence chose his words very carefully, given the growing audience.

"Sokoto has displayed hostility towards Kano for over a hundred years."

"And we have been equally hostile to them," said the Emir. "We live in a rare time of peace and prosperity."

"Respectfully, there are those that resent our prosperity and always have done. Peace time is also strategically the best time to attack one's enemy," countered the minister. "Based on the information fed back by the durbar, the attacks were identical and possibly orchestrated to interfere with his investigation. However, I must concede that there is no concrete proof of this."

"Exactly," said the Emir, turning back to view the hungry crowd. "Unless my hearing is worse than my children complain, the durbar council has found nothing concrete, as you say, to further suspicion beyond what has already come to pass. We have no clearer idea what threat, if any, exists to destabilise our kingdom."

"If our sources are accurate, our army is at least one and a half times the size of Sokoto's forces. With active conscription and recruitment of outside forces, they may well close that gap, sooner rather than later. Given the alleged murder of one of our subjects, two identical but possibly unrelated assaults on another servant of the emirate and most importantly Sokoto's refusal to engage with our terms, it would be prudent to exercise caution."

"Caution in anticipation of what?" asked the Emir.

At this point, the Minister of Defence had the full attention of the Emir and his entire entourage. Everybody had their best guess as to what was on the tip of the minister's tongue and the minister knew it. Careers were made or broken by saying the right or wrong things, at opportune or inopportune times. The minister sensed he was about to be labelled either paranoid or overcautious. He abandoned his original choice of words in favour of something more diplomatic.

"Further aggression."

The Emir smiled. "You are right to be cautious minister. To some, the drum is full to the brim with generations of mistrust and hatred.

Little provocation is needed on either side. Recent events could just be the spark that sets things ablaze," said the Emir. "Unless calm heads prevail, we shall end up burning our own house down."

The noise of the festival crowd was now at a low rumble, muffled by faces being stuffed with meat. The Minister of Defence knew his leader to be a great statesman, possibly one of the greatest, but even he couldn't decipher the man's political rhetoric on this occasion. More importantly, the defence minister appeared to still have his leader's ear. At least for now. "With your permission, I will speak to the generals. In the event that matters escalate, we can at least be battle ready. No aggression will be initiated by Kano but if any is brought upon us, we will retaliate with the full force of the kingdom. My experience and history tell me that this matter is not closed."

"Very good, minister. Let us continue to negotiate with Sokoto via diplomatic channels in the meantime. The Sultan is a reasonable man. He'll soon come round to our terms," replied the Emir.

"As you wish, your excellency. Although I must urge further caution, given the Sultan's reported poor health. If he is as unwell as our sources lead us to believe then the Grand Vizier is an even greater concern. It will be more difficult for his fanatical views to be held in check if his leader is frail. The man is dangerous. Some might say a demagogue in the making."

"Fanatics come and go minister," said the Emir. "What matters is keeping them suitably contained, otherwise they run amok. The Grand Vizier might be no different but he is no fool. Right now he lacks the capability and support to direct any open hostility towards us. Let us continue to be cautious. Inshallah, peace and prosperity will continue. A delegation will go to Sokoto with reissued terms. If Sokoto is not agreeable to them, then we consider further action."

"Yes your excellency."

The Minister of Defence admired the Emir's political pragmatism but didn't share his optimism. In his opinion, the Grand Vizier was a borderline psychopath with unrivalled hatred of others. It was no longer a case of if he would launch an attack on Kano but when.

#

Sergeant at arms Yusuf Dankote was tired. Sleep had evaded him since murdering a man under his command in cold blood. There had been blanket silence since the incident and the more likely it seemed he'd murdered his own man in vain, the heavier it weighed on his conscience. At times the guilt was overwhelming and he walked through some days in a haze. Would he be able to look his wife and children in the eye? Would he see them again if the revolution never came? This revolution, this promise to purge the greed, corruption, and unholy overindulgence that had infected his city. Had he been foolish to go along with the idea? Could the architects of this great change really deliver on their promise to change things for the greater good? Or was he a puppet, hoodwinked into killing an innocent, when in reality the only thing he was certain of was silencing a witness? His stomach turned when he received the latest coded summons from the Minister of Information. Undoubtedly a man of questionable integrity, the minister had mandated the hiatus in communication since the failed operation, since Dankote murdered his own man. Now in the doldrums of Dankote's depression, the minister wanted to meet urgently. Dankote had reached full emotional capacity. He prayed he wouldn't be pushed further.

Two young women walked past Dankote in the passageway to the information minister's chamber. One was tying a wrapper under her armpit, the other was adjusting her messy hair. Both actively avoided eye contact with the sergeant at arms as they hurried past him. Dankote glared at them with contempt. He clenched his giant fist and rapped his knuckles on the minister's chamber door.

"Enter," ordered the information minister.

"My lord…I didn't realise you were…shall I come back later?" asked Dankote. The information minister's tunic was unbuttoned down to his waist, exposing his glistening flabby chest and protruding belly in all its voluminous glory. Minister Danladi wiped beads of sweat from his forehead and seemed a little out of breath.

"No. Your timing is good," said Danladi, in between breaths. "My meeting was very satisfying and my head is clear. Sit."

The sergeant at arms did as he was told and sat on a chair that easily accommodated his gargantuan frame. The room was stuffy and the pungent smell of body odour and other bodily fluids made his nose twitch. There were soiled rags in the corner of the chamber. Dankote momentarily wondered what acts of depravity had taken place before his arrival. Then the thought made him nauseous. The information minister held a jug to his lips and in the candlelight his silhouette resembled a thirsty elephant as water trickled down his cheeks. Minister Danladi looked sideways at his sergeant at arms as he drank. After wiping his mouth with his sleeve, he offered the jug to Dankote.

"No thank you my lord," declined Dankote.

Danladi looked at the sullen enforcer, looked around the room at the aftermath of his liaison and looked back at him. He smiled, sensing the man's discomfort. "You disapprove, don't you?"

"It's not my place to comment on your personal matters, my lord," replied Dankote uncomfortably. History was repeating itself.

Danladi put the jug down, sat down, and let out a satisfied sigh. "You people revere fasting. I believe that a hungry man makes foolish decisions because his mind is elsewhere. We all need to eat sergeant. Even you."

Dankote looked away from the minister, opting not to rise to the bait of a man extolling the virtues of his fornicating ways. "I'm fine my lord."

"So you say. You look like you've seen better days sergeant. Getting enough sleep?"

"Yes my lord."

"Doesn't look like it. Your eyes are redder than a baboon's buttocks. If I didn't know you better I might think you've been seeing my Bori priestess behind my back." The information minister gave his sergeant at arms a devilish grin. "Keeping her for yourself? Getting some visions of your own?"

Dankote's cheeks felt warm. He was both insulted by the minister's taunts and embarrassed that he'd let himself go to the point where others had noticed. "I've been busy," he replied defensively.

"Busy? Busy doing what? Crushing rebellions? Disciplining the cleaners for not emptying his excellency's piss pot frequently enough?"

"Busy with matters of palace security my lord." Dankote hadn't realised he was clenching his teeth until his jaw began to ache. While enduring the toad's wheezy laughter, he pondered whether he could fit one or both hands around the minister's fat neck and silence him for good.

"Of course you have. Suit yourself. If you say you're fine, you must be fine."

"I received your urgent message my lord. You requested this meeting."

"Yes. As I predicted, things are moving along nicely."

"My lord?" Loose ends. Dankote immediately wondered whether he'd been deliberately kept out of the loop. He mentally checked his paranoia and listened for details of the latest revelation.

"I received an update from a reliable source in Sokoto. It seems our durbar caused quite the commotion there," teased Danladi.

"What happened?"

"Five dead, including someone from the Sultan's palace. His exact position escapes me but it doesn't matter. The net result is the same. One of Kano's dead."

"And now one of Sokoto's," said Dankote.

"Exactly."

"And they're certain the durbar is responsible?" asked Dankote.

"That part remains to be seen but my source confirmed that conscription and food stocks to the palace have gone up. This could indicate that retaliation is imminent."

"They're preparing for war." Dankote couldn't quite believe the words coming out of his mouth.

"Quite possibly. As I said, things are moving along nicely. I told you to have a little faith sergeant. I saw good fortune in my visions and it has now come to pass."

"Apparently so my lord. Has Sokoto officially declared war?"

"Not yet. Before we get too carried away with the progress of our plans, there's still some work to be done. The next phase will involve holding talks with Sokoto, as previously requested." Danladi smiled to himself. "Except our goal will be to leverage our position in this conflict between the two kingdoms. By forming an alliance with Sokoto we guarantee regime change if the war is successful and insulate ourselves from retribution if our combined forces are unsuccessful. Regime change will be the net outcome."

"What do you need from me my lord?"

"Arrange a security detail for Sokoto. That is all for now."

"Yes my lord. Forgive me my lord but how do we ensure our excellency will back Sokoto?" asked Dankote.

"Oh he will," replied Minister Danladi. "In any great war, one must choose a side. Or a side is chosen for them. Mark my words sergeant, a great war is coming."

Chapter Fifteen

The rising sun brought excitement. The meeting had special significance for each of them. For Master, the isolating period of enforced leave was over. For Isa, the adventure would resume after a traumatic intermission. Or so he hoped. For Sisoko, the lethargic melancholy that had clouded their compound had officially cleared. That morning everyone moved with renewed purpose and vigour.

The elder statesman of the group and the council chairman, Durbar Master Jibril Asari was the first to arrive at the Emir of Kano's palace gates. Without opening his mouth he was easily identifiable to the guards by his striking appearance. His neatly trimmed white beard perfectly contrasted his dark flawless skin and high cheekbones, while his piercing hazel eyes projected a formidable aura over anyone in his presence. His dark orange robes and brown turban reflected his modest tastes. Despite his advancing years, Master Asari maintained his lean physique and unlike the majority of the durbars, he travelled alone without a ward. The most even-tempered of all the durbars, Jibril Asari waited patiently for the others to arrive.

The Urumu brothers, Kazeem and Hakeem were the next arrivals. Separated by a year in age but almost identical in appearance, the brothers were the only blood relatives within the durbar order. They were fiercely competitive, mostly against each other and being the skilled fighters they were, didn't shy away from the odd physical altercation. If Kazeem was clean-shaven, Hakeem sported facial hair. If Hakeem wore white robes and a blue turban, Kazeem wore colourful attire and a white turban. The Urumu brothers agreed on one thing and one thing only, that the preservation of the durbar order was sacrosanct.

The third arrival was Musa Gindiri. The most flamboyant of the durbars and by far the most well read, Musa glided through the palace gates in his mauve robes and blue turban. The jewelled rings on his fingers glinted in the sun. Often accused by an Urumu brother of being an indulgent poet, Durbar Master Gindiri was as proficient with a blade as he was with a quill. He was unmatched by any durbar within the order as a swordsman and his quick tongue and razor-sharp wit frequently landed him in situations where his unrivalled mastery of any sharp weapon, regardless of its size, had saved his life on more than one occasion. Musa Gindiri's teenage ward travelled in tow and was saddled with the unenviable task of carrying his master's many musings on life, love and the world around him.

Ugo Itojo, the next arrival, was unique among the durbars as being their only member not originally from Hausaland. Born to the Igbo tribe in the southeastern region, he came from a family of nomadic traders who moved around the region and beyond the kingdoms' borders. During a temporary stay in Kano, word of the gifted teenage Itojo's multilingual proficiency had reached the right well-to-do circles. Before he knew it, the boy was frequently called upon as a translator for visiting dignitaries from not only surrounding kingdoms but also abroad. When his family moved on, the adolescent Ugo remained in the employ of the Emir's palace until a decision was made that the logical progression would be for him to join the durbar order. Unfortunately for the polyglot, what he possessed in unparalleled linguistic ability, he sorely lacked in physical prowess. Cursed with a scrawny frame and awkward coordination, young Ugo Itojo spent the majority of his first year of training having his nyash handed to him in the form of regular beatings from even the most mediocre fighters. Ugo's punches landed like wet eba and to make matters worse, he was given the embarrassing nickname *kaza*, the Hausa word for *chicken*, on account of his toothpick-thin legs. The uphill battle to meet the requisite physical standard of a durbar was steep and painful. Unbeknownst to his critics, Ugo Itojo's greatest strength wasn't his mastery of many tongues but his determination for self-improvement. Beating by beating, Ugo took his licks without a word of complaint and slowly built up the wiry strength and agility to first match his opponents, then dole out beatings of his own. In the eyes of his teachers, Ugo Itojo had lived up to two literal meanings of his name, *spirit* and *intelligence*, to become a durbar master.

Isa and Master, or Garba Mansa as he was known to everyone but the boy, arrived just before the remaining durbars. As far as Isa was concerned, his master had the patchiest biography of them all. The gaps in his story were filled by hearsay from other wards claiming privilege to insider information. Some claimed Master's decision to join the durbar order was fuelled by a great bereavement and a never-ending quest for justice. Others believed he was an amnesiac mercenary seeking peace and meaning in the world. The most outlandish theory was that Garba Mansa had been a convicted criminal in a past life and following his execution, juju had confined his spirit to the body of a worthy man to seek redemption in a future life. There were few established facts about Master Garba Mansa. The most controversial one concerned religion. Neither an atheist nor a practising Muslim, the open secret of Garba Mansa's attitudes towards religion seriously went against the grain of the times. If not for Garba Mansa's mentor and occasional defender, Jibril Asari, such a non-conformist ambassador of the emirate would've had his wings clipped and his acceptance into the order curtailed long ago. The long and the short of it was that nobody knew Garba Mansa better than his master and his loyalty to the durbar order and in extension the kingdom of Kano, was unquestionable.

The durbar order was founded one hundred and fifty years before the arrival of the current crop. Recruited from serving ranks in the armed forces, the durbars were originally deployed as a fragmented fighting force to supplement Kano's military might. Skilled horse-riders with unusually high physical and mental aptitude levels and expertise in multiple disciplines, the durbar's role was one of strategy and leadership. With their reputation as uncompromising negotiators, the role was further expanded to a pseudo-diplomatic peace-keeping one to fortify Kano's reach. Over time, these exceptional cavalrymen were separated from regular troops to form their own elite unit, the durbar order, with its own uniquely arduous selection process and self-governing body, the durbar council. Housed within the grounds of the Emir of Kano's palace, the council consisted of the six longest serving durbars, from the total of twelve within the order. Qualification for selection to join the order was defined by very narrow criteria. All women, irrespective of age or ability and all men over the age of thirty-five, deemed too mentally or physically frail by the conventional wisdom of the time, were forbidden from joining. Once accepted in, durbars were allowed to maintain friendships and engage in casual relationships but marriage or cultivating children was strictly prohibited. Any commitment to a significant other or one's progeny was considered too great a distraction and a challenge to the total commitment of loyalty to the order and the Kano emirate. If such rules were broken or the solitary life of a durbar proved too much, expulsion from the order, voluntarily or otherwise, was the next step.

Wards were considered a convenient afterthought. A perk in the mould of an extended houseboy role, with the added bonus of being a potential recruiting pool to maintain the continuity of the order. Unlike their masters, durbar wards were not chosen according to any exhaustive selection criteria and could be relieved of their role if and when their masters felt like it. However, the arrangement was more of a mutual than commensal symbiotic relationship and wards tended to last until they'd outgrown their roles into manhood. Like Isa, some had been rescued from child slavery. The majority were orphans. All the wards considered their servitude to the order to be a stepping stone to a better life. A life without shackles. A life without hunger. A life without fear. A life with purpose.

That day the entire order had assembled for the council meeting. Amongst their number was a familiar face, an older stout man clad in the green of Kano, sat next to Durbar Master Asari. Although clearly an outsider, the man appeared unfazed by the excess of testosterone in the room. After a formal introduction to the group, the man summarised his mandate. As he spoke, the Minister of Defence ignored the politely contemptuous looks from his audience, looks that he'd long grown accustomed to. They could judge him all they wanted to. It mattered not. *They* answered to *him* and he, along with everyone else, answered to the Emir. Master Asari thanked him for his words and opened the floor to questions.

"Forgive me minister," began Musa Gindiri, "for the sake of my brothers who may lack the capacity to comprehend the complexity of what you propose," he flashed Kazeem Urumu a sly glance, "you're saying that you believe Sokoto is actively preparing for war, yet you want us to do nothing?"

The Minister of Defence smiled at Musa Gindiri, the famous swordsman and the most arrogant of them all. "You're mistaken Master Gindiri. His excellency is keen not to interfere with established tension, tension that if provoked will most certainly lead to full-scale war. However, he maintains that we must be battle ready."

"So he wants us to retaliate but not instigate?" asked Ugo Itojo.

"In a sense, yes."

"Minister, Garba Mansa goes to Sokoto and barely makes it out of there alive," said Hakeem Urumu, "yet we're supposed to sit on our hands and wait for them to come and finish off the rest of us?"

"Not exactly. His excellency has requested that a delegation travels to Sokoto to resume separate negotiations with the Sultanate," said the defence minister.

"*Separate negotiations?*" asked Ugo Itojo. Glances were exchanged among the group.

"There are matters of the kingdom that I'm not at liberty to discuss within this forum," replied the defence minister.

"Matters that could force a neighbouring kingdom to wage war as a last resort?" asked Musa Gindiri. "Kazeem, what is the price of starvation on this side of the Rima river?"

The room erupted into laughter.

"*There will be order when the minister speaks,*" interjected Jibril Asari. The laughter died down.

"Please accept my humble apologies minister," said Musa Gindiri. "I meant you no disrespect but I must confess my concern for what might happen when you stop speaking. When negotiations stop."

The minister gave him a wry smile. "The only thing you need to concern yourself with, master durbar, is your duty to the emirate." The two men locked eyes for a few moments before the defence minister continued. "As I said, a delegation will go to Sokoto for further negotiations. The party will consist of the Minister of Trade, palace administrative staff and a security team."

"I'm sorry minister but my handwriting isn't the best and my brother can barely read," quipped Hakeem Urumu.

The minister ignored the jibe and continued. "His excellency agrees that the added presence of two durbars would send the right message. No preference was expressed for who would be the most suitable to travel with the party."

Garba Mansa couldn't hold his tongue any longer. "Minister, would this message be one of more expendable witnesses to further aggression perpetrated by Sokoto or witnesses for the prelude to war?"

Master Jibril Asari frowned. Master Musa Gindiri smiled smugly. The Urumu brothers both folded their arms. The defence minister's veneer of diplomacy finally evaporated. The skepticism in the room had worn thin. He turned to the council chairman, who himself seemed perplexed by the atmosphere. "His excellency's orders are final. Pick two. You can pick the mouthy one plus a friend or the double act brothers, I couldn't care less. Just pick them. The party leaves for Sokoto in two days."

#

"On behalf of his excellency the Emir of Katsina, I am most grateful for this audience."

"Information Minister Danladi, Katsina is most welcome," said the Grand Vizier. The old men in red on either side of him nodded accordingly. "To what end is the Sultanate Council graced with your presence?"

The sweat trickling between his buttocks felt like lizards racing down his nyash. Minister Danladi vowed to thrash his tailor for yet again sizing him up too small for his purple babanriga. Even the turban felt like a vice around his large head. To make matters worse, these religious fanatics had designed the room in such a way that the sun shone directly onto whichever poor soul occupied the floor. While he melted in the heat, the Grand Vizier and his geriatrics sat comfortably in the shade.

"I come at the request of my excellency. As I'm sure you're aware my lord, our kingdom received a visit from Kano." Danladi paused to gauge a response from Vizier Buhari. There was none. "A visit from a durbar and a boy. This durbar made numerous wild claims of murder of a royal messenger, him and the boy themselves being set upon and potential consequences for those suspected of colluding with the events he spoke of. He made many claims and showed no proof." Vizier Buhari's disinterested expression hadn't changed. "Naturally I offered any future assistance that I could give, offered this durbar shelter and relayed as much to my excellency. The durbar rebuked my offer of hospitality and seemed hellbent on coming to your kingdom to further his so-called investigation."

"The council is aware of the durbar's visit to both our kingdoms," said Vizier Buhari. "This is not news. What is the purpose of your visit?"

"Well, while the durbar made no explicit threats, he was rather forceful and seemed convinced of a conspiracy against Kano. My excellency has tasked me to personally see to it that Sokoto receives our full cooperation. I was hoping to offer assistance directly to the Sultan himself."

"The Sultan is in dispose. The council speaks on his behalf."

"That is unfortunate. Is there a more convenient time to seek his direct audience?"

"Whatever you need to tell the Sultan can come through the Sultanate Council. What do you want, Information Minister Danladi?"

"I offer Katsina's full assistance with the durbar's investigation, should Sokoto require it."

"Is that all?" Vizier Buhari was unimpressed. The minister came from a degenerate kingdom, with a degenerate ruler. If Danladi's reputation was anything to go by, the man himself was indeed a degenerate. A degenerate with an agenda. "Do you have any other business?"

"There is one more thing." Danladi looked at the floor before continuing. "My lord, Katsina is struggling. We are ravaged by lawlessness. I doubt that it is merely a coincidence that crime has risen at the same time as the increasing sanctions imposed upon us from our prosperous neighbour. That same neighbour that has sent one of its enforcers, as a reminder of the precipice it holds us over."

Danladi almost missed it. There was a flicker, a momentary change in the stony-faced demeanour of the old man. He was now at least curious about what Danladi had to say.

"On behalf of Katsina, in the face of any anticipated aggression from our neighbour, I seek an alliance with Sokoto. On behalf of Katsina, I seek protection from the kingdom of Kano, should further aggression lead to war."

The old men in red began to mutter amongst themselves. The Grand Vizier scrutinised Minister of Information Atiku Danladi in the meantime and waited for the furore to die down.

"Minister Danladi, what makes you so certain that escalation to war is a possibility?"

"Grand Vizier, my kingdom can only take so much economic hardship. If there is any more, we shall be vulnerable and eventually weak. It would be the natural progression of an aggressor to extend its reach and take that which cannot be held onto any longer."

"And why us?"

"While I do not know the economic health of your kingdom, I do know the history of your relationship with Kano. Sokoto is their greatest rival and by extension their greatest threat. If they come for us, which we fear they will, they will soon come for you."

The rumbling in the room started again. Danladi could smell it. The smell of doubt in the air.

"*Silence*," demanded Vizier Buhari. The room fell silent. "This is a serious request. A serious request deserves a serious response. But before then, serious consideration is needed. The matter will be discussed by the council. Then Katsina will receive a response. Is there anything else?"

"I request private counsel with the Grand Vizier."

#

The Grand Vizier's private chamber let in little light, much to Danladi's relief. However, the four guards in the room left little room to breathe. The old man obviously wasn't leaving his grip on power to chance. He sat in silence behind his desk, appearing to look deep into Danladi's soul, before he finally spoke.

"You requested my private counsel. You have it. What do you want?"

"I'm most grateful Grand Vizier," began Danladi. "Forgive me for the unorthodox request but it seemed pertinent, given the delicate nature of what I'm about to discuss."

"Go on."

"It's no secret that Katsina has become a godless place. While the hungry starve, the wealthy few gorge on their morally bankrupt excesses and unholy practices. Our leadership, or lack thereof, is responsible for the gradual degradation of our society. Things simply cannot continue the way they are. A man of your virtuous nature must understand. If war is inevitable and I believe it is, a new order will need to be established."

"A new order?"

"Yes Grand Vizier."

The Grand Vizier leaned back in his chair. "And if war comes to pass, where would you fit into this established new order, information minister?"

"Grand Vizier, I would not be so arrogant as to proclaim myself a leader. That is God's plan. However, I have the confidence of palace security and the ear of our generals. Both of these would be considerable attributes in the establishment of a new order."

"They would indeed minister, they would indeed."

"Naturally, war would need to pass and Sokoto, as the dominant power, would need to be victorious, inshallah," added Danladi.

"We would indeed minister. Your thoughts have been taken into consideration."

"Katsina is most grateful, Grand Vizier."

Chapter Sixteen

Cautious eyes observed the decelerating carriage and its alien companions outside the main gate of the Gidan Rumfa. The carriage, a heavy plain wooden box, barely five feet tall and three feet wide, had conspicuously travelled with its escort through Kano city, stopping traffic, drawing the attention of hitherto absent-minded pedestrians, not least because of the attire of its companions. In their blood red uniforms and matching turbans, the foreigners avoided antagonising stares and ignored provocative comments, with suspicion unabating as the travelling party progressed to their destination. Upon arrival, the hypervigilance of the royal palace guards, in sentry towers and on ground level, was palpable.

As the men in red and green uniforms eyeballed the visitors, a man sat atop one of two horses bound to the carriage, dismounted. The hands of his colleagues, on a pair of unbound horses, hovered over the hilts of their swords, mirroring the actions of their onlookers. The outsider's heart raced with every step as he approached the main gate. He resisted the urge to grip the scroll in his hand tighter and reach for his own sword with his other hand. His opposite number on horseback lowered his spear to the battle-ready position.

"*Halt! In the name of Kano, who goes there?!*" demanded the palace guard on horseback.

The approaching carriage guard in the blood red uniform obeyed the command and stopped in his tracks. He said a silent prayer and took a deep breath before opening his mouth. "I mean you no harm. On behalf of his majesty the Sultan of Sokoto, I come with a warrant."

The palace guard eyed the document in the foreigner's hand suspiciously, then mumbled to his ground level colleague, who then approached the man from Sokoto. The foot guard kept his hand on his hilt and snatched the warrant with his free hand. He immediately passed the document to his colleague on horseback before returning to the carriage to conduct his own inspection of their cargo. The horse-rider awkwardly unravelled the scroll, maintaining the horizontal position of his spear in the process.

The carriage was suspended on wooden slats attached to wooden wheels at the rear and two horses at the front. A heavy chain locked the carriage door from the outside. At the side of the carriage was a small slit, just big enough for eyes to peep through and a mouth to speak out of. The inspecting palace foot guard slowly and cautiously approached the carriage slit from the side, fearing a projectile might launch from inside. The escorting pair of Sokoto guards on horseback watched him carefully. When the palace guard finally plucked up the courage to confront the carriage passenger, he was surprised by what he found. The box was empty.

"A warrant for what?" snapped the horseback palace guard.

"A warrant for the arrest of the durbar," replied the Sokoto soldier.

The guards looked at each other bewildered. The warrant was passed back and forth between the remaining guards. Each one eyed the stranger suspiciously as he read it. The inspecting foot guard whispered his findings to his horseback colleague. Eventually another foot guard banged on the gate. A few moments later the gate opened and the guard disappeared behind it. The guardsman from Sokoto silently pondered two unfortunate but very possible outcomes. Dying in foreign territory before the warrant was executed, or dying at the hands of the executioner after fleeing back to Sokoto in an act of cowardice.

After an eternity, the gate opened and the palace guard returned with two court officials. The Sokoto guard's heart rate picked up again. Keeping his arms still, he slowly turned to look at his travelling colleagues. One raised his eyebrows. Another frowned. The third one stared ahead blankly. Some more deliberation took place between the two court officials and the guards, with intermittent finger-pointing to add to the confusion. Then one of the officials disappeared back into the palace and the gate opened immediately. The remaining court official beckoned for the party to enter. The men from Sokoto looked at one another and collectively breathed a sigh of relief. The original warrant-bearer slowly wiped the sweat from his forehead as the carriage proceeded.

#

The foreigners' intrusion brought the palace grounds to a standstill. Children were hurriedly ushered indoors by anxious guardians and palace staff cautiously circumnavigated the strangers in the courtyard at a safe distance. More guards materialised to keep a watchful eye on the mysterious carriage. Everyone was on high alert.

"Wait here," ordered a court official. The foreigners soaked up the hostile environment as he scurried away. Beyond the apprehensive stares and the spears pointing in their general direction, the grounds of the Emir's palace were a sight to behold. An incongruently beautiful backdrop to the open hostility. Far more beautiful than anything they were accustomed to. Granted, the Sultan's palace was no mud hut but it was ancient in comparison and not in a good way. The stonework of the Kano structures had obviously been better maintained. As for fine architectural detail, Kano won the contest hands down. The people, frightened onlookers and twitchy guards alike, hadn't exactly been ravaged by hunger. It seemed the other side was living well. The warrant-bearer wondered whether the palace inhabitants were living well enough to surrender one of their own.

#

"Excellency, the royal seal is authentic," said the court official. The atmosphere of the emergency meeting in the main royal courtroom was funereal. All members of the Emir's council had been summoned at short notice to discuss the unexpected arrival of the visitors. Emir Ado Sanusi and his silent entourage faced the court on their elevated platform.

"What are the crimes?" asked the Emir.

"The alleged crimes are as follows. One count of murder of an official in the employ of the Sultan of Sokoto. Four counts of murder of an unidentified individual within the realm of Sokoto. Three counts of murder of an individual beyond the border of the realm of Sokoto. These are the allegations in full, your excellency."

"What is the evidence supporting these alleged crimes?"

"A sword with a uniquely designed hilt, characteristic of and specific to the durbar order, was retrieved at the scene of the murders beyond the realm of Sokoto."

There were gasps among the Emir's entourage and the ministers on the floor beneath them.

"A durbar sword was found?" asked the Emir.

"According to the warrant information excellency, it would seem so."

"What do they want?" asked the Emir.

"Removal of the suspect from where he currently resides or is in the protectorate thereof," continued the court official, "to be transported to the realm of Sokoto, for the purpose of trial for the crimes alleged to have been committed."

There were more mutterings among the meeting attendees. The

court official cleared his throat before continuing. "Forgive me excellency, there is one more thing."

"Continue."

"The warrant states that if the armed escort and the suspect are not returned to the realm of Sokoto within three days, this will be seen as a violation of the treaty between the kingdoms of Sokoto and Kano."

The Minister of Defence stood up. The fabric of his tunic was tight around his thick neck and bulky arms. His appearance confirmed his reputation as a formidable wrestler in his youth, before he was beaten by middle-age spread. "Excellency, this is an obviously telegraphed predicate for—"

"War?" interrupted the Emir. Many heads turned beside him. As usual, the sovereign kept his composure. The defence minister bit his tongue. The Emir turned his attention to his Minister of Justice, a weasley-looking man with pock-marked fair skin and a contemptuous air. "Justice minister. What of these alleged murders beyond the realm?"

"Excellency, this is the first reporting of any additional deaths." The justice minister looked perplexed. "It is either a fabrication," he shot the durbar council chairman a disconcerting look, "or a fact that the durbar failed to disclose."

Durbar Master Jibril Asari stood up. "Excellency, there has been no lack of disclosure. I can assure the justice minister and everyone in this room of that. These accusations are false from start to finish. Durbar Master Garba Mansa is no mass murderer."

"Master Asari, the durbar reported an altercation in Katsina before his arrival in Sokoto," noted the Emir. "Could these be the unidentified deaths beyond the border of the realm of Sokoto to which the warrant refers?"

"No excellency. Master Mansa did not report any fatalities resulting from his altercation in Katsina. As far as I'm aware, Master Mansa didn't even draw his sword when he and the boy were attacked. If there had been deaths, surely those deaths would come under the jurisdiction of Katsina?"

"Not unless Katsina is colluding with Sokoto," said the Minister of Defence abruptly.

"We have no proof of that," corrected the Minister of Justice.

"We also haven't seen this proof that Master Mansa committed these crimes," countered Master Asari. "What Master Mansa reported was the defence of himself and the boy. They were the ones set upon."

"And they were the ones who lived to tell their tale," commented the justice minister. "Unfortunately the burden of proof rests on the durbar's shoulders."

"*Burden of proof?*" Master Asari checked himself, having raised his voice unintentionally.

"Excellency, I would be curious to know how Master Asari or indeed the accused, Master Mansa can explain the discovery of a durbar sword at the scene of the crime?"

"Master Asari?" asked the Emir.

"Excellency, minister, this I cannot explain fully. Perhaps the weapon was stolen or Master Mansa lost the weapon in combat during his altercation."

"The same combat in which he is alleged to have killed three unidentified individuals?" asked the justice minister.

"I'm certain Master Mansa has a plausible explanation. I'm certain he can explain himself fully and acquit himself of these allegations."

"I'm sure he can," said the justice minister. "He will have an opportunity to plead his case at his trial in Sokoto. While we're here Master Asari, do you recall if Master Mansa reported a missing sword?" asked the justice minister.

"No minister."

"Have any durbars reported missing weapons?"

"No minister."

"So what you're saying is that on the balance of probabilities Master Mansa did not simply misplace his weapon at a crime scene where people have been found dead?" pressed the justice minister.

"As I said minister, I cannot fully explain how a durbar weapon ended up at a crime scene but I'm confident Master Mansa can explain in full himself. He doesn't stand a chance of a fair trial if he's tried in a foreign court. His execution will be a certainty. Has his fate already been decided?"

Several pairs of eyes in the Emir's entourage looked at the floor in response to the old durbar's inquisitive plea.

"Nothing has been decided Master Asari," responded the Emir. "What of the party that was to travel to Sokoto?"

The Minister of Trade stood up. He was short with bushy eyebrows, yellow eyes and a grey pencil moustache that clung to his upper lip like a furry slug between his round cheeks. He spoke in a disinterested monotone. "The party was due to travel tomorrow," the trade minister flashed a look at Master Asari, "accompanied by two durbars but given this latest obstacle and Sokoto's flagrant disregard for responding to our recent terms, I'm unsure if the arrival of such a party would be viewed as an aggressive response. Especially if…"

"Especially if what minister?" asked the Emir.

"Especially if the warrant were not executed and the durbar wasn't handed over to the armed escort for transportation back to Sokoto."

"Defence minister, what do you suggest?" asked the Emir.

"Our choices are limited. If we hand over the durbar, war will at best be prevented or in the worst case and more likely scenario, it will be delayed. This durbar incident alone doesn't explain the troop movements and stockpiling of resources that is going on as we speak."

"That we *believe* is going on," corrected the justice minister.

"But if we don't surrender the durbar, is war coming anyway?" continued the defence minister. "Perhaps we view this ultimatum as the premeditated bait that it seems to be and wait things out."

"Minister you're loading my mind with more questions than answers," said the Emir.

"Forgive me. I believe that the outcome of military conflict is inevitable. An old foe doesn't threaten to start a fight that it doesn't believe it has a chance of winning. I say we strike first."

There was more muttering in the courtroom before the Minister of Justice chimed in. "This so-called old foe that my honourable colleague refers to has not explicitly threatened war. They have merely submitted a warrant for the arrest of an alleged criminal to be tried as they see fit."

"Master Mansa is no criminal," interjected Jibril Asari.

"And that shall be determined in his trial," said the justice minister. "We've done our own investigation, let Sokoto do theirs."

"There will be only one outcome," insisted Jibril Asari. "We're signing a man's death warrant. Can you not see that?"

"I urge a different course of action from my honourable colleagues," continued the justice minister. "Military conflict could simply be avoided by submitting to the terms."

Durbar Master Jibril Asari looked at the Emir then the ministers, closed his eyes and shook his head in disbelief. "Are you proposing that we throw one of our own, unquestionably one of our most loyal warriors, a man who has given everything in service for Kano, to the wolves?"

"Durbar Master Mansa's loyal service to the emirate is well known, Master Asari," said the Minister of Justice. "We must put sentimentality to one side."

"*Sentimentality*?" blurted out Master Asari.

"Yes, durbar master, sentimentality. We must not forget that Master Mansa is first and foremost a soldier, a servant of the emirate. We're not sending a lamb to the slaughter. He has spent years preparing for the ultimate sacrifice and has vowed to lay down his life for Kano. This would be his final contribution to the kingdom. Consider his act of surrender and the prevention of war the absolute example of his distinguished service and a fitting tribute to his character."

There was a long uncomfortable silence, as the rationale of the minister's suggestion was absorbed by the council attendees.

"Could we send someone, say a convicted criminal facing execution, in the durbar's place?" asked the defence minister. "A less valuable life could be put to good use."

"Respectfully, the folly of such a fantastical idea is glaringly obvious," said the justice minister, ignoring the defence minister's scowl from across the aisle. "Even if someone strongly resembling the durbar was identified within the next twenty-four hours, he would easily fail a trial by combat if there was any doubt over his identity. Let us not forget that Master Mansa has met the Sultanate Council and the Grand Vizier himself not long ago."

All eyes were on the deflated durbar council chairman, following the politician's hollow plaudits. The room was silent. "What does sacrificing Master Mansa guarantee?" he asked.

"Nothing," replied the justice minister. "But what is one life compared to an entire kingdom?"

"We have nothing to lose by surrendering the durbar. We can still be battle-ready in the meantime," concurred the defence minister.

"Excellency?" asked Jibril Asari. His eyes pleaded desperately.

"Master Asari, do you have an alternative suggestion?" asked the Emir.

Durbar Master Jibril Asari hung his head dejectedly and looked at the floor. He inhaled, exhaled, lifted his head up and composed himself. "No, excellency, I do not."

"Durbar Master Garba Mansa will be remembered greatly," said the Emir. "I know what his life means to you and I understand that it must pain you to accept his fate. But let me assure you, this decision is not taken lightly and it is not a betrayal. His sacrifice will save lives."

"I am most grateful for your words excellency." Jibril Asari's voice faltered as he spoke.

There was a long awkward silence in the courtroom as the decision sank in. The Minister of Justice gauged the sympathetic atmosphere in the room and waited a few moments before speaking. "Master Asari, is Master Mansa within the palace grounds?"

"No," replied Master Asari bluntly.

The justice minister looked at the defence minister and silently delegated the next question to him. "I propose we continue our hospitality for the escort, as a gesture of good faith to Sokoto," said the defence minister. For the first time in the meeting members of the Emir's entourage and the ministers in the room nodded in agreement.

"That leaves one outstanding issue. How do we convey Durbar Master Mansa to the armed escort alive?"

A crestfallen Jibril Asari looked at the defence minister. "Leave him to me."

Chapter Seventeen

The sound of approaching hooves snapped Isa out of his daydream. He ran to the lookout in their compound. The green and brown blur in the shimmering heat haze advanced on the horizon. By the time the royal messenger had reached the compound, Master was already aware of their visitor and waited with Isa to receive him by the open gate.

"Durbar master, the durbar council requests your presence at once," said the emissary. His horse panted with exhaustion but the messenger didn't dismount. "It is a matter of urgency."

"On whose authority?" asked Master casually.

"Durbar Master Asari."

"Understood," said Master. "The boy and I will come at once. You can res—"

"Thank you durbar master but I have strict orders to return to the palace immediately, once your departure has been confirmed."

There was a brief but awkward silence. Master gave Isa a curious almost bemused look before responding to the messenger. "Our departure will be confirmed once my ward gets our horse. His feet appear to have become rooted to the ground."

The messenger stared at Isa. Master flashed Isa an irritated look. Isa looked at Master confused. "My ward has plenty of imagination but not much initiative. *Isa!*"

Isa snapped out of his daze. "Yes Master."

"Don't just stand there. You heard the man. Get Sisoko. We leave for the palace now."

#

Every so often, the messenger looked over his shoulder to ensure that Master and Isa were still in tow. He never slowed down his horse but the messenger was clearly a little on edge. Master said nothing. Isa reflexively held onto him tighter as they rode. After the last council meeting Master had muttered about the possibility of a demeaning trip to Sokoto to babysit another useless politician. Isa hadn't understood what meaning there was in looking after a politician's baby but as usual kept his thoughts to himself. Nothing irritates an irritable man more than irritating questions, Master had said. And Master was definitely more pleasant to be around when he wasn't irritated.

#

The Gidan Rumfa was desolate. A royal ghost town. If not for the usual palace security, one could easily have been forgiven for assuming a great plague or famine had wiped out the palace inhabitants. Even at daybreak after the busiest religious festival, the odd soul could be seen milling around the grounds. Not that day. The palace guards stared solemnly at the visitors as they eerily trotted through the grounds. Only when they reached the stables did the royal emissary give up his escort. He hurriedly dismounted, secured his horse and went off, presumably to report their arrival. For the first durbar council meeting in some time, there were twelve horses including Sisoko in the stables but not a ward in sight. Master looked perplexed but said nothing.

"Master, why is it so quiet?" whispered Isa.

"I don't know," replied Master. "But I suspect we're going to find out."

#

The entire durbar order was present in the council room. Master Garba Mansa was the last arrival. He exchanged nods with his durbar brothers before taking his seat at the table. The mood in the room was serious. Durbar Master Jibril Asari gave his former apprentice a pained smile.

"Thank you for coming at such short notice," began Master Asari. "We meet under the most difficult circumstances. Tensions are high and things have reached a tipping point. As the council members are already aware, a durbar escort has been requested for the trade delegation travelling to Sokoto."

"Who are the lucky two? Who gets to nurse the trade rat in their wrapper?" joked Musa Gindiri. "Or will we be expected to wipe his nyash too?"

There was muffled laughter. Laughter from everyone except Jibril Asari.

"Master Asari, from the expression on your face, it looks like *you* might be going to Sokoto," said Ugo Itojo.

"Only one of you is going to Sokoto," said Jibril Asari bluntly.

The other durbars all looked at one another, surprised by the announcement and unsure why the old man looked so glum.

"Only one of us?" asked Hakeem Urumu.

"I vote for my brother," said Kazeem Urumu.

There was more laughter. The old man was clearly in no mood for levity.

"Why the change of plan?" asked Garba Mansa.

"Our hand has been forced," replied Jibril Asari ominously. "I'm sure you've all noticed the atmosphere in the palace."

"It's like walking among the dead," observed Kazeem Urumu.

"People have taken shelter," said Jibril Asari. There were more looks exchanged among his audience.

"Shelter from what?" asked Ugo Itojo.

"Those fanatics have declared war, haven't they?" asked Musa Gindiri.

"Not exactly." Jibril Asari took a deep breath. "Sokoto has issued the kingdom an arrest warrant and intends to send an armed escort. The Emir's council believes that war could be the next step."

Musa Gindiri smiled to himself and shook his head. "An arrest warrant for what?"

Jibril Asari took a deep breath. "A warrant for the arrest of Durbar Master Garba Mansa for the murders of eight men, including an official of the Sultan's palace."

There was collective head shaking, cursing and other audible signs of outrage.

"*This is insanity*," insisted Garba Mansa. "I reported everything on my return from Sokoto." Master Mansa composed himself for a moment before continuing. "This makes no sense. I fought four men in Sokoto, how can they accuse me of murdering eight?"

"The warrant alleges that you killed three men beyond the border of Sokoto," said Master Asari.

"*Rubbish*," spat Hakeem Urumu. "It's a lie. What proof do they have?"

"They claim to have retrieved a durbar sword from the scene of one of the murders."

"*They claim?*" asked Ugo Itojo. "With the greatest respect Master Asari, our brother's life is worth a lot more than a claim."

"It pains me to say it but the Emir's council believes the burden of proof rests on Master Mansa's shoulders. The council believes he should plead his case at trial in Sokoto."

"*Plead his case?*" said Musa Gindiri incredulously. "Before or after the executioner lines his blade on Garba's neck?"

"Master Asari you can't possibly believe Garba stands any chance of a fair trial?" asked Ugo Itojo. "If he goes to Sokoto his death is a foregone conclusion."

Jibril Asari turned to Garba Mansa. "Believe me Garba, I pleaded your case. I'm as devastated as all of us by the council's decision. I feel I've failed you."

Garba Mansa saw the pain on the old man's face but when he opened his mouth to speak, the words got stuck in his throat.

"And what if Garba stays here? What if we refuse them taking him?" asked Kazeem Urumu.

"The council believes the next escalation will be full scale war," said Jibril Asari.

"Isn't this the same council that believes war is coming anyway?" asked Ugo Itojo. "And yet we get no say in the fate of our brother?"

"We are all servants of the emirate. The Emir has made his decision," said Jibril Asari solemnly.

Garba Mansa spoke in a low volume voice. "When will they get here?"

Jibril Asari looked at the table and appeared lost for words. Everyone waited on tenterhooks for his response.

"Those snakes are already on their way aren't they?" interjected Hakeem Urumu.

"No," said Musa Gindiri suspiciously. "They're already here. That's why everyone is hiding. That's why the palace is like a graveyard. Isn't that right Master Asari?"

Jibril Asari remained silent and nodded his head, unable to look his fellow council members and the remaining durbars in their eyes. "I'm sorry for the deception."

"So it's done," said Garba Mansa. He stared at the table, completely deflated by the judgement on his life. His words hung heavily in the air before a long uncomfortable silence.

"*No,*" said Musa Gindiri. The others looked at him. "It's not done until we say it's done. We are durbars. Brothers. We don't hand over our own for crimes they didn't commit. Garba isn't going anywhere. He'd do the same for us."

"I respect, admire and share your loyalty but loyalty to one another aside, would you risk going to war?" asked Jibril Asari.

"War is coming anyway," said Hakeem Urumu.

"I'd rather go into it with my brothers by my side. All of them," said Kazeem Urumu.

"And die with your brothers?" asked Jibril Asari.

"If I die, so be it. Better to die for something than to live for nothing," responded Kazeem Urumu.

"But what if the sacrifice of one could prevent the death of thousands?" pondered Ugo Itojo.

There was an uncomfortable pause before Musa Gindiri's face contorted into a mask of total apoplexy. "Who's side are you on?" he asked. "Would you betray Garba so easily? Have you no honour?"

"Question my honour again and it will be the last thing you question," warned Ugo Itojo.

"Care to bet on that?" goaded Musa Gindiri.

The opposing durbars both slid their chairs back suddenly as if to launch into a confrontation.

"*Stop it!*" shouted Garba Mansa. He composed himself and lowered his voice before continuing. "Fighting among ourselves changes nothing. We're brothers but we all pledged to sacrifice our lives for Kano if we were ever called upon. As unjust and painful as this is, for all of us, for me especially, that time is now."

"This isn't right Garba," said Musa Gindiri.

"We must accept it. I must accept it."

"We can get you out of the palace. Out of the city," offered Hakeem Urumu.

"To what end brother?" asked Garba Mansa. "To have them come harder, faster and in greater numbers? To erode what little time we've left for this war that everyone feels is coming?"

"First those dogs kill an emissary and now they want to kill one of our best." Kazeem Urumu pounded his fists on the table as he spoke defiantly. "Let them bring their war. I'll enjoy killing as many of them as possible."

There were nods from non-council members around the room. Garba Mansa slumped in his chair and spoke flatly. "Brother, I'm sure you'll have your chance to kill many and you may win the war tomorrow but today is not your day."

The defeated durbar order sat in silence as reality sank in.

#

Advancing heavy footsteps, travelling in tandem, interrupted the morose mood of the durbar meeting. The brotherhood recognised the sound. It was a sound they were all too familiar with. It was a sound they'd once made before their selection to join the durbar order. It was the sound of armed conflict. The sound grew louder and louder until it stopped just outside the meeting room. Then there was a loud *boom* on the heavy oak door.

"*In the name of his excellency, Emir Ado Sanusi of Kano, open this door!*" projected a voice from the other side of the door.

The durbars looked at one another and said nothing. The loud *boom boom boom* came again.

"*In the name of his excellency, Emir Ado Sanusi of Kano, I compel you to open this door!*"

The brotherhood sat in silence.

"*This is your last chance. If you do not open the door, I shall be compelled to break it down!*"

"So they send our own troops to take one of our own." Musa Gindiri shook his head in disgust. "Let them break the door. It's thick enough to keep them sweating for quite some time. They'll earn their keep today."

Resigned smiles were exchanged around the room. They'd each

courted death on at least one occasion, some more so than others. They'd each faced seemingly insurmountable odds and succeeded victoriously. Death was no stranger to a durbar. An absent friend that threatened to reacquaint itself every so often. *When death comes for you, greet your absent friend and tell him the afterlife awaits you another day.* Surrendering felt cheap and cowardly, as if they'd all given up the fight. It was an exit unworthy of a durbar. As despair suffocated their morale, a different voice came from the other side of the door.

"Durbar Master Asari. This is the Minister of Justice. I know Master Mansa is in there. I understand this is difficult but just like you, we have our orders. We have no choice. Lives will be saved, if only in the short term. Kano owes Master Mansa a debt of gratitude and must ask this one last thing of him. Please open the door."

Musa Gindiri forced a smile. "Oh the sad irony. A politician telling you to do the selfless thing. Would *he* surrender to a death sentence?"

"*Durbar Master Asari!*" repeated the justice minister. "This is your last chance to come quietly."

The room stayed silent.

"Very well then," continued the minister. "We'll break the door down."

Shuffling feet were heard behind the door. All eyes within the room were on the heavy oak door in anticipation of the first hit of the battering ram. A minute went by. Not a sound was heard on either side of the door. More shuffling feet were heard. Garba Mansa sighed, slid his chair back, stood up and drew his sword. "Gentlemen, it's been an honour."

#

A gentle rumbling came from the other side of the heavy oak door, as the locking bar slid away. The door drifted slightly ajar, pouring light into the dark passageway. The first man holding the head of the battering ram turned to his hands-free superior. His superior turned to the justice minister. The minister silently motioned for the battering ram to be put down. The message was relayed to the other men doing the heavy lifting, who having carried out the order then reversed the chain of silent messages on how to proceed next. The justice minister pointed for the uniformed commander to enter the council room. The commander partially drew his sword and waited for the justice minister's response. The Minister of Justice nodded affirmatively. Once the remaining uniformed men had all drawn their swords, the senior rank motioned for his subordinates to enter before him.

#

Thirty Kano palace guards piled into the durbar council meeting room with swords at the ready. A few feet short of the meeting room table they stopped abruptly. The senior rank and penultimate arrival shared the same perplexed expression as his battle-ready comrades. It would be a moment to share with his children's children, if he lived to tell the tale. He turned to the last arrival, the justice minister, unsure of how to proceed. Between the armed guards and the meeting room table stood ten well-dressed men, in individual attire, all with their own ornate weapons drawn. Some of the ten even had a blade in each hand. The two men that looked similar, one with a beard and one without, stared menacingly at the intruders. The most flamboyantly dressed one smiled and then winked at the guards. An older more moderately dressed man, presumably the durbar leader, stood by the doorway observing the standoff.

"*Master Asari, what is the meaning of this?*" hissed the justice minister, clearly rattled by the intimidating obstacle in front of him. He had the look of a man who'd realised a second too late that he'd kicked a hornet's nest in a confined space.

Relishing the politician's unease, Durbar Master Jibril Asari gave the justice minister a bemused look. It was probably the closest the weasel had come to the sharp end of justice.

"You asked me to open the door minister. As you can clearly see, I have complied."

"Where is Garba Mansa?" demanded the justice minister.

"Oh he's still here minister. Right on the other side of those men." Jibril Asari nodded in the direction of the wall of durbars. "Please feel free to retrieve him at your leisure."

"I must warn you master durbar, obstructing Garba Mansa's arrest will be seen as an act of sedition, akin to treason," said the justice minister.

"Let it be witnessed that I have fully complied with your request, justice minister. Master Mansa is yours for the taking. My sword is sheathed. I will not stop you."

"And what about them?" The justice minister pointed to the durbar standoff.

"They can speak for themselves," said Jibril Asari. "What I will say is that when considering taking on the most dangerous fighters in the kingdom, one should be aware of one's exits. The windows are rather small and last time I checked, the passageway you came through is only wide enough for one person at a time."

The justice minister went a paler shade of his yellow complexion and swallowed hard. Running away would make him the laughing stock of the council and leave his career in tatters. But he was also no fighter. The durbars were vastly outnumbered but their incredible confidence was deeply unnerving while the palace guards reeked of fear and indecision. The minister turned to the flamboyant loudmouth Musa Gindiri.

"Well then. What do you have to say for yourself?"

Musa Gindiri looked at his brothers-in-arms, looked at the guards and flashed the Minister of Justice his broadest smile. "Good odds. Perhaps you should've brought more men?"

Chapter Eighteen

By nightfall the palace rumour mill was in overdrive. The durbar's arrest had reportedly incurred a high human cost, according to most accounts. The durbar council room had apparently been a slaughterhouse, with the elite soldiers wiping out not one but two batches of palace guards in failed attempts to retrieve their comrades. Some claimed that the justice minister himself had been taken hostage as a bargaining chip for safe passage out of the city. Others believed that upon vanquishing the royal guard, the durbars had taken their uniforms and escaped from the palace in disguise.

As was often the case with such feverish hearsay, the facts of the matter were considerably less dramatic than the fiction. In reality the durbar standoff lasted only a few minutes. The durbars released Master Garba Mansa to his jailers on two conditions. The first was that he wouldn't be shackled in chains and paraded through the Gidan Rumfa like a slave or criminal. The second was that his fellow durbars would escort him to his place of confinement within the palace grounds until such a time came for his conveyance to Sokoto. Upon agreement of the terms Garba Mansa surrendered his weapons to his mentor Jibril Asari.

It was the best outcome for all. Not least of all the palace guards and the justice minister. One of the former had soiled himself while contemplating death at the hands of not one but two Urumu brothers. Once their duties were over, other guards went to embrace loved ones or to the mosque, to praise Allah for his mercy in preventing a durbar massacre. The Minister of Justice was the most relieved of all. His chances of surviving a forty man melee had been slim at best. Having the proficiency of a novice swordsman wouldn't have helped his chances. To celebrate the successful passing of his brush with death, having reported the acquisition of the durbar, the justice minister sent a servant to fetch the largest goatskin of palm wine he could carry and retired to his chamber for the rest of the day. Before passing out in a puddle of his own drool, the justice minister ruminated on exacting revenge on Jibril Asari for the total humiliation he'd suffered.

\#

Isa was oblivious to his master's fate. He'd been kept in a waiting room, as usual, insulated from the numerous rumours flying around the palace. Despite the eerie palace atmosphere Isa was given regular meals and looked after in the usual manner and knew better than to ask any questions. Isa hoped Master's emergency meeting had gone well. Meetings with the Emir's council had a propensity to drag on. It was only as the sun set and Master still hadn't returned that the boy became concerned. Perhaps Master had left the palace urgently and would send word to him. Perhaps there had been several meetings that day or just the one long one. None of Isa's peers were around to glean information from. Whatever it was, he hoped it would be resolved quickly.

\#

Betrayal. Crushing disappointment. Rage. Pushing the emotions to the back of his mind was a struggle. As Durbar Master Garba Mansa sat cross-legged on the floor of his cell, with his eyes closed, his face twitched with failing meditation. The sound of the jailer's key turning in the lock was a welcome distraction. The arrival of his only visitor was an even better one. Jibril Asari had successfully pleaded with the Emir to be granted visiting privileges, despite the fervent objection from the justice minister. Given the grand nature of the durbar's transfer to prison, he had spared what little was left of the justice minister's dignity by banning the rest of the order from any further contact with their incarcerated brother. The mentor and former apprentice faced each other on opposite sides of the prison bars. The old man was the first to yield to the mounting silent tension.

"Say something Garba. Anything."

Garba Mansa kept his eyes shut but dignified the words of the man he'd once revered with a response. "Silence has its own eloquence when the words of others around us are so crass."

The older durbar shook his head. "You're disappointed in me. You feel I've betrayed you, don't you?" said Jibril Asari. "You blame me for them putting you in this cage."

Garba Mansa smiled, still with his eyes closed. "*Disappointed?* I'm definitely disappointed."

"Well at least have the courtesy to express your disappointment like a man, not like some impudent child sat on the floor," snapped Jibril Asari.

The calm was over. Garba Mansa immediately sprang to his feet, eyes wide open. The two men stood nose to nose, separated by the bars.

"*Impudent child?*"

The older durbar smiled, satisfied with his rouse to get his former apprentice's full attention. Garba Mansa stood back from the bars of his cage, took a deep breath and sighed heavily. "I'm disappointed in everyone. Everyone except my brothers who were prepared to spill their own blood, rather than surrender me to the enemy."

"I understand," acknowledged Master Asari, "But to what end? What of the greater good? What of the kingdom? *Our* kingdom. Surely you can see I had no choice."

"You made your choice. You walked me into an ambush then made me choose between killing my own people or preventing my own people from being killed by our enemy. All for crimes I didn't commit."

"Yes, I deceived you. I deceived you to make the difficult choice. Would you rather I'd come to warn you? Would you have surrendered knowing your innocence?"

Garba Mansa silently scrutinised his mentor for a few moments. "We'll never know now will we?" he said.

"If there were a chance…"

"If there were a chance *what?*" snapped Garba Mansa impatiently.

Jibril Asari leaned in closer and lowered his voice. "If there were a chance we could get you back, I would do everything in my power to…"

"*To what? Rescue me?*"

"*Garba, control yourself!*" Jibril Asari glanced over his shoulder at the two guards by the jail entrance. They looked at him suspiciously, each with a hand on the hilt of their sheathed swords. Master Asari raised his hands submissively and smiled before turning round to continue. "You have to stay calm Garba. Stay focussed. All is not yet lost. Your release could still be negotiated via diplomatic channels. Perhaps a delegate could attend your trial."

"A delegate, the same politicians that gave me up?" Garba Mansa smiled and shook his head. "Master, your guilt is clouding your better judgement. How can you be sure there'll even be a trial? How do you know this armed escort won't cut off my head before we even reach Sokoto and have it ready for the Grand Vizier?" Garba paused to compose himself. "It's over. I'm finished. For all his excellency's empty platitudes, only my brothers and my ward will remember me. The loyal servant. The loyal dead servant who was scapegoated in the line of duty to buy weaker men more time."

Jibril Asari felt a wave of great sadness and pity overcome him. It took some time before he felt able to cut through his own painful silence. "The boy will be looked after. I promise you that, as Allah is my witness."

"Thank you. Let him know that I didn't abandon him, that I didn't forget him."

"I will."

Master Garba Mansa stared beyond his mentor for a few seconds before resuming eye contact. "I have one more request. See to it that the boy gets my sword. But remind him that he always has a choice to choose his own path."

"I will see to it Garba."

"So when do they come for me?" asked Garba Mansa.

"Some time in the morning."

"Well I better enjoy my sleep. It could be my last." Garba Mansa forced a pained smile that made his mentor pity him more. His mentor returned the same pained smile. The two men locked their right hands on the other's right forearm through the prison bars. As they did so, tears began to well up in Garba Mansa's eyes.

"Go well brother," said Garba Mansa.

"And you," said Jibril Asari, almost in a whisper as his cracking voice failed to stifle the lump in his throat. "When death comes for you, greet our absent friend and tell him the afterlife awaits you another day."

Garba Mansa nodded, released the older man from his grip and watched him leave. The prison guard locked the door behind him. He was alone again.

#

Isa had been shown to a cool room with a bed near the waiting area. He gratefully received the atypical special treatment but with every passing hour of Master's absence his thoughts were occupied more by anxiety than his imagination. He woke up several times during the night, expecting to hear Master's reassuring voice emerge from the shadows and the promise of an explanation the next day. The shadows stayed silent and his anxiety eventually succumbed to fatigue.

Daybreak brought Isa a full breakfast but no further insight into Master's whereabouts. Shortly after filling his belly with fruits and yam Isa was taken back to the waiting area where he'd spent the better part of the previous day. At first he thought this was a good omen for Master's imminent return. Minute by minute his optimism began to wane and the incongruity of the special treatment for a lowly ward and Master's absence began to weigh on his mind. The palace official monitoring him was an old man with a pleasant tone of voice but a fixed almost constipated facial expression and an apparent inability to smile more than once every few hours. The man looked as though he'd dished out and received his fair share of beatings over the years and brandished a raffia hand broom as if each speck of dust on the floor had committed a crime against hygiene. Every time Isa plucked up the courage to ask the old man if he knew of Master's whereabouts, he considered the possibility of being thrashed with a strip of the raffia across the back of his legs. He waited patiently and kept his mouth shut instead.

A short while later, a silhouette of a tall turbaned man crossed the window of the waiting area. Isa anticipated relief and excitement in equal measure but remained seated lest he incurred the wrath of the raffia broom. Moments later, it was with great disappointment that he greeted the white bearded durbar council chairman. Durbar Master Jibril Asari nodded to the chaperone who, raffia broom in hand, left the two of them alone. The old durbar's face emanated a sympathetic sadness despite the warmth of his smile. After briefly enquiring about palace hospitality Master Asari's smile faded and he explained the purpose of his visit.

#

The stone wall felt cool on his back, despite the stifling lack of air circulation in his temporary confinement. A train of ants came through the cracks in the floor and took a detour around the puddle of urine in the corner of his cell. The guards, having failed to extend the courtesy of providing their detainee with a bucket for defecating, had used the bucket themselves and left it against the bars of the cell. Flies congregated around the container of pungent man-made excrement that was already several hours old. What little natural light there was crept in through three vertical slits in the walls. Rather than the nauseating stench of human waste or the cacophony of hungry flies, it was the sunlight that had woken him. He was immediately reminded that his plight, like his surroundings, was bleak.

Before his few hours of fitful sleep, Garba Mansa repeatedly ran through all possible scenarios of his immediate future. Most were selfish, clearly at odds with the honour code he'd sworn to uphold. The same honour code that had left him facing a potential death sentence. The guards clearly hadn't been rotated overnight and grunted in their sleep. Had there been a means of escape, some other more exploitable lapse in their concentration, he considered subduing them longer term and escaping into the night. Given that the palace seemed on high alert he pondered when such an opportunity might present itself, the lengths he was willing to go to cheat death and the cost to others. Would the alert level be as high now that he was in custody? Or would the palace paranoia die down once he and the outsiders from Sokoto had gone? After ruminating on several permutations of his escape, the crushing reality of his fate gradually set back in. Between leaving his cell and arriving at the Sultan's palace one thing had the highest certainty. He was going to die. Perhaps his exit from this world might be a painless experience. Perhaps his mentor had taken pity on him and would lace his last meal with poison that would render him first unconscious then unrousable, to meet his absent friend in his sleep. In a fit of paranoia, Garba Mansa considered starving himself if there was even a glimmer of hope he would escape. He'd need all his strength and endurance if given the opportunity.

As his eyelids became too heavy, Garba Mansa fought against the bitterness and anger that threatened to consume what little time he had left. Instead he reflected on all the unfinished business leading up to his incarceration. Old wounds were kept firmly closed as he refused to indulge in ruminating on the most painful losses in his life. They'd had their time and were safely buried deep beneath the surface of his emotions. Instead he focussed on the imminent losses, not least of all his own life. He lamented his time with Isa with guilt and frustration. The boy was at an age where he could see the world with his own eyes but still needed guidance on how to interpret it. Garba Mansa's legacy would be that for everything good people achieved, those around them were capable of far worse. Isa would remember a cruel and unjust system that was at odds with the example he'd been set by his longest guardian. Would he grow up to be maladjusted, damaged in some way, only to become the very kind of person that his master abhorred? Or would his kindness of spirit outshine the cruelty around him? If he remained in Master Asari's care there was still hope. Like his current predicament, Isa's future was completely beyond Garba Mansa's control.

Garba Mansa was unsure what the ramifications of his arrest would be for the durbar order. The little standoff with the justice minister had won the order one less friend. Politicians never took kindly to being challenged by mere mortals at the best of times. Master Asari had said the look of panic on the minister's face at the first hint of danger was almost worth his arrest. Unfortunately the minister's embarrassment was bound to have consequences. Beyond the corridors of power, who knew what the arrest of one durbar would do to public opinion of the others? Within the order, loyalty had its limits and his brothers were likely to question their own vulnerability in future political games. Master Asari, for all his patience and wisdom, seemed most shaken by his former apprentice's arrest. The old man's guilt hung heavily around his neck. Being the pillar of integrity he was, Garba Mansa imagined the old man would continue fighting their corner in the political arena. In privacy, he feared some of the old man's fire would die with the death of his former apprentice and that the order would be less resistant to attack in the future.

The looming conflict with Sokoto was at the forefront of Garba Mansa's frustrations. What started as an investigation into the death of a royal emissary and a threat to destabilise his kingdom, had ended up with a principal investigator being wanted for murders he hadn't committed. The absurdity of the escalation of tension, by the party under suspicion, burned him the most. To Garba Mansa his imprisonment reinforced what others had discounted regarding the extraordinary coincidences since the investigation began. There had to be other forces at play, other forces who *wanted* this war to come. The most galling thing for Garba Mansa to admit was that those forces had won.

Most people of his time prayed to one deity or several when they knew their end was near. Most people prayed for forgiveness, some gave thanks, while others asked for comfort and peace on their journey into the next life. Not Garba Mansa. Having lost his faith in the existence of a higher power some time ago, he asked for nothing. Instead he wondered what, if anything, he might encounter beyond the darkness, once he'd met his absent friend. The sound of footsteps, a loud banging on the jail door and the startled guards jumping to their feet, interrupted his meditation on life. One guard hurriedly grabbed the bucket of faeces and tipped the contents through the bars into Garba Mansa's cell. Within moments a key was turning in the lock of the jail entrance door. It was time.

Chapter Nineteen

The muezzin's first call to prayer had seen palace inhabitants tiptoeing around the grounds, not wanting to be seen to be giving in to their natural voyeuristic tendencies but curious all the same to see the outcome of the durbar saga for themselves. The general anxiety following the arrival of the armed escort from Sokoto had diminished significantly. Mosque attendance was at a record high that day. It was almost certain that the attendance for second prayers at noon would be equally as high if not higher. The more savvy worshippers turned up well in advance; just in case they caught a glimpse of the foreigners and the durbar. It had been established by those in the know that the durbar was still in custody.

From the visitors' perspective, they'd been treated remarkably well by their hosts. Better in fact than what they were accustomed to back in Sokoto. Having been thoroughly indoctrinated in the animosity between the two kingdoms, they took shifts in sleeping and those that slept, slept with one eye open. By morning each member of the armed escort was surprised that none of them had contracted food poisoning, some other fatal illness or been sabotaged in some way before their departure. So far so good.

The justice minister, a sickly looking man by anyone's standards, had advised the men from Sokoto that the durbar be brought directly to the escort from his cell. He'd warned that these durbars were a law unto themselves, highly dangerous and could be very unpredictable, regardless of what the law stipulated. He thought it better that strength in numbers from the home side would safeguard against anything untoward befalling their cargo before their arrival in Sokoto. Due to previous engagements, the justice minister advised that he regrettably wouldn't be personally available to oversee the handover. Instead his deputy would be on hand from start to finish. The Sokoto guardsmen nodded enthusiastically in agreement, keen to take on any advice in a strange land that might keep them alive and knowing full well that they had no choice. It was before noon and even if they reached Sokoto after dark, they were sufficiently rested, heavily armed, and prepared to deal with any obstacles along the way.

\#

Onlookers masquerading as early worshippers and palace officials with all too convenient errands had begun to loiter around the resurfaced carriage in the main courtyard of the Emir's palace. Their benign curiosity made the guards from Sokoto in blood red uniforms uneasy, despite the lack of hostility. As time passed, a small crowd had gathered around the carriage to unashamedly observe whatever happened next. The deputy justice minister had attended to the escort and advised them that he would accompany a cadre of the Emir's palace guards to retrieve their prisoner from his cell. To achieve a swift transfer, the Sokoto men were advised to have all means of securing the prisoner ready. A rapid transfer was emphasised as the deputy minister couldn't predict how people might react to the sight of one of their own, with near legendary status, in chains. Not long after the deputy minister had departed, the small crowd moved closer to the carriage, obscuring the wooden box from even a short distance away. As they waited for their prisoner the anxiety of the guardsmen returned.

\#

Almost half an hour later, the crowd's attention was elsewhere. Heads turned away from the carriage as the onlookers were captivated by something else. The Sokoto guards on foot saw the mob slowly start to form a tunnel at first, then give a progressively wider berth to whatever was approaching. The pair of Sokoto guardsmen on horseback had a different view. Thirty armed men in the red and green of Kano, in adjacent rows of ten, marched in unison across the courtyard towards the carriage. The only sound in the vicinity was that of marching feet. The motionless palace guards on the turrets watched their advancing colleagues. The heart rates of the men from Sokoto picked up considerably and the feeling of impending doom returned after a day's hiatus. Anxious glances were exchanged among the foreigners. Had they been fattened up in preparation for a slaughter in front of a home audience?

Just as the visitors' hands hovered over the hilts of their swords in preparation for a last stand, their immediate fate became clearer. From their elevated vantage point, the men on horseback saw a figure halfway along and in the middle row of the approaching guards. The figure stood out from the guards because of his attire, his height, and most subtly the way he moved. Where the guards marched uniformly like nondescript parts of a machine, the man in the middle moved with such unique grace that he almost glided. Furthermore, he didn't move like a criminal, with a head typically weighed down by public shame, only making eye contact with the ground. This man's head was held high, like an exiting dignitary from afar. The tall man's matching grey robes and turban complemented his proud demeanour. The man's description by the Sultanate Council hadn't done him justice. So taken were the outsiders by their first encounter with the durbar, it was only when the armed escort reached the carriage that the visitors realised he wasn't bound by any restraints at all.

The deputy justice minister followed the armed escort at a safe distance behind them and quickly joined the front of the procession once they'd reached the carriage. He immediately nodded for the men from Sokoto to proceed. A foot guardsman unlocked the carriage door and retrieved some wrist and ankle shackles from within the wooden box. The guardsman held them up to the durbar and looked at the deputy minister for confirmation before laying hands on his prisoner. The deputy justice minister nodded affirmatively. A bead of sweat slowly trickled down the guardsman's face onto his trembling hands as he put the durbar in chains. The Sokoto horse guards kept one eye on the crowd and one eye on their prisoner, with one hand firmly around the hilts of their sheathed swords. The crowd, now separated from the carriage by the substantial armed presence of the palace guards, looked at the handover with a mixture of curiosity and disdain. The latter mostly from older onlookers. Surprisingly for the visitors, the durbar was remarkably passive, complying fully with his restraint and staring straight ahead. Once his wrists and ankles were sufficiently bound, the durbar was ushered towards the open wooden box of the carriage. He shuffled forward, crouched then sat down, rolling in awkwardly sideways into his new cell. The door was shut behind him and locked with a chain.

#

Garba Mansa heard movement outside his new cage. He vaguely recognised the whiney tone of the deputy weasel mumbling to the foreigners. There were more footsteps and then the rumbling sound of the Gidan Rumfa main gate opening. The rickety carriage rocked slightly as it began to move forward. The sound of many synchronised footsteps getting fainter was confirmed as those of the palace guards, as Garba Mansa watched them moving away from the carriage, through the slit at the side of the wooden box. As his mobile prison passed through the open gate of the Emir's palace, guards nodded respectfully at the carriage, as one of their own left the palace for the last time.

\#

Unlike his palace jail, the only smell within the wooden box was Garba Mansa's natural scent. Without space to stand or space to lie down, if he'd felt like emptying his bladder or opening his bowels, he'd likely wear his own waste for the rest of the journey to Sokoto. Little light entered the box. The humidity was suffocating. For those religions that buried their dead in coffins this was the closest he'd come to replicating that experience. In spite of the claustrophobic conditions, being able to wipe the streaming sweat from his face was a small mercy. Knowing the local geography as well as he did, he knew he wasn't missing any significant view of the outside world. The rickety sound of the carriage wheels and tired horses were his auditory companions. The escorting guards said nothing.

After calming his mind and acclimatising to his surroundings, Garba Mansa reverted back to his training. *Assess the situation.* The positives were that his shackles weren't chained to the base of the wooden box and other than the carriage being set ablaze or pushed off a cliff, he would see whatever came his way. A major negative was that his limb reach was significantly restricted for anything other than grappling. Furthermore, he also hadn't seen which guard held the key to his chains, meaning his chances of beating each guard while locating the keys were low. The biggest negative of all was the space he was trapped in. He'd literally have to fight in a corner if the door were opened, forcing him to exit as soon as practically possible. Garba Mansa shifted his body from side to side. Nothing. The carriage had been designed in such a way that the box had minimal sway and was evenly balanced on the wooden slats. It was also solid, meaning no amount of strength would prize it open. Unless some accident or means of being ejected from the wooden box materialised, he wasn't getting out by his own hands. The only hope was that the guards might open the box for some reason before they got to Sokoto.

The light in the box faded as the sun set. Garba Mansa had removed his turban but was still soaked to the bone. The carriage had been travelling for hours without a break, so they had to be close to Sokoto. At least the air coming into the box was cooler. Just as he pondered the rapidly closing window for escape, the carriage stopped. Garba Mansa snapped out of his drowsy stupor and immediately pressed his eyes against the box slit, eagerly searching for an opportunity. At first he saw nothing in the dusk light. Then he heard footsteps and buckles being unfastened. A few moments later he heard the sound of water. It came from one, then two, then possibly three sources all out of his field of vision. He waited as the sound of flowing water continued. Garba Mansa silently cursed himself and leaned back in the box. He was listening to nothing more than the sound of Sokoto's finest peeing into the dirt. The heat had added delirium to his desperation. There was no opening for escape.

As he resigned himself to seeing the Grand Vizier's miserable face one more time something passed in front of his side of the carriage. Garba Mansa sat forward and pressed his eyes against the slit again. One of the Sokoto guards stood a few feet in front of the slit facing the box. His uniform looked almost black in the dim light. The soldier unsheathed his sword and a great fear came over Garba Mansa. He was going to be executed, skewered like an animal inside the box. The box that would serve as his final resting place before and after presentation to the Grand Vizier like a trophy. Perhaps they'd hoped he'd pass out with dehydration making him an easy quick kill. Garba Mansa frantically began pulling at his chains, trying to sum up superhuman strength he'd never possessed. Streams of salty sweat ran down his face and stung his eyes and the metal of his shackles tore into his skin as he struggled in vain. Then something most peculiar happened.

The guardsman put his sword down on the ground next to him and unbuckled the scabbard, placing it next to the sword. He then lowered the bottom half of his uniform and sat back in a squat position by a bush. Garba Mansa was baffled. It was only when the gentle sound of faecal matter hitting the earth matched its unique aroma, carried by the breeze a few seconds later, that the reality of what he was watching became clear. The guard had the presence of mind to be battle ready, even if he was interrupted while answering the call of nature. He even had the courtesy or shame not to do his business underneath the noses of his comrades. The absurdity of the situation at first made him chuckle, then he fell back into the box, away from the slit and laughed hysterically. Even if he *was* going to be executed straight after the guardsman had wiped his nyash with bush leaves, he no longer cared. He would die with a smile on his face. Garba Mansa laughed so hard he missed what came next. He caught his breath and leaned against the slit, curious to see if his laughter had put the man off his flow.

The guard was nowhere to be seen. Odd, he thought. The man couldn't have wiped his behind, adjusted his uniform and re-sheathed his sword that quickly and quietly. He scanned the horizon for a silhouette. Nothing. He then heard footsteps.

"Are you done?" mumbled the voice of a guard out of sight.

Silence.

"*Are you done?*" The same voice was less patient the second time round. The silent response was followed up with footsteps. Then Garba Mansa saw the silhouette of a man kneeling where the other guard had dumped his bowel load. In the dim light, the man appeared to be rummaging around on the ground before he froze suddenly. Garba Mansa heard the distinct sound of a sword being drawn and the silhouette jumped to his feet.

"*Ambush!*" screamed the man but it was too late.

This time Garba Mansa heard the sound and saw the end result. Something very fast went through the air and landed in the back of the alarm-raising man.

"*Aargh!*" He let out a blood-curdling scream and staggered, dropping down to one knee. Garba Mansa heard the sound of something whizzing in the air again. As it landed above its predecessor in the back of the wounded man, Garba Mansa was certain what it was. The man slumped to the ground and moved no more.

Garba Mansa moved away from the slit, unsure whether he was about to be liberated or also in danger. If he was captured by someone else, the duration and location of his ongoing bondage could be indeterminate. He laid low in the box and considered his options while the commotion continued around him.

#

The remaining two guards took heed of the warning and scrambled to their horses. One jumped on one of the free horses while the other took the horse attached to the carriage. They set off immediately. The second carriage horse instinctively kept up with its ridden companion. Unable to see their attackers, both guards hastily headed in the direction of Sokoto. If their cargo wasn't brought back to the palace, let alone brought back alive, they knew full well what the price of their failure would be.

#

Garba Mansa was jostled from side to side inside the wooden box, as the pace of the horses picked up. He pressed his back and feet against opposite corners of the box to try and steady himself. Having wedged himself sufficiently in one spot, he looked through the slit to gain some semblance of what was going on in the outside world. He couldn't believe what he saw.

#

With his ears pinned back by his horse's speed, the free-rider scanned the horizon for their attackers. Going mobile instead of standing their ground and being picked off by the silent assassins could prove to be life-saving. There was no sign of their attackers. He looked over his shoulder to check the status of the carriage. It was also still mobile and his comrade was still alive. Good. Two fatalities. Cargo intact. The guardsman on the free horse lifted his right hand up. His colleague did the same from a distance to acknowledge the command. The free-rider then dropped his arm and pointed forward, signalling for the evasion to continue in the same direction. The recipient of the command repeated the signal to complete the message. Just as the free-rider was turning to focus on his own journey, he caught a glimpse of movement out of the corner of his eye. He turned and saw something moving rapidly towards the carriage. He squinted in the darkness to make out the shape. Only when it was too late did he make out the figure in black on horseback approaching the carriage.

#

Was he telling him to stop? The carriage-rider couldn't clearly make out the flailing arm signal of his free-riding colleague. He hadn't slowed down so perhaps he was signalling to change course? The frantic arm waving continued but between the speed of the horses, the darkness and the adrenaline coursing through his veins, nothing was clear. It was only when he felt something whiz past his ear he understood what the signal meant. The carriage-rider dipped forward, pressing his head against the mane of his horse. He turned awkwardly to try and look over his shoulder to see where the projectile had come from. At the last second he made out the silhouette of a figure on horseback. The figure had something in its hands. Then his carriage horse buckled and he was airborne.

#

The free-rider watched the calamity unfold. The carriage horse had been struck in the neck by the assassin's arrow. It buckled, tripped up its partner horse and caused the whole carriage to overturn. The carriage-rider had been thrown clear from the carriage, landing in a heap several feet from the wreckage. His horses were writhing around on the ground but he wasn't moving. The free-rider immediately changed course to give aid to his fallen comrade and protect their cargo. He unsheathed his sword as he gave chase.

#

Garba Mansa was heavily winded and dazed. His head had hit the side of the box as it was thrown one way and his back had been slammed against another side when it landed. Despite the crash, the box was still intact. He heard the sound of whimpering horses and groggily dragged himself to the slit to survey the damage. The motionless body of a guard lay a few feet in front of him. The sound of approaching hooves seemed to rouse the still body. The guardsman rolled onto his front. When he tried to prop himself up, his left arm gave way and the guardsman yelped with pain. He staggered to his feet, initially putting all his bodyweight on both knees and his right arm. As soon as he was up, he drew his sword, spun round and staggered to the wooden box.

"You're hurt," said Garba Mansa. "Get me out of here and I can help you. You won't last long fighting with one arm. Let me help. You've nothing to lose."

The man stared at the aperture in the wooden box, apparently in a daze and staggered round to the side of it. The sound of hooves was getting louder. Garba Mansa heard him slump against the overturned box.

"Let me help you. You're badly hurt," repeated Garba Mansa.

"*Shut up!*" hissed the man. "How do I know they're not with you?"

"You don't," conceded Garba Mansa. "But you don't really have a choice. You can die with my help or without it."

#

The free-rider saw that his colleague had taken shelter behind the broken carriage. Smart. Wait for back-up. It wouldn't be long. He also saw that the assailant in black had stopped. The aggressor then began to slowly circle the carriage. Whoever the assassin was, they had to be there for their cargo. As the free-rider got closer the assassin appeared unfazed by his approach and seemed preoccupied with the carriage. It was only as he felt the excruciating burning pain between his shoulder blades that the free-rider knew why.

#

The carriage-rider saw his brethren's body slump and fall off the approaching horse. Panic kicked in. The free-rider's horse continued moving but slowed down to a trot not far from the overturned carriage. The rider in black had dismounted its horse and was equidistant to the free-rider's riderless horse. The durbar was right. He had nothing to lose. With every ounce of strength he had and his sword in his hand, the carriage-rider from Sokoto dashed to the wandering horse.

#

The man's desperate attempt for the horse was futile. Almost laughable. With a dislocated shoulder or a broken arm or both, his awkward gait was too great a handicap for him to win the race to the horse. The figure in black could've picked him off with an arrow or just shot the horse instead but where would the skill in that be? Besides, the horse wasn't the enemy. The figure broke into a jog en route to the guardsman from Sokoto. Just as the guardsman was closing in on the spare horse, the figure jumped high in the air and thrust a kick sideways into the injured arm of the carriage man. He immediately crumpled in a heap and howled with pain. To his credit he didn't let go of his sword. *Well trained*, thought the figure. The guardsman got up immediately and swung his sword at his opponent. The figure stepped back effortlessly and when the momentum of his swing turned the guard around, the figure stepped back in and swung a kick, connecting an instep with the man's cheekbone. The guard staggered sideways like a drunk on his last legs. Disorientated by the blow, the guardsman swung wildly at thin air, leaving himself open front on. The figure took the opening, skipped side-on and planted a heel square in his chest, sweeping the guard clean off his feet. The time for toying with the guard was over. The figure in black unsheathed a curved blade with a thin hilt, stood over the flattened guard with one foot on his right arm, and plunged the blade straight through his heart.

#

The free-rider rolled over and crawled along the dirt with his elbows. If he could get to his sword perhaps he stood a chance. He couldn't feel his legs and his arms felt like lead but he was hopeful. Everything around him was silent and he wondered if the carriage-rider had escaped. If he had, maybe there was time to get reinforcements, even if the cargo would be gone by the time they came. He'd expected to die in Kano and had made it out of that city, despite being vastly outnumbered. He wasn't going to die in the bush like an animal. His hopes were lifted even higher when he grasped the hilt of his sword with his left hand in the dirt. Then his hopes were immediately dashed by two things. First, he barely had the strength to lift the sword off the ground. Second, the moment he lifted the sword, a foot stood on his left forearm, trapping it. Then he knew his time was up. As he lifted his head up to look his executioner in the eye, unbelievable pain cut through the middle of his torso. His head dropped down and the dirt went moist with his blood.

#

The last thing Garba Mansa heard was the silencing of the whimpering horses. Whoever was fighting had stopped. The concussed guard with the wounded arm had presumably lived for as long as the consequences of his decision had allowed. Garba Mansa waited in the darkness for his rendezvous with the figure in black.

A key turned in the lock of the wooden box and he heard the heavy chain hit the ground. The door swung open. Garba Mansa held his breath and braced himself for the first strike of a blade. Instead, a silhouetted figure stared at him through the open door and he heard a woman's voice.

"Come Garba Mansa. Someone is waiting for you."

She knew his name. She was there for him. He'd been right all along. The figure stepped back and Garba Mansa gingerly climbed out of the broken carriage. In the darkness her face looked young and attractive but she stood with the confidence of an experienced fighter. A bow and separate arrows were slung over her shoulders. Was she from that place? While Garba Mansa stood searching for some semblance of recognition, his rescuer ignored his inquisitive stare and unlocked his shackles. She then immediately mounted her horse and pointed to the vacant saddle on the dead free-rider's horse.

"Follow me. We haven't much time."

Once Garba Mansa had mounted the spare horse, the woman in black immediately set off. Without giving it a second thought Garba Mansa immediately followed. As he did so, out of the corner of his eye, he spotted another figure in black on horseback.

Chapter Twenty

He had so many questions. Now so many more than their first meeting. Who was she? Where was she from? Why had she saved him? Who was their mutual contact? Where were they going? Instead he rode in silence, following his saviour through the moonlit night. Whatever burning desire Garba Mansa had for conversation, the feeling didn't appear mutual. The mysterious woman in black didn't speak again for the rest of the journey. Occasionally she turned and looked in his direction while riding but only for a split-second each time. It seemed to Garba Mansa that his rescue had been a process, an instruction, rather than any personal crusade. Once again he was somebody's cargo. The second rider in black had caught up and rode alongside them with the clueless confused rescued man in the middle. It was difficult to tell riding at speed in the dark but from the little he could see, the second rider also had a slight frame and could also have been a woman. Only the eyes of his second silent escort were exposed. Although it was evening time, Garba Mansa felt as though he'd lived and died several lives in one day.

Garba Mansa had been so mesmerised by the effect of his rescue, he'd given little thought to the consequences of his freedom. The dead were mounting and by default he would carry the blame once the latest bodies from Sokoto were discovered. If this woman and her accomplice were agents of or even allies of Kano, his rescue had all but sealed the justification for war. Even if he somehow returned to the Emir's palace and turned himself in, the damage was already done. His escape from the escort could be seen as treasonous and he could well be executed by his own people. The justice minister for one would be baying for his blood, especially if there was no return on the road to war. Returning to Kano wasn't an immediate option. Whoever had instructed his rescue, Garba Mansa hoped they had a robust plan. If they knew who he was, then they most likely knew of Isa. Even if their paths never crossed again, Garba Mansa hoped that the boy would get word that he was alive.

#

A few hours later, the horses slowed down not far from an unlit compound in an isolated patch of land. Only the sound of hooves and crickets communicating in the arid land could be heard. Bereft of his navigating tools, the durbar was disorientated and oblivious as to their location. They stopped by a tree outside the compound, the riders dismounted and the horses were secured. The freed man was led into the compound.

While Garba Mansa waited in the darkness, an oil lamp was retrieved and within a few minutes several more had been lit and the inside of the compound was bathed in light. The interior of the large compound was sparsely furnished like a temporary home. What little decoration there was inside the compound was functional and of no particular taste. Both riders removed their head wrappers and Garba Mansa's suspicions were confirmed. Both were women of similar physical stature but one looked considerably older. The grey hairs in her cornrows and the scars on her face belied more challenging life experience than her younger counterpart. The women led Garba Mansa into a room with a long table and cloth blinds over the windows.

"Wait here," said the older woman and motioned for Garba Mansa to sit.

"Thank you," said Gsrba Mansa. "But I need answers. I need to know what's going on, who you are and where I am."

"Please be patient," replied the woman. "He'll be here soon."

Garba Mansa reluctantly sat while the younger of the two women disappeared to another room. A few minutes later she returned with a jug of water, a bowl of pepper soup, a knife, a spoon and some bread on a tray. She placed the tray in front of Garba Mansa at the table. It was only when the scent of the spicy dish hit his nostrils that he remembered how hungry he was. He immediately dipped the bread in the soup and shoved in the first mouthful. The taste was invigorating. The hot pepper burned his throat in such a pleasurable way that he was glad to be alive. He wedged some goat meat between two more pieces of bread, doused them in the watery soup and shoved everything in his mouth. It was only when he'd eaten all the solid meat and fish in the soup, put the bowl to his lips with two hands and downed the remainder of its contents, that he stopped and felt self-conscious.

"I'm sorry, I haven't eaten for some time," he said. He wiped his mouth with the back of his hand and grabbed the jug of water.

The younger woman looked at him with the same disinterested distant look she'd given him when she'd opened the carriage box. She said nothing. Garba Mansa downed the jug of water in one continuous effort, while maintaining eyes on his hosts as he drank. He may have just been fed and watered but in the grand scheme of things the gesture meant nothing. His freedom was thus far a relative concept.

"Thank you," said Garba Mansa, stifling the urge to belch. "I needed that."

The older woman nodded curtly. Both women had removed their head wrappers but neither had removed their weapons. They were still waiting, still on edge and Garba Mansa sensed it. He knew that more questions were pointless. Like them, he waited.

#

A short while later the awkward silence was broken by the sound of multiple horses arriving outside the compound. It was obvious that getting up and raising the cloth blinds would elicit a hostile response from his hosts, so Garba Mansa sat still and waited for further instructions. Meanwhile the new arrivals were heard walking outside towards the back of the compound. The only sound they made was with their feet. Garba Mansa waited patiently for his introduction while his two new minders watched over him.

Knock knock knock came a sound from elsewhere in the compound. The younger woman immediately left her post and disappeared into a back room. Two minutes later she resurfaced and nodded to the older woman.

"He's ready for you Garba Mansa," said the older woman. She gestured for him to follow her counterpart. Garba Mansa stood up and cautiously followed the younger woman to the back room. The woman pulled back a cloth curtain in the doorway of the back room and nodded for him to enter. Garba Mansa looked at her hands, scanned her sheathed weapons and looked around the room one more time before entering.

The room was smaller than the dining area, with a solid back door and no windows. There was a long table arranged lengthways from the doorway to the end of the room. All light entered from the preceding room, meaning one could see whoever entered but whoever entered couldn't see whoever was at the other end of the table. Only shadows. Garba Mansa noted two shadows, one small and one large, as he entered the space. Neither made a sound but he knew they were looking at him. He turned round to make sure there was no ambush coming from behind. There was none. Garba Mansa carefully sat down at one end of the table. When the lamp in the room was lit, he was almost floored by what he saw.

#

"*Master Asari?*"

"Master Mansa." The old man smiled. "I told you I'd try and get you back. I also promised to take care of the boy. I even brought the horse."

Garba Mansa looked at Isa, his mouth agape. The boy smiled back at him and he was momentarily speechless. "I…I don't understand."

"It's a lot to take in," acknowledged Jibril Asari. "You must have a lot of questions. Most of which I'm sure I can answer. At least I'll try."

Garba Mansa felt light-headed. It didn't make sense. It *couldn't* make sense. His eyes *had* to be deceiving him. But there they were, his mentor and his ward. Alive in the flesh and both looking very well. Garba Mansa's light-headedness graduated to a gentle pressure, like a tight band around his head. The feeling of relief to see them both was tainted with uneasy confusion and improbable logic.

"There are many questions Master. Very many questions."

"Of course there are," said Jibril Asari. He smiled like a kind uncle acknowledging an innocent question from a child. "Perhaps we should move to the other room. There's more space there and we can do some formal introductions."

Garba Mansa nodded, unable to get the words out of his mouth. Jibril Asari, Isa and Garba Mansa all stood up and followed the younger woman back to the dining room.

#

The old man looked well. It wasn't often that he saw him without his turban. His white hair made him look older but softer, more relaxed. He sat at the end of the table, like the head of a household. Isa sat by his master and his empty bowl of peppersoup. He wore a fresh white tunic and his beaming smile was heartwarming. The only person in the room looking uncharacteristically shabby, with a couple of days' stubble, unkempt hair and soiled clothing, was Garba Mansa. The women in black both stood by the door, on the other side of the table observing the reunion.

"I'm sorry for all the secrecy. I wasn't sure you'd come otherwise."

The old man's apology felt sincere but his smile and his eyes projected content relief more than shame. He still hadn't addressed the two most obvious questions in the room.

"I...I'm confused. I don't know where to start," began Garba Mansa. "How did you know I'd be here?...unless you..." It was difficult to say what he was thinking. It made no sense. "Unless you enlisted mercenaries to achieve my rescue?"

The words made his stomach turn as he said them. In part because it made his gratitude for being alive feel empty but also because it went against everything they'd stood for, for all those years. At least everything he thought they'd stood for.

"Why don't we start with some introductions?" asked the old man.

"Please," replied Garba Mansa.

"Both of these women have saved your life," Master Asari turned to the women by the door, "on more than one occasion before tonight I might add." Jibril Asari spoke with pride of their actions that Garba Mansa found unsettling. "Garba Mansa, Isa, meet Adesua and Amina, my wife and daughter."

The women nodded their heads to acknowledge the introduction. Garba Mansa felt his stomach turn, reeling from his mentor's words, unwilling to accept what was unfolding before his eyes, even though he knew it to be true.

"*Your family?*"

The old man smiled. "I know what you're thinking Garba."

"That you're a hypocrite and a liar?"

"It's totally at odds with the order and you and I have kicked others out for the same desire to cultivate what they felt was their god-given right. You of all people should understand that desire."

"You took an oath," said Garba Mansa, with obvious disappointment in his voice.

"I did but I made it to my family first."

"All those years, all those lies." Garba Mansa shook his head in shock. "Men have trusted you. *I trusted you*."

"And I truly meant it when I said I was sorry for the deception Garba. All the deception, all this time. But I don't regret a second of it."

"And what of the order, Master Asari?"

"The time of the durbars is over," said Jibril Asari.

"*Over? Have you gone mad?*"

Right then Amina Asari reached inside her black tunic and took a step forward. Her mother gently stopped her with an arm across her waist.

"It's okay Amina. Garba has every right to be angry," said Jibril Asari. "I indoctrinated him into the ways of being an agent of dictatorship."

"*Dictatorship?*" laughed Garba Mansa. "Juju has consumed the man I once respected."

For the first time in the exchange, Jibril Asari seemed irked by the words of his former apprentice and frowned. "Juju? You confuse your ignorance with blind loyalty my young friend. Kano has long been a dictatorship, benefiting only those within its walls. If your eyes were truly open, you'd see that people are starving in Sokoto and Katsina, while we serve under a ruler that has lost his way from Allah."

"Coming from the man who's been living a double life. Perhaps you're the one who's lost his way. If you didn't believe in Kano, why haven't you left the order all this time?"

"It wasn't the right time, until now."

"So why me? If we're such a lost cause," asked Garba Mansa.

"I thought someone who had the audacity to renounce his faith would be enlightened enough to see the bigger picture. To understand the need for regime change."

Isa felt Master put something in his hand under the table. It was the wooden handle of the knife. He must've slid it off the table when they first came in.

"*Regime change?* Master Asari I fear that you're in the throes of dementia."

Jibril Asari smiled. "You know, they wanted to kill you. First on your way to Sokoto. I wanted to give you the option of joining us and couldn't let that happen, so I changed the plan. I never told you that my grandfather was in the Katsina royal guard. He knew every inch of that city, all its tunnels and passageways, even the hidden ones. The men from Katsina, probably soldiers, were waiting for you just outside the city." Jibril Asari pointed at his daughter. "It was Amina who kept you safe."

"So *she* killed the men that I was accused of killing beyond the realm?"

"She kept you safe."

"And the durbar sword?"

"One picks up many spares over the years," conceded Jibril Asari with a smile on his face. "The backup plan was to get you in Sokoto on your way back. That was where you first encountered Adesua."

"And then they both murdered innocent men tonight," added Garba Mansa.

"Not innocent. Enemy combatants. Means to an end."

Garba Mansa scrutinised the clinical man that wore the clothes of his former mentor, his former confidant. "You said you changed the plan. So you're now the agent of a foreign power? You realise that in your madness, you're now in league with a more godless kingdom than ours?"

"*Yours.* Not mine."

"So all this talk about the dead emissary...all these investigations...you knew all along what was at play."

"I'm one of many wheels of change that are in motion," said Jibril Asari.

"Wheels of war," countered Garba Mansa.

"A war that will bring about the necessary change."

"And if I don't join you?"

Jibril Asari laughed. "Garba, look around you. Your choices are limited. Even if you aren't part of the new order, do you really think the old one will have you back? You are stateless my friend. An outcast. A fugitive. And in the eyes of many, a murderer."

Garba Mansa banged his fist on the table, shifted his chair back and stood up. Amina and Adesua both immediately stepped forward. Jibril Asari smiled as if he watched sport.

"Isa, cut Sisoko free and wait for me outside," said Garba Mansa. Amina immediately stood in front of the door, blocking his exit in advance.

"Let the boy go," said Jibril Asari. "He's of no consequence."

Amina stepped away from the door. Isa, with hitherto unforeseen initiative and the knife held firmly in his hand, lifted up the cloth blind behind him and jumped out of the window. Garba Mansa picked up the spoon and the peppersoup bowl. Adesua and Amina both produced daggers from their tunics. The three of them squared off across the table.

"Garba, there's no need for this," said Jibril Asari.

"Because you'll just let me go?"

"Of course not. But we can end things quickly. Fighting will just prolong the inevitable. Me on my own, no contest. Two of us, perhaps. *But three?* You barely survived with help in Sokoto. It doesn't have to end like this."

"You're absolutely right Master Asari." Garba Mansa put down the bowl and spoon and took a deep breath. Amina and Adesua eyed him suspiciously with their weapons still at the ready. Garba Mansa then stepped back from the table, picked up the chair he was sitting on and hurled it as hard as he could at his former mentor.

#

The gamble paid off. The old man barely had time to duck the oncoming wooden projectile and it clipped his arm and his head on his way down. Instinctively his wife ran to his aid. The odds were more even, if only for a few moments. Garba Mansa had just enough time to retrieve the spoon and peppersoup bowl from the table before reacting to the retaliatory strike. Amina Asari had propelled herself across the table, using her free hand as a pivot and launched a kick at him. The durbar parried the attack but was caught by the furious swipe of her dagger blade across his right arm. She was angry. Good for adrenaline. Bad for focus. However, she was fast. Very fast. The moment she landed she followed up with a flurry of arcing swipes of her dagger at Garba Mansa's lower limbs and waist. He moved back into a corner, blocking what he could with his forearms and the bowl. As chairs flew out of the way, some slashes caught him on the thighs while he jabbed with the spoon at vital points on her torso, head and neck. Most of his attacks missed their target and he was rewarded with cuts on his arms. Eventually an opening came. Amina Asari weaved away from one jab of the spoon, right into a swipe of the peppersoup bowl. The blow from the pottery caught her in the ear, stunning her long enough for Garba Mansa to launch a front thrust kick into her abdomen. His mentor's daughter flew across the room, dropping her blade in the process and landing next to her father, heavily winded by the durbar's forceful blow.

Adesua Asari had already drawn her sword by the time her daughter crash landed. She jumped onto the table between her and Garba Mansa. When he kicked the table away, she landed gracefully, ready to launch her attack. She was more composed than her daughter and consequently more dangerous. Garba Mansa faced her in a low defensive stance, holding Amina Asari's dagger in one hand, with the blade pointed downwards. Adesua Asari's blade was long but curved, almost like a sickle. The angle of her blade dispelled the illusion that fighting with a sword increased her striking distance. She unleashed several kicks at Garba Mansa's legs, while swiping at his torso with her sword. Garba Mansa gritted his teeth and absorbed the kicks while trying to evade the lacerations from the blade. His attempts at landing his own cuts were mostly unsuccessful, such was her speed. She was patient, darting back and forth, trying to wear him down until he let slip a suitable opening. As the altercation went on this would soon become a reality or her partner would join the fray, significantly reducing Garba Mansa's odds of survival. Behind her Amina Asari was on one knee, holding her abdomen with one hand. Time was running out.

#

What the durbar had in defence, he lacked in the accuracy of his attack. His offensive cuts with Amina's blade only succeeded in cutting the fabric of Adesua's clothing, rather than inflicting any real damage. However, he maintained his guard and low stance, taking his repeated blows as if he felt no pain. He navigated his way around the curved blade admirably and didn't flinch when it cut him. Adesua Asari was impressed by the durbar. Neither reckless nor conservative. Then again, he'd been taught by the best. Sooner or later he'd make a mistake. They always did. It wasn't long before the opening came. Either out of frustration or a futile attempt to break the onslaught of attacks, the durbar launched an ill-judged kick. Adesua stepped inside the kick, ready to bury her blade deep in his abdomen. Then something unforeseen happened. The durbar parried her sword thrust, blade to blade, then immediately dropped lower and grabbed her in a front-on bear hug. Adesua's ribs ached with the vice-like hold. Unable to break free, she was lifted off her feet. As Adesua repeatedly bashed his jaw with the side of her head, she used her curved blade to her advantage and turned the handle to dig the blade into his back. The durbar registered the intense pain audibly. Still suspended in the air, Adesua's back and her head were slammed into the wall with such ferocity that her vision blurred and the air was expelled from her lungs. This happened one more time, causing her to drop her weapon. Then the room spun, as she was thrown across it.

#

As the chaos erupted inside, Isa waited anxiously outside, already in Sisoko's saddle as per Master's instructions. He still had the knife in his trembling hand as he listened to the crashing and banging from inside. He was almost tearful with disbelief when Master emerged from the same compound window he'd fled from. By the way he grimaced and staggered towards them, he looked seriously hurt. He clambered onto Sisoko without any word of explanation and they set off immediately, fleeing into the night.

End of Part Two

Chapter Twenty-One

"We found them my lord."

"And?"

"All dead."

Grand Vizier Gidado Buhari ignored the subsequent rumblings of the old men in red on either side of him and responded to the update with contemptuous indifference. There was a far more pressing, more important question on his mind. A far more newsworthy update. "And what of the durbar?" he asked.

"Gone," replied the scout. It was a relief to finally pass on the news he'd been dreading to deliver. The bodies of the armed escort had been discovered just outside the kingdom that day. The old man's response to the news was expected, given the man's reputation. No anger, no grief. Pretty much no interest in the men who'd lost their lives trying to bring back an enemy of the state.

"*Gone? Escaped?*" asked the Grand Vizier.

"It appears so my lord," replied the scout. "The carriage was damaged but unlocked when we found it. Two bodies were by the carriage. One with arrows, one without. Two horses were also dead. One with arrows, one without. The remaining two members of the escort were a kilometre away. Both dead by arrow my lord."

Arrows. The durbar had his accomplice once again and the bodies were piling up around him. "We thought it best to return and report our preliminary findings as requested my lord," continued the scout. "We haven't given up the se—"

"Leave us."

"Yes my lord." The scout looked at the twelve old men in red as he retreated from his position in front of the Sultanate Council. Nobody batted an eyelid at his abrupt departure. It was true, the Grand Vizier really did speak for the council. The scout left the room as quietly and quickly as he'd entered it.

Vizier Buhari's eyes narrowed as he pursed his lips and rested his hands under his chin. Enough was enough. In his mind, the touch paper had been lit and there was no turning back. "Kano has taxed us into starvation, taunted us with their aggression and shown what scant regard they have for our lives. This latest act, this final act of aggression is the clearest indication of their intent." Vizier Buhari spoke with the conviction of an incensed cleric, with a raised right index finger to emphasise his points. "They intend to dominate us, demoralise us and ultimately destroy us by wiping us off the face of this earth. *Enough is enough.*" There were fervent nods and mumbles from the adjacent elders. "We must strike back before we are no more. I propose the motion that articles of war are drafted immediately and presented to his majesty. Those in favour, raise your right hand."

Given the gravity of the motion, the response was subdued. The Grand Vizier looked left. Slowly hands were raised. Then he looked right. More hands.

"Those against?" No hands were raised. "No abstentions?" There was no further movement among the twelve old men. "Good. The motion has been passed. I will meet with his majesty. Once the articles have been given royal assent, we will declare war on our enemy."

#

Much to his chagrin, there were more weeping family members than usual outside the Sultan's chamber. Under the false pretence of reducing added stress on the invalided monarch, the royal physician had restricted visiting numbers to three relatives, usually wives, at a time. The number appeared to have tripled. The reality was that the royal physician was under very clear instructions from the de facto ruler. The Grand Vizier, in his evolving paranoia, had kept an even tighter grip on information flow, regardless of the ideas, concerns or expectations of the ailing ruler's loved ones. As far as Vizier Buhari was concerned, the fewer people that knew the end was imminent for the Sultan of Sokoto, the better. Like everyone around him, the royal physician was painfully aware that the interim caretaker's powers would expand with the sovereign's passing. With that, the leash around his throat would be even tighter.

The loud banging on the chamber door startled the physician and interrupted the sound of sobbing outside. Such assertive knocking usually indicated a warning of imminent entry, rather than a request for invitation. Within moments the door was opened and several pairs of palace guards piled into the chamber. An equal number waited outside. In the midst of the intrusive beefed up security detail was the Grand Vizier. His paranoia had extended to his personal security, as he got closer to resting both buttocks on the seat of power. The security detail quickly scanned the room for any threats, in a manner most amusing to the royal physician, given that he and the fading Sultan were the only occupants of the chamber. The head of the security detail reported the all clear to the Grand Vizier.

"Leave us. All of you," ordered Vizier Buhari.

"Yes my lord."

"Except you," said Vizier Buhari, as the royal physician hurried past him.

The royal physician stopped in his tracks as the guards left them, silently lamenting the narrow escape. "Yes my lord?"

Vizier Buhari approached the Sultan's bed and assessed him slowly from head to toe, ignoring the physician as he did so. The room stank of body odour and urine, particularly the bed sheets. Choosing his moment carefully, the royal physician joined him by the Sultan's bedside without uttering a word. In the candlelight, the Grand Vizier's forlorn expression was humanising yet peculiar, for a man of such limited benevolent expressed emotion. In his hands the Grand Vizier had three scrolls but all his attention was on the Sultan, whose sluggish breathing at times feigned a recent departure.

"Is he…?" asked Vizier Buhari.

"No my lord," replied the physician. "He's still with us. Barely but just about. In my estimation it won't be long now."

"How long? *Minutes? Hours? Days?*" asked the Grand Vizier impatiently.

"Possibly not up to days my lord. I feel we should prepare for the worst case scenario."

"Is he in pain?"

"No my lord."

"I must speak with him. Now. Can you rouse him?"

"It shouldn't be too difficult. He's been asleep all day."

The royal physician gently rubbed his knuckles on the Sultan's sternum. Nothing. He increased the pressure and rubbed again. Nothing. With the tip of his left thumb he applied pressure to the bony prominence just above the Sultan's right eye. He added more pressure, then more pressure until the Sultan's right eye twitched. The physician continued the vigorous rubbing until a grimace accompanied the twitching.

"My paralysis won't come with me to the next life," said the Sultan in a low volume whisper. "Continue molesting me at your peril, witch doctor."

The royal physician smiled. "As you wish majesty." He stepped back from the bed and the Grand Vizier immediately leaned in to the Sultan.

"Praise Allah that he keeps you here majesty." Vizier Buhari smiled at the Sultan then immediately turned to the royal physician with a complete change of tone. "Leave us."

The royal physician bowed his head deferentially and left the two of them alone.

"Gidado, you came to see me. How nice," said the Sultan dreamily.

"Majesty, I disturb you with three matters of great urgency," began Vizier Buhari. He didn't wait for any acknowledgement from the Sultan and continued. "Kano has continued its aggression against us."

"Kano?" asked the Sultan.

"Yes majesty. The durbar escaped, most likely with the help of an accomplice. Our entire escort was murdered."

"Who is Kano?"

"Majesty?"

"Is Kano your son?" asked the Sultan innocently.

"No majesty. Kano is our enemy."

"Oh, I see. Did he hurt us?"

The conversation was heartbreaking. But the Grand Vizier had to continue. He had to continue in order to do what he planned to do next in good conscience. Even if the man losing his mind in front of him lacked the full mental capacity to comprehend what he was about to propose. Only Allah could judge him.

"Majesty, Kano has done us a great many wrongs. Many wrongs in your time, in your father's time and in your father's father's time. Things cannot continue this way any longer. We must strike back, otherwise nothing will change. "

"Nothing Gidado?"

"Nothing majesty."

"Remind me Gidado, what has Kano done?" asked the Sultan.

"Most recently majesty? An agent of Kano, a durbar, has murdered four of our servants in the last week. An official of the kingdom before that. Then seven unidentified others. These are just the crimes we know of. A warrant was sent for the durbar's arrest."

"And? Did you get him?" asked the Sultan enthusiastically.

"No majesty," replied Vizier Buhari patiently. "He escaped."

"How did he escape Gidado?"

"We don't know majesty. But we believe he had an accomplice. An accomplice that has helped him before. Most likely another agent of Kano."

"I'm sorry to hear that Gidado. Was anybody hurt?"

The Grand Vizier forced a smile and took a deep breath before continuing with the frail old man. "Yes majesty. Four people were killed. Two horses too."

"*Four people?* Terrible. This kind of behaviour cannot go unpunished."

There was a glint in Vizier Buhari's eyes. "*Exactly* majesty."

"So what do you intend to do Gidado?" asked the Sultan.

"That is precisely why I'm here majesty." Vizier Buhari placed one of the three scrolls on the legs of the Sultan, unravelled it and hovered a lamp over it. "We gave Kano an ultimatum. In response, they have spat in our faces. The Sultanate Council has drawn up articles of war. I present them to you majesty."

"Articles of war?"

"Yes majesty, articles of war. If it pleases you majesty, would you like to read the manuscript?"

"*Read?*" The Sultan laughed and then coughed uncontrollably. The Grand Vizier momentarily wondered whether he'd just killed his ruler with unintentional humour. The Sultan regained his composure. "Gidado, my eyes, like the rest of me, are failing me. I see mainly light and dark shadows now. Kindly read the document to me. Better still, summarise it for me."

"With pleasure majesty." The old man wasn't capable of retaining the information in the lengthy manuscript. Instead, Vizier Buhari summarised it as best he could. "Failure to deliver the durbar was an act of war. This document details how we will respond to that act. It details military strategy, timelines of action and the expected outcome."

"And what is the expected outcome?" asked the Sultan.

"That we are victorious majesty," confirmed the Grand Vizier. "The document also details support from our allies."

"Allies?"

"Yes. If you recall I…" Vizier Buhari realised the futility of the reminder. "We have the support of Katsina. The Minister of Inf—"

"*Katsina?* Those dogs? Are you sure Gidado?"

"Majesty, to defeat Kano we will need to enlist assistance from some allies that could be considered…unsavoury. However unsavoury our neighbours, the relationship will be short. Once we've vanquished Kano, there will be plenty of opportunity for re-education of these neighbours. We have a strong contact in the information minister."

"Can we trust him?"

"He has guaranteed us military support, even if he's fuelled by greed and his lust for power."

"I trust your judgement Gidado. What do you want from me?"

"Majesty, in order for articles of war to be approved, royal assent is required."

"You have it."

"Articles of war detail the mechanics of war," continued the Grand Vizier. "In order for those mechanics to proceed, we must declare our intention majesty. We must declare war."

"Yes Gidado, you are right," said the Sultan. "To whom must we declare it?"

"To our enemy majesty. To Kano."

"Yes, to Kano."

The Grand Vizier unravelled the second manuscript in his

possession and placed it on the frail monarch's bed. "This document is the declaration of war in full. It shall be sent by special messenger to the Emir of Kano, with your approval majesty."

"Of course Gidado. I trust your judgement," said the Sultan. "Send it at once. As you say, they will wipe us out otherwise."

"Indeed majesty. There is one more document I must discuss with you majesty. It details something of a great personal nature to you but something that will have a significant bearing on the kingdom in the future."

"What is it Gidado?" asked the Sultan.

"It is an act of succession majesty."

"Thank you Gidado. I wish you also every success." The old man smiled innocently, much to the discomfort of Vizier Buhari, who pitied him greatly.

"Majesty, an act of succession details who will replace you, when the time has come for Allah to receive you."

"Oh I see…I can honestly say I can't wait for Allah to take me Gidado. He must be very busy."

Vizier Buhari forced a smile. "I'm sure Allah will let you know when he is ready majesty. I've taken the liberty of drafting a document based on your expressed wishes." Vizier Buhari unravelled the third and final manuscript, placed it next to the others and began scanning it with his thumb. "My understanding is that Yakubu wouldn't necessarily be your first cho—"

"*First choice?* Are you mad Gidado?" spluttered the Sultan. He was so incensed that he seemed temporarily cured of his illness. "Yakubu is not even impotent, he is *afraid* of women. Useless I tell you. A thorough disgrace. All that fighting ability and conquering a woman is a mysterious concept. If not for my sickness, I would be fathering children for him. Don't mention his name again."

"Of course majesty." Vizier Buhari continued through the motions of scanning the document. "It seems Bitrus might need some assistance with leadership."

"Leadership? He couldn't herd goats. Next."

"Your other sons are very young majesty. The pressure might be too great at such a young age for each of them. May I take the liberty of making a suggestion, a potential safeguard of sorts?"

"Please continue."

"What if there were a caretaker in place for when the right son came of the right age? Someone who knows the royal family well. Someone who can ensure that your legacy is protected. A friend of the royal family. A friend of Sokoto, with no conflict from jealous bloodlines."

"Not a relative?" asked the Sultan.

"Someone close to but unrelated to the royal family. Someone trustworthy majesty."

"The only person I trust with the strength to protect my legacy is you Gidado. Can I trust you to protect the Sultanate?"

"With my life majesty," said Vizier Buhari. "Until of course the time is right to cede power to your appropriate heir."

"Then make it so."

"As you wish majesty." The Grand Vizier bowed his head. "For royal assent to be confirmed, the royal seal is needed on each of these documents."

The Sultan sighed. "My fingers are heavy and my arms useless." He raised a weak right index finger. "Help me Gidado. Where is the seal?"

Vizier Buhari reached under a bedside table and retrieved a stick of red wax and the royal seal. He then grabbed a lit candle and began to heat up the wax. The hot stick quickly melted and dripped onto the first manuscript. Vizier Buhari put the wax and the candle to one side and then placed the seal in the Sultan's cold limp hand and closed his fingers around it.

"If I may, majesty?"

The Sultan grunted in agreement. Vizier Buhari took the Sultan's hand and imprinted the seal on the wax on the first document. He held it in place for a couple of seconds, as the waxy seal set, then lifted the seal up and placed it in a bowl of water. He repeated the process twice more on the remaining manuscripts. When he was done, he released the seal from the Sultan's weak grip and gently placed his hand by his side.

"Thank you majesty," he said, rolling up the manuscripts. "I shall deliver this to the Sultanate Council immediately."

"Goodbye Gidado. May Allah deliver you to me in the next life."

"Mashallah."

The Sultan closed his eyes while the Grand Vizier lingered for a moment, before leaving with the scrolls under his arm. As he left the candlelit bed and entered the darkness, the Sultan turned his head and called for him. "Gidado?"

"Yes majesty?"

"A lot of people are going to die, aren't they?"

"Yes majesty, they will."

Chapter Twenty-Two

Isa feared the worst. They'd been travelling for days, living off river water, the land and whatever insects, wild animals and scraps they could find. Master had initially played down the extent of his injuries but couldn't hide the colour change in the water when he bathed his wounds in the stream. When he thought Isa wasn't watching, Master winced as if every movement was a painful sacrifice. Beneath his ragged clothes, he'd been cut all over his legs, his arms and his belly. Isa was so focussed on the injuries to Master's body, he almost didn't notice the swelling on his face.

As usual, Master had given Isa few details of what had happened with Master Asari and the women in the compound. When Master Asari came to see Isa in the Emir's palace, he'd delicately broken the news of Master's fate but had confided in Isa that he prayed all wasn't lost. Upon leaving the palace, Master Asari had vaguely talked about new beginnings and reiterated his promise to keep Isa safe. Isa hadn't thought to ask where they were going. Just before the reunion with Master, the older durbar had revealed the identity of their nighttime liaison. He immediately cautioned the boy that his master would find the mechanics of his freedom difficult to accept and would most likely feel conflicted. That had clearly been an understatement. From the sound of the commotion that followed and the dramatic exit, Isa concluded that a serious conflict had taken place. For Master to be as badly hurt as he was, the Asaris must've been deadly fighters. Isa wondered if they were still alive.

On the first day since they fled, Master said nothing beyond instructing Isa to eat and drink. At night by the fire he mumbled the words *traitor* and *betrayal* into the flames and seemed so angry at times, he didn't finish his sentences and just shook his head instead. For the first time Master showed a side of himself Isa had never seen before. Isa felt powerless with the disheartening combination of Master's extreme disappointment and sadness. Even worse, it made Master look vulnerable, almost weak. Isa had experienced great loss in his life but had been the lone passenger on his journey of mixed emotions. He had no experience guiding anyone through grief and felt useless. With both of their lips as dry as sand, their urine as dark as dung with dehydration and their stomachs rumbling with every passing day of hunger, it wouldn't have made a difference anyway.

As they continued moving from place to place with no declaration of any clear plan, Isa began to wonder if Master knew where they were going. He was less sure of himself than usual and pointed in opposite directions for them to continue from time to time. Even Sisoko seemed a little less responsive to his conflicting commands. Ever the obedient ward, Isa kept his mouth firmly shut.

The marked decline in Master's health began with rambling in his sleep on night three. As novel as it was, Isa put it down to Master having nightmares, given the catastrophic end to his relationship with his mentor. It also made sense with the tossing and turning in his sleep. The next day Isa respectfully made no mention of Master's restless night. But there were more signs. Master normally sweated after vigorous exercise and typically wasn't bothered by the heat. On that particular day Master was sweating like a criminal in a courthouse. He moved his limbs like an old man, exhausted and breathless just from walking. The sweating came and went, even into the night when the air was considerably cooler. It was the sound of laughter in Master's sleep, broken up by cursing, that alerted Isa that perhaps things might not be alright. When he roused Master from his sleep, the durbar master stared at him blankly then smiled like a fool, before shutting his eyes and lapsing back into delirium. Master slept until afternoon the next day. From then on, he made less and less sense, confirming to Isa that they were in trouble.

With Master's failing health, their chances of starving to death were increasing day by day. The number of settlements they encountered to scrounge food was decreasing and Master was no longer capable of hunting any wild animals for sustenance. They wandered further and further into the wilderness. Isa had initially feared Master was dying. Now he was convinced that they would both perish. As his own consciousness began to cloud over, Isa sought solace in their demise. He took comfort in the fact that contrary to how he'd often felt in his life, he wouldn't die alone. More importantly, he'd lived a life of purpose with companionship. In Master, fate had blessed Isa with the father figure it had cruelly snatched away from him some years before. Master's first great act of kindness had been to rescue him from a destined life of misery. The second had been to provide the nurture and security that had eluded Isa since his family's murder. Isa's apprenticeship had been a life bonus, one great adventure that had wildly exceeded all his expectations. He would never be a durbar but had ridden alongside and fought, by his own definition, with the best of them. Alas, fate had other ideas of how their story would pan out. Isa never imagined that *he* would be the one looking after Master at the end but was grateful for the privilege. If it meant tending to his master as his fever consumed him, so be it. As Master slumped and fell off Sisoko, landing in the dirt unconscious, Isa looked down at him. He knew they were both ready. Ready to meet their absent friend.

#

Sweat trickled down his temples while the huge man stared deep into his soul with his judgemental glare. The royal court of the Katsina emirate had assembled to discuss the growing tension between its adjacent neighbours. Minister of Information Atiku Danladi had been summoned to deliver his thorough and frank appraisal of the situation. The Emir of Katsina was neither impressed nor convinced by what he heard.

"Excellency, my sources inform me that the durbar problem has escalated," said Minister Danladi. "After a warrant was issued for his arrest and he was apprehended, he escaped killing his escort from Sokoto in the process."

"So? What has this got to do with us?" asked the Emir dismissively. "You were tasked with maintaining our peaceful position."

"It seems that the next level of escalation will be war," replied Danladi.

"Is there ground rice in your ears?" mocked the Emir. "*What has this got to do with us?*"

"Excellency, without meaning to oversimplify the matter, we are between both kingdoms."

"Of course we're between both kingdoms! *Idiot!* Do you think I'm a fool?"

Eyes all over the courtroom gravitated towards the floor as Information Minister Danladi's public humiliation continued. Danladi took a deep breath and steadied himself before continuing. "Never, excellency," he lied. "However, if war breaks out, we have no choice but to pick a side."

"This war has nothing to do with us. You were supposed to go to Sokoto and help those fanatics resolve this durbar nonsense quietly."

"And that I did, excellency." Danladi surprised himself with the slight defiance in his tone.

"Did you really?" The Emir smiled, pleasantly caught off guard by the pushback.

"On your behalf I offered our full cooperation with resolving the durbar matter, directly to the Grand Vizier himself."

"And what was the outcome?"

"Our offer was politely rejected. Sokoto sought to resolve the matter directly with Kano." Danladi looked around the room for effect. "And the results have played out."

The Emir's eyes narrowed and he scrutinised his information minister for a few moments. "What are your concerns?"

"Excellency, my first concern is that by being impartial our neighbours will perceive this as weakness. In war, neutrality is a luxury afforded to the few. If we are seen as weak we risk annexation."

"Annexation by who?" asked the Emir.

"Either one."

"Who do you pick?"

"Excellency?"

"Let me be clear, information minister." The Emir scratched his chin. "If your neck was on the line and let me remind you, you have no guarantees it isn't, who would you pick as an ally?"

All eyes in the room, all the ministers, court officials, the Emir's entourage and the sergeant at arms, were on Danladi. He finally had his opportunity to orchestrate the next phase of the takeover. "Excellency, indulge me to explore the benefits and risks of backing each side."

"Go on."

"Kano is the established power. They have the military might and political capital with surrounding kingdoms."

"But?"

"People are starving in weaker kingdoms. Unless the demands imposed on those weaker kingdoms are softened," Danladi was careful not to single out Katsina, "poverty and resentment will continue to thrive for everyone except the established power."

"And Sokoto?" asked the Emir.

"Sokoto is the potential great change. Hope for the hopeless, a champion for the weak." Danladi smiled at the prospect. "Morally, in terms of equality and adherence to religious scripture, as a kingdom they are superior. They have no recent record of oppressing their neighbours but also have no recent political clout. Their forces are undoubtedly outnumbered by those of Kano."

"So if your life depended on it minister," the Emir smiled, "who would be your pick?"

Danladi took a considered breath before responding. "Excellency, ordinarily I would choose Kano but this durbar affair has clouded that line of thinking. We must ask ourselves if we believe it is a coincidence that this story of their murdered messenger, with no hard evidence to confirm it ever really took place, especially with the follow up investigations, allegations and more murders from their side."

"Minister you're speaking in riddles. Get to the point."

"Yes your excellency, please indulge me. I believe it's possible that this whole sequence of events has been engineered by Kano, as a prelude to war."

There were loud murmurs around the courtroom. Some ministers nodded in agreement while others skeptically shook their heads at the bold claim made by the information minister. The largest and most important man in the room seemed most skeptical of all.

"To what end Minister Danladi?" asked the Emir.

"Expansion," replied Danladi. "What better way to bring about rapid expansion than war?"

"Why now?"

"Why not now excellency? Peacetime is the best time to launch any attack. And when one is accused of war-mongering while garnering support, one simply replies that they are preparing for retaliation."

The Emir screwed his eyes up once more and scrutinised what the opportunistic politician was proposing. He waved his left arm to the side and a servant carrying a large jug of water jumped to attention and put it to the Emir's lips. The royal gargantuan audibly gulped the water several times while eyeballing Danladi. He gently nudged the jug and servant away. Another servant stepped forward with a silk handkerchief and the Emir raised a hand to indicate his services weren't needed.

"*War minister*," barked the Emir, "What do you have to say?"

The Minister for War stood up from his pew. A skinny man with big, bulging white eyes and a raspy voice, the war minister begrudgingly joined the information minister in the spotlight.

"Excellency, there has been increased troop movement and conscription on both sides," responded the war minister, "but I have insufficient evidence to confirm the motive suggested by the honourable Minister of Information. Perhaps the Minister for Trade and Commerce could outline the economic risk of going to war?"

The Minister for Trade and Commerce reluctantly took the baton from his colleague and stood up. "Excellency, honourable ministers and royal members," began the flamboyantly dressed minister, "I can categorically state that going to war would be catastrophic for our economy and would sever the trade routes and thus trade links we have with our neighbours. In summary, the economic risk would be most unsatisfactory."

"Honourable minister, surely trade would be protected on one side if we were its ally?" argued Danladi. "Potentially we would be starved on both sides if caught in the middle."

"If there even is a war my honourable friend," smiled the trade and commerce minister. "Excellency, in the event of this great war my honourable colleague speaks of not materialising, we must consider the risk to our economy of favouring one neighbour while being cut off by the other. Considerable trade flows to and from both sides."

Danladi felt exposed as his case for surreptitiously enabling the next phase of the change was weakening by the minute. "Excellency, I take on board the estimations of my esteemed colleagues but I must caution you that these are estimations, opinions that could have disastrous consequences."

"As could yours, information minister," said the Emir bluntly.

"If it pleases his excellency, would it be worth discussing plans for the evacuation of the royal family, in the event of war coming to our gates?" asked Danladi. "Perhaps the war minister could give his valuable input?"

The war minister flashed Danladi a quizzical look, unsure what the man was playing at.

"Only if it pleases his excellency?" asked the war minister awkwardly.

"No it does not," said the Emir. "This obsession with war is making the information minister sound like a loquacious lapdog with the scent of war stuck in his nostrils."

The courtroom erupted with laughter and Danladi felt his face glow warm with embarrassment. He smiled uncomfortably and ignored the smirks from his rivals as the Emir mocked him. He waited for quiet to resume.

"Respectfully excellency, in response to your original question, given the untoward nature of recent events, I would be loath to place trust in Kano. If pressed and I believe we will be shortly, I believe an alliance with Sokoto is the safest option for this imminent war."

"All this talk of war is becoming a bore," said the Emir. "There will be no alliance with either Kano or Sokoto."

"I implore you to—" urged Danladi.

"*Silence*," hissed the Emir. "You've spoken enough. We are not at war and we shall not be entering into any war. I will not hear any more of it."

#

The Minister of Information, the Minister for War and the sergeant at arms all sat in the information minister's private chamber. A couple of hours had passed since the courtroom meeting. Information minister Danladi was still reeling from the ritual humiliation and defeat of his proposal.

"You took your licks well Danladi," said the war minister. "His excellency was in a particularly prickly mood."

"That whale will live to feel the consequences of his words," seethed Danladi.

"Careful Minister Danladi. Such dissent could be considered treasonous," cautioned the war minister. He looked intensely at Danladi then the sergeant at arms, before breaking out into a smile. "It would seem the option of exile is off the table. It was a nice touch."

"I tried my best to pre-empt a less bloody solution," said Danladi. "It's his fault if he's too stupid to plan for the worst. His fate and the fate of his family will now lie in Sokoto's hands."

"The displacement should be quick," said the war minister. "Sergeant?"

"My men are all ready my lord," said Dankote.

"Mine also," said the war minister.

"Excellent," said Danladi. "Will the Minister for Trade be an obstacle?"

"No," replied the war minister. "His loyalty will come at a price but he can be bought all the same. He won't be a problem."

"Good," said the information minister. "Not long to go now."

\#

Isa lay down in the dirt next to his unresponsive master. Sisoko gently nuzzled his dusty cheek but it was futile. He was too weak to move. Had he the strength to stick his tongue out and taste it, the moisture from Sisoko's snout would've been gratifying. Instead his mouth was sealed shut with dried secretions. What little energy he had left was focussed on taking his last breaths. A droplet fell onto his cheek. Before his vision went opaque, Isa looked up to see a tear in Sisoko's eye. Then the black of her eyes blended into the background.

#

A hand caressed his face. Too large for a child, too soft for a man. A female voice called him in the darkness. He recognised it. His mother reassured him. He was safe. They were all safe. The durbar had done a good job. Given him a good life. His job was done. They would all be happy together again.

Isa opened his eyes to see the outline of a woman kneeling over him. The woman gently lifted his head up and put a goatskin of water to his lips. Unsure whether she was real or an angel, Isa complied with the silent instruction. He was so passive that the water went down the wrong way and he began to choke. The woman helped him sit up while he coughed. As his vision came into focus, Isa felt immediate panic and the urge to flee. The woman reassured him with a hand on his cheek and encouraged him to drink more water. He took the woman's goatskin and lubricated his parched throat until he needed to stop for air. Then he remembered.

"Master?"

Isa looked around frantically. Sisoko was still next to him but Master was nowhere to be seen. Then Isa was paralysed by what he saw. Master was being dragged away by two women. Between the two of them, they slung his limp body over a horse and Isa watched, helpless, as his guardian was secured to the saddle. One of the women mounted the same horse, while the other mounted a separate one. The woman by Isa's side noted the fear on the boy's face and smiled at him.

"Come with us," she said. "You'll be safe."

The woman stood up and brushed Sisoko's mane. Then she mounted the horse without any resistance, as if she were her keeper. The woman held out an open hand and waited. Isa looked at Master's lifeless body, looked at the woman and took her hand.

Chapter Twenty-Three

Dying in one's sleep from sickness was a low exit for such a great man. Preferably he'd have died in combat on the battlefield or better still of old age. As he faded from life, death the great thief of hopes, dreams and desires, dictated a different ending. The death he ultimately succumbed to was akin to dying of weakness, not the good death he and others had wished for. The formal recognition of his passing was appropriately grandiose, fit for a king, with hundreds taking part in the funeral procession and ten times as many onlookers lining the streets. Muted kakaki were blown to mark the occasion and the kalangu was beaten slowly as mourners moved languidly, openly expressing their grief with tears. There were no dark colours in sight, in keeping with the custom. The Sultan of Sokoto's surviving wives, children, siblings and extended family accompanied his shrouded body, held aloft by eight turbaned palace guards in blood red uniforms at the front of the procession. They were flanked by a sizable military escort in corresponding colours and closely followed by the imam in white, the Sultanate Council, ministers, dignitaries from other kingdoms and overseeing everything, the Grand Vizier.

The Sultan's journey to the next life marked many different things for many different people. For the public at large it marked the end of months of speculation. The sovereign hadn't been seen in public for over a year and the funeral procession was official confirmation that their supreme leader was dead. It was the end of an era and the beginning of an uncertain future. For his family, dressed in the royal colours of red, white and gold, his passing was an end to painful suffering for all those emotionally invested in his welfare. The Sultan's sons Yakubu and Bitrus, often the objects of a scornful father's abuse, appeared numb while the wives and daughters of the late monarch wept openly. The feelings were mixed for Vizier Buhari. Observing the Sultan's demise had been nothing short of a living humiliation of his revered mentor. It had inwardly sickened him to watch his leader's crippling descent into madness. By the end, all that was left of the Sultan was an incoherent shell of skin and bones. His faculties had been as uncontrollable as his bodily functions and there weren't even brief periods of lucidity in between the stupor. To his own shame, Vizier Buhari had strongly considered tasking the royal physician with hastening the Sultan's onward passage by whatever means were at his disposal. When the royal physician confirmed his passing, Vizier Buhari was grateful to the almighty that the Sultan's spirit had been granted permission to leave his wretched body.

The funeral march lasted several hours and travelled from the Sultan's palace to the city centre and back to the cemetery within the palace gardens. All women and children left the procession before reaching the burial site. Once the procession had reached a standstill, the imam recited passages then prayers from the Qur'an, as the Sultan's body was lowered on his right side facing Mecca, into the ground. The armed escort separated for male members of the royal family to approach and place wood then stones into the grave. Once the shrouded body was sufficiently insulated from the earth, more family men took turns throwing handfuls of soil into the grave while the imam recited one last prayer. As the elements sealed off the Sultan of Sokoto's exit from his former life, the Grand Vizier vowed to honour his legacy with every last drop of his blood.

#

Isa dreamt his way through another journey to another undisclosed location. He dreamt of a happy reunion between his master and Master Jibril Asari. The Asari family had hosted a meal to celebrate the retirement of the older durbar. Master Asari had held court, sharing many embarrassing stories of his younger protégé in training, with his wife, daughter and Isa thoroughly entertained at Master's expense. It had been an honourable end to a long and distinguished career of service. The time had come to pass the mantle of durbar council chairman onto a younger man. That honour had been bestowed upon Master. To mark this metaphorical passing of the torch, Master Asari ceremonially gifted Master his dagger, customised exclusively for the durbar order. As he did so, at the last moment the old man spun the hilt of the weapon and buried the blade deep in Master's abdomen. Master Asari smiled as the younger man shrieked, doubled over and collapsed. As the expanding pool of his own blood surrounded Master, the Asari women looked at their smiling patriarch and began to laugh. Horrified, Isa tried to rush to his master's aide. A firm grip clamped around each of Isa's shoulders and despite struggling, he was rooted to the spot by the hands of Amina Asari. Isa screamed but the laughter only became louder and louder as the blood engulfed the room.

Isa stirred and opened his eyes. He felt something pat his side and looked down to see the stranger's reassuring hand. Knowing that his condition was frail, the woman had strapped him to her waist, so he neither had to hold onto her, nor did she have to monitor him behind her as they rode. Even though Isa had no reason to trust her, she had a kindness in her eyes and her offer had been a better alternative to starving to death in the heat. Also, Sisoko had taken to her and Isa knew she had better judgement than any human. Isa looked across at Master's body, bound to the other stranger's horse riding next to them. The feeling of helplessness returned as his lifeless body bobbed up and down against the side of the animal. Isa closed his eyes. He was alone again.

#

The next time he opened his eyes, the sound of female voices again roused Isa from his sleep. He groggily surveyed his surroundings and at first he thought he was still dreaming. They had reached the edge of a forest and he had a clearer view of his rescuers. They were dressed in beige wrappers and carried wooden staffs, with ends as sharp as spears, slung over their backs. Ivory horns hung around their necks and sheathed swords hung around their waists. A woman carrying a sword. Had it not been for his frenetic encounter with the Asari women, seeing this would have been a first for Isa. The scabbards and hilts were basic but a sword was still a sword. Besides, not everyone had the privilege of appreciating a durbar sword close up like he had. One of the separate riders dismounted, moved a few feet away from them and lifted her ivory horn. The horsewoman gave several short sharp toots into the side of the horn. The other riders waited in silence. A few moments later a similar sound was heard in the distance from inside the forest. The horn-blower turned to the others and nodded. Isa's rider dismounted while the other rider, carrying Master as her cargo, remained on horseback. Isa's rescuer put a hand out to assist him.

"Come with us. You're safe."

Disorientated in time and place, with Sisoko's being the only familiar face, Isa felt resigned to his limited choices. He took the woman's hand and carefully dismounted. On reaching the ground his legs gave way and he fell into the dirt. The woman gave the reins of her horse to the horn-blower and stood beside Isa.

"You're weak," said the woman. "Get on my back." She immediately turned around and dropped to one knee. Isa felt embarrassed and looked at her awkwardly as he got up.

The woman looked over her shoulder and smiled. "They say pride comes before a fall. You've already fallen once, why waste any more pride?"

Isa procrastinated a little longer, as he wondered whether the woman was even strong enough to carry him. After all, she couldn't possibly be as strong as Master and she was a woman.

"*Oya come*," ordered the woman, as she patted her back with both hands impatiently. Isa swallowed what little was left of his pride, did as he was told and accepted the help. To his astonishment the woman carried his weight and stood up with ease. With Isa carried on the stranger's back, the four of them entered the forest with their horses.

#

Some time later they came to a large clearing in the woodland. The vast open space was peppered with multiple shelters, fires and cooking pots. Active signs of life came in the sound of small children playing. Upon spotting Isa they stopped and went quiet, staring at the new arrival. A few women clocked the group and their piggy-backed invalid. As the group advanced to the largest enclosure within the camp more heads slowly popped out of several tents. Some eyed Isa suspiciously, while others smiled and a couple looked indifferent. The net outcome was the same. Isa felt like an unexpected guest at a gathering and didn't know where to look. An older looking stocky woman emerged from the large enclosure with several others. They were dressed in similar attire to the riders, all carried sharpened staffs and had the same ivory horns around their necks. Isa and his new-found companions approached the large tent and the not-so-welcoming committee. The older woman's arms were folded and she didn't look happy.

"You're back too soon," said the older woman. "Who are they?" She gestured with her head towards Isa and Master's body, still attached to the horse.

"I couldn't leave them out there," said Isa's carrier defiantly. "They'd both be dead."

"Amaka, you know the rules," scolded the older woman. "You were meant to be scouting. These two are not your concern. You may have endangered the rest of us just by bringing them here."

"Or I've saved a life," replied Amaka. She turned her attention to the younger members of the reception group momentarily. "Take that one." She pointed at Master. "I'll deal with him later. This one is weak. He needs water, rest and food."

Four of the reception party disappeared inside the large enclosure while the older woman watched with a discerning frown. When the four women returned, each pair carried one end of a cloth stretched and tied over two long branches. Master's body was detached from the horse and flopped onto the stretched cloth. He was carried off immediately out of sight. Amaka turned her head over her shoulder.

"Go with them," she said. "They're my friends. You'll be taken care of."

Another pair carrying a stretcher hovered behind Isa. He let go of Amaka's neck, landed on the cloth cushion and stared upwards. Amaka came into his sky view and smiled at him.

"My name is Chiamaka. Welcome to our community. What is your name?"

"Isa."

"That is a powerful name. I trust that you will honour it. Rest well Isa."

"Thank you."

Amaka left his view as he was carried away. She was kind and made him feel relaxed. She also made him forget his painful new reality. He thought of Master perishing and wondered if they were going to bury him. Tears filled his eyes and rolled down his cheeks.

Amaka watched the boy being carried off. She turned to attend to her next task but the older stocky lady grabbed her arm.

"I hope you know what you're doing?" cautioned the older woman.

"It's the least I can do."

#

The next two days were spent convalescing. Isa's instructions from his hosts were simple. Eat. Drink. Sleep. Use the bucket if needed. He slept through the first day, only getting up to empty his bladder on occasion. It was a small mercy that being dehydrated had left him quite constipated and spared him the experience of a stinking bucket by his bedside. But it was not a pleasant rest. The nightmares continued. Isa saw hazy images of his parents, his brother Ibrahim and Master. In his dreams, the faces of everyone he'd ever loved and lost along the way appeared to be fading from his memory. He was alone in the world again. Occasionally he woke to a reassuring face but not the reassuring presence he was used to. Sometimes it was a stranger from the camp. Other times it was Amaka. Isa wondered how long he'd be cared for and allowed to stay. Having lost another master, he wondered who, if anyone, would fill that void.

On the second day Isa felt alert when he woke up and the strength had returned to his body. When he stood up he was surprised that his legs didn't buckle. Instinctively he immediately took the bucket of his pungent urine outside the tent to empty it. Isa squinted in the bright sunlight as his eyes adjusted to the outside world. He emptied the bucket into the soil a few feet away then took in his surroundings. There were more signs of life around the tent than before. More women weaved in between tents. Some carried pots on their heads. Others carried wood under their arms. A few gave him a cursory glance but he was otherwise invisible. Isa momentarily wondered why he hadn't yet seen any men in the camp before a familiar face materialised.

"How are you today Isa?" asked Amaka.

"I'm fine thank you," said Isa.

"You had quite the rest. After what you've been through I think you needed it."

Isa looked puzzled. He couldn't remember what he'd told her in between dreams. Rather than offend her by questioning her response, he smiled.

"I brought you something to help with your stomach," said Amaka. "It's mint water." She then leaned in close and whispered. "It'll also freshen up your breath."

A little embarrassed, Isa took the cup and drank the cool refreshing water. Amaka gave him a quizzical look. Isa stopped drinking, afraid he had done something wrong.

"I've been a bad host," she said, shaking her head. Isa had no clue what she was talking about. "I haven't given you a tour of our community, like a good host should do."

Isa still held the cup away from his mouth, unsure how to respond appropriately.

"Come. Let's go for a walk." Amaka gestured with her hand for him to follow. "It will be a good opportunity for you to stretch your legs. You can bring the water with you as well."

Amaka set off. Like any good guest, Isa did as he was told and followed.

Along their travels Isa heard women speaking not only Hausa but other tongues he'd never heard before. The camp was a constellation of several tents arranged around a handful of larger enclosures. It was located so deep in the forest that only the birds could view it from above. Isa had so far seen at least fifty women and children. Some of the children were boys as well as girls but none were older than him. Apart from the big woman he'd seen on their arrival, the women were mostly around Amaka's age. Some carried firewood, others chopped it. Some carried fish, while others cooked it. A lot of the women were doing tasks that Isa had never seen a woman do. He wondered whether the men were elsewhere in the forest or running errands. Eventually they walked past a stream where a couple of young women were bathing. Upon seeing that they were naked, Isa's eyes almost popped out of his head. Amaka looked at him with a wry smile but said nothing. They veered right of the stream back towards the largest enclosure.

"I know what you're thinking," said Amaka.

Isa felt his cheeks glowing with embarrassment. She must've seen his reaction to the women in the stream. He didn't know what to say so kept his eyes on the floor and his mouth shut.

"You're wondering why you haven't seen any men here."

Isa said nothing but was relieved and impressed that she knew exactly what he was thinking. At least everything other than his thoughts on the women in the water.

"That's because there aren't any," said Amaka. "Men are not allowed in our community."

They walked past three women practising their archery. The polished woodwork of their bows glistened in the sun. The archers ignored the tourist and his guide and focussed their attention on the three targets in front of them.

"Everything you see around you is a sanctuary, a refuge for women and children," she continued. "A refuge for those fleeing the evil in this world. Our members come from all walks of life. All regions. We keep them safe, help them rebuild their lives and for those that are interested," Amaka pointed to the archers as each of their arrows hit their mark with deadly accuracy, "we teach them how to fight back. Men are not allowed in our community as many men are against us, any woman, having control of her life. For that reason boys must leave when they come of age, we keep our location secret and from time to time we move."

They headed towards a large enclosure. "We don't hate men. You're not all bad." She smiled at Isa. "If not for the kindness of one strong man, my husband would've beaten me to death long ago." There was a glint in her eyes as she reminisced about the life-changing turn of events. "That particular man not only stopped the beatings but gave me the means to get here. It takes a special person to help mend one's courage once it's been broken. I owe him my life." The light behind her eyes dimmed for a second. "Sadly the times we live in are what they are. If our members feel the need for male company or want to have children, or there is something they need that we cannot provide, they're free to leave and come back when they're ready to live by our rules again."

As they approached the large enclosure, they passed an open air stable fashioned from logs and tree branches. An old friend made her presence known from inside the stable. Isa rushed to the stable perimeter and hugged Sisoko over the top of it. He closed his eyes as he gave her neck a gentle embrace.

"I'll be back soon," he whispered.

Isa ran back to his guide and the tour resumed. The stocky woman that had greeted them on Isa's arrival at the camp stood outside the large enclosure. She nodded curtly at Amaka with her hands on her hips then gave Isa a scornful look before walking off.

"That is Nkem," said Amaka. "She's our mother, our leader and the founder of our community. She doesn't mean you any harm. She's just very protective of everyone and everything we have here."

Isa ignored the hostile look from the big woman and followed Amaka to the enclosure entrance. When they got there she stopped abruptly and turned to him with a serious expression on her face. "Isa, there's someone I believe it's time for you to see."

Amaka pulled back the enclosure curtain and a cold shiver ran down Isa's spine.

Chapter Twenty-Four

Large plumes of smoke obscured the skyline illuminated by the fires. The attack had been swift and unexpected in the dead of night, maximising the devastation. Vastly outnumbered, the response was entirely predictable, with the porous defences penetrated easily and the outcome extreme. The advancing soldiers channelled the ruthless bloodlust of their leader with relentless aggression. Those that fled were cut down savagely, without prejudice to age or gender, while those that relented and begged for mercy were either shackled immediately and taken prisoner or hacked down all the same. It wasn't long before the village was razed to the ground and the forces of Sokoto advanced through to the next satellite town. Very few escaped the onslaught. The campaign had begun.

The Grand Vizier watched the destruction from a distance. His promise to bring a new order had been effected immediately, while the seat of power was still warm from its previous occupant. The first strike had occurred within hours of war being declared, reinforcing the statement of intent. The army was at full strength and conscription was in full effect. Mercenaries from the south were actively being recruited, with the added caveat that they could keep whatever they plundered, in addition to their fee. There would be no half measures, no compromises. Stability would be brought to the region, no matter the cost. If he had to, Vizier Buhari was prepared to burn down every village between Sokoto and Kano to vanquish his enemy.

Following the Sultan's death, the extension of his interim caretaker role had been a simple process with no opposition. The Sultan's widows wouldn't dare open their mouths, as long as they were taken care of and his eldest son had thus far shown no interest in continuing his father's legacy. Nevertheless, knowing the seductive nature of power, Vizier Buhari had made Yakubu a military general in the meantime. It was a shrewd move to keep the young man occupied and fully engaged, to keep any future designs on the sultanate at bay. The Sultanate Council had unanimously agreed that succession wouldn't be explored until the current conflict had been resolved and the region was stable. For the time being, Vizier Buhari's house was in order.

#

Master's body was naked except for a cloth protecting his modesty. His eyes were closed and his body was still. Isa stood by his bedside while Amaka watched from in front of the enclosure curtain. With his matted hair, beard and swollen face, Master's resemblance was closer to an athletic beggar than a durbar. Even in the dim light of the enclosure his many wounds were visible all over his body. The multiple lacerations that interrupted the lines of muscle definition on his torso and limbs had stopped bleeding but were covered in some kind of paste with a peculiar smell. Perhaps it was to prepare his body for the burial. Isa's mind immediately raced back to the confrontation at the Asari household where the injuries had been inflicted. Although he knew it to be foolish, Isa considered how the outcome may have been different in some way, had he intervened during the altercation. He wondered if he was responsible in some way for his master's death. Isa held Master's warm hand, hung his head and began to cry.

"The rumours of my death have been greatly exaggerated."

Isa looked up through his tears and couldn't believe what he was hearing.

"*Master?*"

Master Garba Mansa slowly turned his head towards the boy, raised his eyebrows and managed a weak smile. He squeezed Isa's hand to allay any doubt that he was alive. Isa began to sob uncontrollably and hugged his chest. Master winced with pain but didn't resist the boy's embrace. "It's good to see you Isa," he said.

Isa held on tight to his master for a good couple of minutes, neither able to let go nor stop crying. Amaka watched the emotional reunion from a distance then left the two of them alone in the enclosure. Isa lifted his head from Master's chest and looked at his guardian one more time, double-checking that his mind wasn't playing a cruel trick on him.

"It's me Isa. You don't need to worry. These injuries are just for decoration." The exiled durbar smiled at his ward, minimising the extent of his injuries and his level of discomfort. "You did well to come here. I understand they've looked after you well." Master raised an eyebrow. "I trust you've been keeping out of trouble?"

"Yes Master." Isa finally found his voice and a smile.

"Very good. We owe these women our lives." Master's facial expression changed and his tone became sombre, as if he was reminded of a haunting memory. "There aren't many people we can trust. We'll be safe here for now." Master seemed lost in his thoughts for a few moments. "What of Sisoko?"

"She's well Master," said Isa.

"Good. That creature has better instincts than any of us. She's more trustworthy than most humans." Master momentarily had that same haunted look on his face. "I see that you've met Amaka."

"Yes Master."

"Very good. We're old acquaintances." Master's face brightened. "She's a good person." Master's eyelids looked heavy as he smiled. Pangs of guilt gnawed at Isa'a conscience.

"Master?" asked Isa.

"Yes Isa?"

Isa considered his words very carefully. "Would you like some more rest?"

Master looked at Isa with a very stern expression. Then after a long stare, his eyebrow raised and he broke into a smile. "You've grown wise in my absence Isa. More rest is your latest good idea."

#

Isa sat quietly opposite Amaka as she stripped the bark off a tree branch with a short blade. After a few minutes of being observed while she worked, she looked up at him and smiled. "Garba Mansa means a lot to you. Where are your parents Isa?"

"They're dead," replied Isa.

"I'm sorry to hear that. Do you have any family?" asked Amaka.

Isa shook his head and looked at the lighter exposed wood beneath the bark.

"Well at least you and Garba have each other. I'm glad that you found each other. He deserves another chance at a family."

A family. The words jarred as he repeated them in his head. Isa looked at Amaka curiously, with uncomfortable feelings of surprise, bewilderment and a little jealousy. Not only did he dislike the way Amaka, this stranger, casually referred to Master by his first name but now she knew something about his master that he didn't. In Isa's mind she hadn't earned the right for either.

Amaka stopped stripping the wood and looked at the boy. He looked perplexed and scanned the ground. "What's wrong Isa?"

"Nothing."

Amaka pressed her lips together, squeezed one eye shut and cocked her head to one side. "Nothing? Really?" She searched his face for a reaction. "Isa, can I tell you something?"

Isa shrugged his shoulders.

"I have special powers," proclaimed Amaka. She leaned forward, with a serious expression on her face then raised her eyebrows theatrically. "Do you want to know what those powers are?"

It was Isa's turn to scrutinise her. He shook his head slowly, not quite sure what she was on about.

"I have the power to tell when something is bothering someone but they don't want to talk about it," said Amaka. "Sometimes they don't know how to talk about it." Amaka closed her eyes, began to gently rub her right temple with the fingers of her right hand and started to hum. At the same time she stuck out her left palm in Isa's direction.

Isa felt awkward and wondered what juju the woman was trying on him.

"Yes," she whispered, "I see it now."

Isa was fairly confident he could only see madness.

Amaka opened her eyes and put her hands down. "Something is bothering you isn't it Isa?"

Isa looked at the ground again and shrugged his shoulders.

"You didn't know your master had a family did you?"

Isa looked up and shook his head.

"Alright, let me tell you what I know." Amaka put her blade down and sat upright. "Garba Mansa, your master, was married once. And he had a child." Isa sat down to absorb the revelation. "Of course this was long before he became a durbar."

"What happened to them, his family?" asked Isa.

Amaka sighed and looked at the shaved length of wood in front of her before continuing. "Something very tragic happened before Garba Mansa's second child was born. Something that resulted in the death of his family and something that Garba Mansa blamed himself for, for a very long time."

"Why?" asked Isa.

"Because he wasn't there. He blamed himself and was never the same again."

"Was it his fault?" asked Isa.

"Of course not," said Amaka, "but guilt is a powerful poison and longer lasting than bitterness. Their death was an accident. Fate showing its cruel hand. But he blamed himself anyway and lost his faith in many things."

"Like what?"

"Himself...other people...his god."

Isa nodded in recognition of the last point.

"He couldn't see how a loving god could allow innocent people, especially a child, to die. So after some time he channeled that pain and anger into what he felt he could do best."

Isa nodded for Amaka to continue.

"Fighting. At first he fought for money but no matter how many people he defeated or how badly he beat his opponents, he still felt hollow inside. He needed something more. He tried many things. Being a mercenary was a brief distraction."

"*Master was a mercenary?*"

Amaka laughed at his response. "The life of a mercenary is not conducive to living a life with morals. Especially for a man like Garba Mansa. He essentially got paid for more brutal fighting, among other things. He struggled with it. So he found something with more purpose. At least in theory anyway. He joined the army of the Kano emirate. There his aggression was contained, he had responsibilities and his life had structure. A man with no direction in life suddenly had direction. Sooner or later, that part of Garba's mind that felt nourished by a challenge needed something more. And so he found the durbar order. Or rather it found him. He was handpicked by the council chairman to attend the selection process."

Isa was amazed by what he'd learned. Even Master Asari hadn't shared this much with him. "When did you meet Master?"

"I met Garba Mansa when he was already a durbar." Amaka then smirked. "Garba doesn't believe it but my god answered my prayers and brought him into my life when I needed help the most."

"Were you in trouble?" asked Isa.

"The worst kind," replied Amaka matter of factly. "So, Isa the inquisitive. How did you meet your master?"

"He bought me."

"Oh."

"I was a slave."

"So Garba Mansa freed both of us from impossible lives," said Amaka. "So what happened before we found you? How did Garba Mansa end up like he is now?

"The Asaris did that to him," mumbled Isa.

"Why?"

"First they rescued him on his way to prison in Sokoto then they tried to kill him when he wouldn't join them."

"*A-ah! Prison?*" Amaka's jaw hit the floor. "Garba Mansa is no criminal. What happened?"

"They accused Master of killing people in Sokoto. He didn't do it…well he did…but not the way they said he did and not as many. They wanted him to go to court in Sokoto…but the durbar council said he had to go to prison first…Master saved me and the Asari woman was there when it happened."

Amaka stared at Isa as he tied his tongue in knots explaining the convoluted turn of events.

"It all sounds very complicated," she said. "Who are the Asaris?"

"A family."

"They must be a family of very good fighters. Garba Mansa is tough. Very tough."

"There were three of them," said Isa. "My master's master and two women."

237

"*A durbar? His mentor?*" Amaka was shocked. Isa nodded slowly in response. "No wonder Garba looks so sad. Betrayal is like a knife through the heart."

"The women were good fighters," acknowledged Isa, "but Master took on both of them."

"Why do you seem so surprised that women can fight Isa?"

"I've never seen it before."

"Trust me, you'll see it again. You said the Asaris rescued Master. Why would they free him if the durbar council had agreed for him to go to Sokoto?"

"I don't know," replied Isa. "When he took me to meet Master, Master Asari talked about a change coming, leaving the past behind and the start of a new age. He didn't explain what happened to the old age but he was happy. At the house, Master Asari said the time of the durbars was over."

"Hmmm, change can be a good thing. *Radical* change requires caution," mused Amaka. "I can't see a change that requires taking Garba Mansa's life ever being a good thing."

At that precise moment a wide shadow was cast over Isa, disrupting the flow of their conversation. Isa turned around and was greeted by the scornful aura of Nkem. He wondered if she ever smiled.

"Isa, why don't you give us a few minutes?" asked Amaka. "I'll come and get you near your tent."

Isa nodded and left the two women alone, while being careful to walk in the opposite direction of the community mother. Nkem waited until the boy was out of earshot.

"What's your plan with them?" she asked.

"The boy has only just been reunited with his master," pivoted Amaka.

"That's not what I asked you and you know it," countered Nkem.

"Would you rather I'd let them die?"

"You know the rules. The durbar cannot stay. We don't know if he can be trusted. Because of your actions we may have to move. You must put your feelings to one side and think about others Amaka. What makes him so special? What makes him worth risking everything we have here?"

"Where the durbar goes, the boy goes," stressed Amaka. "And he *can* he trusted. If not for him I wouldn't be here talking to you now."

"And you've paid back your debt in full."

"Isn't the whole point of this community to provide refuge for the destitute?"

"We are not a refuge for criminals and fugitives. I heard the boy's story."

"But isn't the essence of what we're doing here, this way of life, choosing who and how we love, considered a crime elsewhere? Aren't we all fugitives and criminals fleeing suffering and pain?"

"Amaka, when a safe space is no longer safe, it serves no purpose. He is a wanted man and by allowing him to stay here, we are his accomplices. Even if he doesn't betray us, a death sentence hangs over us until he's gone. Close your heart and open your eyes. You have until the durbar can ride his horse again. Then he must go."

Chapter Twenty-Five

The hungry crowd packed the sweaty auditorium to the brim. An eclectic mix of the wealthy, well-to-do politicians and aspirational social climbers had all paid the premium to watch the brutal spectacle that was about to take place behind closed doors. Like the space in the room, security was tight and many had brought their own close protection in addition to the armed giants strategically placed on the door and around the exclusive section of the Katsina tavern. A demonstration of wasan sanda, Fulani stick-fighting, occupied the nucleus of the throng and opened the evening's dimly lit entertainment. Two men in tunics, one in brown and one in cream, rhythmically spun a three feet long bamboo cane in one hand, while clashing sticks with an identical cane in the other one. The adversaries weaved and pivoted away from each other's double stick attacks while navigating the torchlit circle in a near-choreographed manner. The intermittent *klak* of the stick contacts punctuated the sound of a flute in the background, faintly audible above the rumbling chatter from the mostly inebriated crowd. Every so often each man winced, frowned or flinched as his opponent's weapon struck him at high speed on the face, torso or legs. After several minutes of the kinetic weapons display, a gong signalled the end of the evening's appetiser.

The stickmen moved to the side of the arena. Two other men that had hitherto been limbering up on the sidelines took centre stage. The first was lean but short in stature and distinctly unusual in his appearance. He wore nothing but a loin cloth, bracelets around both ankles, both wrists, both biceps and a necklace. But these accessories were not a fashion statement. Each item had two inch spikes spaced evenly along the outer surface of each strap. Furthermore it was clear even in the darkness that he'd oiled his entire body. The most striking aspect of his appearance was his long and thick shoulder length dreadlocked hair. It was considered an unusual, somewhat unkempt look in the region. His opponent had a more conventional look, with his scraped bald head, long beard and sleeveless soiled top and long trousers. His striking features were his towering height at almost seven feet tall, taller than any tavern guard and his arms, that were almost equivalent in width to the smaller man's head. As the two men squared up to one another, a referee in a green kaftan stood between them and ostentatiously raised a white towel with his right hand for the crowd to see. Satisfied that he had their full attention, the referee dropped his towel hand and stepped away to the sidelines. Then the drum beat began.

A few members of the crowd grumbled as they were jostled by a small entourage making its way to the front. When the entourage stopped next to an older man accompanied by two women in full face veils, one spectator opened his mouth to voice his objection to the disturbance. Upon seeing the ornate hilts of the swords of the security detail surrounding the interloper, the spectator thought otherwise and turned his attention back to the main event. The older man's veiled companions turned to look at the new arrival.

"Two at once?" asked the interloper. He looked at the veiled women. One was dressed head to toe in red while the other was in purple. "You must be making up for lost time."

The white-haired older man, with flawless obsidian black skin, acknowledged the observation with a bemused smiled. "These are my bodyguards."

Information minister Atiku Danladi gave a wheezy laugh that made his belly shake. When he caught his breath back, he took a few breaths while lecherously looking the two women up and down. "*Bodyguards?* That's a good one! Your retirement is clearly treating you well."

"One cannot complain," said Jibril Asari.

Danladi leaned in to him. "I hear our person of mutual interest never made it to Sokoto. Not that it changes anything but you wouldn't happen to know his whereabouts would you?"

The older man's tone and cordial demeanour changed ever so slightly and he turned to the information minister. "If I did, I'd make sure to put him in the ground myself."

Danladi smiled. "I thought as much."

"What about your rat?" asked the older man. "When will *he* be put in his cage?"

"Very soon. Everything has so far fallen into place, as planned. Now, this is meant to be an evening of pleasure with a sprinkling of business." Danladi rubbed his hands together gleefully as they observed the two fighters pacing hesitantly around one another in front of them. "The mountain versus the man. I know Allah forbids you from betting on your man, so tell me how quickly you think he'll win?"

Jibril Asari smiled. "What makes you think the bigger man is my man, as you put it?"

Danladi raised his eyebrows. "That confident eh? You can take the man out of the order but you can't take the order out of the man. Let's see how long your man with the woman's hair and ugly jewellery lasts."

"You'll find the shanci fighter will acquit himself very well."

Where the stick fighting had been frenetic from the get go, the hand to hand combat was a slow burn in comparison. The mountain and the shanci fighter took their time looking for openings, assessing the movement patterns of their opponent. The shanci fighter moved first, gracefully darting towards and away from the giant. He threw speculative kicks to the shin and knees, dodging blows to his head at the last second. Nothing. The mountain was solid from the ground up. So the shanci fighter went higher. He leapt high in the air and launched a two-footed heel front kick at the giant's chest. The crowd roared as the contact landed. The mountain took a couple of paces back as the shanci fighter landed on his hands and rolled to his feet. The mountain smiled and resumed his slow advance.

"There's no substitute for power," commented Danladi. "Perhaps your man should remove some jewellery and throw it at him."

The mountain threw a right cross at his opponent then followed up with a knee strike off his left side. Having dodged the first attack, the shanci fighter narrowly parried the oncoming knee, absorbed some of the impact and lost his balance but cut the thigh of his opponent with his bracelet in the process. The bigger man grimaced as his opponent got up on all fours and crabbed sideways with his eyes on him.

"The mountain versus the leopard," said Jibril Asari. "Sharp jewellery and all."

The feline fighter leapt up in the air and threw a round kick at the arm of his adversary. While the spike of his anklet lacerated the man's arm, the behemoth had anticipated the attack, closed down the space and caught his leg and torso. He cradled him like a small child before responding in kind with a front on headbutt. The dazed shanci fighter swiped groggily at the big man, catching him on the cheek with his bracelet. The mountain angrily threw him several feet across the auditorium floor and the crowd roared with delight.

The mountain wiped his cheek, looked at the blood on his fingers and advanced slowly towards the fallen fighter.

"It seems the mountain is too high a climb for the leopard," noted Danladi.

The shanci fighter got to his knees, watched and waited for his foe to come closer. When the man mountain was a few feet away he sprang to his feet but maintained a low stance. He fired a sidekick, which hit the concrete abdominal muscles of the gigantic fighter with negligible impact. The smaller fighter then feinted with his leading hand then kicked the mountain below the knee of his leading leg, connecting with the spike of his anklet. This was immediately followed up by a rapid anklet strike to the thigh, prompting the man mountain to step inside and swing a huge fist at the head of the kicker. At that precise moment the shanci fighter pivoted on his landing foot and spun round to launch an almost vertical spinning hook kick where he anticipated the giant's head would be a fraction of a second later. The miracle kick worked. It landed with the smaller man's heel connecting with the bigger man's temple. The mountain stumbled sideways and raised his arms too late to avoid the follow-up jumping knee strike to his jaw. This time he collapsed face down on the ground. The crowd gasped.

The leopard pounced on the felled mountain's back, straddling him in the process and immediately put him in a rear chokehold. The big man frantically grabbed at the feral fighter clinging to him like his life depended on it. He got to his knees, then feet, staggered sideways, forwards and backwards but his dreadlocked assailant clung to him like a second skin. Feeling the life being strangled from him, the mountain threw himself backwards in desperation.

The shanci fighter maintained his chokehold on the mountain as his back hit the ground hard, with the full weight of the mountain on top of him. Rather than releasing his opponent, he dug his heels into the mountain's chest and the anklet spikes penetrated the intercostal spaces between the man's ribs. The mountain screamed a deep guttural scream, as his arms flailed and he rolled side to side, desperately clawing at the shanci fighter's head behind him. Each time he tried to grab his opponent's arms, his hands clumsily slipped off the man's oily skin. The crowd went quiet in anticipation of what could come next. Then the shanci fighter loosened his grip for a split second and rotated both forearms towards himself so his wrist spikes pressed against the flesh of the mountain's thick neck. In one continuous brutal movement, the shanci fighter dug the wrist spikes into the neck of the mountain and crossed each wrist from one opposite side of his neck to the other.

The subsequent spray of arterial blood shot several metres into the crowd and silenced them. The mountain lay still in the shanci fighter's arms. The drum beat stopped as the referee calmly walked to the centre of the floor and stood over the fighters' frozen embrace. He ostentatiously looked over the two men then gestured for the shanci fighter to stand up. With one hand he raised the victorious fighter's hand, with the other the referee raised a red towel. The crowd roared at the victory as the referee dropped the red towel over the dead body of the mountain.

"Perhaps you should be a betting man," said Minister Danladi.

"There's no substitute for resourcefulness, adaptation and determination," said Jibril Asari with a smile on his face. "You should see him with real weapons. He'll serve you well."

"What are the terms?" asked the minister.

"Half now, the rest on completion of the campaign."

"Very well."

The Minister of Information nodded to the head of his security detail, who immediately led him and the rest of the armed entourage out of the room. As they left, two tavern workers grabbed a leg each and dragged the remains of the mountain off the auditorium floor.

A spectator moved into the space left vacant by the minister's departure. He immediately approached Jibril Asari and his two companions.

"You must be a blessed man," said the spectator. His eyes were red with his poison of choice and spittle flew from his lips as he spoke. "Such riches. Surely such a wealthy man is also generous and could spare one of these beauties?"

"They're not mine to give away," replied Jibril Asari.

The spectator leaned in with his malodorous breath and grabbed the old man by the arm. "Everything has its price around here. You just have to name it." The stranger let go of the old man's arm and the trio walked away. The stranger then grabbed the shoulder of the woman in red. "Perhaps I should ask this beau—"

The tip of a sharp blade at the throat curtailed the spectator's advances. He immediately let go of the woman's arm, took a step back and raised his hands defensively. The woman in red lowered her dagger blade and the trio continued their exit from the Katsina tavern.

#

The goje was beautifully haunting. As the woman caressed the strings of the small wooden instrument with the bow, the small gathering of listeners wondered what harrowing tales were being told through the medium of her music. Her expressionless face betrayed no clues as she played. A hand on his shoulder snapped Isa out of his hypnotic trance.

"Mesmerising isn't it?" said Garba Mansa. He looked better but was dressed peculiarly in a woman's wrapper around his waist and over his shoulders. He cottoned on immediately that his ward was looking at him like an alien. "What's wrong Isa?"

"Nothing Master," lied Isa.

The fugitive durbar gave him a curious look and then looked down at his clothes before looking back at the boy. "You're judging my attire? You think I look funny?"

Isa smiled awkwardly. "Aren't those women's clothes Master?"

"And? Does a child choose the colour of the flame that keeps it warm at night?"

As usual Isa wasn't sure whether to answer Master's rhetorical question.

"Isa, these people have brought us in, fed us, kept us warm and kept us safe. Given what they've done for us, why should we choose to look different, to stand out? How does conforming to social conventions help us in our current predicament?" As usual, Master didn't wait for a response. "Come, let's stretch our legs and open your mind."

Garba Mansa and Isa strolled around the camp in the afternoon sunshine. Master was strangely rather upbeat. After his earlier telling off, Isa thought better than to comment. A couple of women holding hands approached them. Isa stared at one of the pair who was bare-chested. Her breasts gently swayed with the movement of her hips. Isa immediately looked at Master, who smiled at him wryly as the couple walked past them.

"Which is it?" he asked. "The fact that they're holding hands or one is half-naked?"

"I've never seen it before. And the…those…things…"

"Those *things*, called breasts, kept you nourished as an infant. Besides, you'll soon be old enough to enjoy the pleasure of a woman's company. Don't be embarrassed or afraid of them."

"But women holding hands, like that? Is it normal?"

"*Normal?*" said Master. "What does that even mean? Don't allow others to imprison your mind with their impositions of what is considered *normal*. Tell me Isa, what harm are those two women doing to others by loving each other in that way? Yet many consider their behaviour sinful, punishable by death. The goje player with her beautiful music would be imprisoned by some because a woman playing music is forbidden. When people's lives are dominated by dogma, instruction without question, they live in dangerous times. You know what the sad thing is, Isa?"

"No Master."

"We're already living in those times."

With the theme of keeping an open mind ringing in his ears, Isa could no longer resist the burning question on his lips. "Master?"

"Yes Isa."

"You don't seem angry. After everything that's happened with Master Asari, the durbar council, Sokoto. Why?"

Master took a deep breath and sighed. "Harbouring rage and resentment is like drinking poison and expecting your enemy to feel sick. A lot has happened. A lot of it has been unfair and beyond our control. But the true path to acceptance has no room for bitterness."

"So if you saw Master Asari again, what would you do?"

Garba Mansa paused and smiled. "I'd be lying if I said I'd greet him with open arms."

Amaka appeared at that precise moment. She was carrying her long spear, her sword was around her waist and the ivory horn was around her neck. She spoke in an almost formal tone. "Garba, Isa. I'm glad I found you. A few of us are going out to scout. We'll be gone for a few hours. I've been asked to invite you. That is of course if you're feeling up to it?"

Amaka wasn't quite her usual warm relaxed self. She was polite but distant. Her words were strained, as if they belonged to someone else. Garba Mansa sensed the change in her demeanour but answered her request, without drawing attention to her presumed duress.

"Of course. The three of us need the exercise. Isa, go and wake up Sisoko."

#

They'd ridden for just over an hour. Although they were healing well, Garba Mansa's thigh wounds chafed in Sisoko's saddle. The stoic durbar in exile said nothing and smiled in his women's clothing but his ward knew him well enough to know when his master was in pain. Amaka's distant behaviour continued and she said nothing to her two female counterparts from the community. Amaka slowed her horse down.

"Have you noticed something?" she asked Garba Mansa.

"From the village up ahead?" he replied.

Amaka nodded. "It's too quiet. I can't hear anything. No people. No animals. Nothing. I can't see any smoke. Something's not right."

They proceeded cautiously. Master occasionally shifted uncomfortably as Isa forgot about his wounds and held him tight. Several minutes later they entered the village. Their questions were answered immediately.

In between the ash where several huts had been, lay burnt utensils, pots and the charred remains of several bodies, both human and animal. Poultry and cattle, as well as pigs hadn't been spared from the blaze. The smell of burnt flesh was unbearable.

"Who could have done this?" asked Amaka, horrified by the grotesque sight of several dismembered bodies lying in the path in front of them. They carefully navigated more dead bodies, a few untouched by the fire, as they continued the recce. The prints of several hooves and feet in the soil meant that the perpetrators of the atrocity had been numerous and recent. All four horses stopped suddenly as they encountered the worst sight of all. Several burnt bodies had been hanged from different branches of the same tree. The victims were large and small, the smallest had been clearly much younger than Isa. While the three riders stared aghast, Isa couldn't control himself any longer and vomited over the side of Sisoko.

Garba Mansa shook his head. "Take a good look Isa. This isn't just the normal behaviour of animals. This is the normal behaviour of evil."

Chapter Twenty-Six

"They can't stay."

"Neither can we. What happened to that village will happen to us if we stay here."

In the aftermath of the village massacre, the journey back to the community had been a sombre affair. Only the horses made a sound. Amaka and the scouts looked stunned. Master looked perplexed. Isa was visibly shaken by yet another encounter with death. The last time he'd seen a child mutilated so horrifically had been when his own village was slaughtered. Many of the images he'd seen beyond the murder of his family had mercifully been suppressed deep in the recesses of his subconscious. Upon the party's return, the community leader and other committee members immediately convened in the largest enclosure to debate the merits of remaining in their current location, with or without the durbar and his apprentice. The other two scouts confirmed Amaka's account of the barbarity they'd witnessed. Given their expiring guest status in the refuge, Master thought it best to wait outside the tent until summoned to give his testimony. The mood in the enclosure was tense.

"The durbar has endangered us all with his presence," said Nkem. "I knew this would happen."

"We don't know if this has anything to do with the durbar and the boy," argued Amaka.

"Sometimes I confuse your naïveté with optimism," said Nkem.

"And sometimes I confuse your complete distrust of others with being protective," retorted Amaka.

"*Enough*," said an old woman with white hair. "We don't have time to argue the *why* of what is coming. We can all agree that it is a case of *when* not *if* it is coming and we need a plan of action." The elder looked at Amaka. "I agree with Nkem. The durbar cannot stay. We have rules for a reason." The old woman turned her attention to Nkem. "However, it's clear that managing this danger is the highest priority. Do you not agree?"

Both Amaka and Nkem nodded.

"What is the plan?" asked the elder.

"Normally we would've found the next location, secured it and ensured our safe passage. Given the nature and potential urgency of the current situation, we don't have that luxury. The situation is unprecedented. We cannot move the entire community at once. One option would be to keep scouting, perhaps give ourselves another week or two and then reassess our options."

"*Week or two?*" protested Amaka. "We could be dead by then."

"You don't know that," snapped Nkem. "The last thing this community needs is panic and fear-mongering being spread by alarmist uncertainty. Let's work with the facts."

"Then let's get an opinion from someone used to dealing with the facts of such acts," said Amaka. "Let's see what the durbar thinks."

"Okay. Bring your durbar."

Amaka's head popped out of the enclosure opening. Isa nudged Master to get his attention.

"*Garba*," she said. "You're up."

Master turned to Isa. "Wait here." He stopped and turned before entering. "If you need anything just call for me."

"Yes Master."

The durbar disappeared inside the large tent for his grilling. Isa remained outside in the open, staring at the flames of the campfire.

Garba Mansa ignored Nkem's stern look as he took a seat next to Amaka in the circle of cross-legged meeting attendees. The committee consisted of half a dozen women spanning the full adult age range. A woman with white hair particularly stood out. All eyes were on the only man in the room.

"What is your appraisal of the situation, master durbar?" asked Nkem.

"Thank you for granting me an audience. I must reiterate our gratitude for everything you've done for us. The boy and I would surely have perished if not for your kindness and generosity."

"You're welcome," said Nkem, "but you may have brought great danger with you. What are your thoughts on the village?"

"What happened to the village wasn't the work of bandits or marauders," began Garba Mansa. "It was the work of an army."

The committee members exchanged concerned glances while Nkem frowned skeptically. "What makes you so sure?"

"Because I'm a soldier. That kind of organised, total devastation, the large number of hoof and footprints, the statement of those slaughtered in the tree. To wipe out a community like that can only come from instruction. An army instructed to wipe out an entire community."

"Tell me master durbar, is that opinion based on experience?" asked Nkem.

"I've lived things…seen things…done things I'm not proud of." Garba Mansa looked at the ground. "But nothing like this." He looked around the circle. "Whatever personal hell you fled to be in this community will be nothing compared to what's coming if you remain here."

"Those are strong words master durbar. How can you be so sure?"

"With the greatest respect, you have many brave people, a few fighters and some weapons but it takes an army to defeat an army. And whichever army is coming must be defeated for you to stand any chance of survival."

"Which army do you speak of?" asked Nkem.

"My suspicion is that Sokoto is responsible. Tensions were high between our kingdoms, before my departure."

"Why not Katsina? Or Kano?" asked Nkem.

"This kind of savagery…it's not our way."

"Don't all aggressors believe in their own benevolence?" countered the white-haired woman.

Garba Mansa nodded to concede the point.

"And what if all they want, all that they're doing this for is you?" asked Nkem.

Garba Mansa smiled. "I doubt that I'm so important that people other than my brothers," he looked around the room, "or sisters-in-arms fighting by my side would kill for me. If I believed for even a second that surrendering would stop all of this, I'd do it in a heartbeat. I've done it before."

"And look where that got you," responded Nkem bluntly. Amaka shot her a death stare.

"So what do you recommend? What is your plan of action?" she pressed.

"Time is against us and we've seen evidence of the severity of the threat. Now we must determine where the threat is coming from."

"*We?*" asked Nkem.

"You, with or without my help, must determine where the threat is coming from, otherwise you'll be leading your people towards their deaths."

"And how would you determine the direction of the threat?" asked the white-haired woman.

"The village was north-west of here, which means the army could either be advancing from our west, north of us or may have bypassed us altogether. You could send scouts in each direction and they could report back on the safest exit route. I would be happy to assist. Even after my departure."

Nkem scrutinised the durbar some more, while the rest of the committee muttered among themselves. "That doesn't address the problem of where we go next."

"I can't say where you'll find refuge but I can offer you assistance. I have friends that can help you."

"You've spoken well Garba Mansa. I don't doubt your sincerity," said the white-haired woman, "but I've known many smooth-talking durbars in my time. Some were helpful when I was the leader of this community some time ago. Others, not so much. Forgive me if it seems that you may be short on friends right now."

"I still have one or two."

"And yet you're here."

"There were forces at play more powerful than any friend I had before I was sent to Sokoto. My friends didn't betray me then and they won't betray me now."

"But didn't one of these so-called friends, a mentor even, not only secure your release but then ultimately betray you?"

There was a long uncomfortable silence. Everyone except Amaka looked at the durbar, waiting for a response.

"You're correct. Nobody was more wounded by his indefensible actions than me," conceded the durbar. "You have my offer of help. Take it or leave it."

#

Two scores of marching feet broke the nighttime silence in the Gidan Korau. The guards in the sentry towers passively watched the lamp-lit incursion by their own, oblivious to the identities of the detainees in waiting. The procession of palace guards, led by sergeant at arms Yusuf

Dankote and accompanied by the Minister for War, passed unchallenged through the main courtyard of the royal palace of the Katsina emirate. The armed enforcers split into two groups, one accompanied by Dankote and the war minister and advanced to opposite sides of the palace. The first stop for the unaccompanied other half was ministerial quarters. There the unaccompanied group splintered further into smaller factions.

A booming knock shook the chamber door of one senior minister. No response. *Boom! Boom! Boom!* Moments later a key turned and the door was opened but held slightly ajar.

"*What is the meaning of this?*" hissed the elderly man. His eyes were bloodshot with fatigue.

"My lord, you must accompany us at once," said the guard.

"*What for? At this hour?*" The old man opened the door a little further to see that in the dark corridor the guard had back up. He counted three more. It was only then that he realised the lead guard had put his foot in the door to prevent him from closing it. The minister's tone changed from irritated to anxious. "Is everything alright?"

"My lord, you must come with us."

"Why? On whose authority are you here?"

"The kingdom of Katsina. It will be easier if you come quietly."

The old man opened the door and the guards entered. Within minutes the old man was being escorted in his nightdress across the palace grounds to an as yet undisclosed location. The process was repeated several more times until the unaccompanied group had removed several other ministers from their beds under cover of darkness.

The other twenty rebel guards approached the royal quarters. There was no group dispersal and everyone, with the exception of the unarmed war minister, had their swords drawn at the ready. Two guards manned the outer gate and were immediately surprised by the advancing group.

"*Stand down,*" ordered Dankote, as his group approached.

The guards looked at each other. One put his hand on his hilt while the other put his hand up to halt the group and negotiate.

"Wait. Wha—"

The response was swift and final. A guard broke off from the advancing procession and drove his sword straight through the negotiator's torso. As the other royal guard drew his sword and blocked one attack, he was neutralised in a similar fashion by another. The procession was already in motion on its way through the outer gate before the second man hit the ground.

This time the group split into two and approached the royal chambers from opposite sides around a smaller inner courtyard. Using speed and darkness to their advantage, much to the rebels' relief they'd so far met little resistance.

Dankote's group reached the focus of the night's operation. Six royal guards stood between them and the Emir of Katsina's chamber. When the armed procession had reunited at opposite ends of the corridor, this time the royal guards were ready.

"*What is the meaning of this?*" demanded one royal guard.

The Minister for War stepped forward to the armed standoff, while maintaining a safe distance from the tip of the guard's raised blade. "As a result of the dereliction of his duties, chiefly as protector of the kingdom in times of war and peace, it has been decided by committee—"

"*Committee? What committee?*" demanded the guard. "*In the middle of the night?*"

"It has been decided by committee," repeated the war minister, "that his excellency is no longer fit to rule the kingdom of Katsina."

"*No longer fit? Who is this committee?*"

The royal guards were almost back to back, defending their position.

"We are here to remove his excellency and take him to a place of safety until such a time comes that he is fit to resume his role as protector of the realm."

The war minister stepped back and the sergeant at arms stepped forward, with his weapon still drawn. "Stand aside. We're here to ensure a smooth handover. There is no need for any more bloodshed."

The panic-stricken guard was unconvinced. "*Then why are your weapons drawn sergeant? Why so many of you?*"

"Dissent is inevitable when change comes. We won't tell you again. Stand aside."

"*Dissent?*" The royal guard shook his head. "*Our loyalty is to his excellency.*"

"So be it."

#

Screaming. Banging. Glass shattering. Every sound indicative of an almighty struggle on the other side of the chamber doors was terrifying. To make matters worse, he could barely breathe, let alone fit under the bed. Then all of a sudden, silence. Silence apart from the terrified whimpering of the three naked concubines on the bed above him. If the intruders got in, as long as they stuck to the plan, he could buy some time before the alarm was sounded and more help came. The Emir slowly turned his head sideways and listened carefully. Nothing except the gentle breeze coming in through the open window. He exhaled audibly, relieved that the insurrection had been averted. He slowly began to crawl sideways, like an obese spider, out from under the bed.

Crack!!! Female screams accompanied the sound of the chamber double doors being burst open. The Emir reflexively scuttled back to his hiding place. *Stamp stamp stamp stamp.* His movement was masked by the sound of many boots entering the chamber. He watched, waited and prayed with his hand over his mouth to muffle his own heavy breathing.

"*Where is he?!*" screamed a voice.

The female whimpering became louder and from his low viewpoint, the Emir watched boots move towards the open window.

"*Go round the back!*" The command was immediately followed by the sound of running feet in the corridor. From his hiding place, he saw the boots of the palace guard move away from the window, back towards the centre of the room. The boots paced up and down the room while others frantically moved around, presumably searching the side-rooms and washroom for him. After a couple of minutes, the majority of the boots left the room. The pair that had first entered now stood still directly in front of the bed. The Emir heard movement above him then the patter of bare feet. One, then two, then three pairs of bare women's legs moved from the side of the bed to stand next to the military boots in front of him. For almost half a minute nobody moved and the room was silent. The Emir held his breath.

The loud *clunk* of shackles dropping to the floor broke the silence. The Emir was so startled he almost hit his head on the bed frame above him. He just about managed to control his bladder despite the fear and remained quiet, ignoring his palpitating heart. Two more boots entered the room and stood next to the first pair. The feet of the concubines moved away from the bed, as did the first pair of boots. Then the Emir of Katsina's bed was lifted above him, like a stone uncovering a tomb.

The sergeant at arms crouched down on both knees and stared at the sovereign, who lay prone, shaking on the spot. The two men made eye contact for only a second before the former stood up and was replaced by two others. More eyes, this time with long ranging arms and strong grips. The Emir was audibly dragged from his hiding place, like a carcass being hauled across an abattoir. In full view of his trembling naked concubines, the Emir of Katsina was shackled like a criminal in his nightdress and dragged from his chamber, through the bloodbath in the corridor to the most secure place in the Gidan Korau.

#

There was a knock on Minister of Information Atiku Danladi's door. He opened it slightly, cautiously confirmed the identity of the late night caller, then opened the door some more. The Minister for War came in and sat down. He had a serious expression on his face.

"And?" asked Danladi anxiously.

The war minister smiled. "It's done."

Danladi gave a sigh of relief. "Any fatalities?"

"Some but negligible."

"Good. Where is he?"

"Safe." The war minister's smile grew wider. "In the cells with the others. The rest of the royal family are under house arrest in their quarters."

"Excellent. Now we send word to Sokoto. We're ready to join the war."

Chapter Twenty-Seven

"*The afterlife awaits you another day durbar master,*" whispered the voice.

Durbar Master Musa Gindiri opened his eyes and lifted his head off the table. He blinked and the grimy wall of the Kano tavern came into focus. He looked down to further orientate himself. His goblet was empty, as were the six jugs next to it. There were several half eaten bowls of chin chin, a quill pen and some paper. Musa picked up a piece of paper and shook his head in disgust at the incoherent scrawl that vaguely resembled his handwriting. As he licked his furry teeth, he wrinkled his nose at the pungent odour of his own ripe sweat. He felt light-headed. Was he still drunk? Did it even matter? He picked up the nearest jug and shook it, just to double-check it was empty. He contemplated getting another.

"*Musa,*" whispered the voice again.

Musa Gindiri froze. Had he drunk so much he'd lost his mind? Apparently one had to drink for many years to start hearing voices. Although he'd become quite proficient at his new past-time, he had some way to go. He reached into his tunic very slowly then spun around immediately. He held a dagger blade in the direction of the man calling his name.

"I don't believe it," he gasped.

"Believe it brother."

Holding the dagger still, Musa reached around with his other hand

and picked up a jug. He immediately threw it at the man. The man caught the jug and placed it on a table next to him.

"I'm seeing a ghost in woman's clothing."

"Don't be so dramatic Musa. It's me!"

"If this is how they greet you, I think you need new friends," said Amaka.

"Just be grateful he didn't throw the knife." said Garba Mansa. "He never misses."

"A ghost with his girlfriend," mused Musa Gindiri. He looked at the two of them suspiciously.

Amaka frowned at him. "A friend."

Musa lowered his knife, cautiously moved closer and touched the tip of Garba Mansa's nose with his index finger. He paused, smiled, dropped the blade and hugged his fellow durbar.

"It's so good to see you! How are you alive?"

The durbar let go of the durbar, held him by the shoulders and looked him up and down.

"Why are you dressed like a woman?"

"I'd normally say you should sit down and pour yourself a drink before I tell you," warned Garba Mansa, "but it looks like you've been doing a lot of that lately."

"A lot has happened," said Musa Gindiri dismissively, "and I've had a lot of time on my hands." He sat down at the table and motioned with both hands for his friend and his companion to join him.

"Why so much time?" asked Garba Mansa.

"It's all over Garba. The order is done." For a man who typically took pride in his appearance, Musa Gindiri looked somewhat dishevelled and deflated to boot.

"What do you mean *done*?"

"After you were sent to Sokoto, Master Asari disappeared without a trace."

Garba Mansa and Amaka exchanged knowing looks.

"The last he was seen was with Isa leaving the palace," continued Musa Gindiri. "Perhaps losing you was too much for him."

"Isa is fine. He's somewhere safe but Musa there's something you ne—"

"Anyway, with your extradition, the chairman of the order disappearing into thin air…it wasn't long before questions started being asked. Some oxygen thieves even believed you were a recalled agent of Sokoto. Thanks to that speckled toad the justice minister, it was decided that the order would be suspended indefinitely."

Garba Mansa leaned across the table. "Musa, this will be hard to take but there's something I need to tell you about Master Asari."

"Nothing you say could possibly surprise me," insisted the drunk durbar.

"Master Asari betrayed us all. He's in league with our enemy. He wants to destroy Kano."

Musa Gindiri chuckled flippantly. "Garba, are you sure *you* haven't been drinking?"

Garba Mansa stood up and took a step back away from the table. He carefully unravelled his wrapper and held one part in place to reveal several healing wounds all over his torso. He then put his right foot on the chair, hoisted up the wrapper on one side and showed more wounds along his leg. Musa Gindiri's eyebrows raised at the catalogue of recent injuries. "Courtesy of Adesua and Amina Asari. The wife and daughter of Jibril Asari."

Musa Gindiri shook his head in disbelief. He opened and closed his mouth a few times, unable to get the words out. "Why?"

"Only he can answer that but the woman in black, Sokoto, my escape, it was all the Asaris."

Musa Gindiri frowned. "Your escape?"

Garba Mansa nodded.

"So let me get this straight. His wife or daughter, whoever, saves your life *in* Sokoto, then he frees you from a death sentence on the way *to* Sokoto and then he tries to kill you *near* Sokoto?"

Garba Mansa nodded. Amaka shrugged her shoulders.

"I need more to drink," sighed Musa Gindiri. He reached across the table for the goblet. Garba Mansa grabbed his arm and frowned.

"Musa, you do know there's a war on don't you?"

The warrior poet shrugged his hand off and yawned. "Of course I know. Sokoto has *officially* declared war."

"So why are you pissing your life away in a tavern instead of fighting like a man?"

Musa Gindiri cocked his head to one side and scrutinised his angry friend. At the same time he reached inside his tunic. Garba Mansa carefully watched him until his hand came out empty. "Disillusionment is the discovery that privilege prevaricates a pariah."

"*Rubbish*. You can do better than that Musa."

"Did you think I would just go back to being a regular soldier?" asked Musa Gindiri. "Digging trenches, lying face to nyash with people who've never washed their nyash before? *I'm a durbar*, not the lowest common denominator."

"Those lunatics want to send us back to the dark ages. People are being slaughtered Musa and all you can think about is your precious ego. You're not a durbar, you're a pathetic drunk wallowing in his own self-pity!"

This time Musa Gindiri put his hand back in his tunic and withdrew a blade. He held it to Garba Mansa's face. The exiled durbar caught his arm by the wrist. The two men stood face to face over the table, staring intensely at one another.

"*Enough!*" said Amaka. The handful of patrons on the other side of the tavern turned round and stared at the trio. They immediately resumed their conversations after a moment's interest. "We don't have time for this."

"Your girlfriend is right."

The durbar let go of the durbar, who concealed his weapon immediately. Both men sat down.

"She's not my girlfriend."

"Why not? She's pretty." Musa Gindiri let out a big sigh. "Garba, you could've just disappeared. Started a new life. Sokoto wanted any excuse for a war. If it hadn't been you, it would've been someone else. The order let you down. Why bother coming back?"

"Because there are bigger things at play Musa."

"We're here because I need your help," interjected Amaka at long last. "I'm Amaka, Garba Mansa's *friend*."

"Chiamaka?" asked Musa Gindiri.

"Yes. You know the name?" she asked.

"It means *god is beautiful*." Musa picked up an empty jug and raised it. "She certainly is."

Amaka smiled while Garba Mansa rolled his eyes. "I need an armed escort," she said.

"Do I look like I'm in a fit state to fight, let alone escort anyone anywhere?" asked Musa Gindiri.

"You look like a man without purpose. A man who's lost his way in life," replied Amaka bluntly.

"*Ouch.*" Musa Gindiri looked at Garba Mansa. "She's pretty but cutting. Sleep with both eyes open brother."

"Master Gindiri, Garba Mansa said that he had the most trustworthy friends, who would give their lives for his if necessary. We're in a desperate situation. We need help urgently but it has to be the right kind. Many lives are at stake."

"Why so urgent and who are *we*?" asked Musa Gindiri.

"We're a community, a refuge for women and children fleeing persecution. Our survival depends on secrecy. That's why we choose help with the greatest discretion. We need an escort to find a new place of safety during the war. A village not far from our location has already been burned to the ground. Garba Mansa can't help us on his own. Will you help him?"

"Why can't Garba help on his own? He fights well and can even come back from the dead."

"There are over fifty of us. A few of us can fight but even with Garba Mansa's help, the odds will be stacked against us."

"Even with the great Garba Mansa," mused Musa Gindiri. "Hypothetically speaking, how many would you need to improve your odds?"

"The more of you the better. We don't just need muscle, your strategy would also be greatly appreciated. We want to avoid conflict."

"I've heard of this community of yours, not from Garba though. Don't worry, I thought it was just a myth. An urban legend to make us men feel better about our worst selves." Musa Gindiri pointed a finger at his friend. "Garba here thought that the mysterious woman in black was from your tribe. Who knows, she may've been at some point. Now we know she was the daughter of our friend before she became the daughter of our enemy."

"So will you help us?"

"I can't do it without you brother," said Garba Mansa.

The dishevelled durbar looked long and hard at his brother in arms and his companion. He looked down at the empty jugs of palm wine and around the tavern at the day drinkers steadily cruising their way to an early grave.

"Why not be kind to strangers, lest they be angels in disguise? The wine in here tastes like cat piss anyway." Musa Gindiri put his right hand out across the table. Garba Mansa shook his forearm in the characteristic durbar handshake and smiled.

"Excellent. What of the others?" asked Garba Mansa.

"The non-council members went back to the army. Ugo took a job in the royal court, interpreting for the linguistically and intellectually challenged."

"Hakeem and Kazeem?" asked Garba Mansa.

"They didn't fancy being average either so they left too."

"To do what?"

"What they do best," replied Musa Gindiri.

Amaka looked confused. "What's that?"

Musa Gindiri smiled. "Fight."

#

The shots to the body barely registered. The punch to the jaw had ached but the real stinger was the one that landed on his nose. The burning pain that radiated up to his eyes and made them water had been a distraction. A distraction from following the script to drag out the fight and risk succumbing to the temptation of pummelling the mediocre fighter in front of him. In between his guard and the head of his opponent, the fight promoter's oafish grin shone in the background and reminded him of what was at stake financially if the fight didn't last the agreed number of rounds. Kazeem Urumu lowered his guard and deliberately telegraphed a wild swing with his left hand by pulling back his left shoulder. His opponent stepped to the side, dropped at the knees to evade the speculative attack and landed two punches on both sides of Kazeem's left kidney. The durbar dropped his guard in response and was rewarded with a right hook to his cheek. The crowd of degenerates roared as he stumbled sideways into the dusty terrain of the field. While on his knees he absorbed a couple of kicks to the ribs before the sound of a horn signalled the end of the round.

Kazeem Urumu wandered to his corner and wiped the sweat from his head with a rag. He bent down, took a swig of warm water from a pouch, gargled it and spat it out. As he got up there was a twinge on his left side. He'd been a little too generous presenting that target and would put his opponent back in his place a little before the end of the next round. Kazeem felt inside his mouth with his index finger and thumb. No wobbly teeth. Excellent. He then pressed one nostril with his thumb, cleared the other one and repeated the process on the other side. One more round to go before he could wrap this up. He checked the strapping on his knuckles and wrists then rolled his neck to the left then the right. The horn sounded again.

As Kazeem Urumu set off to resume the charade, he was rooted to the spot by something. The sound of the low-rent crowd dissipated and the only sense he was tuned in to was the sight of the three late arrivals to the spectacle. For a moment he wondered whether he was hallucinating but his other intact faculties indicated that he hadn't been hit hard or often enough. He rubbed his eyes just to be sure. They were still there, looking at him. The trio stood out from the rest of the crowd with their calm demeanour. They ignored the fight promoter pestering them to place a bet and outwardly appeared disinterested in watching the two grown men beat each other to a pulp. Two of the new arrivals nodded and smiled at him in recognition. The third, a woman, just observed him. Kazeem knew he had to speak to them sooner rather than later.

His opponent, so far comparatively unscathed, came from his corner with a relative spring in his step. He was undoubtedly convinced that he would continue as he'd begun, doling out more of a thrashing to the supposed ex-military fighter, who'd been laughably touted as a real challenge. He'd looked the part with his solid physique and clearly had aerobic fitness but he'd demonstrated nothing other than an ability to take a beating. It would be good to end the fight quickly and if time permitted, get another fight in before the sun went down. As he approached him, his hapless opponent walked towards him with his hands down by his sides like an amateur. It was all too easy.

Kazeem Urumu rapidly walked up to his opponent. Without breaking stride he waited until he was less than arm's length away.

Then, without any shift in bodyweight or major movement of his shoulders, he threw a left straight punch that landed squarely just beneath the nose of his opponent.

The man's eyes rolled back in his head, his right arm went up in a tonic posture and he fell backwards into the dirt, unconscious. The betting crowd fell silent and the fight promoter's jaw dropped in shock. Kazeem Urumu casually returned to his corner, put his top back on, finished his water and went over towards the new arrivals.

"*We had a deal!*" shouted the fight promoter.

"And you now have my match fee as a penalty," said the victorious fighter dismissively. "If you wish to contest it, by all means get strapped up and we can discuss it further."

The exasperated promoter watched the durbar disappear into the crowd before he was accosted by the minority of spectators who'd bet favourably on the durbar fighter.

Kazeem Urumu and Garba Mansa stared at each other for a few moments before the former spoke. "Back from the dead?"

"The afterlife wasn't quite ready for me."

"Welcome back brother." Kazeem Urumu put out a muscular arm and the two men shook hands the durbar way. He nodded at Musa Gindiri.

"This is Garba's girlfriend Amaka," said the poet.

Kazeem nodded at the woman then looked at Garba Mansa, who shook his head.

"Let's walk and talk," said Kazeem. "It's not just the fights round here that have a price. Information also goes to the highest bidder."

The four of them moved away from the disappointed crowd. Garba Mansa explained his disappearance and their betrayal as they walked. Kazeem Urumu shook his head in disbelief at the shocking news and remained silent. As before, Amaka put forward her request for urgent assistance.

"So what do you say?" asked Garba Mansa.

"Master Asari used us…he used you…the emirate has used us to fight their battles and keep the peace…now your friend wants to use us…admittedly for a noble cause," said Kazeem Urumu. "We're everybody's expendable asset. Aren't you tired of being used Garba?"

"Would you rather carry on your theatrical fighting out here?" mocked Musa Gindiri.

"At least my theatrics are in the real world, not on a piece of paper or in the bottom of a jug of cheap wine," countered Kazeem Urumu. "Why don't you put your toys down and see how long you last using your bare hands?"

"What about the war?" asked Garba Mansa, bringing back the fighter's focus.

"What about it? It'll never end," said Kazeem. "If it's not them killing us, it's us killing them or someone else being killed."

"So fight for what's right," said Garba Mansa.

"Right according to who? Me? You?" argued Kazeem.

"My people don't want trophies," interjected Amaka. "They don't want to take anyone's land or impose their beliefs. They just want a chance at survival. But they need help."

"I have to say, Hakeem's going to be pretty disappointed," said Musa Gindiri.

"What do you mean?" asked Kazeem, caught off-guard by the comment.

"Taking all the glory for himself. He didn't take much convincing to join us," continued the durbar poet. "I wouldn't want to be the one to tell him his brother didn't fancy a challenge."

"He agreed?" asked Kazeem.

"Indeed he did." Musa Gindiri winked at Amaka as the confused durbar searched her face for a response. She kept diplomatically quiet.

"Why didn't you say so from the beginning?" said Kazeem.

"I guess we didn't want you to be driven by an unnecessary competitive desire to outdo your nearest and dearest," said Musa Gindiri.

"So you're in?" asked Garba Mansa.

"When do we ride out?"

Chapter Twenty-Eight

He wasn't going fast enough. She looked over her shoulder. They were gaining on her with alarming alacrity. Had there been only one of them, she could've chanced firing a warning shot from her bow. Perhaps a wounding hit would have sufficed to throw him off her tail and force a retreat. Without killing her pursuer, that plan ran the risk of a wounded or angry soldier returning with reinforcements. In reality the scout was outnumbered six to one. Six armed soldiers in blood red uniforms. If they caught up with her it was unimaginable what they'd do to her for her evasion. Of greater concern was what would happen to the others if they found the camp. Survival was now her second priority. She had to warn them before more came. If she reached the community before they closed the gap, she stood a fighting chance. If not, she'd die in the wilderness.

As the scout reached the edge of the forest, she lifted her ivory horn to her lips while awkwardly holding onto the reins with one hand. She blew into the side of it several times to raise the alarm. As her horse continued at full tilt, she prayed that defensive positions would be taken up by the time she reached the base. The scout looked over her shoulder again. Swords were drawn. There was no more shouting. The intention to harm was clear and the aggressors had followed her into the forest. A horn sounded several times in the distance. There was hope but the prolonged sprint was taking its toll on her steed, whose breathing had become laboured and his acceleration impaired. The sound of pursuing hooves crept closer and closer as desperation set in. The clearing in the woods remained a speck of light in the distance between the trees. Suddenly things got worse. As they got closer to help, her horse caught its leg in a divot, causing it to stumble. The momentum from the sudden deceleration threw the scout clear of her saddle.

#

After hearing the multiple distant horn blows and the subsequent replies from within the camp, Isa rushed to the largest enclosure to see what was happening. Something was obviously wrong. The community's most athletic women ran past him. Armed with swords and carrying bows and arrows over their shoulders, they handed each other spears. Everyone was ready for a fight. Once defensive positions had been taken up around the camp, Nkem and the white-haired woman ushered the other community members and their children into the largest enclosure.

"*Get inside!*" ordered Nkem as she stomped her way to the tent. She also carried a spear in one hand and her bow and arrows sat awkwardly on her round shoulders and stocky frame. She didn't stop to listen to Isa's response and carried on marshalling others to safety. It had been a couple of days since Master and Amaka had gone to get help and his gut told him they had some part to play in the frenzy.

The whole camp waited in unsettling silence. Frightened mothers covered the mouths of their chatterbox children within the enclosure, while around the camp perimeter, arrow ends cradled taught bow strings stretched by sweaty fingers. Nobody moved. Isa had followed the advice to seek refuge and sat among the community members at the assembly point. Adults held the hands of other adults and children alike. Everyone was unified by the fear of what threat existed in close proximity to their sanctuary. None of them had taken for granted the privilege of waking up every day feeling safe, since settling in the community. The community leader turned around and motioned for everyone to remain where they were and keep quiet until it was confirmed the coast was clear. Nkem then went to survey the camp for herself.

Her body tensed up as she heard multiple horses approaching. The archer kneeling beside her gently trembled from adrenaline with excitement, fear or both in excess. Not only had Nkem gone through the drills many times in different locations, she'd been instrumental in creating them. Externally she was used to being their rock. Internally she was as susceptible as anyone to the impact of fear resurrecting life's past traumas. Near-death experiences were never forgotten but could be reasonably managed, provided such moments of heightened stress or apparent danger were few and far between thereafter. Today was one of those moments. Her sisters would give a good account of themselves if the fight came to them but deep down, she knew that the resistance would be very short lived if the durbar's prediction came to fruition. For the first time since Amaka had broken the sacred rule and brought him into their midst, Nkem wished the stranger was by their side.

#

The scout landed awkwardly on her shoulder but rolled immediately and got to her feet. There wasn't enough time to get back on the horse. She had to make a stand. The scout pulled her bow off her shoulders, faced her enemies and reached for an arrow. Her plight instantly became clearer. Her fall had broken the weapon. She discarded the broken bow, unsheathed her sword, held it in two hands and stood in a wide low stance. This was it.

The nearest rider accelerated towards his target, while the others slowed down to watch the mismatch. There was a smirk on the rider's face as he closed in on the woman, with his sword raised above his head. The scout managed to block his attack but the impact, together with the speed of his approach, was powerful enough to knock her sword clean out of her hands and drive her backwards. The rider went past her, turned around and observed his defenceless target before setting off again. The scout took off her ivory horn, held it with the pointed end out and prepared herself for the next attack. The rider galloped towards her with his sword held high once more. The other soldiers were stationary, clearly enjoying the spectacle. As the soldier approached, the scout gripped the horn with her right hand as tight as she could and balled a fist with her other hand. She looked the advancing rider dead in the eye and let out an almighty battle cry as her end came nearer.

#

As the soldier's sword came down, his body went limp and he slid off the accelerating horse, falling by the feet of the stunned scout. The horse veered away from its intended target and carried on moving. The scout looked down at the dead soldier in total disbelief. Having spotted the arrow sticking out of his neck, she picked up the dead man's sword and looked around her surroundings immediately. Nothing. The remaining soldiers were equally puzzled and also momentarily looked around for the shooter. Nothing.

"*Aargh!!!*"

An arrow hit the nearest rider square in the shoulder. He dropped his sword and the troupe were immediately shocked out of their static confusion. They turned their horses around and scrambled away from the scout as if she were invisible.

Within seconds more hooves were heard. The scout saw four figures in the distance, closing in on the fleeing soldiers on one side. On the other side a lone familiar figure sat atop a horse, with her bowstring taught and an arrow in the firing position. The figure released the string and a fraction of a second later the wounded soldier was jolted to one side, rolled off his saddle but held onto the reins of his horse in desperation. The attempt to stay on his horse proved fatal. The horse twisted awkwardly and fell, landing on him. The surviving soldiers were now the ones being pursued.

\#

Outside the forest, the four durbar horsemen were in full pursuit of the Sokoto cavalry. One pair had gone in one direction, while the other had fled in another. Hakeem Urumu raced alongside the furthest Sokoto soldier while the man swung wildly at him with his sword. Hakeem reached below his saddle with one hand and unhooked a bullwhip. He waited patiently for the next few swings and allowed the man to commit himself. Then Hakeem edged closer while gripping tightly onto one end of the bull whip and flung it violently out to the side. The other end wrapped around the neck of the Sokoto soldier, causing him to drop his weapon in panic and grab his throat. The struggle was futile, as Hakeem Urumu jerked the whip downwards and pulled the man off his horse. The man hit the ground head-first but his demise continued. He was immediately trampled by the horse of his fellow soldier, which immediately buckled, launching the next soldier airborne. Hakeem slowed his horse down to a canter and set off for the fallen soldier.

By the time Hakeem had dismounted, the fallen soldier was back to his feet and his sword was in hand. Unfortunately for the Sokoto man, the distance to his horse was too great to cover. Specifically, the hulking frame of an armed durbar stood in his way. The man looked terrified. He looked over the durbar's shoulder at an oncoming horse. Hakeem Urumu turned his head slightly to acknowledge the sound of his brother approaching on horseback. He walked slowly towards the Sokoto soldier with his bull whip in hand. The adversaries locked eyes. The durbar shook his head slowly, warning the panicked soldier that armed resistance held only one realistic outcome. The soldier ignored the silent recommendation and charged at the durbar. The sound of hooves grew louder.

The soldier made it within a few steps of his adversary before a sword came down from upon high and landed squarely in his chest. With his movement checked and his face a mask of frozen perplexity, the soldier collapsed. As his brother circled around them to survey his kill and retrieve his sword, Hakeem Urumu raised his hands exasperated.

"*I had that!*" he shouted.

"Of course you did brother," said Kazeem Urumu. He dismounted, nonchalantly rolled the dead soldier over with his foot and pulled his sword out of him. He wiped the blade on the dead man's torso. "But you can never be too careful."

#

Elsewhere the pursuit continued. Musa Gindiri swung two small rocks, connected by chord, rapidly above his head before throwing them forward once they'd gained sufficient momentum. The rocks immediately wrapped around the legs of the fugitive's horse, tying them up and tripping it to unseat its passenger in the process. Garba Mansa's approach was far more direct. He got level with the man he was pursuing, perched on Sisoko's saddle and launched himself from her, directly into the soldier, causing the two of them to tumble into the dirt. Musa shook his head at his colleague's more dramatic approach and casually dismounted to deal with his own evader.

Musa Gindiri yawned and stretched out his arms as the soldier's horse struggled to get to its bound feet. The upright soldier brandished his sword and paced around the durbar.

"Drop your weapon," demanded the durbar lethargically. "It doesn't have to end like this." The durbar poet unsheathed a dagger from his waist. The soldier from Sokoto looked down at the durbar's much smaller weapon then looked up at the man holding it, with a look of sheer incredulity before charging at the durbar with reckless abandon. His attack lasted barely a second. With a sharp flick of his wrist, Musa

Gindiri tossed his dagger blade at the soldier. Upon impact the soldier stopped abruptly, his wide eyes a picture of disbelief and dropped his weapon. He staggered clumsily from side to side and grabbed the ornate hilt of the blade buried in his throat. By the time Musa Gindiri had walked up to him to retrieve his designer dagger, the man was on his knees. He fell to the side with his eyes fixed open.

Garba Mansa and the final soldier grappled on the ground. The man was very strong, very heavy and a very good fighter. He'd landed one headbutt and a couple of elbows to the durbar's face and kneeled astride him, making good progress at choking the life out of him. The soldier seemed impervious to the knees to his ribs. Despite the asphyxiation, Garba Mansa persevered with the knee strikes while defending his airway. Several attempts later, the soldier slid to the side of him and replaced his hands with his forearm against the durbar's throat. From there, with his legs free, Garba Mansa kicked his legs up and scissored them around his assailant's neck. He desperately squeezed as hard as he could with what little strength he had left. Gradually the Sokoto man released the pressure on his throat and appeared distressed himself, grabbing at the durbar's legs. Garba Mansa maintained the hold until the man went limp. He released his legs and gasped for air as the lifeless man rolled off him.

Sisoko sauntered over to where the struggle had taken place. She stopped and looked down at her exhausted master, as he lay on the ground sweating and catching his breath.

"Not a word."

A couple of minutes later the remaining durbars joined them. They each looked down from their horses at their colleague propping himself up on the ground.

"Sometimes it takes a little time to get back in the saddle," said Musa Gindiri.

"I wasn't going to say anything," said Hakeem Urumu.

"Me neither," said Kazeem.

"When Garba has got his breath back after his little tussle, I suggest we go and see his girlfriend and her community."

#

They were getting closer. The sound of screams in the distance had sent chills down her spine. Nkem's heart was beating so fast she began to feel light-headed. Just as the sound of multiple hooves reached a crescendo, the distinct long solitary note of an ivory horn broke the tension. The community leader and several archers exhaled audibly and the extent of the physical and emotional drain of the standoff became clear. Despite everyone's relief, Nkem wasn't ready to lower the alert level until she had visual confirmation that they were out of danger.

Amaka and the scout were the first to arrive. The former looked unscathed, while the latter looked shaken. The archers lowered their weapons as they entered the clearing. Not long afterwards came the strangers, including the one Amaka had brought back some days before. They glided into the camp and stood out, not only because they were male but also their distinct robes, weapons and most remarkably, their aura of confidence. The strangers brought four extra horses. While waiting for the all clear, curiosity had gotten the better of some community members, particularly the boy that had come with the outsider. Isa peeped through the aperture of the main enclosure and saw that his master had returned. Overcome with relief, the boy couldn't help himself and ran out to greet Master and Sisoko. Isa's unannounced sudden appearance triggered the durbars' reflexive flinch for their weapons. The community defenders reacted as they'd been trained and raised their primed weapons in response. Isa stopped in his tracks. The standoff resumed.

"*Wait!*" shouted Amaka. "They're with us."

Several archers looked at her, then looked at Nkem. The four horsemen stayed cool, calm and collected, careful not to make any sudden movements. Isa froze. The community leader looked at the scout for confirmation.

"She's right. They helped us. I'd be dead otherwise."

"Lower your weapons," ordered Nkem calmly. "These are our allies." The archers responded accordingly. Master smiled and nodded at Isa, who looked embarrassed at heightening the anxiety in his orbit. The boy delicately manoeuvred his way past the wall of archers and greeted Sisoko by rubbing her mane. The horse rubbed her snout against his face.

Nkem turned to the scout. "What happened?"

"Soldiers…lots of them…the army…not far away…they followed me…I thought I was going to…" The adrenaline appeared to leave her body and she half collapsed in her saddle. Another archer jumped up to catch her before she hit the ground. The scout came to as she was carefully helped up.

"Get her seen to," said Nkem. Another archer put one of the scout's arms around her neck and with the help of the woman already supporting her weight, both women carried the scout away. The durbars dismounted from their horses and looked around as other community members began to emerge from the main enclosure to judge the outcome for themselves. The community defenders put their bows and arrows away, while a handful of them rounded up the spears, before dispersing to different parts of the camp. A few stayed behind to listen to the exchange with the newcomers. The white-haired elder emerged from the main enclosure and approached them as the conversation continued. Nkem looked at Amaka, her most experienced scout. "The soldiers?"

"All dead."

"Where were they from?" asked Nkem.

"Sokoto," said Garba Mansa. "Their uniforms confirmed it," he continued, pre-empting the next question. "No doubt plenty more will follow."

"Thank you for coming back, durbar master. I see you brought help." Nkem looked at the others, who all nodded a greeting. "You're not many but we are grateful for your help nonetheless. How much time do we have?" she asked.

"Not long. How long was your scout gone for?"

"Only a few hours. Not long."

"Which direction did she travel?" asked Garba Mansa.

"North, north east of here."

Garba Mansa looked at his brothers in arms. Their expressions were grave. Musa Gindiri shook his head ever so slightly.

"What's wrong?" asked Nkem.

"Gather everyone and everything you can. You now have extra horses. We need to leave now."

Chapter Twenty-Nine

The long procession of horses, carts, women and children travelled through the night. Fuelled by hypervigilance and the will to survive, the community pushed through the overwhelming fatigue to reach their destination before sunrise. They settled in a secluded area south-east of Kano, an area that would keep them a safe distance from harm's way. At least for the time being. The community's armed protectors kept watch while the more vulnerable members succumbed to their exhaustion and enjoyed a well-earned rest.

Rejuvenated by a few hours respite from travel, the durbar escort prepared to return to the Gidan Rumfa and rejoin the war effort. As they left, an unexpected recruit volunteered to return with them. Amaka helped unload the belongings of other community members but had left her own horse untouched. Never one to miss a trick, Nkem eyed her deputy curiously and approached her privately.

"Not staying?" asked the matriarch directly.

Amaka's eyes gravitated to the soft earth and betrayed her conflicting feelings of guilt and duty. "I have to do something."

"You *are* doing something," said Nkem. "You're helping keep us safe."

"I can only do so much here and it's only a matter of time before the fight comes to us."

"So you want to take the fight to them?"

"Why not?" argued Amaka.

"Because when they kill you, nothing will have changed and I'll have lost my…" Nkem's voice wavered uncharacteristically. "Did the durbar put you up to this?"

"*Haba*, no!" Amaka looked bemused, if not slightly offended. "I'm not a child."

"But he's made an impression on you."

"You think the durbar has me under some kind of spell?" asked Amaka.

"We're not all as strong as we think we are," cautioned Nkem. "It happens to the best of us."

"Well just so you know, I haven't been bewitched by a durbar and I *am* as strong as I think I am. The durbar fights for what is right. He didn't have to come back and help us and he doesn't have to go back and fight the war but he chooses to. That would leave an impression on anyone."

"We need you here."

"There'll be no here if this war doesn't stop. By staying here, I can't change anything. If I fight with them, maybe I can change something. You'll survive without me."

"Fine." Nkem tried a different approach. "What makes you so sure these men will accept a woman fighting by their side? What if your durbar is not around to protect you?"

"Anyone who believes a woman cannot fight is a fool," said Amaka defiantly. "Women have been instrumental in this war. And you know better than anyone, I'm no longer the frightened girl that came to you."

"And you're just as stubborn now as you were then. Say you survive this war, how will you find us? It's likely we'll move again soon."

"My sister, if I'm meant to find you, I'll find you." Amaka lifted the ivory horn from her chest and smiled. At that moment Garba Mansa came over to them.

"We're ready to go," he said.

Nkem grabbed Amaka unexpectedly and embraced her tightly. Then she whispered in her ear. "Find us soon my sister."

In an emotional farewell, the community members exchanged goodbyes with Amaka and thanked the strangers one last time. Nkem watched the durbars and their latest addition disappear on the horizon. Deep down, she knew she'd never see Amaka again.

#

Heads turned in the sentry towers and on the ground, as the four turbaned horsemen in colourful, almost regal attire passed through the palace main gate. They were accompanied by a familiar looking boy and a slender figure in plain clothing, with dark cloth obscuring the face and head. The guards of the Gidan Rumfa silently applauded the return of the horsemen with measured nods and smiles as they proceeded through the grounds. The durbars responded to the welcoming gestures with modest restraint. After securing their horses, the group headed straight for the main courtroom.

#

The feather's quill furiously etched more names onto the candlelit paper. Its holder's hand hovered over the page, ready for the next entry in the registration book of the main courtroom antechamber. Not expecting anyone of significant importance that day, the official didn't bother looking up from the book as he waited to sign in the new arrivals.

"State your name and business," he said.

There was a long pause. The official sighed a bored sigh, with his head still down and his quill still poised to touch paper. "*State your name and business.*"

"Kazeem Urumu."

"Hakeem Urumu."

"Musa Gindiri."

"Garba Mansa."

The feather's quill never touched the paper. Instead, the official slowly looked up from the registration book, with his mouth agape. Four imposing figures stared back at him in the candlelight.

"We also have Chiamaka and Isa with us," said Garba Mansa. "We demand an audience with his excellency. We know where to wait."

The official nodded and pointed to the side room to his left, with his mouth still open. Once the visitors were out of sight, the official shot out of his chair and ran to report their arrival.

#

Having unwrapped the scarf covering her face, Amaka took in the ornate décor of the waiting room while sipping tea from a pewter cup and ignored the unsubtle stares from the old man in the beige kaftan and green turban. Isa took pleasure in watching someone else bedazzled by the splendour of the palace interior. The moment was abruptly interrupted by the sound of many heavy feet approaching the room. Amaka put her cup down and everyone's attention turned to the side room's entrance. After a few moments of uneasy silence, the registration official awkwardly materialised in the doorway.

"His excellency will receive you now," he said.

The durbars looked at one another. Musa Gindiri nominated himself to articulate what everyone was thinking. "Will that be with or without the armed escort?"

The registration official smiled uncomfortably then bent his knees and shifted his body weight from side to side, like a child doing its best not to pee in its pants. "His excellency will receive you now," repeated the official mechanically.

"Let's get this over with," said Garba Mansa. He turned to Amaka and Isa. "Wait here. This shouldn't take long."

"Famous last words," said Musa Gindiri dryly.

As the durbars followed the official, Amaka grabbed Garba Mansa by the arm.

"Are you sure you want to do this?" she asked him. "They could execute you. You can still fight without them."

"It's the right thing to do," replied Garba Mansa. "I promise I'll be back."

With his parting promise, the durbar and his fellow warriors followed the registration official to the waiting escort of forty palace guards lined up on both sides of the corridor leading to the main courtroom. The old man in the beige kaftan filled two more pewter teacups as Isa and Amaka waited anxiously.

#

Arrogant. Naïve. Stupid. Being around Amaka and her band of persecuted idealists had clouded his judgement. It had been foolish to believe his reappearance would have any outcome other than immediate incarceration. The initial welcoming gestures from the palace security on their arrival had been a smokescreen. An illusion of an anticipated homecoming. A fantasy of military solidarity. The reckless optimism of blind loyalty was immediately dealt a crushing dose of reality. There was no standoff. Musa Gindiri gave the armed escort no witty repartee and the Urumu brothers' carnage count was nil. The final gamble of surrender was a passive process, completely devoid of any bravado. The durbar fugitive was separated from his brethren, put in chains and immediately hauled off to a cell.

In the cold solitude of his cage, Garba Mansa tried in vain to shut out all thoughts of anger, betrayal and the executioner's blade. This time visitors were forbidden. Ordering his thoughts was challenging. Preparing a coherent defence of events since his last incarceration, even more so. His brief time with Amaka's community would need edited highlights, lest he betray their safety in secrecy. Rattled, Garba Mansa closed his eyes and waited.

#

The trial of Durbar Master Garba Mansa was a one-sided affair, with the defendant called as his only witness. The contrary was true for the prosecution, with multiple witnesses ranging from aggrieved palace guards to the Minister of Justice himself testifying. The charge was treason. Punishable by death. The Minister of Defence avoided the gaze of his shackled elite soldier, marooned in the central aisle of the courtroom under the scrutiny of the ministers summoned at short notice surrounding him. When the court official announced the entrance of Emir Ado Sanusi of Kano, it wasn't until the horn-blowers heralded his entrance with the distinct sound of the kakaki, that Garba Mansa snapped out of his meditative state. The final arbiter of justice, in a radiant green babanriga and white turban, sat on his throne with select members of his entourage. The stage was set for the trial to begin.

The justice minister had the scent of blood in his nostrils and the taste of revenge on his lips. "Excellency, honourable attendees. Garba Mansa will have you believe that he, the loyal son of Kano, has returned to serve his kingdom once more. I put it to you that his cowardice, sabotage and treachery, under the tutelage of his master, the traitor and former durbar council chairman Jibril Asari, has plunged this kingdom into a war with our greatest foe. I put it to you that he has returned to guarantee his immunity from harm, while continuing to plot our ongoing downfall, as the disciple of a traitor and an agent of a foreign power."

The minister's opening words were unrepentant in their vitriol. As the veins at the side of his weasley head bulged with unfettered venom, there were nods, scowls and head shakes from the floor. The Emir's people looked largely unmoved by the display, while the monarch himself gave nothing away and watched proceedings with objective neutrality.

Garba Mansa sat through the character assassination expressionless, inwardly bemused by the fervour with which the justice minister pursued his personal vendetta against him. The only words of resonance were those pertaining to Jibril Asari. The scale of his betrayal truly became apparent when Garba Mansa looked around the room and silently acknowledged to himself that everyone present, from the court official to the Emir himself, had been duped by his mentor. Perhaps a guilty proxy would wash their hands of the durbar council chairman's high crimes and remove the spectre of suspicion from all who'd entrusted their faith in him.

More witnesses came and went. Like the justice minister, none offered direct evidence confirming Garba Mansa's guilt and merely piled on further speculation that neither added to nor detracted from the case against him. As his chances of acquittal seemed ever more unlikely, an unexpected voice disrupted the air of inevitability.

"*Excellency, Master Mansa is innocent.*"

Those with their backs to him, including the accused, turned around to identify the sole dissenting voice. Ugo Itojo's lean physique stood tall and proud at the back of the courtroom. The Minister of Justice frowned at the interruption. The attention of the royal stage came alive with the disruption.

"Garba Mansa is no criminal."

"The words of a durbar, albeit one currently employed within the palace grounds where one can keep an eye on him," sneered the justice minister. "The words of this outsider have no place—"

"*Silence,*" said the Emir, opening his mouth for the first time. "Let him speak."

As the justice minister sat down, the durbar linguist stood taller. "I am most grateful excellency. Garba Mansa is innocent of the alleged crimes. These allegations are baseless. If he is guilty of anything at all, Garba Mansa is guilty of loyalty. Loyalty to his kingdom. Loyalty to his brethren. Loyalty to a fault. How quickly have we forgotten this man's service to the emirate? Within the breath of an allegation? This man *willingly* sacrificed himself to our enemy to prevent a war." At that moment, the Minister of Defence caught the speaker's eyes and shifted uncomfortably in his velvet seat. "Upon his betrayal," continued Ugo Itojo, "he *still* came back to where his heart lies. And now we want to reward him by cutting off his head? Jibril Asari betrayed us all and nobody feels greater shame and disgust for this than my brother in chains. Excellency, I urge you not to execute this man."

As Ugo Itojo sat down, Garba Mansa gave him a solemn nod of gratitude, before turning to face his sovereign. There was a long silence before the Emir spoke for a second time.

"Many have spoken against you durbar master," he said in his quiet voice. "Only one has spoken in your favour. What do *you* have to say in your defence?"

All eyes were on the man in the middle.

"Thank you for the opportunity, excellency. Let me start by telling you about my service to the kingdom."

With that, Garba Mansa bowed his head and lifted his bound hands up to his chest. His noisy chains swung with his movements. Then he began to strain. Confusion closely followed by shock permeated the courtroom, as the durbar ripped the clothes from his body. Gasps accompanied the sound of tearing fabric. Garba Mansa tore the clothing around his legs until the remaining intact fabric barely protected his modesty. When he'd finished, the courtroom was divided between those who believed he'd lost his mind and those who thought his behaviour was his last protest before he'd eventually lose his head. Even the justice minister was lost for words. Garba Mansa moved his hands in front of his left flank.

"This wound was courtesy of an assassin in Sokoto, while I fought alongside an observer from the same kingdom. An observer who was unlucky enough to be observing the right man at the wrong time." Garba Mansa stuck his arms out in front of him, as far as his shackles allowed. "The cuts on my arms came courtesy of the blade of Amina Asari, the daughter of Jibril Asari." He waited for the gasps to die down before continuing with his head down and his hands hovering over his thighs. "The same blade did this to my legs. Having freed me from the escort to Sokoto, her father didn't take kindly to my refusal to join their quest for regime change and to lie in bed with our enemies. The skeptical among you may consider that these wounds might be self-inflicted." Garba Mansa smiled briefly. "The pain and the depth of the wounds aside, I challenge the kingdom's greatest contortionist to inflict on themselves the wound on my back, just above my kidney. That was the parting gift of Adesua Asari, the traitor's wife, an even more skilled fighter than her daughter." The courtroom was silent. "All these wounds and many more tell of my history in the service of the emirate. A history it has been the greatest honour of my life to have lived, breathed and suffered. With the clarity of my true purpose and the kindness of strangers, my wounds have healed. Excellency, if I should soon perish, let it be on the battlefield, with a sword in my hand, fighting for Kano, until my last breath."

The ministers, officials and the royal family were speechless. The justice minister evaded the gaze of the ragged half-naked durbar, his scarred skin a tapestry of brutal conflict. Where his confidence in the guilt of the accused had seemed unshakeable earlier, with the pending verdict an almost certainty, even he was moved by Garba Mansa's testimony laid bare. The uncomfortable, infrequent feeling of doubt hung over him like a cloud.

For Ugo Itojo, he felt sick, guilty of betrayal by association. Despite his brother's dignified account of himself restoring some pride to the name of the durbar order, he felt ashamed to be part of a system that punished those that defended it with such disregard for their own wellbeing. If he was to be executed, Garba Mansa's honourable exit from this world would be scant consolation.

"The defendant has spoken well. As has the prosecution," decreed Emir Sanusi. "Both can unequivocally agree that Jibril Asari's heinous betrayal is a stain not only on the durbar order but also our kingdom. Betrayal of this magnitude cannot and will not go unpunished. I have no doubt that the repercussions of his actions have contributed to the shattering of peace and the current reality of war. Indeed in this time of war we must hold onto our allies and bleed ourselves of traitors. If what Garba Mansa says is true, he must be commended for returning to accept responsibility in the part he unwittingly played in Jibril Asari's treachery. He has been a loyal servant of the emirate and his willingness to continue fighting for us is admirable." There was a long pause before the Emir continued. "If Garba Mansa does not speak the truth, he must be punished in the severest way possible. I ask the almighty's guidance before final judgement is passed."

Chapter Thirty

The sky was ominously grey. The clouds quenching the thirst of the dusty plains of Katsina hadn't featured in his last vision. Several months had passed since the last droplet of rainfall had touched the soil, yet the heavens seemed likely to open on that day of all days. His vision of a caged emir had come to fruition, yet nobody had predicted how masterfully he'd manipulate such a powerful ally into declaring all out war on its greatest foe. With the shanci fighter and architects of the new order by his side, Chancellor Atiku Danladi proudly marvelled at their combined forces. In their thousands, in the dark blue and purple of Katsina and the red of Sokoto, peppered by the nondescript colours of assorted mercenaries, they approached the zenith of the campaign.

A blanket of green uniforms covered the opposing plains. A tiny fraction of these opposing forces were in atypical attire. Of those dressed atypically, twelve stood out from the others on horseback. Although heavily armed, with swords, double-ended spears, daggers and the like, their battle dress was more stately than military. This was true for all but one of them. The newest member was heavily kitted out with weaponry but more modest in her appearance, with her face and head obscured by dark cloth. These atypical warriors rode in unity with their swords held high despite all that had recently come to pass. Other than being significantly outnumbered by the combined forces of the enemy, there was one other key difference with the opposing forces. Their ruler was notable for his absence from the battlefield. Unlike his adversary, viewing the conflict from the safety of distant higher ground, the Emir of Kano would hear the story of the battle of Katsina from the mouths of others. In his place, the wards of the elite cavalry watched and waited with a mixture of excitement and trepidation for the latest chapter in the history of the bloody rivalry between the two kingdoms to be written.

Far from the front line, the drummers on both sides squeezed the leather cords of the kalangu, varying its pitch as they beat each talking drum with sticks with curved ends and their fingers. The sound of the drums was heard over the hills long before the armies were visible. The message conveyed long and loud by the instruments was a simple warning. *Turn back, surrender or be destroyed.*

The marching armies came to a standstill in a plateau between the hills. The kalangu stopped. As the drummers retreated further back in their respective lines, there was a temporary eerie silence. With the warning sent out, the drummers were replaced by horn-blowers wielding their kakaki. The time for negotiation had come and gone. On both sides the kakaki were blown long and hard.

#

The clouds responded and the heavens opened. The sound of thunder almost drowned out the thousands of colliding battle cries and stampeding feet. As heavy rain drenched the battlefield, the clattering of metal against metal, bone against bone, the relentless penetration of armour, flesh and the accompanying screams were muffled by the downpour. The torrential rain rapidly nullified the accuracy of any archers and their attack was quickly abandoned as the ever advancing foot soldiers became increasingly likely to be taken out by their own side. With their height advantage at close quarters and superior speed, the cavalry hacked down the opposing infantry. This was where the momentum swung the way of the smaller army. Recruiting horseless mercenaries for the combined forces had been a critical oversight. The cavalry of Kano was greater in number and better trained than their opposition. While Musa Gindiri deftly scythed his way through the enemy with his long blade, the Urumu brothers used axes and bladed clubs designed solely to inflict maximum carnage. And inflict it they did. The rainfall turned red from splatter and limbs flew through the air as the brothers bludgeoned their way through the opposing army. Alongside them Garba Mansa dispatched all comers with ruthless efficiency. Even in the rain his personal objective was crystal clear. He wasn't only fighting for Kano, he was clearing the way to settle the score of all scores. Those that were missed by her master, Sisoko trampled like an ethereal mare, a shadow in the dim light, cutting a path to the afterlife, leaving a swathe of bodies in her wake.

Amaka's first taste of battle was terrifying. Blood, mud and rain obscured her vision while the sound of her heavy breathing was broken up by the screams all around her. Her first kill on the battlefield, her second in life, was a surreal and haunting experience. An infantryman attempted to pull her from her horse and grabbed her shield. Amaka reflexively swiped her spear to knock him away but accidentally caught the man across his throat, slitting it open. She stared at him, her face no longer covered by the headscarf, as he frantically clutched at his throat and stared back at her in disbelief. Killing her husband the day she'd attempted to leave him had been more fraught. Even though it was in self-defence, it had filled her with such shame that to date she'd never told a soul the full details of her escape from her abusive marriage. From the first battlefield kill onwards, Amaka thought of the scorched village and every other image of extreme cruelty she could fill her mind with to distract her from the bloodshed being wreaked around her.

#

From the safety of his raised shelter on the hilltop, Grand Vizier Gidado Buhari watched the advancing tide of the Kano forces with dismay. The enemy was outnumbered but fought with such an unnatural ferocity that a non-believer could almost have been forgiven for thinking that they'd been possessed by spirits. In some cases they were literally tearing apart his forces. The violence wasn't the problem. Violence didn't bother the Grand Vizier. He wasn't phased by pain or suffering. Watching soldiers being mercilessly hacked to pieces or trampled by horses didn't so much as raise an eyebrow. It was the fact that they were losing and the speed at which it was happening. The unforeseen weather conditions had taken them by surprise and slowed down their infantry to a snail's pace. His generals avoided eye contact but he knew what they were thinking. They knew they daren't suggest retreat. Not unless they were prepared to go down there and fight until the cowardice left them. On closer inspection, the Kano horsemen seemed to be the biggest contributors to the bloodbath, apparently carving up the battlefield at will. Something had to change. Then something did.

#

A company of cavalry rode down the hillside, bisected their own combined forces and met the advancing Kano forces head on. The combined cavalry was spearheaded by an older man, with flawless obsidian black skin and a white beard. He wore the colours of Katsina in dark blue robes and a purple turban wrapped around his neck. Two other riders in identical attire, with their faces covered by the high-riding turbans around their necks, rode immediately alongside him. This injection of cavalry was impervious to the weather conditions, better drilled than their predecessors and seemed to lift the spirits of the infantry fighting around them. Their leader fought like a younger man, with the pride of fighting for one's people but with greater efficiency of movement. His companions were precise and deadly. Slowly the momentum began to shift back towards the home side.

As the death toll mounted rapidly on both sides, a direct line of sight with his destiny opened up for Garba Mansa. The object of his retribution was fully engaged in combat and hadn't yet laid eyes on him. He took the advantage while it lasted, sheathed his sword, unhooked a spear from Sisoko's saddle and set off. With the old man locked in his sights, the durbar's tunnel vision blocked out all threats on the battlefield, near and far. In tune with her master, Sisoko accelerated with minimal encouragement, as if she herself had a personal score to settle with the man who'd broken her master's heart. The durbar waited until they were a few metres away, reached back and launched the javelin.

Fate, or a lack of awareness of one's surroundings, intervened at the last second. Sisoko stumbled in a ditch en route to revenge. The spear subsequently narrowly missed its target and landed in the neck of Jibril Asari's horse. As the former durbar's horse and its passenger collapsed in the dirt, Garba Mansa was thrown from Sisoko and landed submerged in the dirty ditch water. When he resurfaced, the old man was already on his feet, smiling at him. Garba Mansa didn't have time to curse himself for being blinded by vengeance. He managed to unsheathe his sword just in time to block the overhead attack from someone much closer. Someone in the colours of Katsina. Someone else wielding a durbar sword.

Adesua Asari hacked at Garba Mansa with unbridled rage. She was stronger than he remembered. The blows kept coming as she stood over him. He defended himself with one arm while propping himself up with the other, with half his body still under the muddy water. Then Garba Mansa's vision blurred and pain radiated from his chin to his ears as her boot connected with his jaw. His head fell back into the water and he choked on the sludge suffocating his mouth and nostrils. Still holding his sword, Garba Mansa lifted his head up and coughed immediately. A couple of moments' disorientation was all she needed. Adesua Asari stood on Garba Mansa's sword arm and pinned it underwater. She then stamped on his abdomen, winding him and held her sword blade downwards in both hands in anticipation of burying it in his chest. Her eyes projected pure hatred as she prepared to send Garba Mansa to the afterlife.

#

Fate intervened once more. As her arms came down to impale the durbar, Adesua Asari felt such an almighty blow to her side, that it knocked her several feet away. She landed on her side in the same large ditch, at first unable to breath. Partly because half her face was underwater but also because breathing was suddenly excruciatingly painful. Several ribs were definitely broken. She slowly got to her knees, propped herself up with one hand and held her broken ribcage. Nobody in her life had ever hit her that hard. And she'd taken her fair share of beatings. On all fours, Adesua Asari surveyed the battlefield for her assailant. There was nothing but men fighting in the rain. And a horse. Then panic gripped her. She no longer had her sword and the durbar was nowhere to be seen. Adesua gingerly stood up and reached inside her tunic for a dagger. It was too late.

#

The smile faded from Jibril Asari's face. There was a sudden softness in his eyes that Garba Mansa hadn't seen in a very long time. The softness that one might show when pleading for their loved one to be spared in their final moments. Garba Mansa stared back at his mentor with no such softness. As he held Adesua Asari and drove his sword right the way through, from her back to her front, the durbar's eyes showed no emotion at all. He withdrew his sword and callously dropped her face down in the ditch. Jibril Asari witnessed his wife's execution with wide-eyed shock and disbelief, then launched himself at his former apprentice with a primaeval fury that surpassed any other living being on the battlefield.

#

Isa's fingers trembled as he held Master's glass and metal eye and watched the two generations of durbar collide from a distance. Moments earlier his eyes had welled up as he was certain he'd witness his master's death at the hands of the Asari woman. Sisoko's intervention had been nothing short of miraculous. The next image would stay with him forever. As his master took the Asari woman's life, the durbar's callous action made his stomach turn. The calm, the ease of it, the statement of the execution. The intent to wound another, with the killing an afterthought, was not his master. These were the actions of a man with hatred in his heart. The actions of a man whose heart bled vengeance.

#

Long blade. Short blade. Kick. Knee. Elbow. Weave. Parry. *Clink. Clank.* Armed with blades in each hand, undeterred by the abysmal weather conditions, their weapons moved in a circular flurry. As they made cuts here and there, both men blocked out the pain. The younger man's fighting style was a carbon copy of his mentor's. A younger version without the immediate pain and anger of an irreparable loss. The fight for Katsina had been abandoned. Jibril Asari had only one objective in mind. Kill Garba Mansa. Wounding the old man had the desired impact. The distractions of rage and the overwhelming desire for revenge would eventually cloud his judgement. If Garba Mansa could stay alive for long enough, an opening would present itself.

#

Chancellor Danladi closed his telescope and sighed. If Jibril Asari fell, the cavalry would lose their shape and it wouldn't be long before the foreigners regained the ascendancy. In the longer term, losing him would be detrimental to the rest of the campaign. After all, he'd skilfully coordinated much of it so far. Danladi tapped the shanci fighter on the shoulder and pointed at the battlefield. With two semi-circular swords attached to his back, the shanci fighter lowered the hood of his cloak and set off on horseback to join the fray.

#

In the haze of heavy rain, thunder and lightning, the dreadlocked fighter glided unchallenged through the piles of bodies on the battlefield like an apparition sent from the afterlife. Despite the ongoing fighting, space had cleared around the old man and the durbar. They were both starting to wane from their lengthy physical confrontation. Bloody and bruised, both were badly injured yet neither was willing to yield. The shanci fighter removed one of his circular swords from the scabbard on his back as he slowed his horse down to take out the unwitting durbar. He got to within a few feet of him before a fast moving shadow appeared in his peripheral vision.

Musa Gindiri's horse collided with the mercenary's and their swords immediately clashed. The two steeds jostled one another as the two men wrestled on horseback. The tussle was short-lived as both men fell into the boggy field. Upon landing in the sodden earth, Musa Gindiri was quick to roll away. Grappling with the spiky fighter was a dangerous prospect. He got to his feet and drew two swords. The shanci fighter discarded his cloak. The warrior poet and the dreadlocked fighter were within several feet of the flagging Jibril Asari and Garba Mansa. Staying close to the former durbar master, the shanci fighter drew his second sword, dropped in a low stance and waited. When Musa Gindiri was close, he launched himself at him. The shanci fighter was a feral whirlwind of kicks and double circular sword attacks. The master swordsman dealt with the bladed attacks but struggled to match the mercenary for footwork. Closing down anyone with weapons was the fastest way to subdue them but the shanci fighter was a special challenge. The ethos of his combat system, with blades designed for close range and spikes all over his body, was to draw opponents near and finish them at close quarters, his exceptional speed notwithstanding. The durbar deftly blocked the circular swords and threw a few kicks of his own. Then the opening came. The shanci fighter feinted a round kick to the durbar's arm then dropped the kick lower to implant one of his anklet spikes in the outside of Musa Gindiri's thigh. The pain inhibition rendered the durbar's leg useless and it immediately gave way. As he fell down, the shanci fighter landed a powerful heel to his chest, knocking him onto his back. Before he knew it, dreadlocks were in his face with two circular swords raised above them and his arms were pinned down by the shanci fighter's knees.

#

As the fallen durbar faced decapitation, something yanked the shanci fighter backwards violently. The nimble fighter rolled in the dirt immediately and got to his knees to hack away at the bullwhip coiled around his wrist, dragging him through the mud. The circular blade was almost through the braided leather when the shanci fighter stopped suddenly. He stared at Hakeem Urumu, the bullwhip bearer, with a startled expression and blinked three times before collapsing. Three durbar daggers, from a wounded master swordsman, were embedded in his back.

#

Their faces were bloody and their eyes almost swollen shut from the battering they'd given each other. But neither of them was going to stop until the other one was dead. Their pursuit of revenge had culminated in a weak clinch on their knees, with one bladed weapon each and the remaining durbar council members within spitting distance as an audience. Having dropped his head onto the younger man's shoulder, Jibril Asari looked like he would be first to give up the fight. Garba Mansa's scream told a different story. He sluggishly shoved the older man away and groaned as the older man released his bite on the durbar, with bloody flesh in between his teeth. This was followed by a straight head butt that finally knocked Garba Mansa down to where the dead shanci fighter lay. Freshly concussed, the durbar dropped his weapon. It was finally time to end it.

As former Durbar Master Jibril Asari brought his sword down to finish off his former apprentice, the blade of a semi-circular sword glanced across his throat. At first he stopped, puzzled and looked at the bloody weapon in the hand of his broken former pupil laid out beneath him. He let go of his sword with one hand and clasped his neck. It was wet. Fluid streamed between his fingers. For confirmation he looked at his hand. It was darker than the rain. Then he collapsed.

Garba Mansa, barely conscious, rolled over and looked face to face at his dying mentor. He got up on his elbows and leaned close to the older man's nearest ear.

"Tell our absent friend the afterlife awaits you now."

With that, Garba Mansa gently released the durbar sword from the old man's grip and drove it deep into his mentor's chest.

#

The repetitive sound of distant kakaki roused everyone from their exhausted stupor. Those that could run did so, back to their respective sides of the battle lines. Others cried out for help or to be put out of their misery. Garba Mansa delicately sat upright and stared into space. A horse approached in the distance. At first he thought it was Amaka.

Then the sudden burning pain from the high speed projectile embedded in his shoulder told him his eyes couldn't be trusted. He fell forward onto the dead man and lethargically rolled him on top of him as a human shield. The next two arrows hit the dead man's body. Then there was a scream. The scream of a woman.

#

Amaka looked down at Amina Asari. The spear protruded from her ribcage. Tears streamed down her cheeks as the traitor's daughter clutched her sword and lay awkwardly on the ground with her bow and arrows next to her. Her breathing was laboured and her horse idled nearby, oblivious to her immediate distress. Kazeem Urumu stood next to Amaka as an endless stream of people ran in different directions around them. Amaka looked pitifully at her crippled enemy.

"I don't know what to do now," said Amaka.

"Get Garba."

Chapter Thirty-One

Every war has casualties. Every victory comes at a price. Those were Master's words before the battle of Katsina. Having witnessed the indiscriminate brutality of war first-hand, Isa counted the cost, with his master one of many critically wounded. Every heroic illusion of valour, every romantic fantasy of glory had been stripped from the boy's imagination. Living with the consequences of such sacrificial servitude was a thoroughly unsatisfactory if not lonely experience. For all the drum-beating, horn-blowing and sword-swinging that had taken place on their adventure, none of it justified the breaking of his near indestructible master.

Having returned from Katsina, Master had declined to be seen by a palace physician or even a healer. The arrow's poison was already coursing through his veins by the time he'd been carried from the battlefield. The Asari woman had been smart enough to hit him near enough to the heart and ensure that death was an almost certainty. The fever came on within a couple of hours and Master was stripped to his bare essentials and dabbed with cold water to keep his temperature down. There was little capacity left to attend to his many other injuries. Perhaps knowing his end was near, Master had requested to return home with his ward and the latest resident of their compound. Amaka's temporary stay was about to be extended as she assisted Isa in caring for the dying durbar. Her upbeat energy, aside from being a little too talkative, was a welcome distraction for the boy.

The remaining durbars escorted their fallen comrade to his final resting place. Musa Gindiri, varnished wooden walking stick in hand, seemed most saddened by Master's demise. The wordsmith was uncharacteristically quiet. All of them pledged to take the boy on, to feed him, educate him and train him. But Master had only one request. One request that was typical of Master. He requested that they dig a grave on fertile soil near the compound. He wanted someone or something to benefit from his passing and what greater beneficiary than the earth that nourished life? When the time came, he suggested, between Amaka, Isa and Sisoko, they could lay his body to rest there. The request was duly obliged and between them, the durbars found an appropriate burial site and dug a grave nearby.

One by one they said their final goodbyes. Musa Gindiri was the last to go and was hampered by more than his injured leg when it came time to leave. He leaned on Master's bed and held his feverish hand.

"Travel well brother," he said in a raspy voice. "When death comes for you, greet our absent friend and..." Musa put his fist to his mouth to fight back the tears.

"I'll tell him I'm going to wreak havoc in the afterlife." Master slowly opened his eyes, turned to his emotional friend and smiled.

Musa Gindiri nodded, squeezed his friend's hand one last time and left his bedside.

#

By sundown everyone had left. Amaka and Isa remained with Garba Mansa in the candlelight. He was clammy and groaned intermittently. Every so often, when the silence was too long, Isa checked his master's breathing by seeing if his chest still rose and fell. He was still alive. Some time later he coughed and Isa sprang to his feet and fetched him some water. He supported Master's swollen head with one hand as he brought the water to his cracked lips.

"The soil must be hungry," said Master.

Isa was unsure quite how to respond to his dark humour but responded nonetheless.

"Do you need anything Master?" he asked.

"Sit down Isa," said Master. The boy did as he was told.

"Let me know if you need anything," said Amaka. Isa nodded and she left them alone.

"How do you feel?" asked Master.

"Master?"

"Is there gari in your ears?" snapped Master. "How do you feel?"

Master's typical impatience was reassuring but his question bizarre, given the circumstances. "I'm fine. I've eaten. Sisoko has been fed."

"That's not what I'm asking Isa. How do you *feel*?"

"Scared," admitted the boy.

"What are you scared of?"

"I'm scared you're in pain," he continued. "I'm scared what will happen to you when…I'm scared of being alone. I'm sorry master."

Isa burst into tears and bowed his head on his master's hand. Garba Mansa looked at him and squeezed his hand.

"Listen to me Isa," he said softly. "There's no shame in being afraid. If it's any consolation, the vivid dreams I've had have been a welcome distraction from the pain." He paused for a moment. "I'm sorry that I won't be continuing our journey together…but I'm grateful for the opportunity to say goodbye. Know that when I leave, the pain will end. Let me reassure you of my final destination."

Isa looked up at his master, clearly confused. Master let go of his hand and pointed downwards to the floor. Isa was unimpressed by his attempt to lighten the mood and couldn't muster a smile.

"Thank you Master."

"I have one last thing to ask of you."

"Yes Master."

"Lead a good life with an open heart," he began. "We live in dangerous times and always will. What gets us through these times is the goodness in people's hearts. Keep my sword and only take it up if absolutely necessary. Anyone can pick up a sword but only the right people should hold them. I know you'll be a good leader. You have a prophet's name."

"Yes Master. Thank you."

"No," said Garba Mansa. "It's you I have to thank."

"Master?"

"Thank you Isa," he continued. "Thank you for allowing me another chance at my greatest pleasure in life. Something I thought I'd lost forever."

Isa looked puzzled but chose not to interrupt Master's most open moment of vulnerability. It was then that he could see the tears welling up in Master's eyes.

"Fatherhood."

A tear rolled down Master's cheek and he smiled. Isa had no words. He held his master's hot hand. The durbar and his apprentice looked at one another in silence.

#

Master died the following day. He left the world as he would have wanted. Silently, with no fuss and his dignity intact. When sunlight woke Isa at his bedside, Master perspired no more. His hand was cold and his chest still. Even before he alerted Amaka, Isa knew he was gone. The compound was quiet. It seemed as though the birds had left with the durbar master's spirit.

After shedding tears that morning, with Sisoko's help they carried out Durbar Master Garba Mansa's wishes to the letter. With hearts as heavy as the man they carried, Isa and Amaka put his body onto a cart.

Sisoko took the honour of leading her master's modest final procession and dragged the simple funeral coach to the burial site. In a manner befitting the straightforwardness of the man, his body was rolled into the grave and returned to the earth as requested. Isa's fingers wrapped around the leather-bound hilt of his master's sword. The pad of his thumb brushed the ornate insignia as his mind flashed back to the first time he'd felt it. Acutely aware of the sentimental value of the weapon to the boy, Amaka reassured him that the rest of Garba Mansa's arsenal and his workshop would be put to good use. As the soil in Master's grave reached level with its surroundings, a warmth filled the palm of Isa's other hand and a soft touch glanced the side of his face. Amaka squeezed his hand tight as Sisoko's mane gently caressed his cheek. With his past, present and future in his hands, Isa was no longer afraid of being alone.

The End

Epilogue

It had been a tumultuous few months. Despite the relative calm, a release was desperately needed before the next stage of the campaign. The knock on his chamber door told him that the new girl had arrived. He put down his feather pen and responded. Chancellor Atiku Danladi looked forward to the evening's entertainment.

"*Enter.*"

The chamber door opened and a young woman entered. She wore a simple hooded robe tied with a cord around her waist and carried a small pouch. Her shape looked reasonable and her face young. So far so good. Her attire was basic but it mattered not. She wouldn't be clothed for much longer. She made no eye contact as she entered the chancellor's chamber. A shy one. Even better. Danladi looked her up and down and smiled.

"Put your belongings down there and empty them," he demanded.

The young woman did as she was told and placed her pouch on a table with gold coins on it by a frosted window. Danladi eyed her as she emptied the pouch. Its sole item was a small bottle of oil. The pouch would be much heavier with payment on her way out.

"If you would be so kind," he said and nodded at the bottle.

An established security protocol for all visitors was to consume a small amount of whatever liquid or culinary gift they brought. This was thought to deter those with particular zeal for poisoning. The evening visitor did as she was told and sipped a small amount of the oily liquid from the bottle. She initially grimaced then smiled at her observer, before putting the bottle back on the table. Danladi waited a few moments then smiled. Excellent. Things could get underway.

"Let's get started. Take off your clothes."

The woman undid the cord of her robe. Danladi's eyes and smile widened as her robe fell to the floor. He scanned her naked body from top to bottom then up again. She was in excellent condition. A long neck, teardrop breasts, a flat stomach, strong hips and long legs. Danladi nodded his head in approval.

"May I get started my lord?" asked the woman. She no longer appeared shy.

Danladi smiled and nodded. His eyes followed her around the room as she picked up a chair and moved it by the window and table. Once happy that the room was arranged to her satisfaction, the woman stood by the chair and smiled at her client.

"If you would be so kind my lord," she said and nodded at his tunic with a smile.

The chancellor removed his tunic in an instant, clearly excited to get things going. The woman motioned for him to sit in the chair. Danladi willingly obliged. From there the woman poured some oil onto her hands then stood behind the seated naked chancellor. She deftly massaged his shoulders. Danladi sighed with pleasure as the stealthy tension was released from his muscles. After a good few minutes, the masseuse poured more oil on her hands from the table bottle and knelt in front of the seated chancellor. With oil on both palms, she massaged his feet then his legs below the knees, taking extra care over his voluminous calves. Danladi smiled with a glazed look of satisfaction, looking down at her as she did so. Playing her part well, the masseuse smiled without eye contact as she worked. She got up one more time to lubricate her hands before resuming her position on her knees. The masseuse massaged his chubby thighs, from outside to inside, working towards his groin with smooth strokes. The chancellor was clearly very aroused.

"What's your name?"

"Chiamaka my lord."

"Igbo?"

"Yes my lord."

"What brings you to these parts?"

"Personal gratification my lord."

Danladi smiled as her hands got closer. "That makes two of us."

The woman looked at his groin then looked up at him and smiled. "I'm definitely going to need more oil my lord. Please close your eyes and relax."

"As you wish my dear."

Danladi closed his eyes and his smile grew wider in anticipation of the entertainment escalating. Within a few seconds he felt a slight tickle around his neck. Then he couldn't breathe.

#

Amaka wedged her shoulders against the wall, with one foot against the back of the chancellor's chair and leaned back with all her body weight as she strangled him from behind with the cord of her robe. The obese minister frantically grabbed at the cord around his neck but her leverage was too great. His weight was to his disadvantage. Danladi's massive frame anchored the chair and aided her leverage. As she maintained the stranglehold, sweat accumulated on her forehead then trickled down her neck onto her chest. Killing for revenge was new to her. It was the least she could do for the man who saved her life. Killing for revenge felt just. Aiding the war effort was an added bonus. Within a minute the obese minister gave up the fight. The stench of human faeces told her that he was probably dead but she held on for another two minutes just to make sure the job was done. When she let go, his head flopped back with his mouth and bloodshot eyes open.

#

Fully clothed, Amaka tied the cord around her robe and put the bottle of oil with the gold coins lifted from the table into her pouch. She looked back at the dead naked minister sat in a pile of his own excrement. It seemed a fitting end for him. Amaka carefully closed the chamber door and approached the guard outside it.

"My lord will need some time to recover from his treatment this evening. He has requested that he not be disturbed tonight."

The guard looked at the woman and turned his nose up at the smell of faeces. His face said he didn't care to know what acts of depravity they'd accomplished behind the door. He grunted curtly for her to leave. Amaka disappeared down a corridor of the Gidan Korau into the darkness.

Acknowledgments

I must thank Andrea Johnson, Chris Major, Lisa Kastner and Alexis August at Rize and Running Wild Press for taking a chance on me. Your patience and kindness in guiding me through the publication process is greatly appreciated. A huge thanks to my 'big brother' and Choi boy all-star from way back when Ian Mahony, Ljuba Naminova and Pooneh Youssefi for taking the time to read my manuscript. Your kind and constructive feedback encouraged me to keep going. I owe a debt of gratitude to Ikenna Azuike for his friendship, enthusiasm and encouragement to explore a passion completely out of my comfort zone. Last but not least, words can't do justice to how grateful I am to have my soulmate, my amorski and my wife Salma in my corner. You encouraged me to begin this journey, kept my chin up and rubbed my back through the knock-backs and have been my biggest cheerleader not just in writing this novel but in my life. You gave us the son that stared at that canvas while I rocked him to sleep with one hand and started writing on my phone with the other. The canvas that inspired this journey. None of this would have been possible without you. Te amo.

About the Author

Remington Blackstaff was born in Nigeria and moved to the United Kingdom with his family at a young age. He was bitten by the martial arts bug in childhood and studied several disciplines into adulthood. Despite his obsession with fight choreography, he set aside any dreams of becoming a stuntman to study medicine at Royal Free and University College Medical School. Remington currently practices medicine in London, where he lives with his wife and son. He remains obsessed with martial arts, rugby and cinema. The Durbar's Apprentice is his debut novel.

RIZE publishes great stories and great writing across genres written by People of Color. Our team consists of:

Lisa Diane Kastner, Founder and Executive Editor
Andrea Johnson, Acquisitions Editor
Chris Major, Editor
Chih Wang, Editor
Laura Huie, Editor
Pulp Art Studios, Cover Design
Standout Books, Interior Design
Polgarus Studio, Interior Design
Alexis August, Product Manager Intern

Learn more about us and our stories at www.runningwildpress.com/rize

Loved this story and want more? Follow us at www.runningwildpress.com/rize, www.facebook/rize, on Twitter @rizerwp and Instagram @rizepress